A BEGINNER'S GUIDE TO BREAKING AND ENTERING

Also by Andrew Hunter Murray

The Last Day
The Sanctuary

A BEGINNER'S GUIDE TO BREAKING AND ENTERING

Andrew Hunter Murray

HUTCHINSON
HEINEMANN

1 3 5 7 9 10 8 6 4 2

Hutchinson Heinemann
20 Vauxhall Bridge Road
London SW1V 2SA

Hutchinson Heinemann is part of the Penguin Random House group of companies whose addresses can be found at global.penguinrandomhouse.com.

Copyright © Andrew Hunter Murray 2024

Andrew Hunter Murray has asserted his right to be identified as the author of this Work in accordance with the Copyright, Designs and Patents Act 1988.

First published by Hutchinson Heinemann in 2024

www.penguin.co.uk

A CIP catalogue record for this book is available from the British Library.

ISBN 9781529152807 (hardback)
ISBN 9781529154382 (trade paperback)

Typeset in 11.75/17.25pt Times New Roman MT Std
by Jouve (UK), Milton Keynes
Printed and bound in Great Britain by Clays Ltd, Elcograf S.p.A.

The authorised representative in the EEA is Penguin Random House Ireland, Morrison Chambers, 32 Nassau Street, Dublin D02 YH68

www.greenpenguin.co.uk

Penguin Random House is committed to a sustainable future for our business, our readers and our planet. This book is made from Forest Stewardship Council® certified paper.

To ALM

Prologue

This is the part where I explain how I ended up here. It's also the point – I think this is right – where I explain how terribly sorry I am about all the poor decisions that landed me here in the first place.

I'm not very remorseful, to be honest, although I hope that fact doesn't come out at trial. I'm rather *embarrassed* to be here, especially given how many lovely homes I've been in over the years, but self-pity is a terrible look, and I had a pretty good run until all this. And as for poor decisions . . . I think I would have ended up here anyway sooner or later. I just came by the scenic route.

Incidentally, you wouldn't believe how easy it is to get access to a computer in here, provided you aren't too fussy about things like 'the internet'. I've signed up for a course in

IT Literacy, meaning I get an hour a day on a whacking great Dell in the badly named Information Suite (it's less a suite than a cupboard, and most people come out of it worse informed than they went in). Not many people want to use the Suite. The PCs in it were forged around the Late Cretaceous, meaning they are a) the size of a room and b) almost completely useless. Also, I guess a lot of my colleagues here were arrested by a PC, so the term has bad associations.

But these ancient, hulking computers – seriously, they're actual desktops, it's like being in the nineteenth century – do have a few things going for them. They have Windows '95, for one, with the full Office set, meaning that I can log on, ignore Gertrude the IT instructor, and type for a solid 57 minutes each day, with a three-minute Solitaire break at the end as a little treat. I might get this published one day, if I play my cards right. Although if anyone pays me for this, will it count as 'proceeds of crime'? Might do. I'll have to circle back to that once the trial is over. And I'll have to think of a decent pen name too. That shouldn't be a problem. My master pseudonym list is currently up to 86 entries.

I *love* a prison opening to a story, by the way. Sorry. That's another distraction, because you're already champing at the bit to get on and find out how I – a bright young man with marketable skills and good prospects – managed to end up in more trouble than anyone else in almost the entire cell block, piss off both the law *and* the criminals, and nearly get himself killed about six times along the way.

But I do love a prison opening. You can't beat them. Just

watch *Kind Hearts and Coronets,* or read the one about that girl who literally murdered all her relatives and still managed to make herself seem like the wronged party. A prison opening tells you this is going to be *fun*. It also gives away that I live to tell the tale, although to preserve a bit of mystery I won't tell you what sort of state I'm in right now. I'll tell you this for free: my skincare routine has seen better months.

Anyway. My current circumstances are south London and medium security. They don't tie you down at night, which is how you can tell it from a maximum security place, but they *do* check the locks on the doors every few days, which is how you can differentiate it from minimum security. I argued that maybe I should be in solitary for my own protection, but they laughed and told me not to be a drama queen. I think solitary must cost them a lot more.

Although I'm actually in the Info Suite right now, typing this up under Gertrude's lazy eye, imagine me sitting in the Visitors' Room. This isn't one of those fancy American set-ups, with the little phone and the wipe-clean screens. No, this is a proper British public-sector environment, which means durable carpet tiles and plastic-coated single-seat armchairs. They have uncomfortably high arms, so it's hard to get at your pockets, and they're positioned nice and far from each other, to make it that little bit harder to hand over any contraband that avoided the friskings.

Right now, I'm waiting for a friend (lawyer) to turn up and tell me how the rest of my story is falling out. My trial is considered much lower priority than the others, but there's also nowhere to bail me to. Not only that, nobody had any inclination to pay my bail, so I'm just waiting around. It's probably the best place to be; the story I set in motion is prompting quite the kerfuffle out there. I'm not surprised, really. Any story featuring luxury property, big-money fraud, international espionage and high treason will snag the attention of even the thickest newspaper editor.

So those are my circumstances. A bit under-vegetabled, a bit short on vitamin D, some split ends (do men get split ends?), but alive, and typing with all the fingers that still work. As for how it all started . . . God. That's harder. I have considered the various points where it 'began'. There's the moment we heard the shot, of course, although that's too neat. Then there was the bit where I met Em and her friends for the first time, although if she and I hadn't already been in the same line of work, we'd never have teamed up.

In fact, I know where it started: 14 Cadbury Lane. My last solo job. If that had gone well – all right, if I hadn't screwed it up so badly – I'd still be a free man now. I wouldn't have encountered Davy, or Mr Bowling Ball, and I wouldn't have found out about the yacht's-worth of money that got me into this whole mess. I wouldn't have met Em, Elle or Jonny, and I wouldn't have become the primary focus of at least three law enforcement agencies and eight criminal gangs. I wouldn't have got someone else shot, or myself banged up.

But much like the Crown Prosecution Service, these things are sent to try us.

Here's how it began.

1

When it comes to breaking into someone else's house, there are rules.

The rules aren't to protect the house, of course. The rules are to protect you. Although confusingly, looking after the place *is* one of the rules. If you're going to be an interloper, which is my term for my highly specific profession, you have to treat the property as if it's your own. If you manage that, more often than not the few people you encounter will genuinely believe you own it, provided they didn't see the rightful owner there last week. The rules will always guide and defend you.

Case in point: here I am, outside one of the nicest houses in the whole of this little Sussex village, about to break in. I should be very tense indeed. But I'm perfectly calm, because I have the rules on my side.

I don't want to make my work as an interloper sound twee, incidentally. I'm not a fucking Borrower. My job is glamorous, enjoyable and yields big rewards, but it does come with risks attached. And one of those risks, not that I know it yet, is about to bite me right on the arse.

Here's how this whole mess started.

10.03 a.m. Paul Lethbridge – prosperous and fifty-something – is leaving for the airport. 'Prosperous' is my polite way of saying he's let himself go a bit in his middle years. But he does look wealthy. He's got a kind of base suntan that you can tell he's proud of, and that he doesn't let get below a certain level even in midwinter. If he has to go to Antigua in January to top it up, then off to Antigua he will go. Even the band where his wedding ring used to lie is now the same uniform honey colour as the rest of his finger.

Paul's not a bad guy, probably. He's a bit short with people, a bit too confident in his own abilities, he's got a high-pressure job, and he's also been a bit too solitary for a few too many years to be considered truly 'socialised' any more. But I could say the same of myself. And I'm *certainly* not a bad guy.

Mr Lethbridge isn't going to Antigua today. He's setting off on a three-week trip to the Middle East to conduct some of the legal work that has paid for so much over the years: this house, mainly, and the primary residence in the city. His work even manages to pay all the maintenance fees now required of him, more or less on time. He's leaving his car at home (a nice, newish proper Porsche; he's sure all this electric nonsense will blow over in a few years) and cabbing to Gatwick. Dev, the minicab driver, has been waiting twenty minutes already, but he doesn't mind. Mr Lethbridge is a reliable customer in an Uber-stricken industry. Dev's freshly vacuumed Toyota is waiting on the drive, inside the slightly overwrought-iron gates.

Out of the front door comes Mr L, frowning a bit when he sees the car and the tracks in his nice clean gravel; he wishes they'd wait on the road like he requested on the phone. He locks the door, checks it, waits while young whatever-his-name-is loads his enormous case into the boot, conscious that it would be improper to offer any assistance, checks the door again for good measure. Then he crunches across the drive and clambers into the back seat. The gate swings ponderously open, and the car – a little lower on its wheel arches thanks to Mr L and his luggage – moves out onto the one-lane road and away.

10.04 a.m. Quiet descends once again on this little back road of this posh little village. In the car, Mr L asks Dev to turn off Magic FM immediately, and checks his phone to see he's booked into the right first-class lounge at the airport. He doesn't even glance at the rear-view mirror. Neither does Dev.

10.05 a.m. Back at the house, I emerge from the nearby lane, and start my day's work.

I hope Mr L has a wonderful time in Jordan, but I'm glad he's gone. He and I would make terrible housemates. And for the next three weeks, his house – gorgeous, Georgian from the look of it, tastelessly modernised but still with some wonderful original features – is mine.

I don't look like much, incidentally. I've got a shirt and jacket on, a Covid mask (the greatest innovation of the last decade as far as my line of work is concerned), and dark blue jeans, tucked into some bog-standard old Dr Martens. I could be literally any member of the gig economy right now, and I'm about as memorable. Consider the last person who delivered a package to your place. Do you remember what they looked like?

Thought not.

Right now, I'm keeping as many of the rules as possible active in my head. You know how most plane crashes happen on take-off and landing? Interloping is just the same. Get in and get out OK, and the time in between practically takes care of itself. Here are just a few of the rules I'm obeying already:

Rule 11: *Daylight is better for getting in.* You'd be amazed how conspicuous you feel at night. It's bad for your nerves. Actually, you just *are* conspicuous – it's much harder to see what you're doing, you might need a light, and the element of plausible deniability when you are found skulking around a basement window at 3 a.m. is almost nil, compared with you getting into the same predicament at 3 p.m. You're practically asking to be caught. No thank you. Let sunshine win the day.

Rule 17: *Approach on foot.* Cars are so easily scanned these days. None of the houses I go for have cameras on – for obvious reasons – but if it comes to the worst and there's a camera nearby, it'll have your plates, and if something goes wrong and the tapes are investigated, you're stuffed. Leave the car nearby and arrive on foot. It all counts towards your 10,000 steps.

Rule 21: *No suitcases.* They drag, they make a hell of a racket on almost any surface, and they catch the eye. 'I didn't know there was someone visiting number 17, dear,' the neighbours will say as they peep out. 'Hang on, aren't they away? And this boy doesn't look like the rightful owner!' Ugh. Instead, go for a casual weekend bag over one shoulder, and slip into the place unnoticed. Many of my interloping rules, incidentally, are subdivisions of Rule 3: *Make yourself as forgettable as possible.*

The Lethbridge gates open at the touch of a button. This isn't surprising: almost all gates open during daylight hours if you press 0. People are far more concerned about the chance of missing a package than they are about someone getting into their home, which is fair enough, because everyone gets deliveries all the time these days, while the odds of me turning up at your house are slim.

What have we got? The house is low, two storeys, and comfortably double-fronted. There will be a few rustic-chic outbuildings round the back, no doubt, via the gate – damn, the *locked* gate – leading to the rear. No keys to be found on an initial sweep of the front, neither beneath the rather bedraggled pots (good, there's clearly no gardener) nor under the doormat (*Welcome to Sin City!* A post-divorce present from a mate, I bet). And, crucially, no alarm. You wouldn't believe how few places actually have alarms, and although there are ways to get around them, there's something much more relaxing about the whole experience when there's no need to fiddle about with wires or override codes.

I give it twenty minutes before I'm in.

I leave my shoulder bag in the front, discreetly hidden behind a huge terracotta urn that's about as authentic as Mr Lethbridge's sparkling front teeth, and after a bit of undignified crawling and wriggling over the side gate, I'm in the back garden. No cat flap; no unlocked doors anywhere. I grudgingly upgrade the owner to a Category 2, or NTC (Not Totally Clueless). But there is a shed, and where there are sheds there are ladders. And ladders are a perfect mechanism for accessing all the roof windows and skylights that nobody ever checks, because what sort of nutter would try to get in via the roof?

Halfway to the shed, I look around. The house is shielded from its neighbours even this far into the garden. This is the back street of the village. At the far end, the garden dips away into a beautiful strip of woodland. I know from Google Maps that there's a golf course beyond the woods, and I'm pleased to report the trees are far too thick to be seen through. It's perfect. God bless you, Mr Lethbridge.

10.38 a.m. Mr L is out of the car. He's paid Dev (£56 one way: Mr L considers this cheeky considering it was only £48 last time, and tips four quid on top of the fee, which expressed as a percentage makes him sound like a stingy bastard but really was just a convenient way of rounding up to £60, and nobody can blame him for that). He retrieves his enormous case and moves onto the travelator towards Departures.

10.42 a.m. This is tougher than I thought it would be.

There wasn't a ladder in the shed. I looked everywhere. The garden is lovely, although it's a bit neglected; Mr L is not an outdoorsy type. Through the windows of one of the side rooms, I can see a gym that is worryingly well equipped for a man living alone. I might have twenty years on him, but I wouldn't like to come up against Mr L in a fight.

Fortunately, what the place lacks in ladders it makes up for in trellises. The trellis leads – with a minimum of breakage and zero footprints in the flower bed – to the first floor, the roof of which slopes up to a lovely slanting skylight. It's been left closed, of course, but these things always have a release catch somewhere. I pull out a few of my favourite tools and get to work.

10.43 a.m. At Gatwick Departures, the automatic check-in is broken – a cyberattack, according to a little paper sign that has been printed on the last working printer in the terminal – and so Mr L joins the queue. It moves briskly enough, and when he gets to the front of it, he announces his name. The girl behind the desk asks him for another key bit of information.

He pats his coat pockets. Then he pats his trouser pockets, followed by his coat pockets again, and frowns.

10.47 a.m. Exactly as Mr L is searching his clothes for the third time, I'm dropping the twelve-ish feet from the skylight window onto the floor of the orangery. (You wouldn't believe how many houses in my line of work come with an orangery. I've never seen one containing so much as a single orange.) Twelve feet is not a *fun* distance to drop, but it's onto a rug thick enough to lose a cat in, and I'm not yet thirty. Despite that, I fumble the landing. As I'm swivelling with feline grace to hit the ground, bend, *roll* and recover, I realise I haven't turned quite far enough. I crash clumsily onto my ankle, and Christ it hurts. *Find ice* goes onto the crowded to-do list. You clown, Al.

Never mind that for the moment, because I'm in. This is the golden half-hour.

I check my watch. I gave myself twenty minutes to get in; it actually took me forty-five. How discomfiting. Three years ago it would have taken me ten. This is the third job in a row where I've taken longer than I predicted. I'm either getting too careful, too careless (as my swelling ankle suggests) or too old. None of these options is comforting.

Never mind that right now. Golden half-hour.

11.14 a.m. Phew. Task list completed, comfortably inside the Golden H-H. That means I've done the following:

One. *Spotted* the exits. In this house there's the big beech front door, which is definitely not the best option. There's also a door out the back of the kitchen, which is a safe bet, some French doors at the back of the living room that I've taken the precaution of unlocking, and a big window in the back wall of the orangery which also looks out over the garden, so I've slipped the catch of that one, just in case. That window is actually my best option, rather than the French doors in the living room, because it leads directly onto the flagstone path running down the middle of the garden towards the woodland gate.

Two. *Sorted* any damage I caused getting in. No problem here. The orangery skylight is sealed again. I've checked the rug for anything I might have dropped, and the room looks as good as it did before I fell through the top of it. Easy.

Three. *Snapped* the arrangement of the key rooms, bedside tables, etc. It might seem like overkill to you, but when you are plotting an orderly departure – in other words, when an interlope has gone according to plan – it really makes a difference to have pictures, so you can get everything back in its rightful place. If anything goes wrong, of course, you'll have more to worry about than whether the alarm clock on the bedside table was facing left or right. As you're about to see.

Four. *Secured* a spare set of keys. No need to explain why these will come in handy. Mr L keeps his in a little leather posing-pouch in the hall table.

Five. *Stashed* my bag by the nearest exit, the orangery window. I know, it seems excessive – the man is going to be a thousand miles away for the best part of a month – but keeping your kit near your chief exit is a useful habit. After all, we're still in the stage of the job when things are likeliest to go wrong. I'll check the flight gets off OK, and once 24 hours have elapsed, I'll unpack a bit.

Six. *Put* the kettle on. The houses I break into – no, that I *make my way* into; 'breaking' only happens one time in three, and I always make good – might all have hi-tech kettles, but the problem is that they almost never have milk. So I've brought a pint with me. Easy.

The interior is lovely. A bit much stripped wood for my liking, but I can see what they were going for. It's the kind of house a banker might have bought in the nineties, if you know what I mean. I can see from the wall chart – God bless you for making my life easy, Mr L – that there's a cleaner coming on Thursday, who I'll have to watch out for. I might just pop out for the morning, give her lots of time. You have to do a double clear-out when the cleaners come – no sense in filling the bins up and creating difficult questions – but that's a small price to pay, because if they do their job right they destroy a lot of evidence that you were ever there.

11.26 a.m. This, in case you were wondering when we'd get to it, is the part where I made my big mistake. We haven't heard from Mr L for a while, have we?

I'm on the corner sofa, which runs to about two acres of plush dark green velvet. I've got my tea made: optimistic WORLD'S BEST DADDY mug, clearly being kept as proof. I've popped some frozen peas on my ankle. I've even – and this is one of the small touches on which I pride myself – got a coaster out from the central stack. *Lighthouses of the North* is the theme. I know he's technically one of my 'victims' (hate that word), but I'm beginning to like Mr L.

The sofa I'm in faces away from the window. I'm not going to sit in the uncomfortable chair opposite me just to keep eyes on the front of the property. That decision will prove to have been a bit stupid.

And then, I hear it. The faint noise of an engine in the lane outside. The problem is, the windows are triple-glazed, so it's extremely quiet, and honestly, I've had a busy few days scoping this place out, getting out of my last place, and it simply doesn't occur to me that anything untoward could have happened.

All of this is sloppy. I do appreciate that.

As I sit there – like a fool, not even twisting around to look – I finally notice the only other object on the table.

Sitting before me, quiet and demure, is a passport, an old-school post-Brexit dark blue set of Her Britannic Majesties.

This feels relevant.

Our two timelines – which I was really hoping would remain parallel – are about to converge.

11.27 a.m. Even as I turn, the gate to the drive is swinging open and I can see the car waiting on the lane. In the driver's seat sits Dev, who has clearly been subjected to some uranium-tipped swearing on the way back from the airport.

Stepping through the gate in an incredibly bad mood is Paul Lethbridge, who has managed over the last forty minutes of illegally fast driving to blame anyone but himself for the stupidity he has shown this morning.

Mr L, all I can say is that I know exactly how you feel.

Shit, shit, shit, shit, *shit*.

OK. So now you're about to see what I call a 'crash exit'. Despite how amateur I'm sure I appear right now, I haven't actually had to do one of these for eighteen months. They're not a lot of fun at the best of times. And right now, I've got a cup of tea in my hand and a twist in my ankle.

Pick up the tea and the peas. Move to the orangery. The good news is that there's a wall between the orangery and the front hall – his footsteps are coming closer across the gravel and they sound seriously pissed off – so assuming he remembers where he left his passport (living room, left off the hall), I'll be fine. Of course, there's a risk he'll go right, to the kitchen, and then pass through the orangery as he runs around the ground floor looking for it.

So: time to leave.

I take two agonised steps into the kitchen, jam the pedal bin open, shove the peas in, hobble back into the orangery. Next, I ease the window open – do the noisy bits first, before he gets in – and then, as I hear his key in the front door, I drop my single kitbag outside, scramble out after it, and stick my head back in to listen. God, it's exposed here. Once he's in the hall, he'll have only a few strides before he's overlooking the garden. It's twenty metres to the far end. And I won't have time to get to the fence without him seeing me.

Wait. I can't move without working out which way he's going. If I know he's going to his left (living room), then I can run to the right of the house, around past the kitchen window, and he won't see me there. Or if he goes right to the kitchen first, I can run *left*, and take shelter in the green of the garden. I'll be camouflaged enough. Glad I'm not wearing my hi-vis today. (Must tweak Rule 34: *Hi-vis jackets help you blend in.*)

Actually, hang on, Mr L is only going to be in the house thirty seconds with any luck, and then I'll be back in possession. He's going to run in, grab his passport, run out again. OK. This can work. I haven't left anything behind he's likely to look at – no debris in the hall, nothing but the milk in the fridge. My bag's by my side out here. OK. Breathe, Al.

Why isn't he in yet? Oh, wait, I know – he's been trying to open the deadlock on the door, which I've already unlocked. He'll think it's jammed or something. I can practically hear how angry he is just from the way he's struggling with it. As he's doing that, I look down, and observe with faint amusement that I'm still holding the WORLD'S BEST DADDY. I pop it on the ground, outside, below the window. He won't see it there, unless he decides he left his passport in the garden.

Eventually, he stops attacking the deadlock – is he thinking? Is he getting suspicious? – and goes for the main lock instead. Now he's coming through the front door. All I have to do is listen out for his direction of travel, *ease* my head out, shut this last window, go the opposite way, and shelter until he's off the premises. Simple. I look up. Good, I shut the skylight window. Even now, I find the time to congratulate myself on sticking to my rules.

Too late, I realise I should have just thrown the passport into the front hall, so he thought he'd dropped it on his way out, and hidden behind the curtains until he left. Well, we are where we are, as they often say in Shit Creek.

He's moving right, towards the kitchen. I think so, anyway. This is a hell of a way to test my directional hearing.

No, he's *definitely* heading into the kitchen; I can hear his footsteps change as they hit tiles. I pull my head out, slide the window shut, grab the bag and the mug from the ground, and run like hell towards the left-hand side of the house, where the shrubs will hide me. I'm in among them. His shadow breezes through the orangery – he's glancing around as he goes – and then he's in the living room. Did I leave anything in there? I'm sure I didn't. Almost sure. If my heart keeps beating this fast, he'll think there's a cat purring in the garden. Breathe, Al, breathe. He won't be able to see me, not from here.

He's spotted his passport. Phew. He's picking it up, pocketing it, then he moves towards the door. My three-week holiday is back on. Oh, I owe the god of blaggers a sacrifice tonight.

He turns around.

He's standing in the living room, looking down at the coffee table in front of the sofa. I want to scream at him: what are you doing, Mr L? Catch that plane! Earn some money! Visit Petra on your day off!

He takes a step towards the table. I can't see what he's looking at. And then I remember it.

The coaster.

He's wondering why, when he left his coasters neatly stacked in the middle of the table, one of them is out now.

He leans down and puts his hand on it, curled into a fist so the backs of his hairy fingers touch it. Then I realise the really bad thing. I only took the mug away about thirty seconds ago. *The coaster will still be warm.*

He picks it up and looks around the room, and then – this is when I know things are about to get spicy – he pretends he hasn't noticed anything. He draws his phone from his pocket, acting nonchalant, and it doesn't take too much wit to guess the three digits he's about to dial.

If I had known then that this was the most relaxed I'd feel

for the next several weeks, I might have lightened up a bit, or possibly just handed myself in then.

But as I don't know any of that, I reason that the most important thing is to stop him ringing the police. There are enough fingerprints in that house to identify me, and they'll go on file, and although that wouldn't mean instant arrest, because nobody's caught me yet, they would create an awful precedent.

So without even thinking about it, I am already moving from the shrubs to the side of the house, out of his field of view. Now I'm glad I unlocked the side gate during the Golden Half-Hour. See? The rules will always protect you.

What am I wearing? A shirt and dark jeans, shoes that wouldn't look out of place on a professional. This outfit will do. I haul the bag over the wall separating the property from next door – I'll come back for it later – and chuck the mug into the overgrown bit of the garden. Then, as I approach the front of the house, I stamp loudly on the gravel before knocking with as much authority as I can on the open front door. My hand is shaking.

'Hello? Is there anyone here?'

Lethbridge pops into the hall. I'm taller than average, but he's taller than me, and it looks like every drop of blood in his body is currently in his face. He lowers his phone.

'Who the fuck are you?'

'Mr Lethbridge? Paul Lethbridge? You're the rightful owner of this property?'

'Yes. Why—'

If you let people finish their questions, you never get anywhere in this life.

'Mr Lethbridge, I'm glad to meet you.' I step forward and offer a hand. 'My name's Rob Lind. I'm with the Metropolitan Police. We've been following a criminal who we have reason to believe has been operating in this area recently. We think this house may have been his next target. Have you been at home all morning?'

'I . . . No, I'm going away. I just came back because . . .' He waves the passport he's holding. I let my expression grow grave.

'I see. It's possible he would have come in just as you left, sir. That's exactly the sort of move we think he'd make. Do you have a few minutes to discuss this?'

The phone in his hand is burbling something. He looks down, dazed, and presses a button to end the call. Excellent. I've got him in a hot state. He doesn't know which way is up.

'I don't understand . . .'

'Are you familiar with the name the Ocelot? No? He's the individual we're after. Nicknamed for a vicious little South American creature. Cat-like, dextrous, and dangerous when cornered. He's an aggressive intruder, very violent when he gets the opportunity. Are there valuables on the property?'

Mr L gestures helplessly behind him. 'There's a safe in the study . . .'

'That would undoubtedly have been his target. Do you have reason to believe the property has been compromised?'

'There was a coaster . . . I'm sorry, this is all a lot to take in. I'm just trying to get a flight . . .'

'I'm sorry, Mr Lethbridge, I don't think you're going to make your flight. In fact, I think it would be best for us to spend a few minutes going over the house. Would that be all right?'

Ten minutes later, I've fixed the whole thing up.

It was a moment's work to rebolt the orangery window I'd climbed out of. He's shown me the coaster, and I've managed to question him about it and its temperature so much that he's not sure of himself any more. Maybe he *did* leave it out. Also, I've put gloves on – I had a pair in my pocket for emergencies (Rule 4) – and I've tried to smudge any fingerprints I might have left around the place, although you'll never catch them all. I've reassured him there's no sign of the sort of forced entry the Ocelot specialises in, and offered him a few home-safety recommendations to boot.

Back in the front hall, I give him my phone number so he can ring if he has any concerns. I also advise him to wait a few days to call ('we're so busy, you see, and this will give us time to get everything together') – that should help degrade any DNA I've left in the place – then shake his hand again. He thanks me. He's going to try and get a night flight, and ask a friend from the village to look in every day or two. No harm done.

As I head down the drive, I pass Dev, still waiting for his

irascible customer. I give him a businesslike nod, then walk on. Once I can see he's safely back on his phone, I slip into the side lane, from which I'll be able to climb into the next-door property to retrieve my bag. Then I lean against an old drystone wall and almost throw up from the postponed terror of it all.

Right. Now I have to find somewhere else to sleep tonight.

2

And that's my job. Fun, eh?

You may be thinking: that doesn't sound fun. That sounds very, very stressful. But when you've successfully got in somewhere, lived like a king for six weeks, and left undetected . . . there's no feeling like it.

I feel like you might have some questions at this point. I also feel like I might have come across a little bit pleased with myself back there. I should probably point out that I have a few likeable qualities too, to balance out all the breaking and entering. So for the avoidance of doubt:

- I'm an interloper, *not* a burglar. I've never taken anything from these places (Rule 14). That would be bad for business. It would create far more trouble than

I need, as well as an entire new job in terms of fencing the stolen goods. Do people still say 'fencing'? Feels a bit Dickens. Anyway, it would cause lots of paperwork and negotiations, and the police would be far more interested in all the places I've visited. No thank you. If you follow the Al method, and the owners can't find anything missing, the odds are the police won't even bother sending anyone round.

- OK, fine: I'd be stretching the truth if I said I'd never had a bottle of the house wine. But I don't take people's personal possessions. There's the line.
- In fact, that's the whole point. I've read descriptions of 'squatters', 'aggressive squatters', 'housebreakers', that kind of thing . . . that's not me at all. Not that I've got anything against squatters. Most of them are just doing their bit under horrendous conditions, dealing with whoever owns the place, with the authorities, sometimes even with organised criminals who are trying to drive them out . . . The squatter's path is a stony one. There are a few in here on short sentences, and they have the slightly dazed look of people who were just trying to house themselves with decency and never thought it would come to this. And while I personally reject the S word, we're doing the same thing. We're taking space that isn't used and making it useful again. Frankly, we're battling the housing crisis. These places are all – *all* – unoccupied. And the ones I go for are all second homes (or third, or fourth). Why not put them to good use?

- I've never hurt anyone physically. I don't have the upper-body strength, for one thing. Again, it's just not me.
- I'm not doing this to make a point. I'm not Robin Hood, I'm not a rebel against the state, I'm just doing what anyone in my (unique) position and with my (unique) skills would do.
- With that said . . . screw it. I may as well write what I think, it's not like they can jail me again. There are so many thousands of beautiful homes around the country, completely unoccupied, and there are so many *millions* of young people who are never going to get themselves anywhere nice, or anywhere near their friends and families, or anywhere better than a mouldy rented two-room they have to spend half their wages on, paying someone else's mortgage . . . so in that sense, yeah. I'm doing it to make a point.

And that's me. I'm Al. Obviously that's not my real name, but I'd be a bit disappointed if you thought I was stupid enough to let that slip. In fact, given what I've told you about myself, Al is the one name you can rule out.

Any questions?

How did you get into this? I'd prefer not to say.

Don't you have a proper job? I certainly do. Or at least, I do at this point in the story, although it only lasts another week because of the huge bucket of trouble about to fall on me as I walk into my next place.

Why don't you just get a place of your own? Can't afford

one. Not to buy, certainly. And once I worked that out some years ago, I reasoned that I had two options: I could spend half my time working to hire a matchbox, saving jack-all, while dealing with some of the worst criminal scum on the planet (lettings agents), or I could take up a new mode of life, stay in some of the country's most beautiful homes, and develop a niche set of skills into the bargain. It's no choice at all.

Any further questions? No? Good. Anyway, it's helpful to remind myself the job is fun, because once I've retrieved my bag and got clear of Casa Lethbridge, it's still about twenty minutes before my heart rate returns to normal. Things don't often get that close. I do a fair bit of blagging, but normally with neighbours, staff, that kind of thing. It's rare to come into contact with the actual homeowner.

I get off the bus in the centre of town around 3 p.m., a couple of hours after leaving Mr Lethbridge to tidy his coasters. I spend a bit of the afternoon in a café, sorting some work emails and rigging up a few jobs (proper jobs, not interloping jobs), and then look at the time. At this time of year – this all happened in April – if I'm going to get to my lodgings in daylight, I'd better hurry.

I'm heading for the one place which has never let me down in the past: good old 17 Balfour Villas. Named for the former PM – haunting to think that one day people might actually live somewhere called Truss Crescent and not even find it funny – it's a beautiful road, even if the stucco's gone a bit soft since the unveiling.

Imagine a row of art deco mansions, looking like ocean liners with their lovely lines and curves. This isn't the famous north London Millionaire's Row of crumbling mega-money mansions, although I do have an occasional bolthole at one end there. Balfour is about half a mile from its famous cousin, but it's much more discreet. Walk halfway along, under the ubiquitous plane trees, and turn left at the tattiest of the lot. That's number 17.

The front garden's a state, and the place is largely unfurnished, barring a few slight improvements I've made. It's been in a probate deep-freeze for years now, surrounded by legal undergrowth – I spotted it in a court report once and worried the press coverage might untangle the thickets and destroy my safe haven. Fortunately, the coverage did absolutely no good and the place remains my private fiefdom.

I know what you're thinking. Why not just live here, Al, if it's perfect and empty? Why not improve this place, do it up, at least until someone finds you and kicks you out?

I wish I knew.

It's sunset as I approach, and although the clouds are promenading before a beautiful tangerine backdrop, somehow the lovely evening only makes me even glummer. My twisted ankle feels the size of a grapefruit. If I'd been cleverer a few hours ago, I'd still be in Mr L's mini-mansion. I could have got onto the golf course at the end of the garden. I've always wanted to try golf.

Really, I'm annoyed with myself. I was so *dumb* back there. How could I have failed to notice the stupid passport on the table during the initial sweep? Have I just got too confident? Or – more troubling thought – am I losing it?

I don't like to admit it, but things have been getting harder for the last couple of years. It's not just the doorbell cameras everywhere, although if I'm honest it's mostly the bloody doorbell cameras. What sort of joyless people need a feed of their front door? What happened to taking a chance, seeing who turns up, taking the universe as it comes? Ugh. People.

Fortunately, plenty of the places I end up in are – weirdly – *too* nice for an Amazon Ring. And their existing security arrangements are very circumnavigable from my point of view. But every year more and more places have upgraded. I've known some absolutely gorgeous houses, about as hard to get into as a poached egg, only to come back a year later and find out they're now off-limits, all because of a couple of rubbishy devices knocked out in China for a total value of about three quid. They're anti-enterprise.

Lately I'm feeling a bit . . . past it. Which is mad, because I'm young, I'm skilled, and I have a lot of fun. But the feeling remains. The last book I read was an old sci-fi novel about a guy who turns out to be the last human alive in a world of vampires, and realises eventually that in the new world, *he's* the freak. All a bit close to home. (I decided to switch and am now on a much more entertaining biography of Princess Margaret, who as far as I can tell spent her entire life staying in other people's houses unchallenged. An icon.)

Maybe it's time to give up. No, Al, don't think like that. 17 Balfour Villas won't let me down.

Except that as I walk the cracked flagstones (Rule 29: *Approach head-on in case of residents*), I spot something I've never seen here before. Something horrifying.

There is a shadow moving back and forth in the front room. It's not a curtain or a door. It's person-shaped.

This was the last moment I could have avoided the whole mess. If I'd turned round at this point and gone to backup #2, a lovely former coach house in Dulwich whose owner is in a Malaysian prison, I would not now be typing this document in the Information Suite of a medium-security prison with Gertie the IT instructor on my left and the Croydon Tram Flasher on my right. But I had to know. Was the probate knot finally untied? Was today about to go from merely bad to totally unsalvageable?

There are always ways to learn what you need without anyone realising you're asking for it. I walk up to the door, grabbing the clipboard from my rucksack, and press the (dumb) doorbell.

Footsteps approach, then pause, as if considering whether to let me in. I feel like I'm being *considered*, in a rather creepy way. Then, at last, a young woman opens the door, and I begin my spiel.

'Hello there, madam. Are you the property's owner, Mrs' – I consult my board again – 'Olive Hooper?'

'I am.'

That's interesting, for two reasons. First, the woman who owns the property isn't called Olive Hooper, as I know perfectly well. And second, unlike the actual owner, this woman has clearly not been dead for eighteen months.

She's a few years younger than me, with dark brown eyes, and dark brown hair too, nearly down to her shoulders. She keeps looping it behind her ear as we talk, as if it's in her way. She's not unattractive – more on that later – but there's something slightly off-centre about her features, and she wears a knowing expression. If I was being bitchy, I'd say she looks sly. Even so, it's an easy face to like.

The other thing about her is that she keeps her eyes on me throughout our conversation. I'm so distracted by how seldom she blinks that I almost forget my next line.

'That's wonderful, Mrs Hooper. My name is Tom Byrne, I'm a representative of the church down the road, the church of Christ Geographer – do you know it? – and although I'm sure you're terribly busy, I was wondering if I might talk to you about our organ pipe campaign? It'll only take a few moments.' I clasp my hands as if in silent prayer that she's free.

'There isn't a church down the road, as far as I'm aware.' She looks at me in a rather discomfiting way. There's a ghost of a European accent in there, but I can't tell for sure which one.

'Forgive me. A figure of speech – we're about three roads over. We find it helps our fundraising efforts to stress that we're local, you see!' I give a little vicarish laugh.

'I didn't think people in the Church were allowed to fib like that. Isn't there a headline somewhere about bearing false witness?'

I get the strangest impression just then that this woman knows exactly what I'm doing. But I also get the impression that she's doing the same thing, that she knows that I know, and that while she doesn't mind us continuing this game, we're both well aware that a game is all it is. It's a bit intoxicating, to tell you the truth. And that's when something else strikes me.

'Mrs Hooper, I hope you don't mind my asking, but is there a chance you and I have met before?'

She smiles then, a wide, knowing grin which has absolutely nothing in common with the demure smile she gave me a minute ago as she opened the door. 'I'm not much of a church-goer.' I'm *sure* I've seen her before. When?

Just then, another woman calls from behind her. 'Em? Are you there? We've found the stopcock—'

She turns, and says rather sharply to the unseen person in the hall, 'I'm just speaking to this gentleman from the local church. I won't be a minute.' The other recedes, and a door slams on their footsteps. The woman turns back to me. 'You were saying, about the organ?'

'I was. It's just . . . Oh, excuse me.' I look down at my notes. 'I seem to have got muddled here. Mrs Olive Hooper actually lives next door, at number nineteen.'

That gives her a knock. She looks at me with a bit of doubt for the first time, paws her hair behind her ear again. So it *is* an anxiety tic.

'And your friend just there called you another name. Em, was it?' I allow the gentlest note of 'sorrowful clergy' into my tone. 'I wonder – is there something going on here that I should know about, madam?'

And that's the point at which she leans out, grabs me by the collar and hauls me into the house.

3

'All right. Who the *fuck* are you?'

The hall – spacious, wood-panelled, permanent aroma of mothballs – is not quite as I remember it. I know, I know, I should probably only be thinking of the young woman half-throttling me, but I'm good at taking in a lot on a first glance, and it seems like someone's done up 17 Balfour a bit since I left it. No debris on the ground, floor tiles scrubbed and sparkling . . . Is that mirror new?

The one thing that's stayed the same is the main feature – a gorgeous old box chair. It's the kind that used to be used for sedans – it still has the iron brackets on the side for the poles. Whenever I come here, I like to spend half an hour sitting in the thing, imagining the total privacy it would have given you. Must have been rare even two hundred years ago. But that's the rich all over, I guess. The whole aim is to shield yourself from the world.

Decor aside, I have to concede I've lost a bit of authority here, given that the girl currently slamming me against the wall is about four inches shorter than I am and slightly built to boot. I break her hold by the undignified 'thrash around' method until she lets go of my shirt, but she keeps her face right up to mine.

'Who are you?' I glance down, because something is pricking my ribs. She's holding a brass blade – how did she get hold of that? – which I dimly recognise as the old-fashioned letter-opener I admired but didn't steal the last time I was staying here. Honestly, you try to have principles about personal property, and this is how the world rewards you.

'Come on. Name? Tell me or you get this.' The letter-opener is pretty blunt, but I don't really fancy learning the hard way whether it can break human skin.

'You won't be able to stab me with that,' I say. 'It struggles with thick card.'

She twists her head and bellows, 'Guys! Intruder!'

Footsteps; then two people enter the scene, respectively stage left and balcony.

The newcomer at stage left is another young woman. There's no polite way of saying it, but she looks like a photocopy of the woman currently waving the letter-opener at me. Her hair is longer and tied up in a bun, and she's slightly shorter, but all the same features are there in different proportions. She's also wearing jeans and a jumper, whereas the one threatening to slit me for my contents is a bit more glammed up. Maybe it's because she's not waving a weapon in my face, but I instantly warm to the second woman more than the one in front of me. I'm prone to that sort of snap judgement.

Up on the first floor – looking over the balustrade – is a tall black guy, broad too. On his top half he's wearing a hoodie that says MACRO DATA REFINEMENT (no idea). He's holding an open laptop plus an extra power pack wedged into his left hand, and two phones in his right.

Both the newcomers converge on centre stage. The tall guy pockets his phones and carefully deposits the laptop on a side table – it's running about eighteen programs, I can see from here – before returning to where the rest of us are standing.

'Em, what is this?'

Em (Letter-Opener) stands back now her friends are here. Unhelpfully, she's still between me and the door. If she wasn't, I'd bolt in a second.

'He tried to trick me into admitting I was the homeowner, and then he told me he knew it wasn't my name. I think he's a cop.'

The air thickens to the point that you could cut it even with a blunt letter-opener. I'm looking at three distinctly angry faces.

The photocopy asks: 'What do we do with him?'

Letter-Opener has a bright idea. 'Knock him out then drive him up to Hampstead Heath and leave him there. By the time he wakes up we'll be gone. We were about to shift to the new gaff anyway.'

The guy speaks. 'I'm not knocking anyone out, Em.'

Photocopy adds, 'Also, if we knock him out we'll need a bigger car. We won't all fit in the Mini with one of us unconscious.'

'We can't just let him go, guys. We don't know what he wants from us. And Jonny, in life sometimes you have to knock people out.'

'I'm just saying, acts of violence are nothing but moments of short-term moral failure, which only ever breed new cycles of pain. I read that in my course.'

'Jonny, please shut up about your course.'

Photocopy says, 'We could go through his pockets. Or just keep asking him. Legally, I think they have to tell you if you ask three times.'

'I don't think the Met operate under that sort of honour system, El.'

At the risk of making things worse, I raise a hand.

'Hello? Can I contribute here?'

All three of them are looking at me. It's time to do what I do best: talk my way out.

'I think I've picked up that there's something going on here. I just want to reassure you that if you think I'm in the police, I'm not. I also won't go *to* the police. You ... uh, Em, was it?' – Letter-Opener scowls assent – 'it sounds like you're worried about me talking to anyone about this. Rest assured I just want to get out of this house conscious and with all my organs in the same place. We can leave it at that.'

The tension in the room slackens a bit. Then Em says,

'Bullshit,' and it tightens again. I try hard not to sigh too obviously.

'Right. Well, if you don't believe me, let's just remember that I'm also clearly not a vicar, as you've worked out. I . . .'

What am I, actually? I didn't have a secondary cover set up after the vicar. Dammit. This place was meant to be empty; why would I need a primary story, let alone a secondary one? Faced with Em's eyebrow, I completely fall apart, and for the first time in a while, I give someone an approximation of the truth.

'. . . I thought this place was empty and that I might be able to stay here for a few nights. Clearly it's not empty, and you were here first, so I can just—'

Photocopy interrupts me. 'Sorry? Are you saying that you do this too?'

Half an hour has passed.

We're in the principal drawing room (baby grand piano, gold brocade curtains with foot-long tassels, tatty Louis Quatorze sofas left by previous owner). We've all got a cuppa, in this arrangement: Al – builder's tea, two sugars; Em – some disgustingly sharp gunpowder concoction; Elle – Sleepytime herbal mix; Jonny – isotonic rehydration drink in ancient Sports Direct mug. Things are much jollier than before, even if Em still has the letter-opener within shanking distance.

'How long did you say you've been doing this?' I ask.

'Six months. We're pretty pleased with how it's been going

so far.' That's Elle, who turns out to be – knew it – Em's younger sister.

'And you call it . . .'

'*Piscining*.'

'Why was that again?'

Em sighs. '*Because* El and I found out about it in France last year. Millions of places in France have their own swimming pools, way more than here. But there's almost no way of enforcing the security of your own pool. Owners keep getting home to find strangers have been enjoying their pools all day. The police can't do anything about it. We started doing that and just, you know, worked our way up to the homes themselves.'

'Via the pool house?' I must have let a bit of scorn into my tone because Em bristles as she answers.

'A lot of pool houses have bedrooms, bathrooms and food supplies. So yes, since you ask, we started in the pool houses before trading up. What about you?'

There's no way I'm going to tell them anything more about myself than I already have. Frankly, I don't even like them knowing my fake name, never mind my real one. Questions about people always deflect their attention back onto themselves, where they feel it naturally belongs, so I turn my focus: 'And, sorry, how did you enter the scene, Jonny?'

'We met online.'

'How do you mean?'

'I met the girls when they needed something done. Security on a bigger place they wanted to get into. They were after a bit of technical support, and they found me via a little Discord server I was running.'

I have no idea what Discord is, but I'm not going to give them the satisfaction of asking. 'So you managed to disable the security . . . remotely, did you say?' He nods. 'And then you just decided to throw in your lot with them.'

Another nod. 'I was suffering some vexed matters of accommodation at that precise time.' Jonny speaks like this a lot. 'And it transpired that our talents are mutually complementary.'

Em hasn't fallen for my new line of enquiry, or taken her eyes off me. 'Anyway. What about you?'

I'll have to tell them something, I suppose. 'I've been *interloping*' – slight emphasis there to show them it's a) a proprietary term and b) the right one – 'for about eight years now. And I've focused on one country. I'm pretty good at it.'

'Hence you turning up and just knocking on the door tonight? That your standard modus operandi?'

'There are plenty of good reasons to do that. Firstly, this place should have been empty . . .'

'Which it wasn't.'

'. . . meaning it was important to ascertain what was going on.'

'And you picked "trendy vicar" as your cover? Jesus.'

'Nothing wrong with that.' I stand by this. Ideally you want to be someone who most people would chew their thumbs off to avoid talking to, and an earnest vicar fundraising for a new pipe is the sweet spot. I've done a lot of Jehovah's Witnessing in my time too.

'How sweet. Guys, it feels like we've met the last of the old-time craftsmen in this business.'

Now it's my turn to bristle. 'For your information, what I do is very precise, it's delicate.'

Em snorts.

'I haven't seen you guys get into a place, but I can guarantee my methods would be an improvement.'

Elle squeaks at that, and claps. 'Well why don't you come along with us tomorrow?'

Em and Jonny's heads both snap round to her. 'Sorry?'

'Yeah, Elle, what the fuck?'

'He wants to see how we work. We should show him. It's not like he's a threat, we know that now. It's only an hour's drive.'

All three of the rest of us have our hands up.

'Excuse me, but I'm not your apprentice . . .'

'No way are we letting this random creep come along . . .'

'My systems are calibrated for the three of us, no more . . .'

'Sorry, did you say "creep"? Because . . .'

'I'd say it again in a heartbeat, you little weirdo . . .'

'I'd rather be a creep than a psycho who can't see a letter-opener without . . .'

'. . . would have to secure alternate transportation, which risks compromising our . . .'

There's a bit more cross-talk, which Elle manages to deal with by marching over to the baby grand and thumping bad chords repeatedly until we shut up. She turns around.

'No more buts. He's in the same line of work, we are friendly people, and if we don't, I'm not coming either. All right?'

I didn't think Elle had much authority in the group, but I was clearly wrong, because after a few seconds of silence, Em shrugs.

'Whatever. I mean, he doesn't even want to, Elle. Look at him.'

This puts me in a bind, because I realise out of nowhere that I really do quite like the idea. And although I'd die before admitting it to these amateurs, I have been feeling a bit – what's the word? – a bit *outmoded* recently. As if my body is joining in with these guys against me, my ankle throbs to remind me, *You could be a bit fitter, too.*

I'm curious about how these guys operate. And, in the unlikely event that they know something I don't – maybe this Jonny guy has some skill, maybe not – I can always learn how to do exactly what they do and replicate it when I'm back on my own. Anyway, they look wet behind the ears. Six months they've been doing it? Rank amateurs. They're lucky they haven't been arrested.

So I shrug too, and say, as nonchalantly as I can manage: 'I wouldn't object to joining you for a place, assuming you have one in mind.'

Em snorts. Jonny raises an eyebrow as if to say, *this won't end well*. It falls to Elle to clap like a schoolgirl and say: 'That's settled, then. How exciting!'

I can't sleep.

I'm lying in the fourth bedroom, on the first floor, with zero idea what's going on. Em and Elle have been in the master bedroom – the one I think of as mine – since they got here a fortnight ago. I've elected to sleep as far away as possible, in the room at the other end of the corridor, overlooking next door's mega-extension. Jonny said he doesn't need a bed because he's semi-nocturnal. So that leaves me in the poky room with the squeaky bed frame and moth-eaten mattress. If I was really paranoid, I could have tried to find another house in the area, but I'm whacked.

Not enough to sleep though, apparently. I can't believe there are other people doing this. In eight years I've met plenty of blaggers defying their landlords, lots of squatters, even a few people squatting their own homes, trying to dodge eviction: but someone else actually interloping? A first. Hard not to feel threatened.

I can hear their voices downstairs still, and the clink of glasses too; they were opening another bottle as I went to bed. I grope around on the floor and eventually manage to jab my phone. Half two. They really must be young.

There wouldn't be any harm in checking out what they're saying. If I'd been thinking properly, I would have hidden my phone downstairs to record the room: as it is, I'll just have to stay quiet.

The door doesn't make a sound as I ease it open, which is a relief, although I'm certainly moving slowly. It takes about five minutes to get it open enough to slip out onto the landing. I should have made a creak-map the last time I was here – instead I just ease along the edge, where most people tend not to tread. As I get to the top of the stairs, I see the light from the main parlour, and lean down to hear the conversation.

'What about the body?' That's Jonny speaking.

'Come on, Jonny. Standard procedure. Once it's been stripped for parts we'll ditch the rest in the reservoir. Guys, this is basic stuff, there's no need to keep on going over it.'

It could be a car they're talking about, of course. Seems likeliest. I nudge down another step or two, just to get their voices clearer.

'I don't like changing plans. Especially as we only secured the asset today.'

Could still be a car. Perfectly possible they've stolen a car and are working out what to do with it.

'All right. But I'm not taking responsibility for it if it goes wrong.'

'What could go wrong?'

'Remember last time? He came round during the procedure, started thrashing about on the table like a tuna. It was awful.'

Doesn't sound like it could be a car, actually, on reflection.

'That was Elle miscalculating the dose. We won't make that mistake again.'

'I have apologised for that, like, fifty times. You weighed him wrong, anyway. But we have this one all sorted. We'll get the dimensions, carry out the procedure, ditch the rest . . . Who wanted this one again?'

Parts of me I haven't thought about for years are starting to break out in perspiration. Have you ever actually experienced a cold sweat? It's real. I lean against the wall for support; the voices carry on.

'I think they were based in Nepal. The inner organs, anyway. The extremities are for that woman in Malawi.'

Oh my God, oh my God, oh my God. I have to stay calm. They'll have bolted the front door, of course. What's paramount now is keeping as much space as possible between me and them.

I thank the god of interloping that I know this building inside out. There's a window in my room which has a tiny ledge outside it, big enough to balance on, and a useful drainpipe by its side. I'll climb out there, clamber as far down as I can, try and hit the ground on my un-fucked ankle, get away from these freaks. Jesus, Mary and Joseph, what have I stumbled into?

'We'd better get started now if we're going to finish before sunrise. The shaman claims she can always tell if the organs have been exposed to sunlight.'

Who are these people?

'Shall we get started, then?' That's Jonny again. I push myself off the wall, as silently as possible.

'All right.' There's Em. 'But we'll have to be fast.'

'Why?'

'He's on the stairs right now, eavesdropping on us.'

A moment's pause, and then the three of them burst out laughing.

I'm so deep in the quicksand of terror that it takes me a few seconds to compute this. Eventually I haul my way out and manage to think a little more clearly. Then, as they keep laughing, I stand and head downstairs. Em looks up, still giggling.

'Oh, I'm sorry. I really am. But it was worth it to see your face. Go and look at the door frame of your room.'

I climb back up the stairs and scan the door. Just at shin level is a little dark circle that looks like a badly repaired hole for a screw. I lean down, pluck it off and inspect it with the light on my phone.

Serves me right for not following Rule 22: *Check for cameras twice – once by day, then again by night. At night, even a well-hidden one will show up if you aim your phone's torch directly at it – the light will reflect off the lens.* I didn't think I'd have to re-check once I was actually in a house, though. I head back down.

'That wasn't funny.'

'I voted against,' says Elle.

Em – clearly the instigator – shakes her head. 'Sorry, Al, but it was. Just wanted to show you how good Jonny's kit is. Probably could have thought of a kinder way of doing it than that.'

Jonny pipes up. 'Really it's a lesson in trusting people.'

Elle adds: 'Exactly. Now that we've got you once, you'll know that we're almost certainly not planning to sell your eyeballs to a shaman in darkest Peru.'

'OK. Very funny, everyone, you got me. Let's not make a big thing out of it.' I'm trying to smile along, but I don't think anyone looking at my face would buy it. So I turn, now with less than zero dignity, and return to my room, pausing only to wedge a small, pointless bookcase under the door handle.

Back in bed, I resolve to give serious thought to whether

it's a good idea to go along with these people. They seem to have a knack of making me feel stupid, right from the moment Em first answered the door. But I'm drifting now, and I can't quite say where I am, and I panic that I can feel myself swaying, because I've been distributed across six separate shipping crates and we're all heading down the Suez Canal, but by that point it's too late and . . .

4

. . . and I wake, late, to the smell of breakfast. I wash, dress, and head down to the kitchen, where Elle is home-making a dish of granola. I didn't even know people made their own granola. In the middle of the kitchen island there's a breakfast so lavish – juice, muffins, scrambled eggs, toast – we could be in an American sitcom.

Jonny is on the ancient armchair in the corner – it's one of those kitchens, the ones so cavernous they need ancillary furniture just to fill up the floor space. He's wearing the clothes he was in last night, and is still on his laptop. I haven't seen him more than a few feet away from that laptop yet.

'Morning.'

'Morning, Al!' I get the sense, faintly, just the overwhelmingly obvious sense, you understand, that Elle might be a morning person. She's not actually wearing a gingham apron, but she'd suit one.

'Where did you get that kit? They don't have any kitchen stuff here.'

'This is all mine,' she says. 'Just because we're in someone else's home doesn't mean we have to live like animals.'

The last time I stayed here, I lived on grubby takeaways, which I ordered to be delivered to – Rule 30 – the corner of the street, always paying in cash. The time before that, I was temporarily on those meal supplement milkshakes, and got through about four buckets of grim grey sludge a day because I was convinced they were a superior means of leaving no trace. I lost half a stone, all joy in mealtimes, and the will to live.

'There's nothing wrong with pre-prepared food,' I say. 'A lot of it is very healthy these days. Actually better for you than home-made stuff.'

Elle smiles and gives my torso the tiniest glance before going back to her pan. I can't help noticing that a lot of the food in the fridge is from Waitrose.

'How do you afford this stuff?'

'We all have jobs as corporate lawyers,' says Elle.

'Really?'

'No.'

'Oh.'

She grins at me. 'Jonny does a lot of work in crypto.'

'Really? Trading it?'

'Don't be silly,' says Jonny. 'Mug's game. I teach other people how to trade it. To be fair, I do warn them they probably won't make any money out of it, but that doesn't seem to stop them paying a hundred and fifty quid a pop for an online course led by a silhouette in a hoodie.' He looks faintly troubled at how gullible people are, then shrugs.

I nod, then look back to Elle. 'What about you two?'

'Oh, we got an inheritance a couple of years ago, but it's a bit vulgar to talk about all that, isn't it?'

Before I can ask further, a voice in my ear says, 'Boo.' I jump, but it's only Em, wearing a ridiculously fluffy dressing gown. A patch on the breast reads: CRIMINAL MEOWSTERMIND, with a picture of a kitten sitting at a nineties computer beneath a rainbow.

'Good morning.'

'Sleep well? No witch doctors visiting you in the night?'

'Ha ha, yeah. No, no voodoo, thanks.' I've resolved to be as personable as possible with these people. It's only going to be a day or so out of my normal run, so I may as well be nice. 'So . . . are you guys going to tell me where we're off to?'

Em sits on one of the stools under the island and grabs a muffin from the central display. 'Jonny, can you show him?'

Jonny swivels the screen as I approach. 'Heard of Bridling?'

'Cotswolds?'

Em nods. 'Little hamlet in Oxfordshire. Always being listed as one of the most beautiful villages in the most stunning part of the loveliest county, blah blah blah. Worth killing to get a place there, all the agents say. About one house in four is a second home. And on the outskirts of Bridling . . .' She leans over and tries to tap at the screen. Jonny, subtly, pulls the laptop away so her finger doesn't grease it up. 'The perfect place.'

Jonny takes over. 'Eight bedrooms. Properly old. Former vicarage. Must have been some vicar, though, because it's *nice*. Fully furnished and maintained, as far as I can tell from satellite photos. And, crucially, owned by someone who we know is going to be out of the country for the next two months.'

'How do you know?'

He toggles a tab. 'Flight data. The owner listed his address as this home on his BA flight. He'll be in Dubai for ten weeks as of yesterday.'

'How'd you access the flight data?'

Jonny wiggles his fingers.

Satellite photos! Flight data! I'm trying to act nonchalant, as though these are all well-worn tools on my own Bat Belt. 'What's the owner called?' I always like to know an owner's name. That way, when someone mistakes you for them and calls you by their name, you can respond appropriately.

'D.H.'

'D.H.?'

Jonny shrugs. 'My database just has initials. I could get the full name, but it would take me a little while. Anyway, we have the flight dates there and back, so we're good.'

'How did you find the place?'

'I've set up little snares for the top twenty postcodes we're especially interested in. Whenever someone books a long trip from one of them, we look at the dates and fit them into the itinerary.'

'I do the diary,' says Elle.

I try to keep looking unimpressed. 'Have you checked the security? Done a ground recce?'

'We do all that later.' Thank God. Something I'm more careful about than they are.

'Have you checked the Land Registry to see who owns the house?'

This, incidentally, is one of my favourite things to do. Did you know about it? You can search for literally any property in the country, and it tells you who last bought it, how much for, what year, and a few other fascinating little details. All that for three quid, and then you can research the owner at your leisure. It's glorious. It's clearly not one of Jonny's favourite pastimes, though.

'We haven't, no. Is that something you do every time?' I nod. 'Doesn't feel strictly necessary. Still,' and here he makes a note, 'accumulating unnecessary data frequently reaps dividends. I'll have a look later.'

'Are you sure it's a second home? I only do second homes.'

'I thought you were interested in how we operated, Al?'

I smile at Em. 'Of course I am. Must be forgetting my manners.'

She smiles back, just as friendly, just as dishonest. And with that politely disagreed, we sit down to breakfast.

Eight hours later, night is throwing its ebon veil over the Ram's Head, a charming pub-with-rooms in the heart of Bridling. It's got an actual skull nailed above the bar, horns and all. A bit forbidding.

I wish we weren't here. I wish we'd made our way into the house in daylight, unpacked, then gone out for dinner. But these guys have their own method and they're convinced I'll convert once I've tried it. I'd never admit it, but I've been impressed enough so far that I'm swallowing my better judgement to go along with them.

Little bit of life advice for you: don't ever, ever swallow your better judgement. If we'd done it my way, there's a chance I wouldn't be writing this document at all, let alone typing it on a computer that has the words HMP BRIXTON SUX carved into the side of the monitor.

But I digress.

The pisciners lazed around at the house until about eleven, then packed up. I did my usual fingerprint scrub, and while they weren't quite as careful, thankfully we have similar notions about not nicking the silverware.

Then, after a lengthy get-out – Jonny remembered he'd forgotten to collect about six internal cameras – we drove to Bridling. Or rather, I drove. As my contribution, I'd rented a van from my regular garage, so these three could leave their car in London. Tariq, who runs Mr Toad's Motors, was clearly surprised at me hiring anything bigger than a Mini, but he's polite enough not to ask questions. Tariq is a proper gentleman.

We stashed the van off a lay-by, off a lane, off the main road linking Bridling to civilisation, then walked to the village and into the Ram's Head.

It's a stunning pub. The windows are mullioned (think I'm using that word right? Each window is made of 150 tiny windows). The tables are huge heavy oak numbers that probably date back to the Civil War, and the menu is in that tiny font which informs older punters, *We're going to flatter you into thinking that you're young enough to read this without your glasses. Also, don't look at the prices.*

Now, I maintain that coming here in the first place was a mistake. But Elle's a foodie and insists we pass for visitors who are just taking in the local area. I'm not convinced. For a start, it is extremely white out here. There's a preppy Asian family at one of the tables, but barring them, it's monochrome. Even Em and Elle look exotic, and Jonny is the only black guy in the place. He doesn't appear to have noticed, though, because he's busy with a screwdriver and the remnants of a Rubik's Cube. The manager looked politely appalled when she brought our mains.

As for Bridling itself: we looked around on our walk through, and Em was right. This is a gorgeous village. They have a *Norman* church, for heaven's sake, surrounded by an unkempt churchyard with crazily angled tombstones and galloping lichens. There is doubtless a functioning bell-ringing society.

The *reses* are *des*, too – the centre's all charming thatched cottages opening onto the lane-and-a-half road, bigger detached places in the 'suburban' bit, then further out a few really grand houses, one of which we'll be breaking into in about half an hour. The high street is a parade of little antique shops and boutiques, plus one upmarket grocer's – it's so posh there isn't even a supermarket, but there's a Waitrose (of course) within a ten-minute drive. I'm impressed.

I can't work these three out, though. I know Em and Elle are sisters, but I can't decide if either of them is with Jonny. Both? I suppose it's possible, but they've given nothing away so far. Although I think Em is single and straight, because contrary to all sensible pre-interlope rules, she has spent the last two pints giving the boy behind the bar a series of remarkably suggestive looks. He – clearly an agricultural student and preoccupied with soil erosion or whatever it is they learn – has not reciprocated at all. Elle has observed with faint amusement but not joined in. Jonny appears to only have eyes for his Rubik's Cube.

Mainly I'm still stunned that these people do exactly what I do, except – and, again, a team of award-winning CIA waterboarders couldn't persuade me to admit this – with rather more technical proficiency. I remind myself: *Soft skills are real, soft skills are real, there's a reason you've never been caught* . . .

'Al?'

'Mm?'

'Time to go.' The light outside has softened enough that

you could doubt your eyesight, and that's the way they like it. The golden hour has given way to rural murk. Jonny picks up the bill, which comes to over a hundred quid – there really must be money in teaching suckers how to trade whatever the latest cryptocurrency is – then we gather our clobber and leave. Em gives the barman a wink as she goes, which prompts a whispered chat with Elle about whether she should pop back here for last orders. As we leave, the ram's skull gives me one final encouraging grin.

It's about a twenty-minute walk to the house, which is called Larksfoot. (I once spent a year trying to stay exclusively in houses with names rather than numbers, just to see if they genuinely are much nicer. Spoiler: they are.) But just before we get there – we're climbing the hill leading out of the village, and thankfully there are no cars around – Elle gives a little squeak, and claps her hand over her mouth.

'Oh, shit.'
'What?' says Em.
'My coat.'
'What about it?'
'It's still in the pub.'
'Oh. Sure?'
Elle gestures at her clearly uncoated torso.
'How did you forget that?'
'It's not cold enough to feel it. And you were distracting me.'
'What?'
'By vamping at that eighteen-year-old behind the bar . . .'
'Right, firstly he was twenty-two, secondly he's called

Marco, and thirdly, if I'd been *vamping* I would already have his legs wrapped—'

'It's all good,' says Jonny. 'I have the kit we need. Elle, just catch up in a bit.'

'Are you sure you don't want to wait? Just in case there's any—'

'Nah, you go for it. You know how boring the first half-hour of most jobs is for you two.'

'Want me to come with?' Em asks.

'Nice try. You stay here and show Al how we do it. I'll tell Marco you say hi.'

Em grins. 'Give me a ring when you're close.'

Elle raises a thumb, and disappears back down the rapidly darkening lane. *Then*, a little voice whispers in my ear, *there were three*. Although I don't think it would have made too much difference to what came next.

The grounds are surrounded by a proper wall, and iron gates ten feet high, with a keypad on the outside. This surprises Jonny, who claims he does at least three virtual walk-throughs before each actual break-in, but who on this occasion was a bit stuck, because the road has become a lane and the Google Maps people clearly got bored or hungry before this point and turned back. The guys only know how nice the house is because of some write-up it got in a glossy architectural mag a few years ago.

None of that gets us through the gates, but 'It's not a problem,' Jonny says, and searches his leather satchel for a little palm computer which he proceeds to plug into the keypad. He also shines a sideways light on the keypad, which shows him which buttons have been most frequently touched and drastically reduces the number of combinations he'll have to cycle.

While he's doing that, I refrain from pointing out that if they'd been here during delivery hours, they wouldn't have had this problem. Annoyingly, I don't need to refrain for long, because after about ninety seconds Jonny murmurs, 'OK,' and the gates moan open. He covers the sensor with a little tab so Elle can get in when she catches up.

Em and Jonny walk up the drive towards the house, and even though every instinct is telling me to skulk through the scrubby trees on either side, I accompany them.

They weren't wrong about the place being a stunner. Red bricks, interrupted by jazzy patterns, and from the size of the place the ceilings inside must be about twenty feet high. I'd guess Victorian – either that or a very faithful reproduction. It has a slight 'medieval keep' feel too – something about the shape of the rooftop, I guess, which is high and slanting. You wouldn't want to have to keep your balance up there. The gardens are well kempt too, and too big for your average wealthy professional to keep in hand. This place definitely *has* got a gardener, if not a few. We'll need to watch out for them.

The curtains are closed, but some lights inside are on. As we get close, I could have sworn that the configuration of lights has changed from when I first saw it, but I'm not sure. Either I've made a mistake, or the timer set by the owner is a more complicated one than usual. I don't say anything, and we start circling the house. You genius, Al.

The security light snaps on at one point in our walkaround, and although I'm pretty used to them, I still jump, before feeling embarrassed about it. No cameras, which is a relief, but Jonny tells me that even if there were any present, he would have ways of dealing with them. He seems a bit disappointed not to show off the full package, to be honest.

The side door is locked, of course, but that's what Jonny's red backpack, patched with a label reading RIGHT TO PICK IT, is for. Three minutes later, the door swings open. Not that I'm threatened, you understand. Probably an easy lock.

I was worried that Em and Jonny would march in chatting away, so it's a relief that they fall silent as we enter the boot room. There's something about your first time in someone else's home that puts you on your best behaviour.

The first proper room we enter is a formal drawing room, lit by the moon. The curtains are twice my height, and the internal wall is lined with books. Not any old stuff, either; big classy volumes coated in the leather of long-dead cows. There is even – dream of dreams – a railed ladder running along the room. These people must be posh. I'm going to really catch up on my reading, although it looks like I won't be reading anything published after 1850.

The rest of the room is beautiful too – cream chairs and chaises longues, an ornate wooden writing table. It's lovely, but despite all its pricey furnishings and decor, the room as a whole feels a bit like it's been stood up for a date; like it's there for show, not for use. It's all rather antiseptic.

The tables are cluttered with ornaments. I'm relieved I brought my camera along to snap the way everything is arranged, so we can do a proper get-out. It's especially useful on longer visits, but even if I leave in a few days – which I almost certainly will – I guess I could send these three the photos, as an aide-memoire. No harm in spreading good practice. Maybe I could become an interloping consultant.

We pass through into the front hall, the core of the house. It's austere and oak-lined, and has that weird double-porch arrangement you get in posh houses, where the outer porch is for the brollies and Barbours and generally stinks of dog. The hall itself is properly grand. The two are linked by a wooden door with a lovely stained-glass window in the top half. Off to the side is a huge modern kitchen, with a stack of abandoned crockery littering one surface in the dark.

From the hall, we drift in different directions. Em glides up the stairs. Jonny turns left into the kitchen – I guess he's intending to scan the ground floor for any internal security. I head further back, to the rear of the house, where a strip of light beneath a door tells me there's another timer switch operating. The light is low, but as I open the door, it's enough to show me I'm in a study, again lined with shelves. Unlike the first room we entered, this one feels properly lived in; the small desk is covered in paperwork, there are heaps of books on the floor, and it's a lot warmer than you'd expect of an empty home in early April.

It's funny, the things you don't see when you're not expecting them. I usually benefit from this quirk of the human brain – if people aren't expecting to see me somewhere, as often as not their gaze will slip right away and they'll forget all about me. But now, looking at this cosy little study, I fall foul of exactly the same quirk, and it takes me several seconds to make sense of the shapes before me.

This really was the last moment I could have extricated myself from the story, if I'd been thinking straight. Turn and run, Al. Just pivot and sprint for the back door, and you'll never have to see any of these people again.

Being – as we've established – too stupid for that, I stand and stare as the room resolves itself.

In the corner is an old, overstuffed armchair. In the armchair there is a middle-aged man, who is looking right at me. And in the middle-aged man's hand is a small, pointy object I eventually recognise as a gun.

5

'Don't move,' he says. This is superfluous. I'm so surprised I couldn't move if he set my jeans on fire.

It's harder than you think to recognise a gun when you're looking directly at it. There's almost nothing to see. It's only when he moves his hand a fraction that I think to myself: *Al, you're now standing at gunpoint.* Weird word, *gunpoint*. If it ever applies to you, you're not the one doing the pointing. Oh my God, Al. Concentrate, will you?

The man gets to his feet, rather unsteadily. He's one of those men who seems a normal height in a chair, only for you to reconsider as he keeps on unfolding upwards. Keeps his height in his legs. The side table has a bottle of wine on it, down to the last inch. A *tipsy* gunman. Today keeps improving.

'Move across there and sit.'

Rule 7 is one of the most important in the entire interloper's bible: *Talk*. When you're talking, you can shape the conversation, and if you can do that, you can usually buy yourself the time you need to improve your situation. When I met Mr Lethbridge yesterday – God, yesterday? – I said so much and so fast that he was putty in my hands. If you keep speaking, people don't notice the cracks in the last sentence you said, because you've just given them a new one to absorb.

But I'm so mesmerised by the pistol's pert little mouth as it follows me that I fail to say a single word, and instead move to the overstuffed sofa he bids me towards. It's one of those really comfortable ones you can fall into if you're not careful, meaning you'll take about thirty seconds to get out of it.

The other thought I have is: *Three*. Three jobs in a row have gone wrong now. The Lethbridge place, Balfour Villas, and now this. The last job that went wrong before these was a year ago, when I was masquerading as an equine physiotherapist and someone asked me a difficult question about horse musculature. What is going on? Maybe I'm cursed. Maybe this is my life now.

The big guy speaks. 'What's that?'

'Just my camera.' My hand goes to my side.

'Slow *down*. Don't get it out. Just unclip it, drop it, and sit.'

I do as he says, and perch on the sofa's edge.

I notice, as I move, that the man's gun hand isn't terribly steady. I'm no marksman, but I can tell when someone is capable at whatever they're doing, and I'd be surprised if this guy had ever held a gun before, from the way he's clutching it.

Half his hand is gripping too tight, and his massive fingers are all squished up in the wrong parts. A tipsy, *inexperienced* gunman. Brilliant, brilliant, brilliant.

Still covering me with a wobbling barrel, he moves across the room and opens the door. 'Call your friends down here. Don't mention me.'

'OK. No problem, man.' Man? What a weird label to affix to someone who might kill me at any moment. An old joke occurs to me. *What do you call a three-hundred-pound gorilla armed with a shotgun? Sir.* God, is that going to be the last dad joke I ever think of? I raise my voice. 'Guys? Can you come here a second?'

Jonny arrives first. He has the same reaction to the gun that I did, and at our new friend's urgent gesture, he sits beside me.

Em arrives last. She's already talking as she comes in: 'What is it, have you found *another* thing you think you can do better than . . .' She tails off.

'Get over there.'

I see her considering making a move, then thinking better of it. At the same moment, her hand goes to her jeans pocket, and I'm pretty sure we're having the same thought. *Elle.* If we get a message to her, she can . . . call the police? Something cleverer than that?

It's getting quite cosy on the sofa.

'All right. Who sent you?'

He's big in every way, this guy. Huge hands – real sausage fingers – and a muffin-top neck mushrooming out of his collar. His shirt buttons are doing the Lord's work keeping the package together. The visible bits of skin above his no-longer-a-neckline have the kind of overboiled redness that you only get with a rigorous regimen of putting away a bottle of wine or two each day for a couple of decades. His accent is Essex, I think, and his short grey hair is incongruously spiked all over. *Maybe he used to be a punk.* God, the irrelevant thoughts you have when someone might be about to shoot you.

I find my voice first. 'Sent? Nobody sent us. We're sorry, we—'

'Don't talk shit. One of the Balham lot? The cops?'

'Sir, we really don't know what you mean.' Jonny is going for the 'sir' option, and good for him. 'We're just squatters.'

'High-end ones,' I'm compelled to add. It's genuinely possible I'm going to get myself shot because I needed to clarify that I'm a cut above your standard home invader. 'We saw your house online. We thought it was empty.'

'Yeah, yeah, and I'm Princess Michael of Kent,' the man says. 'Where's your gun? Or was it going to be some other way? You look like the one who'd do it,' he says, pointing to Jonny.

'Do what?'

'If you guys don't tell me who sent you, I'll start shooting the sofa, and I'm a very bad shot.' He raises his pistol; I raise my hands in the universal gesture for 'please, *please* calm down'.

'Look, we don't know who you are. We don't know anything about this house except that we thought it was empty. We don't know your name, we know nothing about you. If you want us to, we can just go now.'

He laughs. 'Oh, yeah. I see. You guys break in to find out if I'm here, is that it? And someone's waiting at the gate to do me as I leave? No thank you.'

I glance sideways. Em's hand is inching towards her pocket. She doesn't need to type a message – if she can just dial Elle's number, Elle will hear conversation, and . . . I have no idea. Act appropriately. Even the police would be fine. I'd rather be in a cell than under three feet of this guy's back garden.

'I'm serious,' I say. 'We are squatters, quite specialised ones, and we picked your house because it looked nice and we thought you were in Dubai. We don't want any trouble and it looks like you don't either. So we can just—'

'What the *fuck* are you doing?' This is to Em, whose hand freezes halfway into her pocket. 'Give me that. Slowly.'

She hands her phone over. For a second it looks like he's considering shooting it, but then realises how insane that would look and settles for dropping it on the desk, hoisting a brass paperweight in his free hand, and hammering it until the screen smashes. 'No fucking calls. You're staying in this room until I've worked out what to do with you.'

He's clearly appreciating the difficulty of his situation. If all three of us acted at once, we could probably overpower him, but there's no way for us to coordinate when we should go for it. On top of that, we're sitting and he's standing. If we all ran, he'd definitely shoot at least one of us, maybe two. One of us might get away, but there's no telling which one.

Oh, God, am I going to have to *do* something?

Jonny is clearly thinking the same thing. He's the tallest of us, even taller than our new friend, and squashed next to him on the sofa I can tell his entire body is tense. Oh, boy. I don't want Jonny to get himself shot, but I *really* don't want to do anything myself. Why can't I think of the words that will persuade this guy to let us go?

'What's your name?' I ask.

He scowls at me. 'Piss off. Either your story is true, in which case I'm not telling you, or it's not, in which case you already know.'

Jonny is about to move. I can feel it. He's inching his body into a better position. I have to stop him. How? If I move, the man will shoot me. If I don't, he'll shoot Jonny. And even though I hardly know Em and Jonny, I don't want either of them shot. For one thing, the man might miss and hit me.

I speak, aiming my words half at Jonny. I try to sound a bit more RP, too. This character of mine is one I've nicknamed Baffled Man Honestly Wronged. 'I think we should all stay calm. I'm *sure* there's some way we can prove to you that we are who we say, and we can let you go back to your—'

Just then, there's a loud knock at the front door of the house.

Sausage Fingers hears the knock, and it's his turn to freeze. 'Christ. How many of you are there?'

'That's our friend. My sister,' Em says. 'She left her coat at the pub, we told her to come along when she'd got it. She's one of us, she's just another squatter. You'll see, she looks like me.'

Sausage Fingers edges towards the door of the study, still covering us, and opens it. The knock comes again.

As he looks around, two thoughts occur to me.

The first is: *Hang on, Em told Elle to phone when she got here.*

The second is: *Elle wouldn't knock like that.* That was an authoritative knock, as if whoever's outside knows the place well. Elle seems more the sort to call – or ideally text – from the doorstep.

Unfortunately, because I have both of these thoughts at the same time, I'm only halfway through each of them when the man makes up his mind. He goes to the closed curtains, nudges one aside to make sure the window is locked, and looks at us again.

'You might be telling the truth. You might not. You're in the shit either way, I assure you. Don't. Fucking. Move.'

He leaves the study.

We hear his footsteps cross the hall, we hear the door to the outer hall open, we hear a key turn in a deadlock, and we hear a click as the main door to the house opens.

Then we hear a thunderous, booming report, which – I'm no expert – can only have been made by a gun going off at close range.

6

A lot happens in the next few seconds, so I'm going to have to calm down and try to get it in exactly the right order.

Em screams – someone screams, at least, I couldn't swear it wasn't me – and jumps to her feet.

I realise she's about to run into the hall and try to accost a drunk, erratic, armed man, who's just shot someone else by the sound of it and won't have much compunction about firing again. Better stop her. Jonny's between us, but he's had the same thought. Em shakes off his arm, and runs to the door, shouting, 'Elle! Elle!'

She stops shouting a second after she gets through the door, though. Even as I'm scrambling past Jonny, I feel relieved that she's come to her senses, then realise the man might just be pointing the gun right at her.

Then, as I'm running, I realise I might accidentally be running into a situation where I might get *myself* shot – who are these people to me anyway? – and I'm so appalled at my own momentary burst of selflessness that my foot swerves sideways of its own accord, meaning I wobble into a reproduction bust of Julius Caesar by the door, sitting on a fake column. Then the rest of me realises that Jonny's about to cannon into me from the other side, and I push off it into the hall. The pillar and bust start heading to the floor.

All this happens in the eight feet and two seconds between the sofa and the study door. I know, I know, it seems like a lot. I don't know how I fit it all in.

As I get through the door, this is the sight that greets me: Em is standing halfway across the floor. The front door is swinging open, and just inside it, straddling the inner and outer halls, the master of the house is lying on his back. The stained glass from the door between the porch and the hall makes a shattered rainbow around him. Elle must have knocked him out somehow. But how? She's half his height and wouldn't have expected him to open the door.

Then I realise Elle is nowhere to be seen, and weirder still, the man's changed his shirt. The previous one was white and cotton. This new one is scarlet and satin, and absolutely covered in . . . Oh.

Someone has removed a good portion of our new friend's middle. That's the shot we heard. And now Sausage Fingers appears to be stone dead on the stone floor.

Behind me, there is a massive boom, as the marble bust hits the floor and Julius Caesar cops it all over again.

'Nobody move.' That's Jonny, behind me. He approaches Sausage Fingers, steps gingerly over him, nudges his foot out of the way with his own, and rams the front door shut.

'What do we do?' Em.

Jonny says: 'Ambulance?'

'Good shout.' Em's hand goes to her pocket.

'Guys. No.' What sort of bastard denies an ambulance to a man who's just been shot in the chest? Me, it turns out. 'Look at him. They'd take half an hour to get here, you know that. I don't think you can keep going without a middle for that long. He's *dead*.'

Jonny and Em look at each other, then at the body. In my defence, he's clearly not getting up any time soon. Em leans down, and I say – again, it's weird how quickly you can think in these situations – 'Don't touch him. Fingerprints.'

'For Christ's sake, Al. I want to see if he's breathing.'

'And I'm saying you can see he's not. He's *done*.' Em stays where she is, bent over him. 'We have to just get our things together and—'

And then Sausage Fingers heaves a ragged sigh, and I nearly die of fright.

He starts hauling in breath after breath, God knows how. There's so much of his torso missing – what was it, a shotgun? – that I have no idea what he's even breathing with. One of his arms gropes in the air, then flops back like a spent fish across the remains of his chest.

'Hey. Hey.' Em is down next to him. 'You're all right.' (No idea why she says this.)

His eyes wobble towards her, but he's not really with us.

'We're here to help you.' Debatable, in my opinion, but Em's a diplomat.

'Pen?'

'What?'

He's properly drifting now. A corner of his mouth twitches and his wandering eye catches mine for a second. 'Get your money. It's all . . . in the . . . out . . . building.'

And then he dies, this time for good. His breathing tails off, and his eyes film over. I thought it was made up, but there's a tangible moment where the spark of life actually leaves the premises. It's the most horrible thing I've ever seen.

We all fall silent. Nobody wants to be the first to speak. And then a voice comes from behind us.

'What's going on?'

Elle is standing in the doorway leading to the back of the house. And I'm clearly going mad, because I find the time to think: *Ah, good. At least she got her coat.*

Ten minutes later, we're back in the van. Here's what happened between then and now:

We left Sausage Fingers where he was. No paramedic on the planet could do him any good now.

We gathered our things.

We wiped for fingerprints as best we could, but I had no memory of what I'd touched since I'd got there. We were all in shock.

We headed to the back door, because who knew who was lurking around near the front with the same gun they'd used to kill our host.

We slipped out, raced to the end of the garden, scrambled over the fence, and had a horrible muddy slither round the edge of the neighbouring property until we were back on the lane. Then we ran through the village, strung out. I was in front.

Finally we arrived back at the van, tumbled in, fired it up, and started driving in any direction.

The road is unlit and the moon's gone in. It's pitch dark. We're on the outskirts of Bridling, and after that there's nothing but sudden *Blair Witch*-style woodland. The sides of the road rise up ten feet high on either side, the tarmac sunken between them. It feels like we're driving into a grave. I imagine unknown figures lying ahead of us in the dark, waiting for our headlights.

'Al. *Al.*'

'Huh?'

'Can you slow down a bit? There's nobody after us.'

I ease off, and the needle creeps down from sixty to a slightly less suicidal forty. But at the first turning I see, I brake hard, drag the wheel round, nearly overturn the van hauling it off the road, and switch off all the lights.

'Al? What the hell was that, you could have . . .'

'That was very inconsiderate, I have an over-plastic collarbone . . .'

'Who taught you to drive, Vin Diesel?'

'*Shh.*'

We've stopped on a little farm path, which I can see runs about twenty feet before collapsing into spring mud. Nobody's going to be taking this exit tonight.

We stay there for a minute, then two, waiting. I'm looking back along the road as if the tarmac's about to rear up and eat us. And behind all the surface stuff there's a thought nagging at a corner of my mind, but I'm so tense and exhausted and shocked I can't locate it.

'Al, I really think—'

'Shut *up*. Just wait.'

Time passes. Nobody overtakes us.

'OK. OK, we're probably safe for the moment.'

Elle speaks. 'What the hell happened back there?'

Em fills her in. I've thought of a question I can hardly hold back until she's finished:

'Jonny. You said he was in Dubai. Why wasn't he in Dubai?'

'I don't know,' says Jonny.

'You said you had flight data! Did you not check if he'd got on the plane? Why wasn't he in Dubai where he should have been?'

'Obviously he was in hiding,' Em snaps. 'He was waiting in a dark house with a gun. Clearly he thought someone was coming to kill him. Naturally he would have thought it was us.'

'But we weren't.'

'No,' she says, as if explaining to a kid. 'We weren't. So we're going to be all right.'

This feels optimistic.

Em keeps talking. 'Obviously we can't go back. There'll be someone in the house by now. We must have scared the killer off when he was at the door, but by now he might have—'

'Or she.'

'What's that, Jonny?'

'The killer. You assumed it was a he. Could have been a she.'

'Thanks, Jonny. Always good to get a lesson in everyday sexism from an unexpected angle.'

'It's important to remain aware of our unacknowledged biases.'

Em nods, slightly wearily. '. . . Yeah. So what do we do next?'

The thought I can't grasp is still itching away at me. Something, somewhere has gone badly wrong. Not just in the obvious way – that much is clear – but there's another aspect too. Something personal to me. What is it?

Elle says, brightly, 'Well, we're clear of the house. We've got our gear. We can just get out. Nobody saw us go, nobody followed us. Feels to me like that's all fine.'

'The police will definitely turn up,' I say. 'They'll fingerprint the place.'

'So?'

'So has anyone here ever been fingerprinted?'

Em and Elle say no in unison.

'Good. Me neither.'

There's a little gap. Then Jonny says, 'I might have been fingerprinted once.'

'*Might* have, Jonny?'

'I went to a protest and did a bit of property damage. Got arrested, then released. But they got my fingerprints on file. It was eight years ago. Is there a chance they've deleted them?' He's speaking quietly, as if embarrassed by the trouble he's realised he might cause us.

'We can't guarantee it. You know what the Met are like. So this is a problem.'

'What was the protest?' Elle asks, encouragingly.

'It was something called the Campaign to Stop Urban 4x4s.'

'Oh, well, brilliant,' Em says. 'Glad it wasn't a lost cause or anything. Definitely worth sacrificing our liberty for a decade ago. You tit, Jonny.'

'Sorry.'

'What did you touch?'

'Not much. Almost nothing, actually.' Then his eyes widen. 'Oh, shit.'

'What?'

'The keypad. I touched that lots on the way in. And the gateposts. And the back door.'

'OK. Maybe we can deal with that. Any other evidence?'

We all think for a minute. Then Jonny pipes up. 'Pub.'

'What?'

'The pub had CCTV. At least one camera, overlooking the car park. It'll have picked us up as we arrived and left. The lighting levels weren't ideal for it, though, and they might have been using an old system. I didn't pay it much attention.'

'Surely the police won't bother looking at the CCTV of a random nearby pub?' I say.

'They might,' says Em. 'I mean, this is a murder, not a bike theft. Even the police out here will probably pull their heads out of *Hedge Weekly* or whatever they read and do a bit of scouring.'

'OK. Let's think about that in the morning.'

And then I remember the really bad thought. But I don't want to just say it outright, and there's a slim chance that it might be me overreacting, so I ask, 'Er. Did anyone go back into the study after we left it?'

'No.'

'No.'

'Yes.'

'You did? Em, you hero. Did you clear our stuff out?'

'I got my phone. He'd smashed it, remember? Wasn't going to leave that behind.'

'OK. And when you were in there, did you by any chance pick up a black case, about this big' – my hands frame the shape of the object that is going to cook my goose – 'with a little leather strap?'

'Er . . . no, sorry. Was I meant to?'

'Oh, *God*.'

At this point, I think I should admit what I do for a living.

7

Or what I *did* for a living. It seems highly unlikely I'll be able to pick up my old career at this point.

I take photos of nice houses.

It's not a huge money-spinner – even per job it's not spectacular, and if I was trying to pay rent on the proceeds, I'd be in trouble – but for a man with my style of living it pays perfectly well. And it does mean I get to see some of the most beautiful places going (I work at the upper end of the market). Needless to say, it helps with the interloping no end too.

There are agencies for this sort of thing, specifically property photography agencies, and I work for one of the classier ones, meaning the homes on their books tend to be nice. The low end is about £3m, the high end . . . I mean, name your mad property-price excess really. What the agencies want is someone a) willing to travel to remote places at short notice, b) who can make themselves presentable to the rich, and c) who knows which way round a camera goes. I can do all that.

Quite a lot of the photos I take don't end up being made public, of course – they're circulated to a discreet number of poshos looking for their new place. That doesn't matter. It's not like I crave publicity, and I get paid whether or not the pictures go online.

And now I have just realised that my camera – with a memory card full of photos of recognisable homes around the country, homes I have recently been paid to go and snap – is sitting in the house of a murdered man, with no earthly reason to be there. The camera is going to ruin my life. I am literally Canon fodder.

Tremendous.

Back in the van, Em has just asked me a charming question.

'Why the *shit* did you bring a camera, Mister Rules?'

'So I could . . .' I consider telling them all about my job, then remember I have no idea who these three are. Rule 16: *Don't give people anything more than they need.* Embellishing your story is the equivalent of tying a load of tripwires as you're heading into a place. Don't do it, because unless you remember every single wire, they'll mess you up on your way back out.

I'll give them a bit of the truth instead. 'It's part of my process. I take pictures so I'll have a record of the rooms. I do it everywhere I go.'

'So it's just photos of the houses?'

'They're not selfies. But I think you might be able to piece together who I am from the memory card.' That's an understatement. Any copper with half a brain could just look for the properties I've snapped – the main front-of-house shots in particular – reverse-image-search the locations, and work out what ties them together. Might take a thick work-experience kid half an hour.

'Well,' says Elle, slowly, as though she's feeling her way towards the most optimistic possible view of the matter and coming up with nothing, 'that does sound like a problem.'

'I would say so. If you guys want to go on without me, I'll understand.'

'Don't be daft,' says Em. 'Jonny's got his fingerprints problem, you've got the camera problem, we're all on the CCTV. We're all involved.'

Elle says, 'But they might not even look at your camera. If you were the police, which bits of the house would you examine most closely?'

'The hall first. That guy will presumably have been in lots of other rooms, but they'd surely pay most attention to the spot where he was killed, right?'

'So the odds are they'll never even open the camera case.'

Elle is my new favourite member of the group. 'Thank you.'

'Unless, of course . . .' She tails off. 'No. That seems unlikely.'

'What?'

'Well, barring your camera bag, did you leave any trace that you'd been in the study?'

Damn. 'I may have accidentally smashed a marble bust by the door.'

'Oh. Well. In that case, they'll definitely search there.'

'All right,' Em says. 'Enough worrying about Al's holiday snaps. We're in plenty of trouble without having to spend the night agonising over that. Where next?'

'The pub, tomorrow morning,' I say. 'Get that CCTV and get out. If we can secure the footage, that's one bit of evidence linking us to here we can knock out.'

'What about your camera?'

'Ideally we can sort that straight after.'

'The pub opens at ten,' says Elle, looking at her phone. 'That's nice. They must do brunch.'

Cut to 11 a.m. the following morning.

We slept in the van – not recommended; I feel like I've been beaten up by the Yakuza – then tried to avoid detection by driving aimless loops along the back roads of Oxfordshire. Nobody's washed, although we did stop in a field for some discreet changes of clothes, so we're feeling a bit fresher (Jonny and I took the driver's side, Em and El the offside. Anyone observing us would have thought they were watching a party of shy swingers).

And now we're back at the Ram's Head. We're not going in as a four – too conspicuous – so Em and Jonny are doing this one. Em because there's a chance her boyfriend will be on duty again, Jonny because he actually knows what he's talking about with CCTV. Elle and I are waiting in the van, watching the road in the rear-view mirror and jumping whenever a car passes.

'This is something, isn't it?'

I glance at Elle, who is giving me a kind of isn't-life-funny look.

'Elle, don't get me wrong, I'm sincerely glad to have met some people in the same line of work as me, but this is the first time I've ever worked with anyone else, and it's the worst the job has ever gone.'

She nods, sympathetic. 'Us too.'

'It's insane. Were we just in exactly the wrong place at exactly the wrong time?'

She shrugs. 'Must be. Why? Do you think we were set up?'

'Nah. Nobody would have known we were coming, unless one of you three did it.'

'Oh, *no*.' She looks shocked. 'Jonny wouldn't do that to us.' The idea that Em might have dropped her in it seems to be too laughable to even deny. 'It did cross my mind that you might have something to do with it, of course.'

'Me?'

'Yeah. You turn up, and our very next job, not only is the owner on the premises, they get murdered. Hard not to draw a connection.'

'I didn't even know where we were going until you told me, the day before.'

'Well, quite. So we don't need to consider that eventuality.' She looks brighter, then frowns again. 'That poor man. He probably did something wrong, but what an awful way to die.'

I can think of far worse, but Elle's Pollyanna act is strangely comforting, so I don't correct her.

'Shall we talk a bit before they get back? Get to know each other better?'

'Actually, I think that's them.'

I'm lying, to avoid getting to know Elle better, but as we look, the door of the pub opens and two familiar figures pace towards the car.

'Not good,' says Em, hauling the door open.

'Double-plus-ungood.' Jonny follows her in.

'Sorry?'

'Jonny read *Nineteen Eighty-Four* last year,' says Em. 'He hasn't really got over it yet.'

'Was Marco on duty?'

'He was. That's the only good news.'

'So?'

'I told him I wanted footage of us arriving and leaving.'

The main positive was that Em's young barman was not only on site, he was in charge today. He listened with a bit of sympathy to their pretext (some cobblers about a regional tech survey, with an on-the-spot cash inducement of £100 for anyone participating). He trousered Em's fifties, then sneaked Jonny into the office. The bad news was that the chain of pubs, Webb and Mayde, uses the same CCTV system everywhere: an advanced one that uploads the last ten days of footage to a server and then deletes it on a rolling basis. There was no way of deleting it remotely, according to Jonny – he could look at it, even download it, but he couldn't tamper with it.

'So, our options are: firstly we find out which of the world's million servers the data is being held on, then fly to western California or wherever, physically break into the server building, hack the databanks, wipe the data, and come back, all while avoiding detection, which will be hard, because the footage will have been circulated before we even board our flight.'

'Yeah. Was there a "secondly"?'

'Oh. Sorry, no. I was just trying to say what the first and only option was really, which is obviously impossible.'

Clearly Elle's rubbed off on me, because I try to present the positive side. 'Right. So we're on the server. Fine. But there's a good chance the cops won't look, or won't tie it to us even if they do. This place was full last night.'

'Yeah. And there's one other bit of good news, too: from where the camera is, you really only see the entrance and exit to the road. The internal camera's been on the fritz for a year, but nobody's come out from the management firm to fix it.'

'Thank God for lazy landlords.'

'There is more bad news, though.' Jonny and Em give each other a worried look.

'Go on.'

'Someone came here this morning asking for exactly the same thing we were looking for.'

This is how it went, in Marco's telling: a very tall, shaven-headed man, who looked 'a bit like Mark Strong', was waiting at the Ram's Head before opening time. He flashed some ID, told Marco there was a wanted fraudster in the pub's recent clientele, bossed his way into the office, and downloaded the last twenty-four hours of camera footage to a stick. Now that Marco thought about it, he didn't say which law-enforcement agency in particular he'd come from, and he seemed like 'the sort of guy you don't want to piss around with', hence Marco caving immediately and letting him in. The Strong-alike then got back into his car, a low-to-the-ground number clearly beyond the budget of any local police force, and left.

After Em and Jonny have finished relating that, we sit and think.

'He was probably after someone else, I reckon.'

Nobody is quite willing to take the baton off Elle in the optimism relay, and we sit in silence as we drive through the village to drop me off near the house. At least I've dressed for what comes next.

Remember earlier, when I played the vicar before getting into this whole disaster? As I said then, you want someone who's unpopular locally, and the proportion of people in central London genuinely keen to talk to their local clergyman is somewhere between 0 and 1 per cent.

In the countryside, though, you'll get a much better hearing if you're a man of the cloth, which is why I never do it out here. Out here, it's time for the old red rosette. That's right. The one person guaranteed to be unwelcome in the deep Cotswolds: a local Labour candidate.

There is, of course, a risk that if people see a Labour

councillor coming up the drive, they'll pretend not to be in, lulling you into a false sense of security, so I wait to pin the rosette on until I'm safely on the porch and unobserved.

All of this, incidentally, is only made possible by the core principle of what I do, which is this: I fill the gaps in people's minds.

I don't mean to sound mystical about it, but whenever I have to do a bit of this character work, I just make sure I'm as similar as possible to what people expect. That's the real principle: act the part, and people will meet you more than halfway, because they're already expecting something similar from you. All you have to do is anticipate the kind of behaviour *they're* anticipating, then stick to that. If I stood in the middle of the street with a tabard and a big smile, I wouldn't have to do anything else to convince people I was a charity mugger. I tried it once as an experiment in Chelsea, and people started to swerve as though I had an exclusion zone around me, without any further effort on my part.

So now I'm wearing the most Labour-y clothes I had on me – a cheap shirt and dark jeans. I'm also wearing an earnest look and holding the Clipboard of Officialdom. Easy.

As I get to the dead man's gates and press 0 to gain access – smearing the keypad as I go to kill Jonny's fingerprints – I see I'm about to encounter the most naturally conservative people on the planet: the British police. There are three cars on the drive that weren't there last night. Two chequered, the third a Jag fitted with one of the discreet blue lights used by the highups. There's no *Bake Off*-style marquee for forensics but I'm sure it won't be long. I wonder fleetingly whether the police and the *Bake Off* crew get their marquees from the same firm.

At this point, a good chunk of me thinks: *Well, Al, you did your best to score that camera. But look at the place. No dice. Get out now, and start that new life in Andalucia you've always joked about.*

And does the rest of me listen? No. My stupid body over-rules my mind and carries me up the driveway, pulling my rosette from my pocket as I go. As I push the bell button, I realise – maybe I can get into the house. Maybe they haven't found the camera yet, and I'll be able to . . .

'Yes?'

The door hasn't opened. Standing at the side of the house is a man in his mid-fifties: sensible but cheap coat, polished school-style shoes, holding a crappy phone. He also looks as unhappy as only a British detective can. His sandy hair is making an aggrieved rearguard defence against the steady advance of a deeply scored forehead.

I give him my best Things Can Only Get Better smile and 'Good morning! Am I speaking to the homeowner?'

'Not exactly.'

'My name's Liam Baird, representing Labour' – I gesture to the rosette – 'although I hope I haven't come at a bad time?' I nod towards the police cars.

'I'm afraid so. Although you could have been here at an even worse time.'

My smile is glassy as I reply: 'I don't follow you.'

'The *homeowner* was murdered last night.'

I give what I feel is a very convincing gasp. '*No.*'

The detective nods. 'Shot on his doorstep. Most un-Bridling.'

'We haven't had a murder here since . . . I can't remember.'

He glances at me with interest. 'You're from round here?'

'No.' Shit. That was an avoidable error. 'Several villages over. But this is awful.'

The detective looks at my rosette, and frowns. 'What are you campaigning for?'

'Local council elections.'

On hearing that, he somehow crinkles his brow even further. His forehead looks like a McCoy's crisp sitting a maths exam. 'There aren't any local elections this year.' *Double shit.*

'By-election,' I gabble. 'Previous councillor resigned.'

He stays looking at my rosette for a second. Then his brow clears – or returns to its previous level of frown, at least – and he nods. 'I see.'

'Stress of the job, my predecessor said. I said, how stressful is it in Bridling, you know? I mean, clearly it was stressful for poor Mr . . .' I look down at my empty clipboard. 'I'm sorry, I don't have any details for the homeowner. What was the name of the, er, deceased?'

He gives me a brisk nod; with any luck he's completely forgotten me already. 'Thanks for coming by, sir. You'll appreciate we don't have time for the spiel.'

'Of course.' That's a mercy. I didn't look up any Labour or local policies before getting out of the van. My pitch was going to be 'basic woolly fairness', plus heat pumps. The detective is already turning to go. But before he gets working again, I blurt out: 'Anything unusual about the scene of the crime?'

He turns. 'Sorry?'

'Any . . . hot leads?' *Al, you ham.*

'We don't discuss cases, sir. As I'm sure you'll appreciate.'

'Of course.'

Then he leans towards me, looks around to make sure none of his colleagues have appeared outside the building, and says: 'We're all counting on you.'

'Sorry?'

'In the election.'

'Oh. Yes. Of course, yes. The election. We won't let you down.' And I'm so insanely relieved to find out he's just a deep-cover Labour voter that I almost start to laugh.

Three minutes later, I get back to the van. As I clamber in, I shake my head at Elle's expectant look. 'No access. Cops already there. Ergo – no camera.'

Em speaks next. 'Shall we get ourselves back to London?'

'Yeah.'

We drive back in near silence. The one event en route is a phone call from an unknown number. *What the hell?* I think, and accept. 'Hello?'

'Hello, boss, Mr Toad's Motors here!'

'Tariq?'

Tariq is fifteen years older than me, far wealthier, and has had a truly extraordinary life that he's told me about on several occasions, but despite all that he still calls every one of his customers 'boss'.

'That's it, Mr Al. Listen, I got some news. We've had someone snooping around looking for you.'

'Who?'

'Couldn't say, boss. 'E was big, though. Big nasty fucker, you know what I mean? White man, looks like he got a bowling ball for a head. Two little eyes, one mean mouth, rest of him shiny and hard.'

'When did he come by?'

'Half-hour ago, maybe. He said he wanted to find out who rented this van from me.'

'Did you tell him?'

There is a loud, long burst of profanity at the other end of the line. 'Forgive me, Mr Al, but I wouldn't be Mr Toad if I was shopping you all up every time someone asked a question, would I? I told him that van was nicked three weeks ago by some scumbag junkies we got round here.'

'Thanks, Tariq.' I had a hunch he was reliable, but there's nothing like proof. 'Is he still there?'

'Nah. But I'd leave the van somewhere if I was you. Just ditch it, scratch it up a bit, whatever. Tell me where you left it, I'll get the boys to pick it up like we just found it dumped somewhere. You know? Scatter a few needles round if you got any.'

'Thank you so much, Tariq.'

'My friend, it's a pleasure.' And then, because he is an entrepreneur to his core, he extracts another £200 from me for the recovery and repairs.

I tell the others the bad news. The bonus bad news, of course, is that now we have to park at least a mile away from our destination and walk the rest of the way back to Balfour Villas. I trust Tariq implicitly, but there's no way I'm telling him where we're staying.

We ditch the van on Warwick Avenue, and get a black cab across town. Then we break in all over again, and despite the shortcuts we left for ourselves, there's a palpable weariness about the way we do it. Sleeping in a van will do that to you. My spine feels like a broken accordion.

Once we're in, Elle volunteers to make a round of teas, and then we flop in the cavernous front parlour, all on different sofas.

We're all a bit shaken, to be honest. I know I come across cocky, but I've never seen anyone killed before. I'm a housebreaker, not a mobster. That moment – the moment of actual system shutdown, where Sausage Fingers' eyes filmed over and his huge body became just a *thing* – it's been living in my head rent-free, as the kids say, all last night and most of today. Living rent-free. Ha ha. That's how we got into this mess. I think I might be cracking up.

Em opens the batting. 'So, the situation is this: we are the sole almost-witnesses to a murder that happened last night, of a man who'd just been threatening us, in a home we shouldn't have been in.'

'Yes.'

'In the course of leaving, we left behind at least three incriminating pieces of evidence that we'd been there that night.'

'Those are only the ones we thought of, but yes.'

'And now we have inadvertently introduced ourselves to the police investigating the murder . . .'

'Excuse me,' I said. 'We agreed that trying to get the camera back was a good idea at the time. I didn't hear any objections from you three.'

'. . . and are apparently being tracked by a third party, if not the actual killer himself, who would not appear to have our best interests at heart.'

'Yeah.'

Jonny chips in. 'Whoever he is, this guy seems pretty good at tracking us down. We'll be sitting ducks for him if we stay here.'

'Maybe,' Em concedes. 'So we probably shouldn't stay here indefinitely.'

I've been having my own thoughts about this. 'I completely disagree. Assuming he can't track us on a single cab ride across a city – he's not a Jedi – this is the perfect place.'

'Meaning?'

'We should stay here, order some food in, and just keep a low profile. The alternative, of course, would be to get on a cross-Channel ferry – a grim one, from one of the quiet ports – and go abroad for a bit. But wherever we do it, we should just do six weeks of nothing, and hope the cops catch whoever killed the guy without any further involvement from us.'

Em and Elle look at each other. 'Al, that sounds *awful*.' Jonny nods.

'Do you have any better ideas?'

Elle pipes up. 'I think we should go to the police.'

'Really?'

She nods, firmly. 'We didn't kill anyone. We hardly did anything wrong. Maybe we have the evidence that helps the police catch whoever did this. I think we have a duty to help out. Yes, we were breaking in, but this will take priority. And we can always claim he invited us there.'

Jesus, I think. Even the Good Samaritan must have had better self-preservation instincts than this. 'On no previous acquaintance, El? What are we going to say? "We were in the house, we broke in five minutes before he was shot, but the killer was a mysterious fifth person who none of us saw or heard, so now we'll be on our way, you're welcome"?'

Elle thinks about that, and Em chips in. 'So sorry, love, but I think the horrible man is right. It's not much of an option given the circumstantial evidence. Jonny?'

'I've got nothing.'

'All right,' Em says. 'So we can't go to the police. Al's lying-low plan sounds too boring to even imagine. There must be something else.'

We all sit there for a few seconds, too shattered to even think of what other course of action might be open.

Until Em sits up. 'Obviously, we have to find out a bit more.'

'*What?*'

'We find out who this man was—'

'No. I'm sorry, but *absolutely* not,' I say. 'This is the worst idea yet.'

'First we'll find out who he was,' Em continues, 'and then we can work out who would have wanted to kill him.'

'Are you nuts? We're not the Scooby-Doo gang, Em.'

'Why not?'

'We haven't got a dog,' says Elle.

Jonny chips in. 'We haven't even got a van any more.'

'Thank you, Jonny,' I say. 'And the Scooby-Doo gang weren't investigating actual live murderers. They were dealing with . . . I don't know, elderly perverts in fairgrounds. This is serious.'

'Of course it is,' says Em. 'But I'm not proposing doing anything stupid.' (I decide not to interrupt here.) 'We don't have to *solve* the *case*. It might just be worth finding out who this man was and making a few enquiries. Discreet ones. So that when the police inevitably catch up with us – which, I'm sorry Al, they clearly will – we can point them in a different direction.'

It's not the police I'm worried about. I think again of the description Tariq gave of the bowling-ball man who's after us, and get an unnervingly sharp mental image of being head-butted by him.

Em goes on. 'What did he say about money again?'

'Who?'

'The guy. After he was shot. He said the money was in the outbuilding.'

'He was rambling.'

'Might be worth looking into, though.'

'After seeing what they did to him? Are you mad?'

Jonny interrupts. 'There wasn't an outbuilding.'

'What's that?'

'There was none. We went through the garden when we left via the back way. And we walked the entire exterior of the main property. There was no outbuilding.'

'See? He wasn't remotely with it by that point. Guys, this is a terrible idea. I mean no offence at all, but I have no idea who you three are, and from what I've seen, you're sub-competent.' Jonny's eyebrows shoot up. 'I'm serious. If you hadn't been here two nights ago, I'd be fine right now.'

'Why don't we vote on it?' I would bet almost anything Elle was a prefect at school.

'What? What's the constituency here? What's the voting system? We're not a *team*. We just met.'

'You're welcome to make a case for your proposal, Al.'

'I just did. We're not investigators. I don't know what you guys are good at apart from Mr Technical Support here' – Jonny tuts – 'but I doubt "hunting gangland murderers" is in your skill set.'

'From what I understand,' Em says, 'these things are mostly a matter of asking people the right questions, perhaps lying to them a little along the way, and making a few new connections. I thought you were a master of deceit, Al?'

'I am, but—'

'And not getting caught?' That's Elle.

'Yes, but this really is—'

Jonny adds, 'You do keep emphasising your unique talents.'

'Will you all shut up? This is a bad idea, and it will get us caught, or killed, sooner than we otherwise would have been. Frankly I'm amazed the three of you have lasted six months.'

'Very flattering. All right, that's Al's case made, which appears to be predicated on the fact that we haven't done this before. So, all in favour of trying to find out a bit more?'

Three hands go up.

'And those who want to get on a cross-Channel ferry?' There's no point, but I stick my hand in the air anyway.

Em smiles briskly. 'That's settled, then. Let's start in the morning.'

Absolutely no way. I have already made my own mind up: I'm going to ditch these people tonight. I'm going to get across the Channel, or bury myself in a tiny Cornish village, or squat in a bothy in the Cairngorms, and once I've left these lunatics a hundred miles behind me, I won't ever see them again.

8

There are two schools of thought on sneaking out of a building by night:

1) Move like a shadow. Take ten minutes to cover ten metres. Move with all the grace and stealth of a lynx/ninja/stagehand at the National.
2) It's impossible to move quietly. Walk normally, as though you're getting a glass of water, and then just ease the front door shut behind you.

Of these theories, I've always preferred number 2. Sneaking is unnatural. And it always feels loud to you. This might be an illusion caused by your ears straining for any other noises around you; either way, you sound absolutely thunderous compared with your normal gait.

I'm also unpractised at creeping around, partly because wherever I go, I'm the only person in the house, meaning I've never bothered to learn.

So at 3 a.m., I'm dressed, my bag is packed, and I trot downstairs as naturally as I can manage. I flush the downstairs loo – a touch of added *vérité* – and now it's time to go.

The moon is out over the garden. I'm going to my other regular place, in Parson's Green, and although it'll take me two hours, I'm going on foot. I need the walk, and I know the camera-free streets en route.

The girls locked up carefully – just in case anyone tried to get in – but I spotted the cupboard in the front hall where Elle stashed the keys. I make my way across the huge hall now, past the high-winged sedan chair box. A vision of the *other* hall, and Sausage Fingers lying there surrounded by broken glass, recurs to me. I shudder.

The cupboard is tall, and as I ease it open, I grope around inside the upper shelf for . . . Where is it? The keys were on a big bulky ring with a leather luggage tag. They're not here. That's peculiar.

Wait. There is something. A slip of paper folded tight. I pull it out, switch on my phone torch, and open it up.

BEHIND YOU.

A voice comes from the darkness over my shoulder. 'Hi.'

I jump so high I graze the chandelier, and swivel as I land, almost exactly unlike a cat. 'Jesus *Christ*.'

The door of the sedan chair in the corner swings open, and Em clambers out, then puts a finger to her lips. She clearly hasn't told the others she was waiting up. She's wearing purple-and-white-striped pyjamas. In the light of my phone torch she looks like a wholesome version of the girl from *The Ring*.

'Are you trying to give me a heart attack?'

'I'm trying to stop you making a big mistake, Al. Don't leave.'

'Why not?'

'It's not the right thing to do.'

'We're professional intruders and someone's been killed. It's a bit late to start doing the right thing.'

'Well, think about this instead: if you leave, I'll go to the police in the morning and tell them all about you.'

'You know nothing about me.'

'I suppose I don't know the inner you, not your secret heart. But here are a few things I do know about my new friend Al.' She gets a little notebook from her pocket, licks a finger and finds the page.

'You're five foot ten. Light brown hair, grey eyes, birthmark on left temple halfway down ear. There's more, obviously. Managed to get your prints the other day too – Jonny got me a kit – and I suspect those will come in handy. I mean, I don't need any of these details, because I've got lots of photos of you. And even if I didn't have the photos, I've got a list of places you've been recently. Let's see . . .' She turns the pages of her notebook. '18 Pulborough Road, 15 Cavendish Square – Cavendish Square, really? I'm impressed . . .'

'Shut *up*.' I talk over her, a bit too loud. Never mind the sleepers upstairs. I feel light-headed. 'How did you do that?'

She snaps the notebook shut and shrugs. 'You give away more than you think. And I had a little look through your camera the other night, when you left it downstairs here. Then it was just a matter of working back from that. If I can do it, with a little help from Jonny, I think the police will be able to as well, don't you? And if they ask me anything, I'll sing like a fucking canary.'

I take a step or two towards her, trying to serve 'menacing', but to her I probably just look like a panicked man slightly closer up.

'What are you going to do, hit me? That won't do any good, Al. In fact, it'll bolster our version of events. A violent house-breaker gets a lot more time in prison than . . . whatever you are. Also, if you lay a finger on me, Elle will break every bone in your body, and Jonny will then empty all your bank accounts and plant incriminating material on your phone.'

I feel very tired suddenly. 'OK. Just tell me your mad idea again.'

'It's not mad. We're just going to find out a little more about this dead man – maybe enough to keep ourselves ahead of the guy who's so keen to find you, or to send the police in another direction. Nothing huge. We're simply informing ourselves a bit better.'

I give up. 'I give up.'

Em gives me the sweetest smile. 'That's the spirit.' She approaches me, raises her arms as if she's about to wrap them around my neck, and then ... drops the notebook in my jacket pocket. 'I knew you wouldn't let me down.'

She stays close to me for a second. I can see a vein pulsing on her neck. Her heart's beating faster than she lets on. So is mine.

'What's the story, Al? How did you get into all this?'

'You tell me. You know everything.'

'I don't know you. What got you into it?'

In truth, I'm starting to wonder the same thing about her. She seems a lot more practised at all this than I am, even though she claims she's only been doing it a few months. Eventually I manage to regain the initiative. I lean a little closer to her ear, and murmur:

'That's my business.'

She shrugs, steps backwards, and retreats up the stairs, with me watching her go.

I take my jacket back off, ditch my bag in the corner of the hall, and stand for a moment. Part of me wants to climb into the sedan box and stay there for ever. Most of me wants to run anyway, leave the country for good.

Eventually I follow the coward's path and climb the stairs back to bed.

9

The next morning, Jonny's cooking as I get downstairs. He doesn't have Elle's knack of making it seem easy; the kitchen looks like a polecat was left uncaged in it overnight. He has emptied every single cupboard. On the plus side, he's produced a stack of pancakes the size of my head. The flatscreen TV on the other side of the room by the sofas – told you it was a big kitchen – is blaring away with the morning news. Apparently the government is preparing to hold its nose and sign a huge new deal with the dubious foreign trading giant of Qumar, despite significant doubts and internal protests. I know just how the government feels.

'Morning,' he says. 'Sleep well?'

'Oh, like a log. Totally uninterrupted rest, no weird encounters or threats at all.'

'That's good. I'm hacking my sleep at the moment.' I would ask for details, but he's distracted – half his attention is on the TV, which is currently reporting on sewage in rivers, while the rest of him is stirring the remaining batter with a rolling pin, then scraping it off the pin with a Sabatier knife.

'Morning, all!' Elle and Em clatter in and start piling into the pancakes. I take a plate, look in the cutlery drawer – Jonny has managed to use up most of the implements, so I'll be eating mine with an oyster fork – and sit.

'Three have been on the floor,' Jonny says. 'But there's only a fourteen per cent chance you'll pick one of those, assuming you eat two. If you eat more, it rises to—'

'Thanks, Jonny.'

I meet Em's gaze. She smiles as sweetly as if four hours ago she didn't just blackmail me into the worst idea of my life so far. I can feel the notebook still in my top pocket where she tucked it. Elle gives me an equally sweet smile, and I realise I have *no idea at all* whether she knows too.

Em might have my prints, but at least I've kept Rule 1 intact so far. At least she didn't get my name out of me.

'Anyway,' she says, getting out her laptop. 'Task one is to find out who our murder victim was.'

'Land Registry,' I say. 'Simple.'

'Jonny, can you hide our tracks effectively if Al's looking up something here?'

Jonny smears his hands with a tea towel and leans over Em's shoulder. His fingers blur briefly, and when Em swivels the screen, I can see he's opened a browser I've never heard of before with the Land Registry site open.

'Al?'

I log in using my interloping account – nothing like my real name – pay my £3, and put in the address of the house.

'Right. Larksfoot, Bridling. Here we go . . .'

And that's when I get my next surprise.

'It's not here.'

'You said everything was on there.'

'It is, but . . . Well, not everything. A house goes on the Registry when it's sold.'

'When did they start doing that?'

'Long time ago. More than a century, I think.'

'So this house hasn't changed hands since then?'

'Apparently not. Not on the open market, anyway.' This is weird. It's the first place I've ever come across that isn't on the register.

'So it was his ancestral home or something? Does that mean he was posh?'

'It's possible.' I think of Sausage Fingers' spiky grey hair and cross red face. 'But . . . I don't know. He didn't seem posh to me.'

'We'll think of something to track him.'

'How?'

I don't actually have any ideas; the Land Registry was all I had. If we'd only looked at some post, or had time to hunt around the house a bit more . . .

'We could contact Claudia,' says Elle.

'Absolutely not,' Em replies.

'But—'

'No. Sorry. Not doing it. Just shut that down.'

'I know you don't like her, Em, but she's still our—'

'No,' Em interrupts. 'We're not talking to that woman. Move on.'

'Er, guys?' That's Jonny, but I'm so tangled in a new thread of searching *Land Registry property not there* and *unregistered properties* and *secret homes UK* that I don't pay attention. Em and Elle are glaring at each other in a stand-off I don't understand, so they don't notice either. Eventually Jonny has to say it again: '*Guys.*'

We follow his gaze to the screen, where a local news reporter is standing outside Larksfoot, in front of some police tape, and fielding questions from the studio about the Cotswolds gang murder that has shocked this once-peaceful village to its core.

Five minutes later – no thanks to any of us – we know the dead man's name, age and occupation.

David Harcourt was, and now will ever remain, fifty-seven years old. He was a 'beloved part of village life' – fundraiser, church volunteer, a stout pillar of civil society. A series of photos running backwards in time show him gradually becoming less red and portly, until eventually he's quite a handsome young businessman in the late eighties.

More unsettling, he was in my line of work. Davy – I would

call him by his surname ordinarily, but being threatened with a gun puts you on first-name terms in my book, no matter where your relationship goes from there – had been an estate agent at a Mayfair firm. The newsreader, practically salivating at the ratings-winning combo of murder and high-end property, announced that the company he had worked at was one of the UK's most exclusive estate agencies, established in 1987 by a then-buccaneering Davy and his co-founder. A camera crew had been sent to the firm's office – dubious taste, I thought – and a junior reporter was breathlessly relating from the scene that there wasn't anyone there yet, due to it only being 7.34 a.m., and that the police had announced the death was being treated as murder. Nothing gets past those guys.

Eventually, after the ritual declaration that anyone who knows anything at all should blah blah, the anchor lets go of the juicy murder and moves on to the busting of an Iranian spy ring operating on the south coast, and we switch off.

'Who would want to kill a luxury estate agent?'

We all sit and ponder Elle's question for a bit.

'All right, who would *not* want to kill a luxury estate agent?'

Em stands. 'Well, the first thing we have to do is get into his firm somehow. Find out what was going on there. Maybe a rival agent shot him.'

'What, over a five-bed semi in Walthamstow? Be real, Em.'

She shrugs. 'Doesn't matter. Worth checking anyway. Al, have you heard of this firm before, Harcourt and Wallace?'

'Never. They must be tiny.'

'Office in Mayfair,' says Jonny. 'Somewhere called Kennel

Row. They can't be unsuccessful. In fact' – more tap-dancing fingers – 'oh, yeah, they're doing all right for themselves. Look at these figures.'

'Can you summarise?' I've never been much good with balance sheets.

'Pretty decent profits at the end of the last two years. Big increases in pay to the directors. Yeah, they're doing great.'

'I hope for their sake it's above board,' says Em. 'Although if one of their senior people has just turned up dead, I suspect it won't be. We'd better find out.'

'How?'

'One of us will have to go along and make a few enquiries.' She's looking at the ceiling, speaking as if to herself. 'If only we had someone who knew anything about estate agents, or would know the right questions to ask. And someone who was brilliant at coming up with cover stories.' Her gaze lands on me.

'You're *joking*.'

She grins. 'You wish.'

10

Three hours later, Em and I are in a Pret round the corner from Kennel Row, in the West End.

The street name is a bit of a misnomer; this whole area is seriously nice. It probably got its name back in the 1600s when an immensely wealthy aristocrat kept his hunting dogs on site, or when the fourth Lady Buckingham decreed the place was such a pigsty she wouldn't even keep her spaniels there. It's come up in the world since then.

The area is full of the tall terraced buildings that housed high society three centuries ago, and that are now offices for all the dubious businesses that keep high society afloat today. It's west of Harley Street, north of Oxford Street. Kennel Row itself is a tiny spur off the main road. It's a cul-de-sac too – meaning, of course, the office probably has no back door, or not one that would allow a quick exit.

The lack of an escape route is just one of the things making me uncomfortable right now. The others are, in order:

1) My shirt. Em has forced me through John Lewis and into something smart, saying it would only be appropriate for a young man turning up to convey his condolences for an industry giant.
2) The bunch of flowers under my arm, with half the label still glued to the cellophane. They're white, but tulips seem a bit jolly for a death.
3) Em, who is sitting at my right elbow. She is half helping me prepare, and half making sure I don't abscond. There's no need for the second role. I'm well aware I'm going to have to be a joiner-in for a few days more.

'The TV crew has gone, at least. I glanced in as we walked past and there's no sign of them.'

'Perfect. The less attention on me, the better.'

'You ready?'

'A bit nervous. I'm normally the only person in the buildings I get into. And if someone else turns up, I take evasive action.'

'None of this fretting. You'll be fine.' She takes our empties to the bin and comes back. 'Also, if you can't do this, nobody can. Seems like you know the property industry best out of all of us. You'll work out how to find out what was going on with our man Davy. Or see if anyone in the office is shouting about how they're glad they did it and he got what was coming to him.'

'Very funny.'

I give Em one last baleful look and head round the corner to the London office of Harcourt and Wallace.

Kennel Row is high and narrow, and still cold in the shadows at this time of year. As I enter, a hideous sculpture of an enormous, distended copper eye watches me approach. Cameras everywhere, too. If anyone's looking for evidence I've been here – I think of Mr Bowling Ball from yesterday – they won't have to look for long.

The office itself is going to be old-fashioned, you can tell that even from street level. At the brass plate of buzzers, I mumble something about condolences and wave my flowers at the lens, trying to obscure my face.

My performance for whoever's at the other end of the camera seems to convince, because the door clicks. The hall is clean and distinguished; marble underfoot, and a lift that must be a century old. It's one of the ones where you have to press the button, haul open a normal wooden door, slide the grille back, press the button, close the door, haul the grille again, and risk losing a hand, all for the dubious pleasure of standing in a box the size of a coffin as it moans and judders upwards.

After roughly three minutes of gentle ascent, I'm on the fifth floor, and after one more door, I'm in Dead Man Davy's workplace.

This bit is an antechamber. The rest of the office – which looks like it occupies the whole floor of the building – is on the other side of a partition wall. This section has a desk, with a woman sitting at it, and she looks rather pleased to see me for some reason. Maybe she just likes the flowers.

'Can I help you?'

I let a bit of countryside into my accent. 'I'm here for Mr Harcourt. Well, not here for him. I'm sorry, I'm a bit flustered . . .' I genuinely am, so I may as well acknowledge it. This isn't the sort of environment my cover would be happy in either.

'That's all right, dear. We're all upset today.' She must be a few years older than Davy was, somewhere in her early sixties. She's quite mumsy – strong cashmere vibes – but she's also clearly in mourning, because she's dressed top-to-toe in black. I wonder whether she saw the news before picking her clothes this morning. More likely, they got word about Davy's death yesterday. The cops would have contacted the office and any next of kin before they released the news to the press. That's a point, I think – the TV report didn't mention any family. Another thing to find out here.

'How did you know David?' The woman gestures at a vase – she's already lined up half a dozen on the desk, three of which are full – and I busy myself putting the flowers in there. 'Oh, dear, you haven't done this before, have you? Let me.'

As she takes them off me, shears the cellophane with an inch-long nail and gets arranging, I look at the other bouquets. *Always – C*, which is tied to a sumptuous bunch of lilies. *Regards Dave from the Balham Brats*, which is on a petrol-station bunch of wilting daisies and gerberas. And finally, appended to the biggest, most ostentatiously mournful bouquet of the lot, SORRY FOR YOUR LOSS DAVID. I check the label: Foxtons.

'Sorry, how did you know him? I hope you don't mind my asking. We've had two journalists try to get in already.'

'How awful,' I say. God, I hope they didn't try the line I'm about to. 'My name's Ted. I know him from the village – Bridling, I mean. We used to play tennis together.'

'You came all this way just to see us?'

Don't push it. 'Oh, I was in town anyway. But I saw it on the news this morning . . . I couldn't believe it.'

'I know. I know, dear. I've been here with him since the start. We went through so much, and now this . . .' She looks like she's about to cry. Whatever Davy's crimes might have been in life, this woman had clearly forgiven him or never known about them. 'I'm so sorry. Please forgive me.' She gets out an actual lace handkerchief and starts dabbing her eyes.

'No, I'm the one who's sorry. He was a wonderful man. We didn't see much of him in the village, what with his work, but he was always popular at the Head.'

'The Head?'

'The local pub.' Rule 24: *Speak casually and familiarly about whatever you do know, and they'll assume you know the rest*. 'We didn't know too much about his work, of course, but we knew he was important.'

'Oh, yes. Yes indeed. He was the core of this place . . .' Her lip wobbles again, but she pulls herself back. I think I see the way forward with her, though. Full crawling, full Davy-was-the-best, and see what she reveals.

So I continue: 'I can't think why anyone would want to murder him. He didn't have an enemy in the world, not down where we were.'

'No, dear. No indeed.'

'It doesn't make sense.'

'Oh, I know, I know.' She's wringing her hands. I've never seen anyone actually do that before.

'To be honest, it made me curious about who could possibly have wanted to. It wouldn't have been anyone in Bridling. I wish I knew a little more about it.'

'Of course, dear, of course. Although when you say he had no enemies . . . well . . .' She leans forward suddenly, conspiratorial, and suddenly she's a different woman – glancing around, ears attuned for any approaching footsteps, mouth framing the opening words of some really good gossip. 'I can tell you this much . . .'

The moment doesn't last, because a young Asian guy rounds the partition from the office proper, and within an instant she's reverted again to her role of the grieving office widow. As I watch her transform, I realise she's a magnificent actor. 'Sami!' she practically shouts. 'You must meet Ted. Sami, Ted is a country friend of David.'

Sami is twenty-something – sharp suit, sharper beard, small stud in one ear – but beneath the youthful features he seems deeply tired. 'Hello, Mrs P. Hello, Ted. You knew David, then?'

Before I can get my story out, 'Mrs P' turns back to me. 'Where are my manners? I'm Hetty, I run the office here. Ted, Sami is one of David's brilliant young men. David does – did – so much for the young people just starting out . . .' The use of the past tense sets her off again – although given her extraordinary performance a moment ago, I have no idea if any of it's real.

Either way, Sami says, 'I'll look after him, Mrs P,' and gestures me through into the main office.

It's decent, this place – the sort of place where you imagine millionaires buy their homes. Cream walls and carpet, fancy plaster mouldings on the ceiling, the occasional bit of disturbing plastic modern art between the desks. Most of the open-plan workstations are occupied by sleek young people. From just one look you can tell they have meal-box subscriptions, Zone 1 gym memberships, and airy studio flats with railings instead of wardrobes. The far wall is a row of private offices, with that sheet glass that you can turn opaque or transparent at the touch of a button. Harcourt and Wallace are doing all right for themselves. Well, half of them are, anyway.

One of the offices has its windows blacked out, and there's a sad bunch of flowers wedged into the aluminium handle. In the next one along – currently transparent – is a big, broad man I recognise from the website – Rob Wallace, Davy's co-founder. He's the one I want to talk to next. But Sami has escorted me to his desk and gestured me casually to the client's chair beside it, and I don't want to arouse suspicion by abandoning him now.

'Sorry about her,' he's saying. *Cheeky boy*, I think. If one of your colleagues of nearly four decades had died, you'd be in bits too. 'She was a bit obsessed with Dave. They used to be a thing.' He makes a disgusted face.

'Wow. When?'

'Dunno. I probably wasn't alive; I think in the eighties or some shit.' He grins, and I suddenly feel rather sorry for Mrs P, working with these jackals.

'When she said David's brilliant young men, what did that mean?'

'Dave ran a mentoring scheme. Charity thing.'

'Sounds good of him. What did it involve?'

'Nothing really. Just taking on young agents from disadvantaged backgrounds for six months, then farming them out to other firms, but with experience of high-end clients, high-end properties, that kind of thing. We followed him around' – Sami clearly has no problem at all with the past tense as far as his former boss goes – 'and we said nothing, just observed. It was all right.'

I can't picture Davy doing that voluntarily. He didn't seem charitable to me during our brief acquaintance. 'Sounds like good experience.'

'Yeah. Although at the end of it most of his people went off to shit firms. Firms that do bad places, you know? Like, ninety per cent of lettings in the city, and about half the sales, all that.'

I think of the last few rental places I tried in London before

I took up this line of work. 'I know the sort you mean. Mould and rats?'

'Yeah. Although I guess that's normal. There isn't enough prime resi in the city to get everyone jobs at agencies like this.' I'd have said 'to house the population', but I guess when you're an agent you see things differently.

'You said "disadvantaged". What was your background? Before you came here, I mean?'

Sami gives me a cryptic smile. 'That's classified.' I smile back.

Looking around the office, most of the staff are subdued, although I can't see any obvious signs of distress. It certainly doesn't seem like the place has lost its beating heart. One person catches my eye, though, two desks away and facing us. He's balding, bespectacled, and he looks more anxious than anyone else here. He's reading some paperwork in great agitation – turning to his screen, back to the papers, not focusing on anything for more than three seconds.

'Who's that?'

'That's Tench. He's the chief solicitor. Did all Dave's cases.'

'He always that stressed?'

Sami looks at me a little longer than before, then grins. 'Who did you say you were again?'

This long into the job, you get a sense for these things. As I look into his eyes, I can tell I've been rumbled. Fortunately, at that point a pane of glass swings open at the other end of the office, and my main target emerges.

Rob Wallace is a few years older than Davy was, and posher too. His hair is a similar grey, but it's longer and still bouffant, swept to a side parting. He's got a beak you could break an ice floe with, and deep lines running down from it to the corners of his mouth. He would have made a good Roman emperor, I think, which takes me back to the bust in Davy's office.

Is he a killer? No time to judge that now. There is only time to approach.

'Mr Wallace?' I'm up from Sami's desk like a shot, and before Wallace can get to wherever he was going, I'm by his side. 'My name's Ted Marx. I'm here as a representative of one of London's leading reputation management firms, and I can assure you, you need my help. Can we talk?' I gesture to his personal office. 'Alone?'

He looks a bit startled by the speed of my approach, which is exactly what I usually go for. 'I'm sorry – who did you say you were?' He looks at me, trying to get my measure from my clothes. I'm glad I wore the smarter shirt.

'I'm a reputation manager. And you need one.' I try to look forceful. It's hard to do when talking to someone twice my age who's probably screwed over more rivals than I've had hot Prets, but I don't wobble. I know I can blag this one. I read a lengthy BBC Explainer on reputation managers a month ago in a Tudor manor house in Norfolk. That was a happy time.

'Um . . . all right . . .' It's bloody worked. As I glance back, Sami is looking totally bewildered. It doesn't matter. Rule 10 has come into its own again. *Approach people sideways, and fast enough, and they'll go along with whatever you say.*

Now Wallace is closing the door of the office. He taps a screen beside it, embedded into the glass. Nothing happens. He taps it again.

'Why won't this *fucking* thing . . .' He taps it a third time, and it goes opaque. The door clicks at the same time. Rob Wallace has a temper on him. He turns, sits, and gestures me to sit at the other side of the desk. I realise I'm now in a locked, opaque room with a man who might have committed a murder the day before yesterday. Brilliant.

'Mr . . .'

'Marx. Like Karl, not "and Spencer". No relation. And please call me Ted.' He opens his mouth, so I plough on. Rule 26: *Never let them ask two questions in a row.* 'Mr Wallace, I gather your co-founder lost his life in tragic circumstances about' – I consult my watch – 'thirty-six hours ago. Have you got any reputation management in place?'

'We already have some.'

I give a sorrowful chuckle. 'You'll need a top-up, Mr Wallace. Has anyone approached from one of the mainstream agencies? Wickham and Brandon, for example? Or Wentworth and Tilney?'

'I don't think—'

'Good. Keep it that way. They'll try to offer you their boilerplate crisis package and you deserve much better. My firm is Rillette Marx. We deal in crisis management for individual firms that have been marked by—'

'Wait a second. Let me look you up.' He pulls over a laptop. *Shit*. Why on earth did I give a company name?

Because I wanted to sound convincing. Idiot. 'Rill . . . ette . . . and . . .'

Time for evasive action. 'Mr Wallace. I'm well aware that Mr Harcourt had enemies in this firm. Any whiff that his death was in any way related to the business could cause you catastrophic reputational damage.'

Never mind bluffing on a bad hand, this is like betting on a dog when I'm not even sure it's a greyhound. But it gets his attention. He stops typing and looks at me. 'Go on.'

'For example. You and Mr Harcourt had difficulties in your working relationship.' Bluff, bluff, bluff. This is taking years off my life. But I suspect that when you've been colleagues as long as Wallace and Harcourt were, there will be ways in which you cordially hate each other. Sure enough, he goes pale.

'That's absurd. We built this business from nothing.'

'I know you did.'

'Anyway, heaps of people hated him. Ask his ex-wife. Ask the daughter he was practically estranged from.'

'That may well be. But you have to show the world how loved he was, how close you all were. Commission a statue of the man if you have to. Anything to make clear that the firm has taken a terrible blow but will carry on the way he would have wanted it.'

That makes him smile for the first time, rather grimly. He says, more to himself than me, 'Oh, we won't be carrying on the way he would have wanted it.' Then he remembers my presence and his smile fades. 'And you would offer?'

'Ongoing advice for the first few months to ensure your

business remains reputable, which in turn will ensure it remains profitable. There is always a rubberneckers' premium at first, but when that fades you want your clients to know you can provide the service you always have done. Better than ever before. We can be on call twenty-four hours a day. And when the police come by, we can advise how to handle that.'

Is it me, or did his eyes flicker when I mentioned the police? 'I'll consider this, Mr Marx.' He seems to have forgotten about his laptop for the moment, at least. And then there's a tap at the opaque glass, and the door opens. It's Mrs P, from the front desk.

'Mr Wallace? Oh, hello there . . .' She looks at me as if she's groping for my name.

'Ted,' I say firmly.

'. . . but I'm afraid I need Mr Wallace's attention. There's someone from the police here for you.'

'Where?'

'They're just coming up now.'

This sounds like my cue to leave. I rise from the chair.

'I'll be in touch, Mr Wallace, with my details. I'm sure we can work something out.'

And with that, I get out, cross the office – giving Sami a wide berth – and head towards the lift. As I'm approaching it, the grille slides back, the door opens, and I'm face to face with the detective I spoke to yesterday, outside Davy's house.

11

His eyes meet mine. They're only on me for a second, but time turns to treacle, my guts turn to water, and I think my heart . . . stops?

And then, for whatever reason – different context, different clothes, lack of red rosette? – he doesn't recognise me. Maybe he's preoccupied, or grumpy after that lift journey. Whatever the reason, I thank the blaggers' god, stand aside, and watch him sweep into the office. He's got a colleague with him, and the lift is so tiny that to see even two people getting out of it looks like a magic trick. They head in, followed by two uniformed colleagues who took the stairs and consequently got here about a minute before the detectives did.

I let the procession pass. Once they've gone, I slowly walk down the first flight of stairs, then throw myself bodily down the next four. I'm just about to burst into the courtyard and run back to Pret when I remember my second most important rule. Rule 2: *Never run.* Not ever. If you're running, you've already lost.

Just as well I didn't, for two reasons:

1) There's *another* uniformed officer waiting in the courtyard. Why have they sent so many cops? It's not like anyone else is going to get murdered.
2) As I walk, cool and calm, into the courtyard, just like a flash young estate agent would, the intercom crackles behind me.

'Ted?'

I almost keep going until I remember that was the name I used upstairs. I turn, and look at the fish-eye of the camera lens. It crackles again.

'Wait there.' I can hear it's Mrs P from upstairs. 'I have something for you.'

'All right.' She's already broken the connection. So I stand as nonchalantly as I can, and get my phone out as if I've just had a message. The police officer isn't paying me any overt attention, but when I'm not looking at her, I can feel her gaze on the back of my neck, and when she's looking away, I'm certain she can feel mine on hers, as I try to work out whether she's taking an interest in me.

After about a minute, I know she's about to come over and start asking questions. It's cold in this courtyard, but I'm still sweating. *Al, calm down.* You're only eyeballing each other because there's nobody else here. It's just good old-fashioned British awkwardness, rather than murder-inquiry-related suspicion. God. I'm beginning to understand what that guy in *Crime and Punishment* was on about.

The cop presses a button on her shoulder radio, responds to a squawk from it. What was it saying? *That young man who just left, did you see which way he went? We need to question him. Pretending to be a friend of the deceased, then a reputation manager. Detain immediately, Tase if you like. Go on, treat yourself, you've done the training.* She doesn't move yet, but she's clearly still aware of me.

Oh God. She's turning. She's about to come over. Where is that lift? The cop takes a slow step in my direction, then one more, and—

'Ted! Come in here.' Mrs P is leaning out of the door. The cop stops, stymied suddenly. I slip into reception. Thank Christ. Mrs P stands in front of me, looking nervous.

'You said you wanted to find out more about David. I just needed to make sure. You do . . . you would have his best interests at heart, wouldn't you?'

Oh, dear. She's trying to quiz my morals, which is a non-starter. But she's looking at me with such pathetic hope in her eyes. All I say in reply is: 'Believe me, Mrs P. I never wanted David to come to any harm.' For once, I'm telling the truth. Even when he was pointing a gun at me, I just wanted to talk my way out of his house and back into my old solitary life.

'All right.' She comes to some conclusion and purses her lips. 'You might go to his London home.'

Play along, Al. 'Where was that? Somewhere central, wasn't it?'

'There used to be a couple. There was the one he shared with that woman . . .'

'That woman?'

'His former wife. But if I were you, I'd start in his private flat.' She gets a lime Post-it pad from her pocket, clicks a pen and starts writing. 'Nobody else knew about it, you see. It was just for him and . . . well, never mind that now. His neighbours might know something, you see.'

I look at her, and although I never knew Davy as anything other than a red-faced bully who might blow a hole in me, and I've only known Mrs P five minutes, suddenly I see the pair of them as they might have been a couple of decades ago, young and besotted and out to make their fortunes. And I see him through her eyes: a rogue, sure, but a lovely man deep down, and one who loved her in his way. I take the Post-it from her, and our fingers brush.

'Thank you, Mrs P. I'll keep this to myself.'

'Good. He deserves so much better than he got.'

I suspect Davy may have got exactly what he deserved. But I keep the thought to myself.

'One last thing, dear. I might not know who you are, but I can assure you nobody up there is to be trusted.' She jerks her head towards the fifth floor. 'I got in early the other day and David and Rob were having a screaming row.'

'Mr Wallace?' She nods. 'When was this?'

'Two weeks ago. I'm the first one in, normally. Well, I wasn't that day. And I left again as soon as I realised they needed privacy.' Not before overhearing everything you could, I bet. 'Anyway. I'll be off. Look after yourself, dear. Love to Bridling.' She gets back into the lift, and begins the long climb back to level five.

Out in the square, the cop seems to have decided I'm just an estate agent, because she pays me no further attention. I get back to Em in the café, now doing the *Guardian* Killer puzzle (in dubious taste, given our current circumstances) and on her third Americano.

'How did it go?'

'Quite . . . busy. Oh, before we do anything else, can you ring Jonny?'

She gets out her phone, dials, and hands it over.

'Hello?'

'Jonny? How quickly can you knock up a website for a reputation management firm?'

12

Two hours later, we're late-lunching in Hampstead. I suggested we stay in the house and rest there, because Mr Bowling Ball – aka the thug who's been searching for us at the pub and at Mr Toad's Motors – might walk by, but I have been outvoted again. This is why I like working alone, by the way. When it was just me, I was never outvoted *once*. The others have taken pity on my nerves, though, and got us a booth where I can cower unseen.

The restaurant/bar/event space we're in is modelled on a ski chalet. Jonny, a man of unexpected gastronomic depth, has informed us that this is part of a London restaurant microtrend called 'Alpine Fusion', where the foods are permitted to come from all round the world provided they originated above an altitude of 4,000 feet. So there's a clean pine bar and funky neon signs, but there's also a Japanese wooden temple in the corner and, towards the loos, a Rocky Mountains shack. The booths are designed to look like ski lifts. I don't love it. But Jonny's paying, so that's something.

Our food is here, and with one hand, Jonny is halfway down a bowl of something called *Erdäpfelgulasch*; with the other, he's on his laptop, building the website for Rillette Marx, which is already looking decent. I think there is a reasonable chance Jonny has an IQ of over 200.

From the outside, the four of us probably look like the team at a buzzy new fintech disruptor, rather than four wanted housebreakers trying to simultaneously avoid arrest and murder.

Something else is strange, too. I know that last night I was literally on the verge of leaving these three to their mad plan. And yet I can't lie, I had a lot of fun in the offices of Harcourt and Wallace, even if the arrival of the police gave me a coronary. It's been a while since I spent this long with anyone. There are the people I meet through my day job, but they never ring, it's all done via the photo agency app. And I have a few professional contacts, of course, but they're mostly glaziers and locksmiths scattered around the country who I can trust to be discreet when I need a window patching up or a deadbolt repairing. I don't know how many would call me a *friend*.

But eating lunch with these three feels almost . . . normal. Nothing about this situation is normal, of course, and it's probably a good rule of thumb that if being on the run from a murderer and the police in the company of three professional squatters is the first time you've felt normal in a few months, maybe it's time to re-examine the choices that brought you to this point.

Obviously, if I'd known where things were going to go from here, I'd have got up and walked away, but that's my magical hindsight binoculars talking.

'So – this is what we have.' Elle has written everything out neatly on index cards. She has strong 'pencil case' energy about her, Elle. The top card reads ODD MENTORING SCHEME, one says SECRET SEX NEST?, one says BOSS FURY ROW?, and one says WIFE DAUGHTER ESTRANGED?. All these surround a central card with DEAD MAN DAVY written on it, accompanied by a pencil sketch and a list of personal attributes:

- Gun owner
- Hair plugs?
- No manners
- Generous lover?
- Wine lover?
- Big hole in chest

'So clearly Davy's business partner, this Wallace guy, did it,' said Jonny. 'That would be my initial assessment. Or this Mrs P woman, in a jealous rage.'

'What about Sami, the mentee?'

'Nah. Not the type.'

'Well, let's try and keep an open mind,' says Em. 'Maybe

we can track down the ex-wife and daughter. What was the ex-wife called, Al?'

'Dunno. Wallace didn't say.'

'Charli,' says Jonny, swivelling his screen and licking his fingers at the same time. 'Charli Ray, previously Harcourt, before *that* Charlotte Raymond. Married twenty-six years ago, divorced seven years ago. They have one daughter, Lulu, who's studying textiles in Brighton.'

'Amazing. Where is Charli right now?'

'Looks like she's migratory.' He taps a bit more, and an Instagram feed fills the screen. 'Look at this. Mustique, Verbier, Fiji . . .' Charli appears to have visited almost every luxury resort in the world, and from the look of her feed she buys a new kaftan each time. In close-up shots of her face she's an equal blend of sunglasses, skin cream and surgery. Imagine a sentient set of cheekbones and you've got the vibe. 'Dunno where she is now. Last post was a week ago in the UAE.'

'All right, well, let's put her and the daughter on the list.'

I've been a bit worried ever since the index cards came out, but I've bitten my tongue until now. I'd better say something. 'Guys, are we sure we *need* to do more of this?' They all look at me. 'I mean, I don't want to sound like a . . .' I fumble for the word.

'Coward?' That's Elle.

'Pussy?' That's Em.

'Faintheart?' One nice thing about Jonny, I decide, is that you have no idea what word he's going to say next.

'I don't want to sound *lame*, but we've been to Dead Man

Davy's workplace and found out there was a lot going on with him – rows with colleagues and family life and all that. Are we sure this is a good idea? Now we know there's lots for the police to get their teeth into?'

'Thinking of going somewhere, Al?' Em throws me a wicked little glance.

Elle and Jonny look blank, and I suddenly feel a bit grateful to Em for not telling them about what happened last night, which is obviously insane. Is this how Stockholm syndrome starts? She continues: 'Still got that notebook I showed you?'

'Yeah, I think so,' I say, as casually as I can manage.

'What did you do with it after our chat?' I get it out, and she nods. 'Take a closer look.'

I look again, and realise it's a page-per-week diary for the year.

Inside the first page:

If lost, please return to:
David.Harcourt@btinternet.com.
Reward: £15

Jonny asks, 'What is this?'

'It was on the desk in Davy's home office, next to my phone,' Em says. 'I thought it might be useful.'

'You appropriated an item that explicitly links us to the murder location?'

'We're already linked to the place about four different ways, Jonny. If they catch us, this won't make any difference.'

'I still think it's a grave error.'

Em leans forward and taps the diary. 'Let's just let Al look inside.'

I flip through the diary, and notice a couple of things. Firstly, what a skinflint. £15 for the convenience of recovering a year's diary? The main thing, though, is that there are hardly any appointments, across the entire year. One is *Pen Bday*, one is *Wed Ann*, another is *Div Ann*, but in the coming month there are just two events. The first is in two days' time, and it says *215 Feathers*. The second is two days after that: *BB AGM*.

'OK. This is clearly his personal diary, not work. So he was boring. So what? That's just being in your fifties, isn't it?'

'Come on. Two appointments in the next month? He was hiding away in that house, Al, you said so yourself. He was waiting, with a gun, for whoever turned up because he thought they'd be coming to kill him. And he was right. These appointments are relevant somehow.'

I look at them. *BB* rings a faint bell. 'I've seen those letters before. Recently, I mean.'

'Where?'

I can't quite scratch the itch just now. 'Not sure. What about this one, day after tomorrow? *215 Feathers*.'

'Must be a sex thing. Dirty old man.'

'I mean, maybe. Would you write a sex thing in your diary if you were in hiding in your country place in fear of your life?'

Em gives a shrug, as if to say, *Men*. But she has something else to show me too. 'Look at the inside back page.'

I flip to it. Crossed out, there is a series of initials – none I can identify – with sums of money appended to them. £12.4m. £7.3m. £3.8m. £9.1m. I look up. Em gives me a nod, as if to say: *That's right, Al. Now you see what the stakes are.*

'Bloody hell. What is all this? What was Davy up to?'

'Who knows. But there was clearly a lot of money sloshing around his life. Would it be the worst thing if we managed to work out where some of it went? Even if it means asking a few awkward questions?'

'It won't be in stacks of fifties in his flat.'

Em shrugs. 'Only one way to find out.'

'The police might be there.' But even as I say it, I know that that detective won't have got the address from Mrs P. There was something conspiratorial about the way she told me, as if the place might contain some information that wouldn't reflect well on Davy but which she trusted me with anyway. God knows why people put so much faith in me. Maybe I looked like her nice nephew or something.

'I have a strange feeling I know which one of us will be going in,' I say.

Em smiles again.

You've heard of 'poor doors', I'm sure? They're the back entrances to the crap bits of swanky blocks of flats, the entrances reserved for you and me. You won't be surprised to hear that Davy's secret London flat, a high-rise ultra-prime block of converted Battersea, has a poor door and a not-so-poor door (a splen-door? A Di-oor? Needs work).

Most of the building is fancy-pants flats. I'd guess the starting-gun prices are £1m for a studio, double it if you want a couple of bedrooms. The poor doors tend to crop up when developers can't get away with exclusively building luxe homes. The council extracts a promise that on top of, say, five hundred swish apartments for the rich, the grudging developer will include fifty – all right, forty, thirty-five once we've left room for the triple-height aqua-gym – normal flats for normal people.

If you're walking into the building on the fancy side, you're walking among people who didn't just pay silly money – this is Battersea, everyone did that – you're now among people who have paid the kind of cash you only ever see written on giant prop cheques from the lottery.

I saw recently a *Guardian* long read all about how appalling poor doors were, because they were *segregation*, and actually disgraceful when you think about it. The counterpoint: if it wasn't for the flats they get suckers to pay big money for, most developers would be building no affordable flats at all. I'd rather they knocked up at least a few places that some poor flipping nurse or teacher or whoever might be able to afford than none. The real answer is a revolution, of course, but I haven't the time to organise one, and even if I did, with my luck I would 100 per cent be the first one guillotined when the snake got around to its own tail.

Personally, I'm a fan of poor doors. For one thing, they offer a much more convenient route into a block of flats – far fewer cameras and gatekeepers. And there is *always* a way of getting from the normal bit of the building to the absurdly nice bit. Might be an unadvertised staircase, might be a fire escape, but there'll be something. For example: the developers usually build to the assumption that the eventual management company will be contracting all its cleaning out to one firm. Granted, the cleaners might be paid to spend more time polishing the swanky bits, but the same people will be scrubbing the floors. They'll be on exactly the same crummy subcontracted wage wherever they are.

And *that* means I simply have to get in through the PD, work out where the cleaners' special tunnels are, then wriggle through to the bit with the expensive, generally empty homes. Usually you won't be noticed, and even if you are, you'll have your hi-vis on. And once you're in the nice bit of the building, it's just a matter of getting through a flat's front door.

Plus, once you're in, you can whip off your hi-vis, walk out past the reception at the luxury door, and deliberately greet the receptionist, who will automatically fill in the blanks and assume you're a new resident. Do that a few times and then, once you've nicked a pass, you can start walking in through the marble entrance, and that feels great.

This is the Al Method of Interloping Central London Prime Apartments. It's never failed me yet. The only downside is that most flats have just one door. It's easy to panic if you hear a key in the lock and realise you have no time whatsoever to pack up your stuff, nor a good escape method. Most windows in these places don't open; even if they did, you could reach the ground floor in three seconds flat but you wouldn't be in great shape to walk away.

One solution is to open the hatch to the stopcock or gas meter or whatever when you're inside a home. It's the barest fig leaf of an excuse, but if you're in your hi-vis, you *might* get away with telling the owner you're here from the power company to adjust the polyphase doodah because there have been warnings from central office of a dangerous leak of gas, or electricity, or whatever. The owner will be alarmed for at least thirty seconds – you've put them in a hot state, just like I did with Mr Lethbridge when I introduced myself as the police – and you can use that time to clear up and clear off.

Final thing on poor doors: a few years back, the bloody developers started reading the *Guardian* and realising they were copping some reputational damage, so now they've replaced them with poor *floors*. They work almost the same way: everyone comes into the building via the same hall, but the people in the really nice flats are on separate floors of the building, accessed by separate lifts. These have made my job harder, and as such I can confirm they are highly regressive and actively harmful to my radical pro-equality agenda.

Back to Dead Man Davy's flat. Jonny's with me this time. As before, I'll blag; Jonny will get us into the flat itself. He's found photos of the inside of the building on Instagram, and while I don't recognise the keypad system on the doors, Jonny has dismissed it as almost embarrassingly off-the-shelf. He disappeared into the Tottenham Court Road electrical supply swamp for two hours, and came back with a big thumbs-up, so at least one of us is confident.

I'm nervous, but there again there's that feeling of . . . what is it? Intrigue? Oh, God, I'm clearly losing it. Focus, Al. There is nothing to be interested in here except saving your own skin. The thought of staying out of prison for a murder I didn't commit helps me concentrate.

We found the cleaning station OK, run by a harassed woman in her mid-forties who couldn't find any record of us being booked for the afternoon shift (unsurprising), but who was so short-staffed and so used to chaotic management from above her that she was willing to hand us our kit with no questions asked. Rule 13: *Play dumb.* Most people are so used to dealing with idiots that if you pretend to be one, they'll probably do everything for you out of the desire for a quiet life.

Our new boss gave us detailed instructions about which corridor to clean first, in the 'poor' bit of the building. My job now is to get us to the fancy half. We're currently in the corridors, pushing our cart aimlessly and nodding like idiots at any other maintenance people we see. The other advantage is: we're in cleaning gear, masked and gloved, so no fingerprints and no CCTV footage.

Jonny's in a chatty mood. 'Who's your money on so far?'

'What?'

'Davy. Out of all the possibilities, who do you think did it?'

'Jesus, Jonny, I don't know. Probably Mr Bowling Ball, who's apparently convinced that we're involved somehow and is trying to track us down and murder us so we don't blab.'

'I suspect you're right.' Jonny nods, solemn. 'But it's too premature to judge.'

'Then why did you . . . Never mind.'

'The question, of course, is why Mr Harcourt didn't fire, if he was going to his door holding a gun. You wouldn't open the door at all unless it was someone you trusted.'

'That's true.'

'And the other question is who knew Mr Harcourt wasn't actually out of the country, as his flight booking suggested. Once you find that out, you've presumably got who killed him. Or who allowed him to be killed.'

'Food for thought, Jonny.'

'Yeah.'

We've come to another lift, halfway across the building. Before us is the side looking out onto the riverfront; the side the posher apartments will be on. 'This will be it.'

The thing about these new apartment buildings is that they're designed to be as impersonally wipe-clean as a beautiful hotel. The designers try their utmost to showcase the nice parts and hide the shabby ones, including me and Jonny in our fluorescent tabards. It's not unlike those country houses with secret passages between the walls to conceal the staff.

Anyway, as we step out of the lift onto Davy's floor, I look back, and sure enough, the service lift has been carefully designed almost out of existence. It's concealed round a fold in the wall, a subtle partition that any resident here would subconsciously know not to look behind, in case they tripped over someone on minimum wage. Jonny and I have moved from the grubby side – cracked concrete, ill-smelling air, a kind of *aroma* of poverty – to the thickly carpeted corridors Davy would have walked. It's so plush underfoot the sound is deadened, and the lights are gentle enough to make you think you've died and are being gently cradled on the journey from this world to the next.

You know, it's thoughts like the above that make me conclude that in another life I'd have written a cracking update of *Down and Out in Paris and London*. Although on reflection, that's a bit gritty for my taste, and my own provisional title, *Fucking Lovely Homes I've Sneaked Into*, doesn't quite have the same moral force.

My point is, this building is so luxurious it's hard to imagine any residents ever having a bad day, or a breakdown, or a divorce. *Or being murdered*, a little voice murmurs, and I look over my shoulder.

Outside Davy's door, Jonny reaches into our cart's bin bag and pulls out a credit-card machine with a dozen leads dangling off it. He plugs one into the keypad, and after about thirty seconds (which I spend doing the most obviously fake dusting you've ever seen), there's a *bzzz-click*. The door swings open.

'Take the cart in?'

'Definitely.' If the supervisor has already seen on the building CCTV where we've ended up, it's too late; but if not, there's no sense in leaving a big THIEVES AT WORK sign in the corridor. We push it through, into Davy's London flat, and gasp.

It's breathtaking. I thought a river view was something nice to have; I realise in this moment that I want nothing else in the world. The apartment's entire front wall is sheet glass, so clear you feel like you could step out onto the glittering water. A few boats are bobbing at anchor, or chugging between the sparkling wavelets. It looks like one of those paintings of Venice by that guy . . . Cornetto? That can't be it.

It's open-plan. The bedroom is separated from the rest of the room only by a black Crittall window. The bed consists of a huge mattress–headboard combo on a wide podium, making it faintly sacrificial. The decor is impersonal, though. You couldn't tell from this place whether Davy had liked collecting Victoria Crosses and visiting Flanders war graves, whether he was a wine buff, whether he was a punk as a teenager. There's almost no character here. I find it hard to picture that big chaotic man living in a flat like this.

The kitchen is ultra-stylish – not a cupboard handle in sight, and the stripped-back cupboards contain some spotless grey Le Creusets. The tap is one of those boiling-water ones where you can scald yourself while making tea – far more convenient than scalding yourself with a kettle – and the fridge door is about fifteen feet square. The countertop also contains one unusual built-in feature – one of those grill devices you get in Japanese restaurants. Davy fancied himself a chef.

Maybe not all the time, though. The only bum note is a half-eaten supermarket lasagne, still in the foil, sitting on the counter with unwashed cutlery beside it. It's clearly been there a few days. There aren't enough bacteria in this place to have rotted it yet, but it smells of cold grease.

Jonny nods at the lasagne. 'Left in a hurry.'

I've just had the same thought, although I was considerate enough to keep it to myself. 'Mm.'

'Probably worried he was going to get murdered.'

'Let's look around, shall we?'

The river wall does have a desk on it, which I gravitate towards. It's one of those standing ones. Maybe Davy was trying to get in shape, get his life together. I stand at it, grasp the adjustable handles on the sides and—

'What's this?' Jonny has approached from the other side, and reaches into the desk's innards.

This is an old MacBook, which was sitting in a recessed pocket on the desk.

'Could be useful?' he asks.

'Very.'

'Should we steal it?'

'*Remove*. Remove for further study. Yes, Jonny. Good idea.' Into the base of our cart it goes.

Next to the desk is a bookcase. Finally, a bit of Davy's personality. I look through it: a lot of historical novels (Patrick O'Brien and *Sharpe* both strongly represented), plenty of horror, some popular science, an entire shelf of dull-looking property books. The cookbooks are here, too, and are almost exclusively Japanese: *Hibachi at Home*, *Further Journeys in Okonomiyaki*, *Make Your Own Shirako*. I pull titles off and start flipping through, looking for notes, for lists. TEN MORTAL ENEMIES WHO WISH ME DEAD. That sort of thing.

None of the books contains any notes. I keep looking. 'Who were you?' I murmur. 'Why were you so scared?'

And then it pops out at me: a brown leather case, at the end of the property shelf. I pull it out, open it up, and see the same expansive, confident handwriting that was in Davy's diary.

10 Leinster Avenue
14 Manfred Court
27 Jupiter Gardens

. . . and so on. It's a sort of ledger, and all the addresses have a date next to them. The dates are ancient – the first entries in the book are ten years old. I flip until the pages go blank – there must be several hundred properties here, although oddly there have been no new entries in the last three years. But it's *something*.

'Hey, Jonny? Take a look at this.'

But as I'm in the process of handing it over, there's a *bzzz-click* behind us. We turn around. Somehow, the hairs on the back of my neck have already informed me the news is bad.

Standing in the doorway – let's not forget, the only way out of the room – is an extremely tall man, with a shiny dome of a head. If you were feeling whimsical, you might say he looks a bit like a bowling ball.

13

Now, there's a bit coming up where I do a generic Eastern European accent. I'm not proud of it, but I'm just letting you know in case you're worried it's cultural appropriation or something. I justify it because I know that if I get it wrong, this man will kill me and Jonny with his bare hands. He could probably do us both simultaneously. So that kind of takes priority. I'm not going to patronise you by saying lots of my best friends are from Eastern Europe, because as you've been reading for the last however many pages, I don't have many friends of any nationality.

Back to the room. This man is *tall*. Jonny's about six three, and this guy has a couple of inches even on him. He also lacks Jonny's expression of gentle benevolence.

He opens the batting. 'Who are you?' English, I think, slightly middle class but that doesn't do any good. Even if he spoke like the Duke of Westminster, there's no mistaking the violence in his face.

'We cleaners,' I say. 'We clean.' (I told you I wasn't proud.)

'What about you?'

Jonny decides not to pretend to be from downtown Bucharest, and slips into multicultural London English. 'We're just cleaning, man. Why, you own the place? This your flat? You want us to get out?'

Bowling Ball looks at us for a second, takes another step into the room.

'You're not cleaners.'

Suddenly I'm glad I kept my mask and Marigolds on. I gesture at our cart, baffled but cheerful. 'Yes,' I say, loudly, as if I'm used to dealing with the rich and deaf every day. 'We clean.' Is my accent slipping?

'You.' He points at me. 'Take your mask off.'

'You want mask?' I reach into my pocket. 'We have extra mask.'

'No. I said, take your mask off.'

He takes another step towards us. If we ran . . . it wouldn't do any good. He's quite clearly the most athletic person in the apartment.

'Me . . . mask?' I gesture to my face. Has he seen me before? Think, Al. Think. Has he got you on CCTV? The cameras at the Bridling village pub didn't show our faces. Has he found out what we look like? Did he discover my camera before the police did? Does he already know exactly who I am? Oh Christ. I'm starting to panic. And he's just stepped towards me again.

'Take. Your. Mask. Off.' He accompanies it with a mime. Quite hard to pretend I don't understand that one. I'm going to have to go along with it. I raise my hands, loop one finger around my ear, and—

'What the *fuck* is going on here?'

All three of us look around. Standing there, framed by the doorway and looking like a pissed-off Boadicea, is Em. I have never been happier to see her. Nobody replies for a second, and she follows up: 'Hello? Does anyone in this room speak *English*?' The fury in her voice could scour a pan.

I pipe up. 'We cleaners.'

'I get that, dope. My question is, who are *you*?' This is to Bowling Ball.

'I'm the owner.' He doesn't sound terribly sure.

'Fuck off you're the owner. My boyfriend owns this place. And you're not him.' She gives a little wobble, just the kind you might show if you were the unacknowledged kept woman of a senior estate agent who had been murdered and now your very livelihood was under threat. That sort of wobble.

'Listen, madam, I'm with the authorities, and—'

'Authorities? Get to shit. You haven't got a warrant, that much is clear. Are you a fucking *journalist* or something?' To be clear, this guy would make the least convincing newspaper journalist since Clark Kent. He looks like his sole reading matter is the manuals of small, expensive German firearms, or niche CIA magazines with titles like *Enhanced Interrogation Quarterly*.

But Em has evidently decided that's the most palatable interpretation she could make to get this guy out of the room, so she goes on. 'You are, aren't you? You're a bloody tabloid rat. Well you can just get out. First my boyfriend is murdered and now you worms have to come in and snoop around . . . Just get out, all of you. Get out. You too, cleaners. Go on. Out. *Out!*'

This last word is thrown at us in a key and register I didn't know Em had in her. She's unstoppable. And before we know what's going on, the three of us are standing in the corridor, and she's slamming the door behind us, her face streaked with tears.

There's a pause, as we all recalibrate in the light of what's just happened. I'm the first one to speak.

'We clean next place now.'

And I drag Jonny away to the neighbouring flat, where he busies himself fiddling with the entry keypad while I rearrange our cart. Bowling Ball looks at us for a few seconds, and then decides we're not worth the effort. Either that, or he's too embarrassed about what just happened to attempt a second questioning. Whatever the reason, after a final baleful look he stalks away down the corridor towards the posh lifts, and I breathe freely for the first time in about three minutes.

'Jeeeesus.'

Jonny gestures back along the corridor. 'Shall we go and see Em?'

'No. She'll join us when she can. Let's just get out.'

As we're walking back to the service lift, another thought strikes me.

'Jonny. What happened to the ledger? The one I gave you in there with the addresses in?'

'I dropped it.'

'What? Where?'

He grins, and reaches into his bin bag.

About five hours later, we're back in Balfour Villas, finishing an unbelievable stir-fry courtesy of Jonny. I didn't think people actually made stir-fry except the stuff the supermarkets sell pre-prepared. I should learn to cook, I think, before dismissing the thought as ridiculous. Interlopers don't cook. *Why not?* I turn my attention back to our two finds from the afternoon.

'A laptop and a ledger,' I say.

'Hope they're worth it,' says Em. 'That thug has seen my face now.'

Em joined us an hour or so ago, having skulked in Davy's flat all afternoon. She managed to get in by informing the receptionist that she was the PA of the resident in flat 227 and she had been notified of a breach in security by his internal security systems. God knows how convincing she would have had to be to get through on that lie, but the receptionist bought it and it worked. As for why she did it . . . she was waiting outside the building and saw Mr Bowling Ball heading in. I've been too embarrassed to thank her properly so far, because what can you say to someone who's just saved you from an agonising death?

'Seriously,' says Elle, 'can't we just report this guy to the police?'

'And say what? "Yes, this man is following us, we recognise him because he's been chasing us since the morning after the murder. What's that, officer? Why's he after us in particular? Well, we were in the building when Mr Harcourt was shot, you see. No, we didn't have anything to do with it, we were just . . . Hey, why are you handcuffing me?"'

Em gives me an annoyed look, but she doesn't disagree. 'Let's look at the properties on the list.'

'They're all classy, as far as I can tell. Barely a double-digit postcode among them. Must have been sales Davy made.'

'Al, did you say something about the register?'

'Registry. The Land Registry will show who owns all these places. Let's have a look.'

Jonny opens up his laptop, gets us secure access, and starting from the top, we look up the list of properties. By the fifth one down, a pattern emerges.

Arthurian Capital
Sid Wayne MNP
Kidd Orpington Ltd
J. Besley
T. Grantham

About half these properties are owned by companies – none of which I've ever heard of, although that's hardly surprising. Looking at the ones that aren't, the dates of sale don't match the handwritten dates in Davy's ledger. But the properties that do come up on the Registry as being company-owned correspond exactly with the dates Davy wrote.

'These ones' – Em points to the properties that don't match Davy's dates – 'must have been resold. But these company ones are the sales he was responsible for.'

'Does his laptop have any more information, Jonny?'

Jonny sucks some sauce off a finger. 'Dunno. It's locked, properly. Going to take a few days to get into that one. First difficult job I've had for months.'

'Suspicious?'

He shrugs. 'Maybe just careful. Lot of money sliding around here, clearly.'

'So what are we saying?' says Elle. 'Davy represented companies that were buying property?'

'Looks like it. Nothing automatically dodgy there. Might have been his speciality.'

'All right. I guess the next step is to look at the companies.'

'Yeah.' Em frowns. 'Maybe we ask that friend of yours at the firm, Al.'

'Mrs P.'

'Exactly. Try your superficial charm on her.'

'Thank you.' I look at the lists Elle wrote in the pub at lunch. 'What about these appointments from the diary you nicked off his desk?'

I'm worried about these. The first engagement, *215 Feathers*, is in thirty-six hours. 2.15 is clearly the time, but as for the location, we're nowhere. Before supper we spent an hour looking up feather merchants, pubs called the Feathers, chicken farmers . . . but none of it seemed to have any connection to Davy. We even did some cold-calling of everywhere in London with 'feathers' in the name, and various places in the Bridling area. Nobody had even heard the name David Harcourt.

'Still nada,' says Jonny. 'I'm up to a five-mile radius around the three known locations we have for Mr Harcourt.'

'Damn.'

'Yes. Finding out what this meeting is – assuming it's meaningful – would be by far the easiest way of working out Davy's business interests, but at the moment there's no indication whatsoever where it would have taken place.' Jonny has a knack for delivering the worst possible news in the poshest possible way.

'How about the wife? What was her name again?'

'Ex-wife. Charli. And nothing doing,' says Elle. 'I've been on her Instagram account all afternoon trying to map where she might be. There's no pattern. Seems like she lives in the UK – somewhere in west London, I think, but she's private about that. No job, as far as I can tell.'

'And right now she could be halfway around the world. Where do rich people go in April?'

'I'm not sure there's a particular place. Maybe there's a horse race or something? It's too early for tennis.'

'Coachella's on,' says Elle.

I look over her shoulder at Charli Harcourt's Instagram feed. Not many followers, but it's full of the stuff influencers like posting. A few shots of her holding a doughnut or a steak near her mouth, beaches, heavily filtered close-ups. It looks silly enough when teenagers post this stuff. 'She's a bit old for Coachella, surely?'

Elle shrugs. 'Looks like she's been everywhere else.'

In my pocket, my phone buzzes. I ignore it, and a few seconds later, it buzzes again. That's odd. I don't normally message anyone from this phone, and the photographic agency I work for never texts me, let alone after hours. I look at my watch: it's almost 10 p.m.

Out in the corridor, I look down at the screen: two new messages.

The first one reads:

Hello Al. You are still going by 'Al', I'm guessing? Sweet. But I know who you really are.

The second:

I don't know exactly where you are, Al, but it doesn't matter. Because wherever you are, you're in deep, deep shit.

14

I don't recognise the number. I google it (you'd be amazed how often you can find out who owns a phone number that way), but get nothing.

So this is either someone from Davy's life, or it's Mr Bowling Ball, or . . . or it's something completely unconnected and I'm just in a whole new variety of trouble. None of the options is especially cheering.

I tap: *Sorry wrong number mate this is Finn who is this?*

Three little dots appear, then vanish.

I stand there for another five minutes, waiting for the typing to resume. But whoever it is has decided not to reply.

I'm first up the next morning, even though it's heading for 10 a.m.

A Beginner's Guide to Breaking and Entering

Downstairs, I make a cup of tea and look at the pathetic investigation we've pulled together so far. We have a list of properties, all owned by different firms nobody's heard of. We have two appointments that Davy seems to have kept secret and that we haven't managed to crack – the first one tomorrow. And we have a stick-man outline of his life: arguments with his co-founder, a long-dead affair with a secretary, a secret flat in Battersea, an ex-wife. Maybe his whole existence was pretty bare. In which case, why shoot him?

I also can't help noticing they opened two . . . no, *three* more bottles of Merlot after I went to bed, and am briefly haunted by the idea that I'm the kind of person who has to leave before everyone else can start enjoying their night. No, that can't be. They just go back ages, they're old friends. *They only go back six months, Al.* Thinking about it now, I know almost nothing about any of these people either.

For want of anything better to do, I pull up Charli Harcourt's Instagram feed again. There's a new post.

She's in a walk-in wardrobe, which features in a lot of her stories – in fact, all the stories based in the UK. She's *So excited to be heading to my beautiful friend Guggy's newtiquel rebirthing centre for its grand unveilage! Going to treat myself to some #ultraprime #selfcare. For a week from tomorrow EVERYTHING is at a 15% discount if you use code #GugCharl at checkout.* You can tell she's older than the average Instagrammer, despite all the tweakments, because she's not quite been able to let go of writing in full sentences.

I look up the venue on Google Maps. Then, in lieu of

waking them all up individually, I go to the hall and shout: 'Guys! Something relevant!'

Forty minutes later, we're in a black cab heading to Chelsea. Jonny's on his laptop, wearing a T-shirt that says 33 REVOLUTIONS PER MINUTE above a Black Power fist. Elle is helping Em with her hair. I'm on one of the backward seats, trying not to slide into Em's lap.

'So everyone knows what they're doing?' Em asks.

Two 'yeah's, from Elle and Jonny. Em's not going to get a third out of me. 'I still don't think I should be doing this,' I say.

'Nonsense,' says Em. 'I won't get in unless I turn up with a gopher.'

'I think Elle would make a better gopher.'

'I'm not a performer,' says Elle.

'Have you ever tried?'

'I was in our school play once. I had a panic attack on the opening night.'

'Who were you playing?'

'I was in the front row doing the prompts.'

'Jonny, then.'

'No way. I pretended to be a cleaner yesterday and that's my acting for the year. I was bricking it then and all I had to do was mop.'

The three of them do kind of *work* together, I have to admit. Not that I want to join their little gang. Quite the reverse. I mean, Jonny's very skilful, and I'm sure it took him years to teach himself all this stuff. And Em and Elle complement each other nicely. They seem like a proper unit, though. All of which leaves me on the outside. Again.

I sigh. 'Any sign of our new friend?'

There's nobody on the street as we pull over, although our killer – sorry, burden of proof, he may not have killed Davy, he's merely the guy who wants to kill us – wouldn't be stupid enough to wait out in the open. There's a novelty café across the road, but there's nobody sitting inside. It's easy to tell whether anyone is lurking in there; the entire place is deserted, barring one teenage staffer who's clearly wondering whether people will turn up for the place's gimmick, which appears from the sign to be 'Disrupted Yorkshire Puds'.

'No sign of Bowling Ball.'

'Police?'

I look again. The few people passing by are the sort of poshos you get on the King's Road at 10.30 on a Friday morning – trim, bored women click-clacking along, the occasional traffic warden.

'We're good.'

'All right.' Em opens the door and pops out. 'Let's find the Widow Harcourt.'

Charli's friend Guggy's new place is called *trust*, and it's mobbed. I'm a bit surprised the opening is on a weekday morning – do none of these people have jobs? That's unfair, I suppose, as my own job isn't exactly office-based either. But the bar in the far corner is rammed and the volume is high. It doesn't exactly scream 'wellness'.

trust is . . . all right, I was going to say 'ridiculous', and that's not fair, because I have no idea by what standards these places are judged. But it's certainly a *lot*. The door from the street opens into the shop bit, the 'newtique'. At the back of the room there's a door that must lead to the rebirthing/tweakment rooms, with the words *trust your self* in lime neon above it. The newtique is the sort of place where an entire table is devoted to a small black clutch bag, and if you turn over a price label it just reads 'no'. The whole enterprise is in a converted King's Road townhouse which clearly has no idea what's hit it.

We had prepared an elaborate story for how to get in, but I think Em's a bit disappointed when we realise nobody is checking names on the door. That would be a bit déclassé – the guests at these parties function as white blood cells, which can simply tell when someone's not meant to be there. I may be a born liar, but even I find myself uncomfortable around people who are this confident.

Actually, I'm wrong. There is a clipboard, the unmistakable spoor of some poor twenty-year-old intern, but it has been abandoned. Em picks it up, ticks off two random names, and we head into the party.

I've decided to lean back and let Em run this. And I'm annoyed to find out she does exactly what I would have done. She is about to ace Rule 19: *Lean in to whatever you think you should avoid.* If you're trying to get in somewhere and the neighbours have just spotted you, don't skulk, go and introduce yourself. Stick your head into the lion's mouth, and if you're holding a dental mirror it will obediently say 'aah'. In short: allay suspicion by courting it, and Em is doing her bit by sweeping the room for our hostess. After a minute she murmurs to me, 'Bingo.'

'Guggy' is the place's owner. I looked her up after seeing Charli's post, and as far as I can tell, she's a kind of ultra-blue-blood fashionista, the kind of old-school Cruella who used to be big in the nineties and whose tribe are now clinging to shreds of their former terrain after the rest of the world realised the money was good and muscled in, armed with confidence and cocaine.

Em approaches all six foot two of her and shouts up: 'Guggy! My God, it's been too long. Tiff, remember? I was on the travel desk at *Snatch* magazine. Polly mentioned it, and then I heard Adrienne was coming and I just couldn't resist. I hope you don't mind?' I should have guessed after her performance at Davy's flat yesterday, but I had no idea how good Em would be at this. Rule 15: *Don't have one reference, have three.* 'Who's this?' She caresses the upper arm of Guggy's dress.

'It's Alok.'

'*Love* Alok. I haven't seen him for ages.'

'Well, he died two years ago. This is from his Posthumous collection.'

Em doesn't flinch. 'Mm. *Too* awful.'

'And who's *this*?' Guggy is looking at me. I am suddenly aware how shabby I appear compared with most of the other men present.

'This is Dom. Well, he's more of a sub, actually.' Em gives

a little musical laugh. 'My assistant. Dom, coat.' She gestures to her shoulders, and I take her coat, while she pays me – and this is exactly how she should behave – no attention whatsoever. Having worked out my status here (zero), Guggy disregards me too, meaning I'm free to look around as Em continues. 'Now. I need to know. Have you seen Charli Harcourt?'

'She's in there somewhere.' Guggy sweeps a claw across the crowd.

'So *awful* about her husband. Just tragic.'

'Ex-husband. But yes. Terrible. And she *hates* wearing black.'

'She's not doing that, is she? I mean . . . black? For an ex?'

'Oh, they still saw a lot of each other. That's co-parenting for you. She was despairing of him the other week. Said he was like a wardrobe that's too ugly to look at but too big to get out of the house.' *Interesting.* 'Still, it was bound to happen one day.'

Em leans in. 'Really? Why's that?'

'Well, he was involved in all that . . . Ricca, you angel!' Guggy breaks off as another guest – a woman who appears to be half puma – arrives behind us. 'Get yourself a drink. And *buy something*!'

We melt into the crowd, and Em murmurs: 'Well done, Dom. Mind that coat.' I'm both impressed and annoyed at how impressed I am. What the hell was Davy involved in? We won't get another chance to chat to Guggy now.

As we go, I try to take a little bit from the snatches of conversation all around me:

'The guys in R&D keep telling us skiing as an industry is effectively defunct due to this climate nonsense, so we're diversifying to beachwear. No, I know it's all a hoax, but . . .'

'. . . been trading about three months now. Our backer is Mac, do you know him? He's my uncle, but only by marriage, so it's all above . . .'

'. . . one of the bigger islands. What was it called? Oh, I'm so annoyed, it's on the tip of my tongue. What *was* its name? Anyway, the hotel was gorgeous, so we didn't see much of the . . .'

'. . . Yes, but these are heritage gooseberries, that's the difference. Anyway, they juice them, put them in the pessary and then insert the whole thing . . .'

'. . . Fifty grand, to go to some poxy dinner where you have to sit next to a nobody like the Culture Secretary. I mean . . .'

It's about 85–15 women to men. The few men are divided: they're either *very* fashion or they seem like bemused uncles, with a distinct vibe of 'the Garrick isn't open yet so I may as well be here'. The women are tightly clothed, exuberant, and as skinny as whips.

We stand in the middle of the room for a second, looking around, and then:

'There.'

We make our way through the crowd to the bar, where a highly trained barman is wasting his career pouring endless low-calorie vodka tonics with sprigs of juniper in.

'Hi. Hello? Hi. Vodka tonic,' Em snaps. 'No juniper, they're just little sugar pouches.'

I start to speak and she cuts across me. 'No, Dom, absolutely not, you're driving.' And then she notices the woman next to her. 'Oh my God. Charli Harcourt?'

She turns.

Charli Harcourt is a beautiful woman. She was about eight years Davy's junior when they got together, I read that in one of the newspaper obits, and from the photo of the pair of them I thought: *Lucky Davy.* Today she's still quite something. Don't let anyone tell you surgery can't yield incredible results – in Charli's case, the procedures have dovetailed magnificently. She could be in her mid-thirties, even though I know she's grazing fifty. As always when I meet someone really expensively assembled, I marvel at the amount of effort people are willing to spend getting other people to look at them. I've spent my whole career trying to achieve the opposite.

Despite all the work, there's something vulnerable about her too, some air of late tragedies around the corners of her eyes. She's no killer, I can tell that much instantly.

'Tiff,' Em says. 'Tiff Branagh.' (This is a nice touch. Pick a surname just famous enough that people think: 'Surely not a cousin of . . . ?') 'I used to write on *Snatch* when Guggy was editor. We met at the opening of the Palm in Mustique. You probably don't remember.' Nice one, Em. That was on Charli's Instagram, but three years ago, and you could forget anything in that time.

Charli's brow furrows slightly, in a manner consistent with the life-of-a-thousand-cuts I reckon her face has been through. 'Did we?' Oh, shit. I hope Em got the reference right.

'Pretty sure we did. You were wearing this amazing Balmain gown, I remember that much.'

Charli nods, vaguely; then – and it's a lovely bit of acting on both sides, actually – her brow clears. 'Oh, *Tiff*. Sorry, I was miles away. God, that was fun. Didn't we watch the fireworks display together? They sent us all up to the roof? And then the lifts broke down?'

'Yeah, that's right. Absolute chaos.' Em looks round as if she's noticed me for the first time. 'Oh, this is, um . . .' She flaps a hand.

'Dom,' I say.

'Dom. He's my latest fucktotum. The last one was actually flogging my old clothes on Vinted, can you believe?'

Charli frowns at me, as if to say *Watch your step, pal*. There's a certain flintiness about her, alongside the grief. Maybe it's just the frost-coating of recent bereavement I'm detecting, but there's something there that chimes within me. I sense she wasn't born to the world of newtiques or tweakments, and she's spent a long time making damn sure she looks the part.

She turns back to Em. 'So what are you up to now?'

'Oh, I'm running my own travel thing. Trips of a lifetime. But each one takes about three years to put together. Anyway.' Em leans a little closer. 'I just wanted to say. It's so brave of you to be here, given everything. I saw the news and I just wanted to offer my condolences. I didn't know him, but . . .'

The image of Davy dying before our eyes reappears to me

against my will, and I imagine the same thing is happening to Em, because there's a little *vérité* in the way her voice catches.

'... but I just thought of you straight away. I've been through something similar myself.'

Charli nods. 'Thank you. You're very kind.'

'How did you find out?'

'I was away, in—'

Em interrupts her. 'Actually, I'm so sorry, if you just want to enjoy the party . . .'

'No, that's fine.'

A couple of guests have arrived behind us, waggling empty glasses at the poor barman. 'Shall we get away from the bar?'

'Let's.'

We move to a corner room of the newtique, which is either so expensive or so cheap that nobody's in there. We're out of the canapé firing line, so nobody's going to interrupt. Charli fiddles with one of the expensive bags, sips her drink through a straw (corner of the mouth, no lipstick loss). Outside the context of the party, she looks exhausted suddenly.

Em prompts her. 'Sorry, love, you go on. You were away. Anywhere nice?'

'Dubai,' says Charli. I'm avoiding everyone's gaze, but I see Em glance at me.

'Wasn't Davy meant to be there? They said on the news he had a ticket.'

'That's right,' Charli says, after a pause. 'But he was already late to meet me. I flew back as soon as I heard. Bunny put me on her plane. You know Bunny Winthrop?'

Em nods. 'Only socially.' Winthrop is the owner of the Frame Magazine Group. Even I've heard of her; it's the kind of publication my more fashionable interlopees tend to have lying around. All the mags have about 350 pages, consisting of three features (a deep-dive on Bronzers of Tomorrow, a new Fijian resort you haven't heard of yet, and something about a posh woman rewilding her estate). To bulk it out there are some horoscopes, a sex column, and the rest is ads.

'Why was he coming out?'

'We were on the brink of . . . of reconciling, to tell you the truth. It's been years in the making. We kept the Ealing place and we were always close, because of our daughter, but this time it felt better. And now this . . .'

I feel a pang for Charli Harcourt. Her husband was clearly involved in something or other, and she may have no taste in holiday destinations, but she didn't deserve this.

'How terrible. Have the police been to see you?' Charli nods. 'Do they have any . . . leads?'

Another pause. It feels like Charli's being quite careful in what she admits. 'They wouldn't tell me. I did ask. A few people were spotted near the house, but they're still investigating.'

That's good. Em keeps talking. 'That's terrible. Is your daughter all right?'

'Oh, she will be.' Charli seems a bit more preoccupied with her own mental state than her daughter's. 'It's not like it wasn't a shock for me too. And I see a lot more of Lulu than he ever did. He was useless at keeping up with her life.'

'Are there financial implications?' That's a bit on the nose, but I've found that when asked a blunt question, more often than not people are so surprised that they answer.

'Are you a journalist or something?' Charli's eyes are narrow now. Dammit, Em, you shouldn't have pushed her.

'Of course I'm a journalist,' Em says. 'A travel journalist.' Again, she's steering in the direction of the skid. She is, in that moment, extremely attractive. 'But I wouldn't write about this. I am discreet, you know.'

'Well, it's none of your fucking business what the financial implications are,' Charli snaps. Ah. But after a few seconds – I've seen this happen so many times – it's as if she's been thinking about it so much she's relieved to be asked. 'Our daughter will be fine. She's in his will. At least she'll be all right.'

So no more maintenance for me is her implication. And her life is clearly expensive. I bet she wishes she'd personally escorted him to Dubai now.

'I'm so, so sorry. When I lost my husband—' Em begins.

Charli interrupts. 'He died?'

'Kitesurfing accident in Tanzania. Big gust, sharp rocks . . . it was terrible.' I think Em's pushing it here, but I'm in no position to say anything. It seems to work on Charli.

'How *awful*.'

'The hotel was negligent, but the authorities hushed it up. And I let them do it. Don't let anyone keep you quiet. In fact . . .' Em wavers for a second. 'Look, I dare say you've already thought of this, but if you want someone to look into it further . . . my sister investigates this kind of thing. Discreetly.'

Charli looks dubious. 'Won't the police be enough?'

'Well, yes and no.' Em scribbles a phone number on a bit of card. 'I mean, you hear so much about them screwing up investigations and taking backhanders and copping off with mob leaders. Sometimes you want peace of mind, you know? It's kind of like going private. Here's me, if you want to get in touch. My sister's agency is female-led. None of that willy-waving copper stuff.' This is catnip for Charli, I can tell, because her face has assumed the expression that the wealthy always get when they've just heard about an exclusive new service they can get in on. She reaches out and takes the card Em proffers.

'Excuse me?' One of the Amazons running the party is leaning round into our corner. 'Guggy's about to speak. Would you care for a top-up?'

Twenty-seven minutes later – Guggy had one or two people to thank – we slip out into the street and round the corner. Elle and Jonny are waiting for us in a cab. Jonny is halfway down one of the Yorkshire puddings from the posh place opposite the newtique (whipped feta and oregano). We fill them in; Elle gets out her index cards and starts writing.

'Jonny, can you check her claim about the flight?' asks Em. 'This Bunny Winthrop thing?'

'Most private planes have trackers, so I can see if it took off. Although you'd have to be very stupid to claim it had when it hadn't.'

'Yeah.'

'But so far she seems to have had an interest in Davy staying alive,' I say. 'Which is more than we can say for his co-founder at the agency. Or Bowling Ball.'

'All right,' says Em. 'Oh, Elle, if you get a call from an unknown number, it's probably Charli wanting to hire you as a private investigator. If you get flustered, just hand over to me.'

'*Em.*'

'I'm sorry. It was the only thing I could think of to keep her on the hook. We might need her again. All right, what next?'

Elle deals the index cards out onto her lap like a gambler with one pair. 'Well. We could have another crack at Mr Wallace from Harcourt and Wallace, especially if he had a big row with Davy a few weeks ago. There's these properties in the ledger, which we should check out. Plus the appointments, one tomorrow and one two days later, which we still haven't cracked.'

'215 Feathers and BB AGM.'

'Exactly. And that's about it.'

'What about the daughter?' I say.

'Lulu?'

'Yeah. I mean, if she inherits everything, that makes her a person of interest, doesn't it?'

15

I like Brighton enormously, for a few reasons:

1) Hotbed of progressive housing policy. This would ordinarily be bad for me, as they've actually managed to fill quite a few homes, but:
2) Squat-friendly vibes. There are great stretches where you can't walk fifty metres without inhaling the aroma of mung bean stew and strong lager. It's either students or squatters, if not both.
3) The strongly liberal, anti-capitalist instincts of the general population have given them a pronounced prejudice against Amazon Ring devices and the like, meaning that the places I've established as my sort of house are still as interlope-able as ever they were. Finally:

4) Great cafés. You can't beat that little warren of streets, whatever it's called. The Arcades? The Follies? The Lanes, that's it. Dull name. But you could go to a new place every hour and not run out for days.

I'm quite glad to be having a day out of London, given that Bowling Ball is still presumably interested in our whereabouts. We got the train out of Victoria (cash tickets), moved around the station separately to avoid attracting attention, and Jonny went full mask-and-hoodie to avoid the cameras. 'Got to avoid the Thinkpol, man,' he kept saying. I don't know about Thinkpol, but I had to resist turning and fleeing when a standard, dozy, un-special constable ambled past me. Living as a murder suspect puts you on edge.

When I had a moment to myself on the train, I took another look at those two texts I got last night. *I know who you really are*, and *Wherever you are, you're in deep, deep shit*. Who would be interested in telling me they know who I am, trying to scare me that way? Could it be that Bowling Ball has worked out my identity? That's likeliest, I suppose, but he doesn't seem the type to play psychological games.

Something else happened on the train down, too. We were travelling in pairs, to avoid attracting attention. God knows if any of this stuff works. Presumably the police are looking for four people who look like us, and if they've managed to trace us – via the van, or via some other camera we didn't clock – we'll be caught as easily in two groups of two. I haven't seen any more headlines about the murder, although I have been on a bit of an involuntary news detox these last few days, so I haven't really been paying attention.

I was sitting with Elle. I was actually relieved it fell that way. Jonny is a bit of a challenge to have a normal conversation with, and as for Em, I think she's best in small doses. I like thunderstorms, but I wouldn't like to live in the middle of one.

Anyway. This is how it went. I'm only making a big deal out of it because I never tell anyone about my early life. Maybe I was feeling a bit wobbly because of those weird texts, and the seamless transition I seemed to be making from 'basically benign uninvited house-sitter' to 'murder suspect and future mob victim'.

The reason I never tell anyone is not that I'm a man of mystery or anything. It's just that, under normal circumstances, nobody *asks*. My closest interactions over the last several years have been with a) my colleagues at the photographic agency, who I see perhaps five times a year; b) a few hook-ups when I'm in Cornwall in the off season, and none of those girls seemed especially interested in finding out more about me; c) Tariq from the van hire place, and d) Ilya the glazier, who is one of my most reliable guys when I've broken a window in London in the course of a job. He travels anywhere inside Zone 6, he works for cash, and he has never once asked to see any ID, or proof that I am allowed to be in the fabulous homes I've called him out to. Until recently, I'd probably have said Ilya was my closest friend.

Put like that, it sounds a bit tragic, doesn't it? Which it

isn't. It would only be tragic if I was in any way unhappy with that arrangement. But as it happens, I was content, always improving my skill set, and getting a lot of reading done to boot.

Anyway. We were on the train down, with our station coffees and our Nero snacks, and Elle said, 'So, how did you get into all this in the first place?'

I'd known she was going to ask me, because – I think this is Elle's superpower – she has a knack of getting information out of you, simply by directly requesting that information, tilting her head to one side and waiting. I had seen the tilt coming. What's more, I had guessed for a couple of days that as the member of the group most interested in other people in general, Elle would be the one to ask. I thought about stonewalling, but something made me want to talk. So I finished my mouthful of flapjack, and began:

I didn't ever know my birth parents. From what the institution intimated, I would never have known my father anyway; he was gone in roughly the time it took to put his trousers back on and write a fake number in my mother's address book. There's no question he'd done it before and would do it again. Occasionally I'll see someone who looks a bit like me, not too far from my own age, and wonder if I've crossed paths with one of the half-siblings who must be out there.

My mother was young, in her early twenties, living in a beaten-up mining town up north that had been thoroughly Thatchered over the previous decade and never quite recovered. From what I've gathered, Mum wasn't one of life's copers. Remarkably, someone noticed before she did anything drastic like leaving me in a basket, and relieved her of me. I do wonder how bad it must have got for someone to have intervened, but those kinds of details weren't made available to me, which is probably for the best.

So in lieu of any other relatives – my mum didn't have much family of her own – it was off into the glorious carousel wheel of residential social care for me. This isn't going to be a sob story, by the way, but it wasn't especially enjoyable. I'll spare you the details. It wasn't like *Oliver!*, which is probably as close as most middle-class families get to the care system.

I got one very lucky break: Mr Eliot. In a pool of staff who were underpaid, under-slept, under-resourced and under-motivated, Mr Eliot was the one who taught us, or the willing ones among us, to read. Those of us who showed an interest he kept teaching, and kept providing with all the things we needed to carry on educating ourselves. He would do lessons in the morning. Even now I like the morning more than the afternoon.

If it wasn't for him, I don't know what I'd be doing now. I know what you're thinking – what I'm doing now is hardly a noble calling. But I know it would be even worse if it wasn't for Mr Eliot spotting some glimmer of curiosity or interest in me, and nurturing it. He brought in books for us – I think he paid for them himself. I visited him once, on a day out – well, I went to his home, anyway. Not to break in. He lived by himself, in an old terraced cottage in the rather tatty nearby village, and even from the other side of a rainy street I could see his place was crammed wall-to-wall with books. He was well-spoken too. I learned my accent from him, practised it at night. I never found out what his story was – disgraced teacher? Penitent banker? Simply a decent man trying to mend the world with broken tools? I suppose it doesn't matter what the cause was. He saved me from a nothing life.

Mr Eliot was the one who got me into photography. From somewhere, I have no idea how, he procured my first camera, a battered old Olympus that taught me everything I needed. That Olympus was the making of me. I took a few pictures of life inside the home – surreptitiously – and he sent them off to a newspaper, which printed them as part of an exposé on boys in care. It started my career down the runway – the money got me a better camera – but the subsequent investigation got Mr Eliot sacked. I didn't know how to thank him, or apologise properly, but I did keep in touch from time to time. He didn't know my real career, of course, but the fake one impressed him just as much. He died last year. I miss him.

By the time that all happened, I was in my final year in care, and after a woefully inadequate briefing on life outside, I was triaged into a hostel. I don't really think the conditions there were the council's fault either. They were a few years into the financial crisis by that point, and it was becoming clear that the tide of money (never very high) had gone out for good. But the effect was: take a moderately self-taught boy who has lots of energy, give him a scabby room he doesn't want to be in, and see how he gets out. Some of the building's graduates chose drinking and fighting; I chose interloping.

A Beginner's Guide to Breaking and Entering

It started small, of course. The first time I did it, I didn't even stay the night; I just got into one of the posh houses in a nearby village, stood there for twenty minutes taking photographs, and left. What a weird kid. But I got better at it, and eventually I decided to take it up full-time, just until I secured enough money to rent somewhere decent. Well, that's never happened, not with my expenses.

I pause, and glance at Elle, to see how she's taken all this. She's looking at me sympathetically, head still cocked at a 'poor you' angle. Does she believe any of it? Hard to tell. I shrug, bravely.

'So here I am,' I say.

16

And now we're at the seaside. I don't remember the last time I just hung out at the seaside with a few friends.

Not that this lot are friends, of course. But they're not exactly colleagues, they're certainly not family, and 'acquaintances' sounds a bit Victorian. Ugh. Whatever. We're at the seaside together and that's good enough for me.

Also, we're not really 'hanging out', given our to-do list for the next few days (avoid detection by angry shaven-headed thug, avoid police, trace killer). But I'm not feeling unhappier than before we got into this mess. I expected to feel horrible after spending a few days with the same people. Very discomfiting.

Part of that is Em's influence. I've never met anyone who does what I do. She's not quite as good, of course, but it's still interesting, like seeing yourself from outside. There's a kind of 'raw performer' element about her that I'm sure I used to have, before I started twisting my ankle on short drops or leaving coasters everywhere. And if I'm honest, I'm curious about her too. Where did she and her sister come from? I don't quite buy their 'piscining' story, which seems a bit semi-baked to me – the sort I might trot out to deter annoying questions. They mentioned someone called Claudia a couple of days ago, but that's hardly a lead, and I don't have any leverage to ask.

Worth keeping an eye on, our Em.

We know – thanks, Jonny – that Lulu Harcourt is studying textiles, and he's somehow got into her (private) BeReal too. She goes to a lot of gigs, and she seems to spend the rest of her free time in a three-storey café deep in the Lanes. It's one of those places where students can turn up and play a board game for five hours straight on one latte without the management throwing them out.

One other thing we know is that her mother's alibi is watertight. On the train journey, Jonny logged in to a website he uses sometimes when he and the girls are planning their own interlopes. It's a flight tracker for private planes, and he confirmed that Bunny Winthrop's Embraer private jet had indeed made the journey back to the UK the day before yesterday. So Charli seems to have told us the truth there.

It's a fair way from the King's Road to Brighton's Lanes. I guess in both places you'll have your idea of what a functioning human society looks like fundamentally challenged. But the vibe in the Lanes is a trifle more laid-back, and getting served in Six Sides of Sourdough is taking a while.

The place is lined with faintly international wall-hangings. There's a noticeboard covered in yellowing adverts for events: 'Vibraphone lessons', 'Uric therapy workshop', 'Syndicalist crochet slam'. The terracotta tip pot by the till looks like it was thrown by an employee: on the side, glazed in wobbly writing, is the word RESIST. It's very, very studenty here. If I'd been to uni, I bet I'd be nostalgic now. Elle wanders off while we queue, and a few minutes later comes back excited.

'She's here,' she says. 'Upstairs, with a friend.'

'What's she doing?'

'Playing a board game. Couldn't see which one. Should I go back and check?'

'No, Elle. No, that's great. OK, how shall we do this?' We talked on the way down about how we might make our approach, but we didn't come up with the final answer.

I was all for playing student welfare officers – I could just about pass for a PhD who had taken his time over his studies, and the other three are so fresh-faced they could plausibly be doing master's degrees and making cash on the side by asking troubled undergraduates how they're *doing*. Em wanted to go in harder – pretending to be from the authorities – because she reckons that as the heiress, Lulu's got a good chance of having killed her father, or having him killed. I said that was risky; I have a faint memory that impersonating a police officer is a crime that comes with an especially long sentence. The police don't like it when you do impressions of them. (I find this particularly unfair, because apparently they're allowed to do impressions of normal people and that's just 'undercover work'.) In the end, we persuaded Em round to my view.

The other thing hobbling us is what we're actually going to say. Em wanted to ask about the death; I think we should just gently enquire about Dead Man Davy and lead her onwards from there.

We head upstairs as two unconnected couples. Elle and Jonny go first, flump themselves down in the corner on a pair of beanbags, and start playing an incredibly involved board game that looks from the box like it's about the glass-blowing industry in fifteenth-century Europe.

Once Em and I have got our teas (fennel and lemongrass for me; builder's for her, with what the pencil-moustache and pencil-neck barista disapprovingly refers to as 'teat milk'), we follow along. Upstairs we spot our mark immediately. *Poor thing*, I think.

Lulu Harcourt doesn't look terribly sad from the outside, but that's not what grief is like, of course. She's nineteen years old, I know that, and although I don't know much about textiles, you wouldn't think she did either. She's in a big, shapeless grey top over black leggings, capped with massive trainers the size of snowshoes.

'Lulu?' She looks up.

'Hi. I'm Kiki, from Student Services,' says Em. 'This is my colleague, Kevin.'

I wave, awkwardly. 'Hi.'

'Do you mind if we have a little chat with you?' Lulu shrugs, and Em glances at the girl with her. 'I mean . . . in private?'

Lulu gives us a flat look, then looks at her friend and rolls her eyes. 'Does it have to be?'

I nod. 'I'm so sorry. GDPR rules. We'd go to prison if we discussed personal Student Service details in front of anyone else.'

'Can you come back another time?'

'No,' says Em. 'We're wall-to-wall this week.'

'It's all right,' says the other girl. 'I have to get to a class anyway.'

After a lot of coat-gathering and one final throw of the dice, Lulu's friend gives her a big hug, and leaves. Lulu takes a photo of the board set-up, then starts packing away the pieces. From the box, the aim of the game appears to be to decarbonise the power grid while simultaneously avoiding blackouts and any investment in new nuclear. What's wrong with Uno?

Eventually we have Lulu Harcourt to ourselves. She's sitting in the tatty remains of a huge imperial wicker chair. Em and I are on a squashy sofa facing her. Nobody is sitting upright.

'Thank you for your time, Lulu. I know this can't be easy.'

'If you're here about Faisal, I told you guys everything I know. Then I told the police twice.'

I'm about to reassure her that we're not here to talk about Faisal, like an idiot, and then I feel gentle pressure from my side.

'I'm so sorry,' says Em. 'There was a burst tap at the office. Your notes got a bit mushy. Do you think you could bear to tell us again?'

A Beginner's Guide to Breaking and Entering

Lulu sighs, Em clicks her pen, I surreptitiously hit 'record' on my Dictaphone app, and we're off to the races.

Here's how it went. Oh, incidentally, if you're ever involved in this kind of situation, do try to sweep your phone for anything incriminating before your arrest. I have a hunch that a fifty-minute chat with the daughter of the deceased on my Voice Memos will make a pretty strong plank of circumstantial evidence at trial.

Lulu was just out of a relationship. Now, I know what you're thinking. Students are always in or out of a relationship. If you're over a certain age reading this, you'll be thinking: *Students these days, they're all polysexual or something, aren't they, not like when we were young, when our icons were normal, straightforward, male-presenting males and womanly women, like Mick Jagger and David Bowie and Grace Jones and . . . er . . . er . . .*

Well, Lulu's had been an old-fashioned hetero love match, or so she'd thought at first. Faisal was Iranian – sorry, Persian, she explained (about five minutes of my recording from the first mention of the P word is a severely garbled history of Middle Eastern politics) – and he was over here studying for a master's.

I never went to university. I put York on my CV – I reasoned I should go Russell Group, but not get cocky and claim Oxbridge (partly because I've seen just how much other Oxbridge types enjoy quizzing you about exactly what sort of gown you wore to breakfast). So I have no experience of this world. But apparently, a master's student seems very glamorous and worldly-wise to the average undergraduate. Looked at from the other end of the telescope, of course, you can see that all these people are basically twelve. But Faisal had impressed Lulu. He'd taken her to restaurants. He'd bought her a few presents: clothes from decent shops, jewellery a cut above the costume stuff most students can afford. He'd been *wooing* her.

And then he'd turned.

One night, they'd been in her room. He'd come over around six, they'd slept together straight away, and then they'd spent the rest of the evening chatting, ordering a takeaway (more largesse by Faisal), and watching other teenagers play video games online. Faisal was religious, but he drank, and they'd both had a fair bit to drink when he fell asleep in her bed.

Lulu wanted to retrieve a photo from Faisal's phone. Her bright idea was that she'd send herself some of the photos on his camera roll, then get them printed out onto some bunting to celebrate their six-week anniversary. (I know, I know. The sheer amount of *free time* students have.)

So she'd held up his phone to his sleeping face to unlock it and gone into the camera roll. Faisal was always cagey about handing over his phone during the hours of consciousness. To kids Lulu's age, it's like putting your kidney in someone else's hand and hoping they don't squeeze. She'd just assumed there was disgraceful filth on there and considered it no further.

The first thing Lulu saw on Faisal's unlocked phone was herself. *That's sweet,* she thought, *he's taken a photo of me while I sleep*. Then she clicked on the thumbnail. She was asleep in the image, and he was awake. More than that, he was looking at the camera.

She scrolled back through the images.

They'd been going out five weeks by this time, but five pretty intense weeks, and they'd spent a lot of nights together in her room. His room, he'd explained, was some way out of town, and also it was in a disgusting shared house, so she'd never actually been back to his place. So maybe there had been twenty nights, tops, that they'd spent together, in her room.

Every single night, there was a photo of her in bed, asleep. The picture had been taken as a selfie, and by her side, in every shot, was a wide-awake Faisal, staring at the camera dead-eyed.

In one of them, he was holding a knife.

Now, Lulu was pretty scared at this point, but she was a smart girl, and she knew what she should do. She checked his sent messages, and found he was sending these pictures to a strange email address consisting of jumbled letters and numbers. Twenty of these messages, all sent off, to be used by someone else as ... what? They weren't nearly revealing enough to be pornographic. Erotica, then? Maybe. Power-play stuff. Or was it kompromat? Was she being set up as an acquaintance of this guy? Who, really, was Faisal?

A less together girl than Lulu would have deleted everything in the shock of the moment, woken her new ex, dumped him and kicked him out. But she poured herself a glass of water, went to the window, looked out at the cold light of the

English Channel, and worked out a better plan. Then, as he slept, she sent the photos to her own phone from Faisal's, forwarded the emails, then deleted them from his 'sent' folder, put the phone back by his side, dressed, left, and walked through the night to the nearest police station.

Luckily for Lulu, the local police force was recovering from a recent scandal involving one of their officers, and were especially keen to 'hear women's voices' right now. Before Faisal could wake up for a hung-over piss, Brighton's best and brightest had set Tasers to stun, gone to the flat, and taken him into custody, and that had been that as far as Lulu was concerned. The wheels of – well, not justice, but university administration – had moved quickly. Within a few days she had been moved into alternative accommodation and had a new phone number. When offered the chance to go home for a bit, she hadn't taken it. Silently, I reckoned that made sense. Charli Harcourt seemed to have many qualities, but I couldn't see her playing the doting mum for long.

Lulu told us this with faint boredom, and I could hear in her voice the bits of the story she'd relayed half a dozen times already. Maybe that's how people get over trauma – they just repeat the words until it's banal. Or maybe her father's death had put this incident in the shade. In any case, the Faisal Fiasco seemed to have already faded and assumed the importance of a rather dull old anecdote Lulu dug out occasionally because she knew other people might like to hear it. But we needed something else from her: which is why, when she'd finished, Em took her risk.

I've always hated the phrase 'don't change horses in midstream'. I mean, back in the day, were enough people really escorting more than one horse across a stream and finding it necessary to change, only for it to go wrong? Why would you even want to change horses in the first place? But it's much more lyrical than my updated version, Rule 20. *Stick with the story you've got.*

Em breaks that rule in three . . . two . . . one . . .

She leans forward. 'Thank you for telling us that, Lulu. It's all very helpful. But the truth is, we're not from Student Services.'

Lulu raises her eyes. 'You're not?'

Em shakes her head. 'Not even close. Can we trust you, Lulu?'

Lulu nods. She's interested suddenly.

Em leans further forward still, until her torso is practically horizontal. 'I'm sorry to mention this. I know the last few days will have been terrible. And ordinarily I'd love to be able to leave you alone. But the fact is: we worked for your father.'

Oh, *shit*. And now, like a chump, *I* have to play along, and give a little nod, like I knew she would say this. What is she playing at?

Whatever it is, Lulu's digging it. She nods again, enthusiastic. 'What did you do for him?'

'We were investigating who might want to kill him.'

It's all I can do not to let my eyes widen and my head slowly swivel round like an owl's. *Em, Em, Em, abort, let's just ask a few questions and get out. We had a good cover story, which you've now torpedoed. For Christ's sake.* But she keeps going. 'He paid us, and I know we let him down. Both of us, and our associates. But he hired us, and we want to work until we have an answer.'

Lulu is eating this up with a spoon. 'I knew it,' she mutters.

'We were actually in Bridling on the night, but we didn't get there in time.' Oh my God. We may as well handcuff ourselves now. 'But we're determined to do the right thing for him. Do you mind if we ask you a few questions?'

'No, of course.' For someone who's lost her father, there's something a little unnerving about how calm Lulu seems about this whole volte-face of Em's. Maybe she's in shock. I certainly am.

'Richard – my colleague is called Richard, Lulu, he's not really Kevin – you're taking the lead on the case. Perhaps you can start us off.' It takes me a moment to realise Em is talking to me. And as I glance sideways, she's looking at me, and on the side of her face tilted away from Lulu, there's the ghost of a twitch at the corner of her mouth. We will have words after this is over.

But Lulu's looking at me too, expectant, so here goes nothing. I start off by mumbling a condolence, and she nods briskly, as if to say, *Yes, that's read, get on with the intrigue.* She's tougher than her appearance suggests.

'How was your relationship with your father?'

'It was fine. I live with Mum in the holidays, when she's around, that is.'

'Where's that?'

'West London.' She says it dismissively, as though everyone lives in west London. For a second, I enjoy judging her, then I remember: she's a child, she's probably never known anything else, and considering what her parents are like, she's refreshingly normal.

'Did you see much of your father?'

'Not really. They broke up when I was, like, twelve. He would come over a few times a year, for Christmas and the like.'

'That sounds very mature.'

'It wasn't. They argued like children, then he would drink too much to drive home, she would walk out, we'd have an awkward conversation where he apologised to me over and over, then he'd fall asleep on the sofa and was gone by the time we woke up on Boxing Day. Every year.'

The Harcourt family Christmas reminds me why I'm glad to operate alone.

'How was his relationship with your mother?'

'How does it sound? They didn't like each other. I mean, they literally called me by separate names.'

'How's that?'

'She called me Lulu, because that's the name she picked. He got the consolation prize of my middle name. From as long ago as I can remember, Mum's called me Lu and Dad's called me Pen. They're messed up. Seriously.'

'Pen?'

'Penelope.'

'Did you ever imagine that they might . . . reconcile?'

She laughs. 'Why would they do that?'

Em chips in. 'Sometimes people resort to hating each other because they can't admit the alternative.'

Lulu looks at her. 'I'm their daughter. I'm pretty sure they just classic hated each other.' Either Charli was lying, or there was more going on in Lulu's absence than they'd let on to their daughter.

'How has your mother been since your father's death?'

'I mean, fine. She's got super-clingy, though, as if someone's going to, like, come after me. I guess this thing with Faisal and then the thing with Dad have got to her a bit.'

'What about his work? Did you know any of his colleagues?'

'There was Rob – Rob Wallace. He came over all the time when I was little. But he and Dad fell out in a big way a few years ago. Dad was livid. Rob said he wasn't pulling his weight. Wanted to take his name off the firm. He only kept it there because Dad legally owned enough of it to stop him. And he admitted it sounded better having two names. Made it sound distinguished.' Another row between Harcourt and Wallace. First this one, then the one Mrs P eavesdropped on a few weeks ago.

'Can you imagine anyone wanting to take his life?' I ask. 'Anyone he argued with?'

She shakes her head. 'I mean, he argued with everyone. But no, I can't imagine anyone wanting to murder him.' The M word brings us all up short, as if his body is in the room with us.

Em moves things along. 'Do you know anything about your father's finances?'

'I know he was broke. He wasn't earning much at the firm

because Rob kept him off the good jobs. He threatened to leave but never did anything about it. He was always telling me that Mum got everything but the country house in the divorce, and if it wasn't for that he'd have nothing.'

'Where did he live in London?'

She shrugs. 'Hotels, I think? He was in the country most of the time.' Interesting. Clearly Lulu didn't know about the flat in Battersea, and I bet Charli didn't either.

'Are you aware of what will happen to his estate?'

'I saw his will a few years ago. I'm pretty sure it all goes to me.'

'You're right, Lulu.'

'Does that make me a *suspect*?' There's a slight tremor in her voice, but despite that, she sounds bored saying it. I have to say, we've properly screwed up the Gen-Zedders. They can't even be a lead suspect in a murder investigation without treating the whole thing with heavy irony.

'We're not the police, Lulu. We just want the truth. And I don't think you're really a suspect at all.' It's a good line of Em's, especially because she doesn't mention *why* we want the truth (to save our own necks). 'So, you're the main beneficiary of your father's will?'

'Yeah.' Lulu gets out her phone and scrolls through a few photos. I can see from her screen that there's text on there.

'Is that your father's will?' I ask.

'Yeah. My godfather sent it over, he's doing all the executor shit. He's being a real pain, actually. Keeps on getting in touch, telling me it's important we find some time to catch up. Dad wanted me to be properly close with him, too. He kept banging on about it lately. Even a few days before he . . . before it happened, he rang me up telling me he was going to take me and Ben to lunch so we could reconnect. Hang on, here's the will. "The principal residence, any other properties and outbuildings—"'

'Wait. What?'

She looks baffled. 'He's left me all his stuff.'

'Yes, but did you say outbuildings?'

'Yeah. I mean, there isn't one, not at the house in Bridling. It's probably just, like, a legal term or something? Like, if he had built one, or whatever.' I stare at her as hard as I decently can, but I'm convinced she doesn't have any secret knowledge. Nobody's that good a liar, and I should know, because I've been working on it my whole life and even I would struggle to summon up the complete bovine disinterest Lulu's currently dishing out.

Em takes over before the pause gets awkward. 'Have you spoken to the police?'

'On the phone. They're coming down tomorrow.'

Em holds out her phone. 'You ever seen this guy?'

'No. Should I have?'

'He's a person of interest.' As Em draws her arm back, I can see she's got a photo of Mr Bowling Ball, taken outside what looks like Davy's building in London. How on earth did she have the presence of mind to get that shot? 'If you see him, he's trouble.'

'Worse than Faisal?'

'Much worse. One to avoid.' Em looks down at her phone.

'I'm out of questions. Richard, do you have any more?' I have none, and she takes over again. 'Can you keep this to yourself, Lulu? There are good reasons why your father wouldn't want it known that he'd hired us. And there are good reasons for us to do our work undisturbed by anyone. Including the police.'

Lulu nods. Oh dear. The poor girl thinks we're going to get justice for her father, when the most she can reasonably expect is that we get away with breaking into his house and are never seen again. 'Can I call you if I think of anything?'

'Of course you can. Rich, take her details.'

Another tie to this family. More evidence, all the time. I feel like we're just doing a future jury's work for them now, but I hit 'stop' on my voice recorder, hand over my phone, tap her number in, then give her a missed call.

'Thank you, Lulu. You won't regret talking to us.' And with that Em stands, gives the grieving girl a brief but enormous hug, then walks out, with me trailing behind her.

17

'You weren't very kind earlier, you know.'

We're back in London, at Balfour Villas. When we got back Elle looked in the fridge, which contained two onions and three rashers of bacon, and somehow produced a huge and nutritious stew. She's now doing the washing-up, on the grounds that 'It's unfair for one person to make a mess and for other people to have to clear.' Jonny's retreated to check the footage from his cameras around the house, to see if anyone paid us a visit while we were gone. Em and I are looking for any possible ideas about Dead Man Davy's appointment tomorrow. 215 Feathers. So far, we have nothing, yet again.

'Not kind? How so?'

'Giving that girl hope. Telling her we'd find out who killed her father.'

'Are we not going to do that then?' Em is scrolling through an online thesaurus for any words even slightly related to 'feathers', and is not-quite-listening to me.

'Em. *Em.* This is crazy. Why are you doing it?'

'It's our best hope of getting out of this intact. At some point, Bowling Ball or the police are going to find us. That's inevitable. If we can give them something, they might let us go.'

'It must be nice having such simple faith that the police would ignore massive circumstantial evidence and an easy conviction in favour of the truth.'

'I guess I'm just an old-fashioned believer in civil society.'

My phone buzzes again, and before I get it out, I look at my watch. It's twenty-four hours, almost exactly, since the last messages came through. I glance down so it unlocks. *You've spent your whole life running away from your own life, Al. And now it's catching up.* Ugh. Straight onto flight mode, back in the pocket.

'Someone trying to get hold of you?' I look at Em, who is after all holding her own phone. She couldn't be, could she? Sending something through a spoof number? No. Not possible. Don't be paranoid, Al.

'No. Look, why don't we go to the police now? It's far less suspicious if we approach them. And we know lots. We know Davy had a huge row with his co-founder. We know his daughter will benefit from his death. We know he was on the brink of reconciling with Charli. Maybe he had another woman who was worried she was going to lose everything.'

'And turned up to blow him away? That's not normal jilt-ee behaviour, Al. That's gangland stuff.'

'It's high-end London. Or posh country. These people are all nutters and half of them have shotgun licences. Maybe Lulu—'

'Lulu plays board games about renewable energy. The overlap between her sort and shotgun murderers is nil.' Em smiles. 'Why are you so determined we stop doing this?'

'Because I'm not sure I can trust any of you, let alone anyone we're talking to. It's just a terrible idea.'

'You can't trust me?'

'This afternoon you changed our story halfway through the interview without warning me in advance. You stitched me up and then expected me to go along with it. You think that's trustworthy?'

'I knew you'd cope.'

This is as good a time as any to ask the question I've been wanting to since Em was threatening to bisect my diaphragm with a letter-opener. 'Where do you two even come from, anyway?'

'Why should I tell you?'

I can't think of a good enough answer, but there must be something I can say that'll get her to open up. 'Because it might make things easier. I told Elle a little about myself on the way down.' I don't mention how much of it was accurate.

'Yes, she said you'd given her your version of events.' Em yawns. 'All right. If you're so desperate to know, our dad is British, and our mum's from Nîmes.'

'Oh right.' I clearly don't sound as confident as intended here, because she rolls her eyes.

'In the south of France.' I nod sagely: *Of course I knew where Nîmes is.*

'No accent?'

'Educated here, mostly. Plenty of trips back. But Dad only got one of us in the divorce and then we went back home with Mum. I was ten and Elle was eight.'

'Wait, which one of you went with him in the divorce?'

'Neither of us. We have a third sibling.'

'OK. So who are they – a brother, a . . .'

She glides past that. 'We stayed with Mum, and then she died a year ago, and we were doing a lot of this stuff already by then, just for fun. Plenty of nice and under-occupied places on the Mediterranean coast. And then we just thought we'd . . . *piscine* our way around for a bit, spending our limited inheritance all the way. We picked Jonny up in Paris.' It sounds a bit glib to me, the way she puts it, but she does have a way of making things seem easy.

'How much of this is true?'

She cocks her head, just like her sister does sometimes, and leans closer to me. Provocatively close. 'You tell me. You're the great deceiver.'

'Me being able to tell whether you're lying is hardly the point.'

'Yeah? What is the point?'

'I don't . . .' We really are quite close to each other now, and I lose my train of thought. 'I don't know what the point is.'

'Stop talking, then.' She leans in an inch or two further, and kisses me.

Now. I'm not going to pretend I hadn't noticed there was something between me and Em. I'm not stupid. And I'm not going to pretend I hadn't liked the idea, when it occurred to me. But it was still a shock. I haven't been with anyone for a while now – not *with* with, I mean. I don't think the occasional drunken thing at the end of a night in the pub counts. If you only go ever back to the other person's place because you don't want to compromise your own accommodation, and if you make sure to leave before they wake up, and if you make sure you have two specific cover stories lined up, it probably doesn't count as a 'relationship'.

But Rule 8 is *If the situation changes, change faster*, and I do my best to adapt now.

About thirty seconds pass. If we hadn't heard Jonny clumping down the stairs, I don't know what would have happened next, but by the time he can see into the main room, we're at opposite ends of the sofa, maybe slightly readjusting our clothes.

'Any progress?' Jonny asks. He's changed into a T-shirt that reads: WE HAVE ALWAYS BEEN AT WAR WITH EURASIA.

'Er,' I say. 'Yeah, some.'

'Oh really? What?'

Em frowns at me. 'Actually, Al's being a bit optimistic there. We don't have anything new.'

I remember what Jonny's actually asking about. 'Oh. Yeah. Er, 215 Feathers. No, there's nothing. I've tried Davy's name in connection with every species of bird. I've tried looking up pillow shops, bed shops. There's a road about three miles from his flat called Horse and Feathers Lane but it doesn't have anywhere you'd want to meet someone on it. Maybe we just go there at two fifteen tomorrow.'

'Possible he was meeting someone at two fifteen in the morning?'

I think back to our brief encounter with Davy. I know he was a drinker, but he seemed like an in-bed-before-*Newsnight* kind of guy. 'Not his style, I reckon.'

'All right. I'm getting some tea. Anyone want some?'

Jonny goes off to the kitchen. On the back of his T-shirt are the words WE HAVE ALWAYS BEEN AT WAR WITH EASTASIA.

Em and I look at each other. I couldn't stand up right now without making a fool of myself.

She breaks the silence. 'I'm not going to try and blackmail you into staying again, Al. I'm really not. If you run, I won't go to the police. But I like having you around. And I really think we can work out what happened to Davy as collateral for when things catch up with us.' She wakes her laptop up, and the screen's glare lights her face. 'Maybe we can even work out what happened to that money that he mentioned before he died.'

'Is that what you want? The money?'

'No, Al. What I want is for my sister to be safe. She's not built like us. We've always looked after each other. I got her into this piscining stuff . . .'

'Interloping.'

'... whatever, this *interloping* stuff in the first place, so now it's my job to look after her.' I feel a bit chastened, until her serious look cracks into a smile. 'Although if there's any money going...'

18

It's the next morning. I spent half the night wondering if I should knock on Em's door, the other half wondering if she was going to knock on mine. In the end, nobody knocked on anybody's door. I look terrible. When she comes downstairs to join the rest of us, she looks completely fresh.

Jonny's cooking again this morning, a kind of porridge-with-everything. I think he's reversed his T-shirt since last night but I couldn't say for sure.

'Morning all,' Em says. 'What's on the agenda today?'

'Oh, you know, more dodging the police, avoiding thugs who want to kill us, all of that. The usual. Although Davy's first appointment is at two fifteen and we have no idea who it's with, where it's supposed to be, or what's so important about it, so I imagine we ought to spend a bit of time on that.'

I'm trying to meet Em's eye, to suss out what she's thinking, but she's acting like she didn't kiss me, like nothing happened at all, and she's so good at it that I almost start to doubt myself.

'215 Feathers,' she says. 'Feathers.'

'By now we've tried everywhere called "Feathers" in a ten-mile radius of here and a twenty-mile radius of Bridling,' I say. 'Nobody's heard of Davy Harcourt, nobody took a booking from him. So either he booked under an assumed name, in which case we're stuffed, or Feathers is his little joke, and we can't work it out because we didn't know him, in which case we're equally stuffed.'

'Feathers,' Elle says. 'Can I use your computer for Google Maps, Jonny?'

Jonny waves an oaty hand. 'Help yourself. I've added you to the face recognition. Don't use any browsers you don't recognise. But the porridge is almost ready, I can't keep it fluid much longer, so . . .'

Elle opens Jonny's laptop up and taps away.

'Feathers,' says Em. 'Maybe it's an aviary.'

'An aviary.'

'London Zoo has an aviary. Maybe he's supposed to be meeting whoever it is there.'

Elle interrupts us. 'Guys. "Down" is another word for feathers, isn't it?'

'Yeah.'

'I remembered because of "eiderdown".'

'Yes, well done. So?'

A Beginner's Guide to Breaking and Entering

'So if there was a street near Davy's office called, say, Down Lane . . .'

Em and I scramble to the laptop. I get there first. There, opposite Davy's cul-de-sac, is a tiny little spur of an alley, almost unnoticeable. But when you zoom right up on it, two little words appear. *Down Lane.* You could knock me down with 215 feathers.

'Is there anywhere Davy might meet someone?'

'There's, let's see . . . a shipbroker's, probably not that. A few offices, just insurers and things. Hang on.' Elle turns Street View on and sits back. 'There doesn't seem to be anything here.'

'Guys, the porridge really is—'

Em interrupts Jonny. 'Wait. Go back.' Elle swivels the virtual viewfinder round – God bless the Google Street View team for bothering to stop off at the shortest street in London – and Em says, 'There. What's that?'

'It looks like the top of a staircase.'

'And at the bottom?'

There's a brass plate. You can't read it from here, but Em's already looking on a different screen. 'That's it. It's a restaurant. Pretty well-hidden one, too. St Francis.'

'Maybe he ate there?' says Elle.

'Got to be worth a try,' I say.

'They don't open until noon,' says Em.

'Jonny can hack in, can't he?'

'I'll have a crack,' says Jonny. 'But would it kill you to pause while I serve up the—'

'No, love,' Elle says. 'You can't book online. They don't have a website. Gosh, they like making it difficult.'

'Maybe when your whole clientele come from within two hundred metres, you don't need a website,' I say.

'*Someone* must know if he ate there,' says Em. 'Think of who that would be, Al.'

'Not Charli or Lulu. This looks like it's his work restaurant. If it even is the place.'

'So who would know, then?'

I've got it. 'Give me the general number of Harcourt and Wallace.'

Thirty seconds later, Davy's office phone is picked up by – *yes* – Mrs P. I try not to sound too relieved. 'Hello? It's Ted here, Davy's friend from Bridling. I hope you remember me?'

'I do,' says Mrs P. 'Although I know you're not who you say you are.'

'I . . . Sorry?' *Shit*. Someone must have blabbed. Or did the police recognise me after we crossed paths on my way out?

'You told Mr Wallace you were from a reputation management firm.' Her tone is frosty.

'I . . .' The thing to do in these cases is to be honest, by which I mean, as honest as your circumstances permit you to be. Regrettably, mine permit almost no honesty whatsoever. 'I'm sorry, Mrs P. I had to lie to him to get into the room. He wouldn't have listened to a random friend of Mr Harcourt's from Bridling. Did he find out?'

'Almost immediately,' she says. But she sounds a little warmer. So much for Jonny's flawless web design. 'He phoned his own reputation manager, who said he'd never heard of . . . what was it, Gillette Marx?'

'Rillette. But yes. I wasn't telling him the truth, Mrs P. I'm sorry.'

'Oh, I don't mind,' she says, and suddenly she's sounding rather flirtatious. First Em last night and now her. Is imminent arrest on suspicion of murder a powerful aphrodisiac? Whatever it is, it's working. 'Just as long as you're telling me the truth.'

'I am, Mrs P. But I do need to know one or two things from you. Did Mr Harcourt ever eat at St Francis on Down Lane?'

'Of course.' She sounds insulted at the suggestion he might not have. 'It was his home from home. He'd have had breakfast there if they did it.'

'You don't know if he had any bookings coming up, do you?'

'He made all his bookings through me, dear. He'd just tell me when he needed to eat there and I'd make the call. Although he was there so often they had a special table for him. "Booth three," they'd say, whenever I called. "Booth three is available for Mr Harcourt whenever he needs it." He took me for Christmas every year. It's *very* chic in there.'

'Is there a chance he'd have booked himself?'

'He'd hardly have done that. I don't think you realise quite how clueless David was, with computers and so on. He never had the time. Even with his mobile phone I had to take out a contract in his name for him, the silly old bear. They still deliver me the itemised bills each month. Now, is there anything else I can help you with?'

'There is one thing, actually,' I say, slowly, and I mouth the word *ledger* at Elle and Em. It turns out that 'ledger' is an unbelievably difficult word to mouth clearly, so I end up havering while I get up and look around the room for it. There it is. 'Do you recognise any of these addresses? Were they maybe properties Mr Harcourt would have sold?' I reel off a few of the names. 'This would have been several years ago now.'

'No, I don't think I . . . Wait. Say them again.'

'10 Leinster Avenue. 14 Manfred Court. 27 Jupiter Gardens . . .'

'Yes. That was it. 14 Manfred Court. Beautiful mews house in Chelsea. I've always wanted to live in a mews, that's why I remember it. Do you know *Mews of the World*? Industry magazine.'

'Right. Yes. But . . . did Mr Harcourt sell it?'

'No. It came to us for a pitch, and David went along, but we didn't get the job. He was furious at losing it because he knew how much it was worth. It went to another firm in the end, I don't know which one. We don't keep track of that. Leinster Avenue rings a bell for the same reason. There was a big row with Mr Wallace over that.' It's always *David*, I notice, but *Mr Wallace*. She couldn't be much clearer whose side she's on.

'So Mr Harcourt definitely didn't sell those two?'

'That's right. In fact, let me check . . .' *Clack-clack-clack.*

'Nor any of the others. None of them are coming up on the system, dear. Which means that none of them was ever officially a Harcourt and Wallace sale.'

'Can you think of a reason he might have written the address down?'

'Maybe he was annoyed at missing out. Or maybe he wrote it before he got the brief.'

'Thank you, Mrs P. Oh, one last thing.'

'Go on.'

'Did Mr Harcourt know anyone who was about six foot five, totally bald, and rather unpleasant-looking? Maybe someone from the firm?'

'We tend to hire more carefully than that.'

'Might someone like that work for Mr Wallace?'

'I don't think so. He's quite unpleasant enough on his own. And as for David, there was nobody in his life like that, as far as I know. Knew.'

Oh, Mrs P. Davy clearly had a rather busier life than met the eye, hence him currently lying in a police morgue somewhere. 'Thank you again. Really.'

'Good luck with your project, dear. And,' here her voice lowers, 'be extremely cautious if you come to see Mr Wallace again.' Then there's a click, and the line goes dead.

I wonder why Mrs P is so willing to share the details of Davy's life. She made that last call rather easy. Is it just because she thinks she's the only one in that place who really knew and loved him?

She might be right about that. She certainly seems to hate

Wallace, for reasons unknown. I have a horrible feeling I'll have to see Wallace again before the end of this, and I don't like the prospect. When I met him, he seemed somehow like a polite version of the bowling-ball thug. Maybe they're cousins.

'So what now?' says Em.

'We have a lunch booking,' I say. '215, St Francis, on Down Lane.'

'*No*,' says Jonny, who is standing before four bowls of almost totally cemented porridge. 'Now we have breakfast.'

19

The rest of the morning is a blur of inactivity.

There's little to do for four hours, and I'm a bit cagey about going out onto the street without good reason. As we clear up the breakfast things, I spend a little while attempting to flirt with Em, but I'm clearly out of practice, because everything I think of saying would come out either too boring or arrestably lecherous. This is my punishment for being single for eight years, barring the odd drunken clinch.

The others revert to type. Jonny plots all the properties in Davy's book on a home-built web map, which he's assured us is 'operationally secure', and creates a complicated spreadsheet with all their details to see if any patterns sing out. Elle does a bit of background reading about Davy's life, once Jonny's boosted her over all the newspaper paywalls, because she thinks the psychological angle is bound to yield results and because she wants to 'get to *know* him a bit better'. Em ostentatiously lies back, puts her copy of *Emma* on her chest and her hand behinds her head, and naps.

And me? I stare at my phone, trying to work out every possible angle of approach to St Francis, every possible risk, and every way this late lunch could end up with me being arrested, captured or knocked off. This is the sort of preparatory work that distinguishes a merely good interloper from a great one. From time to time, I look at Em, sleeping without a care in the world, and feel faintly annoyed that she seems to be just as good at this stuff as me without putting in half the effort.

Eventually, I snap and suggest a walk in the garden to the room at large.

'No,' says Jonny. 'Spring pollen is worse than white asbestos.'

'That would be lovely,' says Elle. 'Just let me finish these few articles.'

'Yeah, OK.' I didn't think Em was awake, but she was clearly just resting her eyes, because she's already sitting upright and stretching.

The garden at Balfour Villas is how you can tell the owners are properly posh. Down the green-slimed steps from the house there's a broad but shallow lawn, and then a few paths lead off into the scrubby undergrowth. Somewhere in there is a fountain with a naked bronze statuette, which contains such stagnant water that even London's birds – not hygiene sticklers – don't wash in it any more.

In other words, it's the garden equivalent of the genuine

aristos who go everywhere in the same twenty-year-old coat and the same battered Land Rover, and who would treat the suggestion of home renovation as an appalling breach of etiquette. Anyone even slightly middle class would never dream of letting such a beautiful garden get this bad. But that's how you can tell people of true quality. They let things go to the dogs and everyone else still tells them they're marvellous. My pet theory is that that's why some people like rewilding so much: they can pretend to be scruffy poshos.

Em and I walk gingerly down the deathtrap steps, holding the rusted rail, and then take one of the wooded paths.

'So . . .'

'So.' Em's not giving me anything here.

'Who do you think killed Davy?'

'Obviously, Bowling Ball is the prime suspect. But even if it was him, we don't know why. Or who ordered him to pull the trigger.'

'Would you open your front door to a man who looked that threatening?'

'No. But Davy had a gun. Maybe he didn't realise Bowling Ball was armed too. Or maybe they knew each other. Or maybe it wasn't him at the door at all. Maybe the person at the door was the business partner he'd fallen out with.'

I remember something. 'Or his chief solicitor.'

'Who?'

I describe the solicitor at Davy's firm, the one who looked so nervous when I was sitting next to his mentee, Sami. Tench, was that his name?

'It's to do with the properties in that ledger of his,' Em says. 'You'll have to go back to his office sometime, you know.'

'I suppose so.' I kick moodily at a bramble which is getting ideas above its station.

'You still thinking of leaving us for Zeebrugge or wherever?' She says it casually, without looking at me.

'Not imminently.'

'What changed your mind?'

'It wasn't . . . whatever this is, I'd like to make that clear.'

'Of course.' She stops walking, so I do too, and swing round to face her.

This would be a terrible place for anything romantic. There are brambles and roots underfoot and a heavy aroma of vegetable decay in the air. But in that moment I can think of nothing else but her. Ridiculous. It's not the way she looks, or not just that. It's everything about her. My main thought is of the look on her face when we were in Davy's city flat, and Bowling Ball had just caught up with us. She was in total, absolute control of the situation. *She still is*, says a little voice, and I turn and keep walking. She follows.

'I'm not leaving because you guys are clearly going to keep investigating this, and the more you're left to muff it up, the likelier it is I'll get caught. OK?'

'Oh, I wouldn't want to tread on your toes,' she says. 'Not the best infiltrator in the business.'

'Interloper.'

'Sure.'

And with me more frustrated than before, and Em more

amused, we swing back round to the house and start preparing for a late, expensive lunch.

At ten past two, the four of us are in the same branch of Pret we visited before I went to Davy's office, and Em and I are about to head to St Francis. I do wonder what amazing, passionate, criminal, life-saving schemes are planned and executed from Prets all over the country each day.

Em has procured a silky dress from somewhere; I've just gone for a smart shirt, casual jacket and jeans, plus a pair of discreet dark trainers in case we have to run.

'Ready?' asks Elle.

'Think so,' I say.

'Don't put your arms above your head,' Jonny tells Em. 'It'll pull the wire out of place and I won't hear anything.'

'What if someone has me at gunpoint?'

'Try to surrender verbally. Ideally don't move anything above your elbows.'

As we approach the restaurant, I see the sign – a stained, worn picture of St Francis himself, his outstretched arms covered in birds. He looks like one of those tourists in St James's Park who take genuine pleasure in feeding the pigeons and who are clearly either very unwell or soon will be. But now I see why Davy wrote *Feathers* as his private code for this place.

'Ready?'

'Can't wait,' Em says. 'Which table are we heading for again?'

'Booth three.'

As we head down the stairs, it does feel uncomfortably like we're walking into a trap. You could block the steep iron stairwell with one medium-sized special constable. And although I've done my homework on the exits, it was on an old map. Hope they haven't moved things around.

The place itself is not just chichi, it's old-money posh. I've eaten in some nice places in my time – when you save so much money on rent, you do find yourself splashing out in other ways – but this place feels *generationally* expensive. It's not old-fashioned, though; it's definitely had some discreet work done over the decades.

It's also incredibly dark. You can hardly see the clientele, and the staff are moving between faint pools of light as if they've memorised all the routes. Even at the front, in the relative light from the stairwell, I can't tell the sex of the person standing behind the mahogany lectern.

'Good afternoon, sir, madam,' says a fruity Mitteleuropean baritone voice. 'Welcome to St Francis. Your reservation?'

I can see him a little clearer now. He must be nearly seventy, and what remains of his dark hair is slicked austerely back. There are deep grooves running from his nose to the corners of his mouth. He sounds Swiss, Austrian maybe, and it only takes one look to know he is a restaurant-industry lifer, the kind of pro from somewhere they take hospitality seriously. I would be willing to bet he's been working here as long as I've been alive, scrambling up the truffle-oiled pole all the way from the potboy's kennel to the maître d's eyrie.

'We're joining an existing table,' says Em. 'Mr Harcourt's party.'

'Ah, yes,' he says, unruffled. 'You are honouring his appointment, I assume?'

'That's right.'

'So sad,' he murmurs. 'Thirty years I have known Mr Harcourt.'

'How awful,' Em says. 'Our condolences . . . Gustave.' She leans forward and gently brushes her fingers over the brass name-plate on his desk.

He bows his head. 'You are family?'

'Business associates,' she explains. 'We are representing his interests today.'

Gustave nods. 'Your dining companion is here already. I will have another place laid at table.' And then he moves closer and murmurs something in Em's ear, while I stand there, lemon-ish.

'That's fine,' she replies. She takes one of the restaurant's cards from the little stand on Gustave's booth, and grabs the biro there too.

'This way.' He picks up two menus and glides into the gloom of the restaurant. Em begins to follow him.

'What did he say to you?'

'Tell you later.' She loves to tease, Em.

Gustave pauses to let a waiter glide across his path, moving like a barracuda through the darkness. Then he leads us on to the third booth on the left, where a figure is sitting. The figure stands as we approach.

'Sir. Madam,' Gustave says, and withdraws.

The woman standing in the booth is a few years older than I am, maybe mid-thirties. She's plainly dressed considering how fancy this place is, in a simple pearl shirt and high-waisted black trousers. Her hair is blonde and her expression illegible. She could be about to pull out a bazooka or tell us we've won the lottery, and I wouldn't be surprised by either.

'Have a seat.'

Normal voice. She's not from London – she sounds a bit Scottish, but if so, she's been down south a long time.

We sit. There's room for all three of us on the round banquette. I let Em in first, partly from manners and partly because I might need easy access to the exit. Em, in turn, gives me a look to communicate that she's well aware why I'm doing it.

There is a temporary pause while a young waiter – most austere, he could be Gustave's son – arrives and lays a third place. There is a bit of a rigmarole with water glasses, wine glasses, the ceremonial folding of a new napkin. Everyone keeps quiet for this bit. Meanwhile, I'm looking around in the gloom, trying to see who else is here. I can't see light reflecting off a shiny domed head, so I'm going to assume we haven't kept an appointment with Mr Bowling Ball by mistake.

Eventually the waiter leaves, and the woman opposite us speaks.

'My name's Kate. Who are you?'

'I'm Josephine,' says Em, 'and this is Al.' So annoying. I know it's not my real name, but I wish she'd make an effort.

'Hello, Josephine and Al,' says Kate. 'Neither of you is David Harcourt.'

'Sorry about that,' says Em. 'But we're friends of his.'

'I see. Do you want to explain what's going on?'

'We think we should ascertain who you are first,' I say. 'If you don't mind.'

'Certainly,' she says, and flips her wallet open onto the table. 'My name is Kate McAdams, I'm with the National Crime Agency, and I'm here to see Mr Harcourt for a personal chat. But he's dead, of course. As I suspect you both know.' She does not smile.

So now we really are in trouble.

20

'Keep your seats,' Kate continues. 'You're not under arrest, yet.'

'But—'

'I'm just curious how you knew about his appointment. How you knew about him at all, in fact. You were two of the crew at his house, I take it?'

I'm going through my list of rules, but absolutely nothing I can find applies here. Rule 23 is *Take more care with new places than you thought necessary*. Didn't manage that. Rule 6 is *Prep your exits as soon as you're in*, which I have done, but which won't do me much good while I'm sitting here. Ah, wait, Rule 7, as previously mentioned: *Talk, talk, talk*. Keep talking.

'Are we having lunch, or what?' Em has clearly intuited the same rule.

'Here? Not on my department's budget.'

'Ah,' says Em. 'Yes, of course, this should have been on Mr Harcourt. Well, I'm sure we can cover it. Al?'

'Absolutely.' I've got about £200 in my wallet – in notes, thank goodness. Use a traceable credit card in front of a police officer at a meeting this incriminating, and I may as well just drop myself off at Wormwood Scrubs and ask if they have any rooms going. 'What sort of crime do you specialise in, by the way?'

'Financial.'

Well, that's useful to know, at least. 'Shall we have a drink before we start?'

'This is a work meeting.'

'A non-alcoholic beer?' I gesture into the abyss, and within a few seconds a waiter has beached by our table. We place our order (two glasses of Soave, one lemonade for Kate). I've now spent about thirty quid and bought us precisely sixty seconds. At my current budget, I can afford for us to kill time for just over five more minutes. It's not sustainable.

'Financial crime,' says Em. 'And you wanted to see Mr Harcourt about that.'

Kate frowns. 'No. He wanted to see me.'

'Sorry?'

'He made the appointment. I was coming here as a favour to him. Except that he was killed a few days ago. As you know.'

Davy made the appointment. Davy was the one wanting to speak to the police about whatever he was up to. That makes no sense. I had thought he might be in enough trouble for the police to be after him, hence the detectives getting to his place so fast, but . . . what?

Em speaks again. 'Sorry, if you know he's dead, why are you here to have lunch with him?'

'Because I thought someone he was associated with might come along. Or the people who killed him.' Kate smiles, and I blench.

Em isn't fazed in the slightest. 'Did he tell you what it was about?'

Kate purses her lips. 'I'm not going to discuss private police business with two people who've just turned up claiming a vague personal connection with a murdered man.'

'All right,' says Em. 'That's fair enough. Let's order, and then we'll talk.'

I look down at the menu. It's one of the ones where every dish contains one ingredient you're comfortable with (lamb), two you've vaguely heard of (*brassica, pommes à la Chantal*), a few totally unfamiliar ones (*aliguelles, smadellas, beresali*), and a number of terms that seem entirely out of place in a culinary environment (*wet-shaved, caressed, Alsatian*). At the end of each two-line description is a frighteningly large two-digit number.

We order, between us, a number of dishes we are destined never to eat. I still wonder what became of my foamed scallop with slacklined *crontili*. I hope someone in the kitchen got to enjoy it at least. The waiter glides off.

'So?' Kate says. She's very demanding.

'We were working with Mr Harcourt,' I say. 'He told us about the appointment. That's why we're here.'

Now. 'Working with' is my euphemism for 'being held at

gunpoint by'. And he obviously told us nothing. But persuading Kate that we were genuinely involved with Davy is the only way I can see her divulging any information about what he was up to. And it bloody works. She leans forward.

'Go on.'

'We worked at the agency,' Em says. 'Harcourt and Wallace.'

'In what capacity?' Kate has produced a notebook from nowhere and is scribbling.

'We were on his mentoring programme,' Em continues. 'He told us he had a proposal for a job for the two of us. And he mentioned this meeting. It felt like he wanted us to be here. Almost like he needed witnesses.'

Kate is interested and doing a rotten job of hiding it. 'Did he say anything about the work he wanted you to do?'

'No. He invited us the night before he . . .' Em's head drops, and she does a good impression of someone overwhelmed by emotion. I put my hand on her shoulder, and she reaches up and wrings it, painfully hard. I almost believe her in the moment, even though I realise after a second what she's actually doing.

'I'm going to get your pills. They're in your bag, aren't they? Did you leave it in the cloakroom?' She nods through her sobs, and I slip from the table before Kate can reply.

I glance around as I make my way across the restaurant. It's the usual clientele you'd expect at 2.20 on a weekday afternoon: good-timers nearing the end of their careers, a couple of discreet pairs of lovers doing some preliminary carb-loading before their *cinq à sept*. But there's one table that is almost blindingly out of place.

Two men, blending in about as well as Mary Whitehouse at the Notting Hill Carnival. They're drinking tap water, and they're dressed in ill-fitting dark suits. They're even sitting facing the same direction, for God's sake, so they can both watch Kate at her table. I don't know why they bothered changing out of their uniforms. As I pass, one turns his head a fraction to see which way I'm going.

It's no good unfolding the piece of card Em slipped into my hand in the gloom of the restaurant. But under the dim lights of the Gents, I can just about read it.

Go now. I'll catch up.

A few options present themselves, all of them bad.

The window in the Gents is so small that a big ferret would struggle to get through it. If I stay in here much longer, either of the two coppers outside will come in to scoop me up.

The main restaurant door: well, I could theoretically go that way. But I feel like Em will need a clear path in that direction to get herself out, and if I do escape by the route I have in mind, that might create enough confusion to give her an easier time leaving. *Odd*, I think. *Consideration for another*.

So that leaves option three.

I have never escaped via a kitchen before. It's clichéd, and I wouldn't touch a cliché with a nine-foot pole. But at least I did all that research. And there's a trick I've always hoped to try. Now seems as good a time as any.

I remove my jacket and bundle it up, take my phone from my jeans pocket, find the right app, and . . . oh, thank God. Even in a basement surrounded by thick brick, I have just enough signal. As the phone, now cradled in the heart of my bundled jacket, starts playing a YouTube video called NEWBORN CRYING SIX HOURS NO ADS at full blast, I plunge back into the gloom of the restaurant.

The cop's head swivels round as he hears the noise, then he sees a torso hurrying by wearing different clothes to the ones I went in with, and hears a horrible shrieking, and just thinks an unwise new dad has tried treating himself to a fancy lunch. He turns his attention back towards Kate and Em. I turn right, head for the kitchen door, and shoulder through it.

Now, in most movies, the kitchen is a hive of activity, right? A maze of gleaming steel and white ceramics, with chefs screaming at sous-chefs, sous-chefs kicking apprentices, waiters yelling for service *now* . . . Ideally the camera pans the whole place in one single tracking shot, weaving between flames and people bandaging the thumb they've just sliced off and a few others racking up lines of cocaine to snort before mopping a rogue dot of *jus* off an eighteen-inch plate because the Michelin man is in and their ass is on the line.

That may be the case normally. All I can say is this: if you turn up midweek at 2.30, after the lunch rush is comfortably over, you don't get that sort of thing at all. There are three people in here – one presumably cooking our mains, the other two dealing with some late puddings for another table. The three of them are, at least, wearing chef's whites, so that's one point for the cliché crowd.

One of the two junior ones focusing on the pudding looks up and sees a dishevelled young man holding a screaming bundle. On the plus side, I bet lots of new parents look like slightly tired, wired scarecrows, so really the last several days of stress have just been deep cover.

'Back door?'

She jerks her thumb.

'Thanks.'

Before anyone can challenge me, I'm walking confidently through towards the exit. Time and again, that's the most important rule of all. Take the initiative, and everyone else just . . . lets you take it. It's magic, really.

And then, just as I'm at the fire door, about to open it into the little basement courtyard that I know from my research has a stairwell leading up to street level, from where I can get back to the main road . . . one of the two plain-clothes officers pushes through the door to the kitchen.

Our eyes meet for a second, and then he starts walking briskly towards me. He's reaching for something at his belt, too. Whatever he's getting out, I don't want to be on the other end of it. So, bundle and all, I shoulder through the door and speed up.

Courtyard: check. Stairwell: check. I run up the stairs, trying to fold my jacket as tightly in on itself as possible for what I'm about to do next, and as I get to the top, the police officer bursts through the door from the kitchen. He is halfway across the courtyard when I shout a warning, holding the bundle up in front of me. He pauses.

'Catch.'

And then, still holding onto my phone, I chuck the rest of the baby-bundle over the edge of the stairwell down to the concrete floor behind him.

His face in that moment is a mask of sheer terror. He's a good copper, but he's only human. He swivels like a cat trying to get to it. And I don't wait to see his reaction when he finds out he's just given himself a heart attack preventing a £45 jacket from Next getting slightly grubby, because I'm already running along the alley back to civilisation.

Out onto the street. Good. The more street, the more people, the better my chance of blending in. The Tube is a couple of hundred metres away. That's my best option. I can't stay on foot: I'm willing to bet the copper runs faster than me, once he's recovered from the baby-shock. The traffic is gridlocked, and I don't have the swagger to steal a motorbike and race off on it. Also, I can't ride a motorbike. Tube it is.

Through the crowds, keeping my head forward (looking back will just give him something to lock onto). Oxford Circus is its usual lovely self. There's a scruffy street preacher explaining through a low-quality tannoy that we're all saved already – good news, I guess, although I personally would have shaved if I had such glad tidings to impart – and about a thousand shoppers milling around.

Down the first stairs, jump half the second flight, vault the barrier – no time for the Oyster card here, and the staff aren't legally allowed to chase you any more – and onto the left escalator. I risk a look back. There's a bit of a kerfuffle at the barrier. Shit. He's still after me. Where to go? Wherever gets me above ground soonest. No, forget that. Wherever will shake this guy off most effectively. Which train is coming first?

I spent a few miserable evenings hanging around in Oxford Circus for warmth eight years ago, and I know the station quite well. There's a passage linking the left-hand tunnels – heading to the northbound Victoria and Bakerloo platforms – where you can jerk through to the right-hand ones, heading southbound. But even better, you can run through from left to right, then double back on yourself and head along the narrow pipeline leading to the Central Line. And once you're down there, you can peg it along the platform and loop back if you need to.

So that's what I do. Down, dodge right, double back, and through, until the Central Line opens up and, *brilliant*, I smell the warm sewer breath of an approaching train. I keep going towards the other end of the platform as it comes in, then risk a look.

Unbelievable. He's about four carriages behind, and he's got his eyes on me. It's not crowded enough to lose him. And if he gets on the train, he can make his way through the carriages between this stop and the next one, and by the time we're at Tottenham Court Road I'll be his.

The doors open. I dive onto the train, and from a corner by the doors I can just see him heading up the platform, trying to get as close to me as he can before they close.

Now he's on, at the other end of the carriage from me, and starting down the first section. Wait for it . . . wait for it . . .

The doors start beeping, and I throw myself at them before they close.

He buys it. He dives off the train, just as I grab the rail above me and almost dislocate my shoulder hauling myself backwards. He's on the platform, skidding towards the wall like a cartoon character. I'm still on. The doors close. And by the time he's stopped and turned back towards me, the train is moving.

We're still separated, but he's running alongside the train, pulling something out. As he gets closer to me, he holds it up; a camera phone. I don't have time to turn away before he's got a shot, and then he's pulling up, because we're plunging into the tunnel. *Great*. Now he's got a decent picture of me.

I slump back against the carriage door, and look around for the first time. I'm getting a lot of weird looks, and someone is wailing. Am I covered in blood or something? Did I hurt myself?

It takes me about thirty seconds to realise my phone is still playing the screaming noise, and switch it off.

I wonder what's happened to Em.

21

I don't know much about CCTV, but I expect every station has it. Or every carriage? Either way, I feel distinctly observed. I get off at the next stop, then spend an hour or so walking the quietest streets I can find. I cross a few parks, which are great for shaking cameras, and head into a couple of department stores I know, which will a) sell me clothes to change into, and which b) have more than one exit, also handy. (If your local department store is closing down, fight to keep it open. Think of the fugitives.)

I can't help noticing I'm running short on cash, though. The wedge I took out a few days ago is crumbling. At least I didn't pay at the restaurant.

After two and a half hours of walking, I'm back at Balfour

Villas. It's an unhappy Al who trudges through the decaying front garden and up the steps.

Elle answers at my knock, and looks worried sick.

'Oh, at last. How did it go?'

'Poorly.' I walk past her into the hall, and she shuts the door behind me.

'Wait. Where's Em?'

I turn. 'She's not back yet?'

Elle shakes her head.

You see, this is why you shouldn't get involved with people. The sheer terror when they don't show up is more trouble than it's worth.

We've made about twelve cups of tea since I got back, and watched them cool, and then Elle has thrown away the old teas and asked if anyone would like a new one, and Jonny's forcibly sat her down and gone and made new ones for us all to sit and watch cool. Nobody's eaten anything.

It's close to 8 p.m. now. Elle and Jonny had already waited three hours when I got back – initially in the café, then they realised something must have gone awry and came home to Balfour Villas. Elle's spent the rest of the day obsessively sorting the house out as a displacement activity, and Jonny has been re-categorising and listing every house in Davy's ledger. The weather has turned grim. I hope Em's not out in it.

As for me, I'm wondering how we could have been so stupid

as just to turn up somewhere again. It worked for days in a row – just turning up at Davy's office, at Guggy's boutique, to see Lulu – but our luck was bound to run out eventually.

And then . . . there's a knock at the door.

Elle's up first. 'Thank God.'

'Wait.' I run to the bay window that overlooks the front door. It's her. 'OK, open up.'

She's wearing a grubby jumper and jeans instead of the dress I saw her in last, her hair's a mess, and she's got a bruise on one cheek. She's trembling with cold.

'Where the hell have you been?'

'Getting away. Took a while.'

'Are you OK?'

She looks down at her shaking hand, then up. 'Is anyone going to make me a cup of tea?'

Half an hour later, things are a bit clearer.

Em kept Kate talking until there was a disturbance in the restaurant – that was me leaving. When that happened, Kate and the remaining officer got up for a moment and took their eye off her. Em made the most of their distraction by walking swiftly to the front of the room and urgently pleading with Gustave to help a friend of Davy's. Rather than just steering her out of the building, he turned off the three remaining lights in the place, then hustled her into the nearby cloakroom and left her there. She banged into a shelf – hence the bruise – but couldn't even cry out. She had to stand in the dark for an hour, wondering what the hell was going on.

Eventually Gustave opened the door again. He'd told the remaining police – Kate and the officer who hadn't chased after me – that when the lights had gone out, someone had run past him up the stairwell, someone of about Em's build. They'd asked him a few more questions, and he had listened, and answered in his impossibly grave manner, and they'd believed him. Kate had left her phone number, and they'd departed. But they'd stationed a plain-clothes officer on the street corner outside for an hour, so Em was trapped.

As she left, Em thanked Gustave, and asked why he'd been so willing to help her. Turns out Davy had helped Gustave onto the property ladder when he'd arrived in London in 1989 – got him his first little flat in Streatham, despite him having no deposit whatsoever – and Gustave remained forever in his debt. It's feeling more and more like Davy's an actual work contact of ours.

Then, as Em left St Francis, she thought she saw someone else following her, so she ran for it, and spent even longer than I did changing her clothes and her route.

'So who's this Kate McAdams then?' Elle asks.

'She told us she works for the . . . what was it, Al?'

'National Crime Agency.'

'Sounds made up,' says Elle. 'Bit on the nose, isn't it?'

'It is, a bit. Any further details about her?' asks Em.

'They don't do extensive personal biographies on the NCA website,' says Jonny.

'How annoying,' says Em. 'Would it kill them to write "Kate rounded up the Fulham Forgers" or whatever? Anyway, doesn't matter. Davy contacted her and wanted to confess. Or to grass someone else up.'

'Someone like his co-founder at the firm?' says Elle. 'What was he called again?'

'Rob Wallace?' I say. 'Yeah, possibly. But the main thing is that whoever knew about the appointment must be the one who killed him. They must have found out both that Davy wasn't actually in Dubai, and that he was going to meet the police.'

'And they were willing to kill him just to protect themselves.'

'Yeah.'

'Could that be Mr Bowling Ball?'

'Yes, but it still doesn't answer why, unless he was in business with Davy and was going to be grassed up,' I say.

'You know who we should ring about this?' Em says.

'Who?'

She holds up a card with a phone number written on it in Gustave's stern Austrian script. 'Kate McAdams.'

'Em, *no*.'

So five minutes later, Jonny's rigged up what he assures us is a 'double-plus-good' phone connection that can't possibly be hacked, and the four of us are WhatsApping Kate.

She picks up. She's at home; TV noises, and a baby gurgling in the background. 'Hello?'

'Hi, Kate! It's Josephine from earlier,' says Em. 'Good moment? I can call back if not.'

There is a gasp, some footsteps interrupted by Kate saying, 'Keep feeding him,' and a door slamming. 'How did you get this number?'

'It's your work number, isn't it?'

'Yes, but—'

'OK, great. First of all, don't bother tracing the call. If you do, the computer will swear blind we're ringing from central French Guiana, which we're obviously not. Secondly, can you tell us who knew about your appointment with Mr Harcourt, please?'

'I'm not telling you anything. I should—'

'Kate, Kate, I know, love, but we're all trying to get to the bottom of this one, and we think whoever you told at the police might be involved somehow, or might have given the game away, which is why Mr Harcourt wound up dead. You know?'

'I'm sorry, I found out this afternoon that you two are wanted for questioning in relation to Mr Harcourt's death as a matter of priority. I shouldn't be on the phone to you at all. You have to come in. Where are you?'

'*Absolutely*, Kate, but we just have a couple more questions, because whoever *you* told that you were off to meet Mr Harcourt is much more involved than we are, right? And we know that person is the one you need to be questioning.' Em has a good telephone manner, brisk but friendly too, and I can see why Kate makes her mistake here.

'Listen,' she snaps. 'Nobody knew. Harcourt came directly to me, and I didn't even record his name in our system. OK? Which is why you two are persons of interest. Are you and your friends the people who were spotted near his house the next day?'

Em carries on. 'And did he want anything from you? Protection, that sort of thing?'

'Of course he did. Protection for three was what he said. Everyone wants protection when they make this sort of appointment. Look, you *need* to come in, we can sort all this out . . .' She's sounding increasingly Scottish.

'Yeah, completely, totally *totally*, thanks for your help on this one, Kate, but I'm afraid we won't be able to do that, thank you so much, that's really helpful, and if you didn't tell anyone Mr Harcourt's name then you're looking for someone else he told, unless it was you who killed him – no, only joking – all right, thank you, bye, love, bye, take care now' – and as Kate threatens to explode at the other end of the line, Em hangs up.

'Strange,' she says, as Jonny takes the laptop and continues the work of making it look like we're in French Guiana. 'If she's telling the truth, then Davy must have told someone else he was meeting the police. And that's the person who killed him, or got him killed.'

'*If* she's telling the truth. Coppers are allowed to lie.'

'Encouraged,' says Jonny. 'Ministry of Truth.'

'So, what next?' says Elle.

'Well, his other appointment is the day after tomorrow,' Em says.

'BB AGM,' murmurs Jonny. 'If we take as long to solve it as we did Feathers, we won't get there until next year's AGM.'

It keeps nagging my brain. *BB*. Where did I see it? In Davy's house, in an obituary? Ugh. I'm too tired to rifle through my mind.

'What else is there?'

'We need to keep on at Davy's work contacts,' says Em. 'Find out anything more about Rob Wallace, see what's going on with him. What did they argue about? Is he violent? All that stuff.'

To be honest, the idea of setting foot back in the Harcourt and Wallace office fills me with dread. But I think I might have another way of finding out more – the photography agency I work for. I wonder if a colleague there might be able to help.

I keep a second phone for my photography work. It's off most of the time, but I turn it on twice a day to pick up messages when I'm not on a job. Even turning it on that infrequently still probably leaves a yeti-sized digital footprint that could be used to trace me to any number of homes I've interloped, but I need a work number. I also turn it off because it's nice being a bit less contactable, you know? You've got to be mindful about your screen time these days.

Anyway, it's been several days since I switched it on, so there are bound to be lots of emails from the firm, offers of jobs, that kind of thing. On the principle that a hungry dog stays loyal, the agency contacts a whole mailing list of photographers about each gig and then they scramble to secure the booking. So I go to my room and grab the phone, then come back and sit with the other three and turn it on. Along with all the GDPR updates and mandatory courses and other HR crud, there's something unusual – three voicemails from Jasmine, our office manager.

The first came in yesterday afternoon, when we were all in Brighton:

'Hello, Al! You got a minute? We've got a job that's come in and I think you'd be perfect for it. Basically, bit of a weird one, the client wants to interview a few selected photographers for it, ask you about your shooting style, that sort of thing. I know it all sounds a bit mad, but guess we've just got a fusspot on our hands! Give me a ring when you get this and I'll see if we can hook you up. Should be a nice earner, though.'

The next one arrived this morning:

'Hey, Al! Jasmine again. Just to let you know, thought you ought to be aware, this one is *huge*. The guy owns some estate in Scotland and he's offering up to ten grand for you to head up and spend a couple of days snapping. Sounds good, right? Anyway, give me a bell today and we'll see if we can get you in the same room together.'

And this afternoon:

'Hey, Al! Jasmine here. Can you ring when you get this? You've probably seen my other messages but I really don't want you to miss out on this one. Between you and me, this one is as good as yours. Apparently he saw your portfolio and just thinks it's got to be you. But he still wants a face-to-face, so I need to set it up. OK, bye, give me a ring!'

Now. Jasmine and I could have been great friends. We're the same age, the same class, the same background (not that she knows anything about my background). But we fumbled it, and our relationship is now best described as 'mutual lifelong enmity'. We took against each other on day one, when we had a disagreement about Ed Sheeran as I was waiting by her desk before my interview, and it only got worse from there. She's declined to acknowledge me at office get-togethers, she's given me cold stares throughout business Zooms, she once cut me dead for an entire Christmas lunch when we were sitting next to each other.

So there is no way, no way in hell, Jasmine would sound that nice when offering me a lucrative job for an eccentric millionaire. She'd do her best to sabotage me getting the gig, and if she did have to notify me about the offer, she'd put it in small print at the bottom of an eighteen-paragraph email about a new JPEG protocol.

All of which means that my workplace are on to me.

And that, in turn, means the police know my real name.

22

'Are you certain?' says Elle. 'You know, it's possible people can just wake up one morning and turn over a new leaf. Maybe Jasmine's finally seeing you for who you really are.'

I give this comment the reception it deserves.

'Yeah, I think that's not quite right, hun,' Em chips in. 'I think the problem was she always could see Al and his personality clearly, which is why she's disliked him for years.' Elle's brow wrinkles.

'In that case,' says Jonny, 'you're completely compromised.'

They don't know the half of it. Here's the truth: I'm a fraud even at being an interloper.

I have a name, a real one, I mean. I don't ever use it. Nobody knows it. Not the agency, certainly not my interlope contacts, nor my new friends either. But to go fully off grid is harder than ever these days, unless you're buying a mobile home in north Norfolk for a cash deposit and living on baked beans. So I half-arsed it, like I have done everything else.

My bank account is in my real name, although I told the agency my fake name and they've never queried the disparity. I also have somewhere for my post to go, an old mate's house from which I pick it up sporadically. I dropped off the census last time they conducted one, which made me very happy – I was staying in a beautiful shepherd's hut in a famous writer's garden (he had no idea I was there). But that's as far as I've gone. I'm not Robin Hood. It's much easier to slip between the cracks than to build yourself a brand-new identity.

All of that means there's a little thread for the police to pull. If they are in touch with my agency, they'll be all over my bank account, and from that they'll find my real name. Not only that, thanks to the Terminator cop from the restaurant and his stupid phone, they have my face too.

I'm starting to feel like a fox, halfway through a bracing and easy escape from some dumb dogs and red-coated poshos, who has just smelled a second set of dogs coming from the direction he was headed in, and has realised: *Ah. This might get a bit complicated before the day is out.*

I realise I haven't replied to Jonny's comment.

'Yeah. "Completely compromised" is a good way of putting it. Thanks, Jonny.'

'Oh, leave him alone,' says Em. 'We'll work out what to do in the morning.'

'Sure.' I turn off my work phone – was it on long enough

that the police could work out which mast the messages were delivered to? Probably. Either way, for all the good it will do me, I take the SIM card out, disassemble it, and chuck the lot in the kitchen bin.

'OK, guys, I think I've had enough excitement for one day. I'm going to turn in.'

As I stand, my pocket buzzes. My main phone – thankfully bought off the shelf and with no link to me whatsoever – has received a new text message.

Time is running short, Al.

Tremendous.

Not the best night's sleep I've ever had.

I can't swear, but I think someone faintly tapped on my door around midnight. The tap seemed much more 'Elle coming to say how sorry she is that you're probably going to prison' than 'Em coming to ravish you'. Even if it had been the latter, I wasn't quite in the ravishee's mindset, so I just waited, patiently, until whoever was on the landing gave up and left.

At breakfast the next morning, we work out what we're going to do next.

The reasoning goes as follows: there is clearly something going on at Davy's firm. These addresses he kept – all with dates and sizeable sums of money next to them – must have meant something to him. And several are within an hour's walk of here. So we may as well start asking questions there.

Elle says she doesn't fancy coming along, although she's a bit vague about why. Not like her – she has strong 'joiner-in' energy. Maybe Em's told her to give us some alone time. Dream on, Al.

Jonny doesn't want to come either – he's still trying to access Davy's laptop, which is apparently unbelievably hard to crack. He's tried about fifteen tricks so far, with zero luck, and the fact he's been failing all this time makes him think there must be something significant in it, especially as Davy didn't seem the type to bother with strong security.

But he does produce a list of the properties that haven't been resold since the date in Davy's ledger, and an itinerary of the fastest route between them. We've got our cover story in place, and our petticoat story beneath that in case the first one blows away.

And, fuelled with nothing but toast and nerves, off we go.

The first place is in Chalk Farm. There's a square near the Tube station that is honestly ridiculous. It looks like the sort of place they'd film a Paddington movie, or any other heritage Brit culture to trick the world into thinking London's a nice place to live. It's exactly that kind of dependable Georgian brickwork, trussed up with wisteria lingerie. I'm just relieved we started at a reasonable hour and have beaten the Instagrammers to it.

Number 33 is the prettiest of the lot. Sky-blue door, delicate iron balconies, and at least five storeys on the inside. I'm willing to bet the basement is one of the iceberg jobs (enormous, cold and lifeless. The owners are often similar, with the added similarity that they're more dangerous than you think). The places on this square all have that weird stone bridge from the street to the front door, with spiky railings on either side, good for keeping the outside world that little bit further away.

We've dressed smartly enough – nothing too fancy, but the sort of thing that might make you think we were from Harcourt and Wallace, London's premier boutique super-prime property agency.

We ring the bell, and step back a few paces.

There's a long wait before the door opens, and when it does, the woman inside is clearly unthrilled to see us. She's East Asian, still in what looks like a proper silk dressing gown. Behind her, I get a glimpse of some expensive-looking art on the wall, and children's voices are shouting happily in the back.

'Yes?'

'Hi there. We're from Harcourt and Wallace, the estate agent who sold this home five years ago. We just have a few questions for you. It's a long-running customer satisfaction survey, we can offer a substantial reward for taking part, and . . .'

. . . and I'm talking to sky-blue wood. At the word 'survey', the woman shook her head and softly closed the door.

'Nice one.'

'Come on. There's no combination of words that would have opened her up.'

Two floors up, as we step back to the street, there's a movement in the window, but by the time I'm looking, I can only see reflected sky. The woman would have to have been an Olympic hill-runner to get up there in time. Maybe she is. But it seems likelier that someone else was observing us from within.

'Strange.'

'Yeah,' says Em. 'Well, that's one off the list. We have about twenty more. Good to get the rubbish talkers out of the way. Maybe we'll have done ten by lunch and then we can knock off for a drink.'

If only we'd known how the morning would go, we would have gone to the pub right then.

I'm not going to say exactly how many times the exact same scene plays out over the next few hours. But it's a lot. Nobody tells us *anything*. Here's the playbook:

1. We walk to the door, looking smart, presentable and – yes – a little flirtatious. We knock.
2. Someone opens the door. This might be an attractive young woman in yoga gear, a tattooed man restraining a bulldog, a skullcapped butler, an impatient Sub-Saharan imam, an Englishman, a Scotsman, an Irishman . . . doesn't matter. They vary, is my point, in the kind of way you only get in a few cities of the world. The one thing they all have in common is that they look like they're doing all right for themselves.
3. They listen to whichever of us is pitching, and after about fifteen seconds they shake their head and the door drifts shut. We try everything. We try naming the firm. We try naming Davy. We try holding up a *picture* of Davy. We try pretending we are his grieving

children, collecting evidence for his memorial. *None of it works.*

4. Nobody has heard of the companies that own the properties. We start mentioning them halfway through the list, thinking we've got nothing left to lose. If anything, when people hear the name Tritone ALM or Phoebus Moonbase Partners, or whatever, they close the door even faster.
5. As we leave – and this happens particularly in the places where we've named the company that owns the building – we get the queasy feeling of being watched.

By 3 p.m., we've knocked on the doors of – at a conservative estimate – £100m-worth of central London. We've gone without lunch, we are in South Kensington, and we are furious with each other and ourselves. I've observed that Em isn't selling our line quite right, and she's observed that I'm a condescending twat. Eventually we give up and get crêpes.

'This is hopeless.' I nod agreement, and Em keeps thinking aloud. 'What does it mean? Does it prove we're on to something?'

'Doesn't matter if it does prove that if nobody's talking. Just means we screwed up our chance to find out what's going on.'

'I keep having a horrible premonition that Mr Bowling Ball's going to be behind the next door.'

'Me too.'

'Ugh.' Em sighs and spears her galette. 'What do we do next?'

'Don't know. Davy's got this other meeting tomorrow.'

'The one you're convinced you saw the answer to somewhere. **BB AGM**.'

'Yeah.'

'Well, why not think about that? What does B stand for in the property market?'

'Bricks, bedrooms. Buyers. Er, bad landlords. I don't know.'

'What about places?' Em says. 'Bedfordshire. Battersea. Balham.'

'Fuck!' I shout this a bit too loud. The school trip at the next table give me a look that is 90 per cent delighted (the nine-year-olds) and 10 per cent furious (their teacher). 'Sorry. Balham. That's it. It was on one of the bouquets in his office. There was a card saying something about the Balham Brats. That's the meeting. Balham Brats AGM.'

'Amazing. OK, let's look it up.' She fiddles with her phone. 'Balham Brats Harcourt . . . Hey, here's something.' She holds it up for me to see – a web story from the *South London News*.

The Balham Brats are not children. They are all blokes, though. They're a charitable organisation dedicated to inner-city kids. The money they raise goes to supporting underprivileged youths in the borough of Balham. The local news story is from two years ago, almost to the day. It's a profile of the Brats and what they do. It's capped by a photo of five men, all roughly Davy's age and weight class.

One of the men present is Davy himself. He's in a wood-lined dining room, glowering at the camera from the other side of a table. His cheeks are flushed and his thick white shirt is undone by one button too many, revealing a lily-white slab of chest. Another of the men is his co-founder, Rob Wallace. Two of the men in the photo – the ones nearest the camera – look happy at being snapped. Wallace, our Davy and the fifth man aren't quite so sure. The table they're sitting around is awash with bottles and glasses.

'This is the steering committee,' says Em. 'There's a senior police officer, an MP, Davy *and* Wallace . . . These are pretty eminent boys.' She keeps reading. 'It says here they all come from the area, all grew up poor, and are determined to give underprivileged young men and women the opportunities they wish they could have had themselves.'

'Very laudable,' I say. 'Does it say anything about Davy's potential involvement in criminal activities that might get him murdered and ruin the lives of four underprivileged young people who just happened to be present?'

'Oddly, no.' She keeps scrolling. 'Hey. Good news. They meet every year at the same pub for a trough. The Bombardier. More Putney than Balham, not that that matters. We have to go along.'

'Why do I do get the sense that you're enjoying this a lot more than I am?'

'I get the sense that I enjoy almost everything more than you do, Al.'

It's that kind of comment that really gets my back up. 'Can we stick to talking about what we're actually trying to work out here?'

'Al.' She drops her fork and puts her hand on mine. 'Don't

be weird. We're having fun, admittedly under trying circumstances. And this could be a step forward. Maybe these guys will know something.'

'But I—'

'No. Stop. Can't you just . . . relax a bit?'

I am about to answer, huffily, that someone's got to keep an eye on the exits in case the police or Bowling Ball show up, and it's clearly not going to be someone as slapdash as her, and if it wasn't for her and her amateur friends we wouldn't be in this mess, and if they'd only listened to me, we would never have even tried Davy's place without doing proper checks. In short, I've spotted my high horse and I'm just reaching for my stepladder, and then . . . I just don't say any of that. It feels unbelievably freeing to not be defending myself all the time.

Looking back, that was probably the moment I properly fell for her. It didn't last more than a couple of seconds, because her phone rang, but . . .

Em's phone rings.

'Yeah? No, total washout . . . What? Slow down . . . Really? You're kidding. Where are you? . . . OK, yeah. If we come, can we see them?' She looks at her watch, which has Mickey Mouse on it. Never noticed that before. 'About forty minutes if we pace it. You genius, darling. Well done. In a bit.' She hangs up.

'That was Elle. While we've been doing our little door-to-door act, she's actually worked something out. Clever girl.

Come on.' She fishes in her wallet, pins twenty quid under her ginger beer, and stands, wiping her mouth with her hand.

'What's she found out?'

'Tell you halfway across Hyde Park.'

The park route is longer, but, as Em points out before I get the chance, there are fewer cameras that way. So across we go. I'd forgotten how nice it is in the spring. I also get to tell her my favourite bit of London history as we walk. It's true, as well. This is how it goes:

Ann Hicks was an apple-seller in London in the 1830s. Originally she just has a stall selling her apples in the middle of Hyde Park. Tiny shack, you know? Nothing to look at. But Ann is a smart woman. At some point, her cloth awning is replaced with a proper lock-up, and she starts selling cakes and drinks too. Then, without anyone noticing, she tacks a little enclosure onto the back of the shack, a proper building with windows and a door. Then she extends upwards. So now she has a two-storey house with a shopfront. Then, in the course of repairing the roof, a chimney appears too. Soon she manages somehow to fence off the building, and for her next trick, the fence keeps creeping outwards. This is all right in the middle of *Hyde Park*.

Finally, the authorities notice that there is a brand-new house in the middle of the poshest park in London. Ann's response is that her family were granted life tenancy in the park after her grandfather saved George II from drowning in the Serpentine at least seventy years before. It's bullshit, of course, but long enough ago that records are patchy. The authorities are planning the Great Exhibition and they really, really need the space for their great big crystal palace. Eventually *the Duke of Wellington himself* has to go over there and promise her a weekly allowance if she promises to leave. Ann Hicks has managed to secure herself a lifetime pension from the most powerful man in the country just by chancing her luck.'

As I finish, Em smiles. 'You're a romantic, Al.'

I shrug. 'She's a personal hero, that's all.' And although I would not have admitted it then, and I'm reluctant even to type the words now, sitting in the IT Suite in medium security, I feel a bit warmed to have told her about something I care about, and not to have been knocked back.

Em seems to be in a reflective mood, and it doesn't take long before she's reflecting it my way too. 'What do you think of him?'

'Who? Dead Man Davy?'

'Yeah.'

I've been considering that too, strangely. 'I can't help sort of . . . liking him.' It's true. In my memory, he's practically holding a toy gun.

'Why do you like him?'

'Because . . .' A number of inaccurate answers tumble together. 'Because he seems a bit like us.'

'I don't identify with out-of-shape middle-aged con artists. I've never threatened anyone with a gun, and I'll bet you haven't either.'

'No, but . . . Think about him. He was basically a small-time crook. Whatever he was doing with all these homes, I don't think he was the chief beneficiary of it.'

Em nods. 'He was another parasite living off people with too much money.'

'Exactly.'

'Just like you.'

'As before, I prefer "uninvited house-sitter" to "parasite" and "interloper" to both, but yes.' It feels like Em is going to interrupt and gainsay me again, so I cut across her. 'And clearly he was more of a crook than we are, and he must have got involved in something really bad, but . . . I don't know. I just like him. Opportunistic yet un-malicious. He has – had, rather – an energy about him that I think I could acquire in thirty years.'

'Maybe you could,' says Em.

'Thank you.'

'If you really let yourself go.'

I ignore the insult. 'You feel it too, though, don't you? It's because he was murdered. And obviously I *know* murder is wrong, but seeing it actually happen . . .' I shrug, and we pause as some kids on scooters cross our path. 'He won't see any of this. Not this lovely day, this week, nothing ever again. He won't have a chance to confess, or get arrested, or change. Someone took it all from him.'

'I know.' Em nods.

And with that established, we walk in silence until we reach the western gate, where a distant but cheerful stick figure is waiting for us.

A Beginner's Guide to Breaking and Entering

Elle greets us both with hugs, and together the three of us walk to Holland Park. This is one of the *really* fancy bits of town. I used to interlope here, but honestly, the places are just so big that you feel a bit of a fool by yourself, and if you hear a distant door slam you have no idea which way to run. These are streets where the main neighbourly arguments are not over parking permits, but over whether one decrepit rock star is allowed to excavate a four-storey basement for his supercar collection despite the objections of the decrepit rock star who lives next door. You might have enough money to move to the moon, but if you don't like your neighbours, life is hell.

Palace Gardens is a street of honest-to-goodness mansions, right near Kensington Palace itself. A couple of them have national flags dangling out of the front. If your immediate neighbour is an actual embassy, you're probably doing all right for yourself. The houses on this street are so big that you think you can't possibly be in central London. If you went out as far as, say, Croydon, and saw how tight the city packs people in all the way out there, and then you saw this place, you'd laugh and laugh.

Number 34 is in just this mould. It's covered in stucco – that's the white plaster stuff, I think? – and it's got a rounded porch sticking out of the front, with a balcony above it on the first floor. The front garden also has immaculate palms, although I'm guessing the people who live here don't. Elle presses CALL HOUSE on the buzzer by the gates.

'Dial 0. It'll let you in automatically.'

There's something about the house I find familiar, but I

can't place it at the moment. Before I can pull my keypad trick, the gates swing open, and the three of us walk to the porch. God, what is it? I'm getting serious déjà vu. Footsteps approach the door, and a man opens it.

He's in his mid-seventies, I'd guess, but one of those vigorous oldies who are constantly climbing dangerous mountains or launching charity campaigns on behalf of small hunger-struck nations you couldn't even find on a map. His hair is a thick white shock, all still present and correct, and his eyes are a crisp pale blue.

'You must be Elle! And these are . . . ?'

'This is my sister, Emara, and this is our friend A—'

'Francis,' I say. I mean really, how hard is it to just come up with a name?

'Wonderful.' His accent is thoroughbred public-school-Oxbridge. He's probably never even *thought* about sanding the edges off his vowels to fit in anywhere. He turns and raises his voice. 'Patricia! Those people have arrived!'

He steps back to let us into the hall – chequered tiles on the floor, some surprisingly modern art on the walls, a little lacquered table that doubtless costs as much as a small flat – and I realise with a lurch why I've had déjà vu for the last ninety seconds.

I've interloped this place before.

23

Rule 5: *Never go back to the scene of a previous interlope.*

This is a Top Ten rule. Once you've interloped a place, don't ever, *ever* return to it.

Let's say you did a perfect job. Nobody noticed you were ever there. Great. Well done. But if you got something even *slightly* wrong, if you aroused a suspicion, if a single fingerprint was taken and kept on file, and you go back? Maybe the owners have installed more security, which you don't notice. Maybe you're cocky because you know the way in and you pay less attention. Whatever it is, the odds of you being caught go up tenfold on a return visit. I've learned this the hard way (Cornwall, off season, 2019) and it nearly ruined everything.

There are a couple of exceptions. If you've left something behind, and you realise within about half an hour, *and it's safe to*, then go back. But if you're doing your job, you won't have left anything. And normally I've locked up the place perfectly behind me, or as perfectly as possible, so getting in again will be a pain.

Balfour Villas is the other exception to this rule, but that's only because I know about the unique legal limbo it sits in. Even then I try to treat it like a new place each time. And although this isn't exactly a return interlope, here I am now, staring at the rightful owner of a home I broke into a few years ago, as he shuffles down the hall and through a door I already know leads into a green-wallpapered drawing room.

When was it? I haven't been in this part of town for years. Were these people the owners at the time? I have a horrible feeling they were: I remember all the decor, for one. It's not déjà vu, which is apparently just getting some wires crossed in your brain. I have literally *vu'd* this place *déjà*.

All these thoughts go through my head in the seconds between recognising the house and Em turning to look at me as I stand gawping. 'What's the matter with you?'

'I'm just . . . remembering something.'

'OK, well, you just sit quietly. We'll talk.'

Elle is glancing at both of us from the doorway and beckoning. As we approach, she asks her sister: 'Is he all right?'

'He's having a madeleine moment. *In Search of Lost Crime.*'

'Very funny,' I croak.

We cross the threshold into the reception room. It's full of those extremely posh sofas that start to hurt your spine after five minutes, and tatty cushions that might turn out to be sleeping terriers. Elle does the introductions. 'These are my colleagues, Mr Denton. Or is it Sir Simon?'

He waves a mahogany hand. 'Please. Simon.'

We smile and murmur our names. It's all coming back to me now. This was their secondary residence when I was here. He's some sort of aged industrialist, mineral rights and things like that. He and his family were living in France full-time. It was a safe bet.

Behind him, a woman maybe ten years younger than Sir Simon enters, holding a tray. She's got a cooler and more calculating eye than her husband, even when she's just handing out cups of tea and offering round the biscuits. 'Lady Patricia,' Denton says, taking a cup and twinkling.

'Well,' Elle begins, 'these are my – oh, thank you, lovely – these are my colleagues. We're conducting an internal review of Harcourt and Wallace, and your property – your previous London residence, that is – came up as being one of concern.'

'Chepstow Crescent?'

'Exactly. We gather you sold it through this man.' Elle holds up her phone.

'Oh, yes. Don't remember his name. Nice chap.' Sir Simon crunches a Garibaldi.

'David,' Lady Patricia says.

'That's right. David was one of our agents until recently. Could you tell my colleagues about your discussions with him? What you just told me?'

'I'm sorry, why are we discussing this?' Lady Patricia is

hawkish suddenly. She looks sideways at her husband: *You old fool, what have you told them?*

'These people are investigating something about the agency, dear,' says Sir Simon. 'This agent man is dead. They think something was awry.'

'It won't go any further than an internal investigation,' says Elle. 'And you'll be strictly anonymised.'

I wouldn't buy this line myself, nor try to sell it, but Elle is so demure that she's actually kind of convincing.

'We'll tell you as much as we know,' Lady Denton says. Those words are only ever said by people who are about to give you a deeply partial version of the truth. 'The firm came highly recommended, you see. By some dear friends.'

'Roger and Jean,' Sir Simon murmurs.

'Yes, exactly. We can ask them if they'll talk to you. They said we had to specifically ask for David. Well, we did, and he came round, looked at the place, told us what he thought it was worth – I think it was about twelve, he said, wasn't it?'

I will never stop being astonished by the way some people casually mention eight-figure sums of money.

'Well, he said that if we sold the place through him direct, he'd cut the commission in half. More than, actually. Obviously the standard commission on a place like Chepstow Crescent – what is it, one or two per cent normally? – would have been a serious sum of money.'

'Hundreds of thousands,' Sir Simon chimes in.

Yes, I want to scream, *but it doesn't matter when you're selling your home for twelve million quid.* Good thing I don't scream it, because Elle picks up the baton: 'So naturally you wanted to save a bit of money if you could.'

'Well, yes,' Lady Patricia says. 'He said we could do it using his solicitor at the firm, that it would all be arranged. Who was buying it again?'

'Some consortium,' Sir Simon says. 'We wanted to know it was all above board, of course, and we quizzed David on how it could be. He said it was due to him playing a slightly different role in the transaction – what was it, a search agent, an introductions agent? Something like that, anyway.'

Lady Patricia nods. 'Yes. He knew of a buyer who wanted just that sort of place. They had their own lawyers, and they were pukka too. So that was fine. It all went through just like he said. And we had saved a really good amount of commission. I'm sure he wasn't doing it out of the kindness of his heart, but . . .' She trails off. *But you were careful not to look too hard in case he pulled the offer away. And you made sure to ask just enough questions so he could assure you it was proper, for deniability's sake later on.* Honestly.

'Well,' Em says. 'That *is* interesting. Thank you for telling us.'

'Obviously, if we'd even thought there was any impropriety going on . . .' *You obviously did think that.*

'I understand,' says Elle. 'This won't go any further. We're just trying to ascertain what Mr Harcourt's practices were like, and this is very helpful indeed.'

'Well, he did a great job for us. Got us quite a bit more than we thought we'd get. And we've been jolly happy here.'

'It's a beautiful place,' I say.

'Thank you.'

I can't stop myself talking. 'It must need a lot of security, I'd imagine?'

'Oh, yes.' Sir Simon is oblivious. 'But we've never had any trouble.'

Lady Patricia looks at him rather sharply. 'Yes we have, Simon.'

'When?'

'The . . .' She tails off and glances at us.

I try to stare back blankly, but I have to know. I just have to know if they know I got in. I think it was about a fortnight I was here.

She continues. 'We had squatters once.'

'*No.*' Em sounds appalled, and looks at me. 'Did you hear that, Francis?'

'About five years back. They covered their tracks well, but we could tell the place had been ransacked.'

'Nasty business,' said Sir Simon. 'They must have got frightened and left. Just as well for them.'

'Did they take anything?' I ask.

'Yes, a few lovely objects. We're just lucky we weren't here at the time.'

That's robbers, I want to say. *You're confusing us with robbers.* I certainly didn't take anything, despite there being a lot of rather vulgar jewellery lying around the place. I bet they claimed on the insurance.

Did I leave things in a bit of disarray? I wasn't quite as careful back then. For God's sake, who's careful aged twenty-three?

'The police were useless,' says Sir Simon, and I breathe again. 'We've tightened security since then. We got you all on camera arriving, and we'll get you again as you leave!'

Elle and Em laugh. I need to splash some cold water on my face. I ask directions to the cloakroom, and listen carefully as Lady Patricia tells me where to go, despite knowing it's the second door down on the left.

After some polite thanks and goodbyes, Lady Patricia retreats, and Call Me Simon sees us to the door.

'Oh. One last thing,' says Em, in her best Columbo. 'Did you ever find out who bought your former home? Chepstow Crescent?'

'Knocked on the door a few years later, just to say hello and see what they'd done with the garden. I must say, I was not impressed. Middle Eastern lot. I wouldn't be surprised if they were dodgy.' Sir Simon leans closer. 'I just think they're very *different* to us, don't you? Societally, I mean?'

'Oh, I wouldn't say that,' says Em, stepping back and looking at the marble porch. 'I think you find corruption everywhere under the sun if you know where to look.' She smiles guilelessly at Sir Simon. And with that minor parting shot against a thousand years of jingoism, we take our leave. I clock three separate cameras on our way to the street.

Back outside the gates, Em hugs her sister. 'Elle, you genius. How did you get the details of the last house and Dead Man Davy being involved? No, don't tell me. Jonny.'

'Yeah. He found the cached Land Registry files.'

'So Davy had his own little operation, selling homes with hardly any commission, avoiding the actual firm.'

'That's why Mrs P says none of those properties were Harcourt and Wallace ones,' I say.

'And if he did that for all the homes in that ledger . . .'

'That's a lot of money Harcourt and Wallace would have missed out on.'

'And Wallace had a big row with him a few weeks ago. Maybe he'd found out what was going on.'

Elle's brow crinkles. 'So then Wallace . . . killed him?'

'It's possible, I suppose.'

I think of something else. 'That's why his solicitor looked so terrified when I visited the office. He might have been the weak link. Perhaps Wallace used his evidence to confront Davy.'

'Wow.'

'But it still doesn't make sense for Davy to slash the commission,' I say. 'Even if he was getting a much bigger chunk all for himself, that's a thumping discount. Davy had an expensive life. He must have had another way of making the cash back.'

'Yeah.'

'Probably something to do with those companies.'

'Yeah. Let's ring Jonny.'

We all agree this is a great idea and we've done a great day's work. As we head home, I switch on my main phone. A message bumps onto the screen:

You're going to pay for everything you've done, Al. And more.

I glance at Em. She's on her phone, but when she looks up in response to my hard stare, she seems totally oblivious. I don't suppose . . . No. Just so unlikely. It can't be her sending them. Nobody's that good an actor.

Of course, if it's not her, or Elle, or Jonny – although now I'm starting to have worries – then it's another bit of my past catching up with me.

Either way, great stuff.

24

Four hours later, we're sitting in the wreckage of a big Korean takeaway and doing our homework. Jonny's sitting on the floor with his laptop and two phones; Elle's in a solo armchair; Em and I are on the sofa. Her bare feet are quite near mine. Focus, Al. Jonny is talking us through something. He's also told us he's got exciting news, but he won't tell us until he's sure we understand the basics. He's such a dad.

'All right,' says Em. 'These companies listed in Davy's ledger – every one of them owns one property, right? And you're saying the properties are worth at least five million quid each.'

'Much more, in some cases,' says Jonny. 'So now we find out who owns the companies. Anyone?'

I feel like this is a trick question. 'You can just look that up, can't you?'

Jonny sighs. '*No.* As I said a few minutes ago, these are firms registered overseas under a variety of complicated structures. It's impossible to see at a glance who the ultimate owner is. Have you heard of the Paradise Papers?'

I shake my head.

'Pandora Papers? Panama Papers? Mossack Fonseca?'

'I'm more of a practical housebreaker than a theorist,' I say, a bit defensively. 'But you're saying the owners of all these places are . . . crooks? Overseas crooks?'

'Not necessarily. Plenty of people in Britain use complicated overseas structures as well, to own properties in Britain. Not that they're automatically *not* crooks. The whole point is that it completely disguises your identity. And it used to be unbelievably easy.'

'How easy?'

'Until a few years ago, if you were an overseas buyer, you could hide under three or four nested companies and buy twenty million pounds' worth of property without anyone blinking. Then they tightened the rules, so now estate agents have to gather detailed information on buyers before proceeding with a sale. You can't just buy a place under a company name any more. They need proof of ID, address . . . all of it.'

'But Davy must have known whose companies he was dealing with, surely?'

'Of course, but he doesn't seem to have written it down anywhere, unless it's on this laptop of his.'

'So assuming he was knowingly helping people who wanted to stay anonymous buy properties, how would he help them get around the rules?'

'Easy,' Jonny says. 'He'd use a cut-out. You hire a stooge, get them to sign the paperwork in exchange for a few hundred quid, and they go on the agent's forms as the property's new owner. Most likely the forms won't be checked.'

'Nice racket.'

'Very nice. But here's the thing – last year the government introduced a Register of Overseas Entities to try and shut the racket down. Every overseas company that owns a property in the UK now has to identify the "ultimate beneficial owner", log their details with Companies House, and keep the details updated.'

'And what's the ultimate aim here?'

'Well, it's all to stop money-laundering.'

'Sorry, Jonny,' I say. 'Can you just . . . remind me what that is again?'

Jonny puts his hand to his face. 'I have explained that twice already.' He would not make a good teacher.

'Yes, I know. But if you could just . . .' To be fair, I didn't ever make a good student. Em and Elle groan, and Em takes the reins.

'Al, it's for people with hot money. Let's say you're the recipient of ten million quid in bribes from a dodgy mine scheme in, say, Angola.'

'Good for me.'

'Not if you can't spend it. You need to keep it somewhere safe. You want it to look impeccable. So if you can buy into the British property market, maybe hold on to your investment for a few years, then sell it, suddenly you've changed "dodgy Angolan mining money" into "Knightsbridge townhouse money". Just by using Davy – assuming that's what he was doing.'

'So Davy was laundering dodgy money into prime properties. And to get custom from the people legitimately *selling* the properties, he slashed his commission and did it off the books at his firm.'

'Right. He doesn't need the commission on the sale, because he's looking out for a much bigger pay packet, paid to him some other way.'

'Wait,' I say. 'What about that notebook of his? Did you have it last, Em?' She goes to her bag, in the corner of the room, and fishes it out. 'Look in the back page again.'

She opens it up and passes it round. As I remembered. There are large sums of money scattered all over the place – some in the millions, a few in the tens of millions. Each one has initials scrawled next to it. Most of the sums are crossed out. 'I can't believe we didn't remember this. Maybe these are his commissions. Jonny, have you checked them?'

'No. Hand them over. Nice one, Al.'

For a moment, I feel genuinely useful, and I pass him the notebook.

'All right, Jonny, can you just tell us the exciting news?'

'Not until I'm sure you get it.'

'I get it,' I say, a trifle defensively. 'Criminal A has dodgy money. He approaches our Davy. Davy finds a sellable property, thanks to his impeccable connections in the property world and thanks to his name being on the plate at Harcourt and Wallace. He discreetly secures sellers by playing on their greed, like Sir Simon from earlier. The sellers are now his clients. But the crooks buying the places are the *real* clients, because they'll pay a bonus price to conduct a transaction secretly. Dodgy solicitors at either end of the deal help it all go through. Then Davy helps Crim A set up an anonymous company based in a secretive Caribbean island somewhere . . .'

'Or the Channel Islands.'

'. . . right, or the Channel Islands, and Crim A is the ultimate beneficial owner of that company. Crim A pays their dodgy money into that company, and the company buys the huge property.'

'All right so far.'

'And *that company* is the one registered with the authorities, and the company's ultimate owner now has to go in the Register of Overseas Entities. And you're saying that's how we'll find the ultimate owners, right? Through this register?'

'It's not quite that simple, unfortunately.'

'Thought so. Why?'

'Because anyone really determined to hide their identity will probably just port over their stooge, their fake "ultimate beneficial owner", and put them on the register.'

'Oh. Won't anyone check?'

Jonny shrugs. 'Not much. Even worse, if you claim your dodgy overseas company is owned by a trust and nobody owns more than twenty-five per cent of it, you don't have to declare the identities of *any* of the people with control.'

'Jesus.'

'Yeah. It stinks.'

'OK, Jonny, I'm really genuinely on top of it now. Can you please just tell us what you've found?'

He grins. 'All right. After Elle went off on her trip today to find some of Davy's sellers rather than his buyers, I just made a list of the companies and went through the register to see the listed beneficial owners. And they're all the same guy.'

'What?'

'Yeah.'

'The same guy owns *all these properties*?'

Em groans. 'Oh my God, Al. No. The same guy is *listed* as the owner of all these places. Meaning he's the stooge Davy relied on and provided to his dodgy clients.'

'Oh. Yes. Got it.'

'Exactly,' says Jonny. 'He changes the address and the details around so it won't be too obvious to any software crawling the system to find duplicates, but basically that's it. We know who Davy's stooge is.'

'And who is he?'

He turns his screen around. On it is a picture of a pallid-looking young man sitting in front of a concrete wall. The shot looks like the cover of an album for a genre of music too cool for you to have even heard of. 'His name is Wolfgang Eisenlohr. German-based.'

'Nice name. Extremely metal.'

'You know the even better thing?'

'What?'

'I've tracked him down.'

'Shut up. How?'

Jonny gives his standard finger-waggle. 'Computer stuff.'

Elle pipes up. 'Don't be mean, J.' She leans towards me. 'He just took a punt and emailed wolfgang.eisenlohr@gmail.com. Got a reply in three minutes.'

'Often it's hardest to work out the simplest thing,' Jonny says.

'Sure. Well done either way, Jonny, that's amazing. Think he'll answer any questions from us?'

'It's worth a try. He's said he can Zoom us at seven tomorrow evening.'

'And, I'm sorry, does all this help us work out who killed Davy?' I gesture at Jonny's screen.

'Might do. The killer could be one of the crooks who found out they were about to be identified. Or it could be someone Davy was working on the scheme with. Thieves falling out.'

'Someone else in property, you mean. Someone Davy argued with. Someone like . . . Rob Wallace?'

'Could be.'

'Amazing. Well done, everybody. Jonny for finding all that. Elle for finding Sir Simon earlier. Em for putting up with me all day.'

'OK, enough Oscars stuff,' says Elle. 'What's tomorrow?'

'Well,' Em says, 'there's the Balham Brats AGM, which was clearly important enough that Davy was going to try and attend even with this hanging over him.'

'What's that?'

'Oh, sorry, Jonny, you didn't come and get crêpes. Neither did you, Elle. Take a look at this.'

The pair of them read the *South London News* piece on Em's phone.

'Wait a second,' says Jonny. 'Wallace is here. Would you go to a meeting with someone you thought was trying to kill you?'

'Depends on the biscuits.'

'Be serious.'

'All right, no, I suppose I wouldn't,' I say. 'But he might have put it in his diary before he was afraid for his life. Who were last year's attendees again, apart from Davy and Wallace?'

'Let's see,' says Elle. 'OK, we have an MP, a senior police officer, and a fifth guy, Ben Westcott, who seems to have no achievements at all beyond his name. That's it. Just five blokes allegedly running this charity and having a nice lunch once a year.'

'We should go along,' says Em.

'That's your answer for everything.'

'We should, though. It's obvious.'

'Well it can't be me who goes,' I say.

'Why not?'

'Because I sat in Wallace's office pretending to be a reputation manager. He didn't seem like a genius but I think he might just about clock me if he sees me again.'

'I can handle it,' says Em. She gives me an arch little look. 'If Al wants the day off.'

25

The Bombardier is almost a fantasy pub. If George Orwell had drunk here, he'd never have named his dream place the Moon Under Water, and half the crummy chain pubs in the country would now be called the Bombardier instead.

It's off a large common in south London – presumably two hundred years ago it was the only building of any size around, barring the church – and even with the city now sprawled out for miles around, the common has kept it isolated, so as you arrive it feels like you're deep in the countryside.

It doesn't feel dangerous, which is good, given that the last time the four of us approached a large rural building together on foot was when we got into this mess in the first place. Although that didn't feel dangerous either, so who am I to judge?

Anyway, it's lovely. Huge triangular awnings looking like sails shield the outdoor tables from the spring sun. Insects are already buzzing their way around the flowers in the borders. The car park is a hundred yards away, so you're not inhaling fumes with your pint. And on the inside, it's that beautiful combination of dark wood, old prints, crisp linen and – somewhere – a highly stressed kitchen team, all of which combine to make the Bombardier 'the perfect place to meet old friends or make new ones' (credit to the website writers). Huge fireplaces, too. I bet they do obscene business at Christmas.

I can see why Davy and his friends come here every year for their AGM.

We arrive on foot. We thought about getting the bus, then realised buses all have CCTV cameras and switched horses to a big Uber, booked in Elle's name for more anonymity. Finally, as a bit of magnificent subterfuge, we got ourselves dropped off at the edge of the heath, only to realise we'd miscalculated just how far away the pub was, and spent the next twenty minutes walking, steadily getting warmer and crosser.

Em's cross because she's worried she won't look at all like a staff member by the time we arrive, as her uniform will be all crumpled. When I point out that probably the staff's uniforms will also be quite crumpled, given that they're running around a pub all day, she snaps at me that she's the one taking the risk here and if I'm not going to be helpful I should just go back to Balfour Villas.

I'm cross because I wanted to show willing by coming

along and I'm only unable to do the risky bit because I took the risk last time, and because that appears to have gained me no brownie points whatsoever, and also because Em appears to have gone cold on me.

Jonny's cross because he's the one with the heaviest bag. Today's T-shirt is a picture of an Ancient Greek bloke and the slogan WE SHOULD HAVE STAYED IN THE CAVE. I swear they're getting weirder.

Elle's not cross at all, which is – I'm starting to realise – classic Elle.

We arrive at 12.15. That gives us plenty of time to get a secluded booth, and time to check the serving staff are dressed exactly like the clothes Em bought this morning – white shirt, black trousers, dark brown apron – so to any inattentive punter she'll look just like a waitress. The other advantage of this place is that it's massively overstaffed. She'll blend right in.

We all order drinks (Doom Bar for me, double vodka tonic for Em, pint of Diet Coke for Jonny, heavily diluted lemonade for Elle). Elle gets 'lost' on the way to the Ladies, and reports back that the table is already laid for five in the pub's private dining room upstairs. Jonny looks in his bag and makes sure the tech is working. Em rehearses her role again. And, in the time between us and our targets arriving, I open my phone and try to unpick the tangled history of the Balham Brats.

Now, anyone who knows south London knows what the leafy suburb of Balham is like these days. It's chic. There are pizza restaurants where sometimes they don't even put any tomato on. There are still grocer's shops, and a butcher, but they're the posh modern sort who know about graphic design and have given themselves whimsical names like *Mr Barney's Meat Emporium*. There are lots, and lots, and lots of prams.

Basically, for Balham virgins (rare commodity), it's where the young lawyers and management consultants go when they've tired of Clapham, the next staging post on the way out to the Home Counties. As inevitable as salmon, the well-to-do start in Zone 2, in posh places their parents have helped them with because even a top law firm position won't get you a flat these days. Then they gradually head outwards to spawn. Eventually their own young will wriggle against the ferocious tidal wave of money sloshing back the other way, and – with a bit of help from their parents – secure their own starter flats in the centre of town, and the cycle will begin once more.

It hasn't always been like this. Forty years ago, Balham was *rough*.

A colleague from my snappers' agency lived there back in the eighties. Red lights in every other window, red and blue lights flashing down the street every five minutes. Fights spilling over from the pubs to the street and from Fridays to school nights. Sometimes, if you didn't have any cash, the minicab firm by the station would give you a lift home for free just because they didn't want you getting in any trouble, my colleague told me.

This is the Balham that Davy and his friends started out in. A foundation to help the area's poor boys and girls probably made sense at the time, even though these days it seems a bit like a sick joke.

The other thing I often think is: how the hell were all these places so shabby within living memory? I've had people tell me that when they were young, Clapham was edgy, that you wouldn't go to Notting Hill without an armed escort. Some have even told me that Wimbledon used to be a bit ragged round the edges, although that one I find hard to believe. Were people just not aware how lovely all the homes in these places were? I guess not.

I suppose people a few decades ago weren't to know about the right to buy and about the government not building any more social housing, and about 2008, and about the tripling of assets since then because of all the money being pumped into the economy, and about the failure to sort out planning, or council tax, or the bank of Mum and Dad setting up shop, or the Boomers getting a nice seat at the table then clearing the other places off it before anyone else arrived.

Anyway. Here are the Balham Brats, one by one:

Rob Wallace we know already. Swish agent, angry man. Killer? No idea. I wonder if he's planning to tell his friends today what Davy was up to, and why they had such a furious row. Now that Davy's dead, I suppose the relations between the four survivors are going to start evolving a bit. They must have had all sorts of arrangements over the years – Davy keeping a nice flat back for someone here and there, maybe without Wallace knowing? Don't know.

Jay Hawthorne is one of the two men who was smiling in the *South London Gazette* snap. He's a senior police officer in the Met. I get briefly excited that maybe he's in fraud like our new friend Kate McAdams, but he isn't. From the little I can tell, he's simply a senior officer, with all sorts of phrases like 'operational command' and 'urban pacification unit' swirling round him in news reports. At the few public appearances we've been able to find, he's either been explaining that this or that corrupt police officer is positively the last in the force and it's all going to be fine from here, or stonily refusing to answer the questions of a parliamentary committee who are trying to find out why the bad apples keep on tumbling out of the barrel. He must have been a very good copper or a very bad one to get this far.

Conor Vane is an MP, and the other man smiling in the publicity shot. Lots of the newspapers call him 'Weather Vane' because in the last fifteen years since he entered Parliament he's somehow managed to stay on the right side of almost everyone. (I'm actually impressed that anyone with the words 'con' and 'vain' in their name went into a career where it would be referenced every single day. I guess that's nominative determinism for you.) He's had three ministerial jobs of increasing seniority, and he's on a staggering number of committees. Horse-racing, manufacturers, European relations, defence . . . he has left no pie un-fingered on his way to the top. He's a member of the All-Party Parliamentary Group for at least fifteen different countries, lots of them vibrant beacons of autocracy across the Middle East and north Africa. He's frequently written up as 'one to watch', presumably because if you don't keep an eye on him, he'll go through your stuff.

A Beginner's Guide to Breaking and Entering

The one I can't work out is Ben Westcott. I've searched for him online. He pops up a bit in the nineties, in the newspaper archives Jonny helped me look through. He appears to have made a stack of money with a gambling firm when the industry was starting to deregulate – he came up with some clever new ways of undercutting the old-school bookies – but sold up for a colossal amount of money in about 2004 and has hardly appeared anywhere since. Maybe he retired.

The final member of the group, of course, is David Harcourt (deceased). Going on his diary, he really wanted to be here with his mates today. I wonder why.

These men are all in their mid- to late fifties. I suppose the story of the Balham Brats is the story of a whole cohort of people in this country in the last few decades. They found a bubble, almost without knowing it, and rode it all the way to the top. I'd have done the same in their loafers, given half a chance.

We have a nice view from the window of our booth of the four surviving Brats as they turn up.

Officer Hawthorne arrives first. He's round and ruddy, with a wily look about him, as if Fantastic Mr Fox has let himself go a bit. He emerges from the back seat of a Range Rover with tinted black windows, so it's safe to say his career in the Met is going all right. He greets the barman like a local, loud and coarse, before hauling his way up the stairs.

Rob Wallace walks in next. He's still in a suit, even at the weekend, although this one is more 'sophisticated urbane countryman' than 'killer estate agent'. He's much lower-profile than Hawthorne, murmuring his arrival to a waitress and waiting for her to lead him to the private room. He doesn't spot me. There's a lot of anger in his movements – Elle notes with some concern that he's 'really carrying the week he's been through in his lower back'. I don't care, as long as he keeps the tension in his lumbar region and doesn't take it out on me.

The third man to arrive is Vane, the MP. He's in a shirt and jeans with a preppy jumper draped round his shoulders, and he looks highly moisturised. He glances around as he crosses the threshold with the confident smirk of a man who knows he's been recognised by at least a few people in the room. Nobody comes over to say as much, though, and eventually he decides the court of public opinion has failed in its duty and sidles upstairs unacknowledged.

Vane's got two security men with him, I note, the sort of shaven-headed Statham-alikes who doubtless spent some time in the SAS, SBS or another Acronymic Agency for Hardmen (AAH).

Much to my relief, after conducting a walkaround of the room, dismissing us entirely in the process, the two goons settle themselves at the bar, where they start leafing appreciatively through the *Sun* and spending taxpayers' money on pork scratchings.

Finally, Ben Westcott shambles in, hardly recognisable from last year's photo. Shabby cords, grubby boots, ancient Barbour. A scruffy beard is scaling his cheekbones, and the only things missing that would complete the impoverished-gamekeeper look are a shotgun under his arm and a brace of pheasants on his back. He walks straight through to the stairs, apparently neither expecting nor desiring a greeting from anyone.

'Right,' says Jonny. 'I suppose now they're all assembled it might be worth our while actually doing something, eh?'

'Good idea, Jonny,' says Em.

I should explain, there's a bit of tension between the four of us at the moment.

When we got here, Em decided she would place the flowers herself, but that she wouldn't do it yet. She's had plenty of time – especially once Elle had checked out the room – but she still hasn't got it done. She says she wants to do it right, and for that to happen all the Brats have to be here first. The rest of us – particularly Jonny, who is as calm and relaxed about his expensive equipment as a mother with her newborn baby – politely asked her to get on with it, but she dug her heels in and said she was the one taking the risk so she'd be the one to decide when to move. Also, the four men were hardly going to start saying the juicy stuff as they were still taking their coats off.

Hence Jonny now saying: 'Can we get on with it then?'

Em gives him a look. 'Yes, we can. Thanks for being so nice about it.'

Jonny murmurs something that sounds like *newspeak* under his breath. But Em disregards it, and extracts the flowers from her bag.

We got them at the flower stall at Embankment station. Florists take cash, thank goodness, because three of us are now operating cash-only for security reasons. (Jonny works exclusively in crypto, and in the week I've known him has twice told me that any currency that hasn't been blockchained is a barbarous relic and I may as well be buying things with silver florins or cowrie shells.)

'Got the vase?'

She digs out the vase.

Most of the waiting staff here aren't anything to worry about, because they're about fourteen. There are a few who look more experienced, though, and one obvious manager – he's wearing a tucked-in shirt and jeans, and moving around directing staff, greeting guests, occasionally pouring a pint for a favoured customer if there's nobody else available. He's got an air of efficiency and a trimmed beard, neither of which I like the look of. We'll have to make sure he's out of the way before Em goes in.

The most innocuous tasks seem horribly conspicuous when you're doing them in the wrong place: in this case, filling a jar with flowers at a pub table. Jonny takes over, once Elle has finished fussing over the *placement*, and fits what he needs to. Once he's done what she calls the 'technical bit', Elle requests a slight adjustment for aesthetics' sake – two adjacent tulips should be balanced and separated by some old man's beard – only to be told 'absolutely not'.

Nobody interrupts us during this transaction. None of the staff have noticed the flowers; the manager is busy elsewhere. Em whips off her jumper, revealing her Bombardier-ish shirt and apron, slides out of the booth, and takes the vase upstairs. Jonny opens his computer and hands round AirPods.

Here – as we have it – is a perfect transcript of what went on in the upstairs room, until the point where it all went wrong.

[Thirty seconds of swishy walking. A knock. A door swinging open.]

HAWTHORNE: . . . just horseshit. If we had someone, we'd have to announce it. It's not like there's not been any . . . *[He tails off.]*

VANE: Can we help you, miss?

EM: I'm so sorry to interrupt you. Just wanted to bring you this. It's a gift from the management.

HAWTHORNE: What for?

EM: I think everyone just wanted to say how sorry they were about Mr Harcourt.

[Vane makes some comment here, but it's too indistinct for the microphone to pick up. The person next to him – Rob Wallace, according to Em's later memory – snorts.]

WESTCOTT: Thank you. That's kind.

EM: Can I leave them here?

WALLACE: Don't put them in the middle, love, they're massive. Our friend over here is so short he won't be able to see over them.

EM: Oh, sorry, I—

VANE: Fuck off, Rob. They're fine on the table, love.

[A moment's pause.]

At this point, those of us listening downstairs are registering: if you're going to use a floral display as a surveillance device, make the flowers big enough to hide the microphone, rather than 'so huge they make the vase an encumbrance'. In the room, Em takes cover behind Vane's ego, which is much larger than the man himself. She steps forward, and – as Vane suggests – plants the vase in the middle of the table.

WESTCOTT: Would it be all right to order some wine?
EM: Yes, of course.

I don't know exactly what Em's playing at here, but I'm sure she's on top of it. I'm starting to understand that she's usually got a plan.

WESTCOTT: All right, we'll have two bottles of the Picpoul to start, then the—
HAWTHORNE: Not Picpoul, Ben. You know I can't have gaseous drinks.
VANE: Gaseous bullshit. It's hardly even sparkling. It's not like it's Tizer. You're not stopping us getting some fizz anyway.
WESTCOTT: Can you give us a minute, please?
EM: Of course. I'll be back.
[Footsteps. Slam.]
HAWTHORNE: Jesus, Ben, what's wrong with Sauvignon Blanc?
WESTCOTT: We can get Sauvignon Blanc if you like.
VANE: She was a bit of something, wasn't she?
WALLACE: Grow up, Con. She looked younger than your Becky.
VANE: Don't be a prude. I'll tell you something about Becky's friends . . .

A Beginner's Guide to Breaking and Entering

[There are a few further comments here that I've edited out for reasons of taste. Then there's some inconsequential chat for a few minutes, while the actual wine waitress turns up and takes their order, then a bit more desultory stuff about Hawthorne's recent bout of gout, Vane's 'absolutely rank' constituents and their boring problems, and so on. The drinks arrive; the waitress leaves.]

WESTCOTT: Shall we have a toast?

[A moment's silence falls upon the room.]

VANE: Good idea.

WALLACE: Yeah.

WESTCOTT: Shall I say something?

[A chorus of 'no'.]

VANE: Too sentimental.

HAWTHORNE: Yeah. Wanker.

WESTCOTT: I did know him longest.

WALLACE: And he picked you as his best man. We know, Ben. You were closest. God.

HAWTHORNE: I'll say something. *[The others grunt; Westcott apparently gives up.]* All right. Dave, we're going to miss you. You were a pain in the arse most of the time, but you were a good mate, and we're going to find the scumbags who did it.

[Glasses clink.]

WESTCOTT: Short and sweet.

VANE: Short, anyway.

HAWTHORNE: You're welcome to have a go at improving on that. But there's nothing else to say. And we will catch the little rats responsible.

WESTCOTT: How's the investigation going?

HAWTHORNE: Well, it's not my patch. But I'm keeping an eye on it. There's a group of people they're trying to track down who broke into the house on the night . . .

VANE: Are we getting on with today's business or what?

WESTCOTT: Shut up, Con. Jay's telling us how the investigation's going.

HAWTHORNE: Like I say, there's a group. Four people. Two men, two women. All in their twenties.

WALLACE: What's the motive?

VANE: Wouldn't have thought you'd need a motive to kill Dave. Just talk to him for five minutes. Wait for him to start banging on about Japanese food or the Napoleonic Wars.

HAWTHORNE: We're still working on motive. But we have a lot of evidence piling up. They were definitely there on the night. Prints, belongings, DNA . . . One of them even left his camera, the silly twat. Who has a camera these days?

Not me any more. I wonder briefly how the police's journey through my memory card went, then remember the messages from Jasmine at my agency, and feel sick.

WESTCOTT: Why, though? Why kill him?

HAWTHORNE: Oh, who knows. It's all so depressing. Maybe they were anarchists. Maybe they were climate protesters angry at his Jeep. No good reasons for anything these days.

VANE: It's true. The kids are all mental. I read the other day that there's a group of student lawyers who are prosecuting all men over the age of forty-five for crimes against the rainforest.

WESTCOTT: Con, you have got to stop reading the *Express*.

HAWTHORNE: No, I saw that too. And some students are saying they identify as soups. Soups!

WESTCOTT: It's not like Dave would have even been armed. Just such a waste.

They all pause for a moment. It sounds to me like they're grappling with the brute fact of mortality; the idea that their friend, so long in their lives that he's really a small part of themselves, has been taken from them, and that all four survivors are diminished as a result, in different and unpredictable ways. And now they know the fragility of life a little better than before, and any one of them might be next, for as we pass through this vale of tears, we cannot tell—

There's a grunt, and a pop as a champagne cork ricochets off a wall. Two of the four say 'weyyyy', and glugging noises follow. Oh well.

WESTCOTT: Well, what are you going to do next?

HAWTHORNE: As I say, it's not directly my case. But I'm overseeing, and we're offering all the help we can. We know these kids are in London somewhere.

WALLACE: Where, exactly?

HAWTHORNE: It'll be within Zone 2. Spoiled lot of trusties like them can't imagine going somewhere honest like Rayners Lane. Or . . . or . . . Epping.

I'm so annoyed about this. I get to live in Zone 2 due to a lot of highly criminal behaviour, not because I'm spoiled.

WESTCOTT: Have you got protection for Charli and Lulu?
HAWTHORNE: I hardly think they'll need that, Ben. Aren't you the girl's godfather?
WESTCOTT: Yeah. But she hasn't been returning my calls.
HAWTHORNE: What you ringing for?
WESTCOTT: Her father's been murdered. I'm her godfather.
HAWTHORNE: So?
WESTCOTT: She might just want a bit of support. Davy was very keen that we have a good relationship, although she's been a bit—

At this point, the door opens.

VOICE 5: Good afternoon, gents. I just wanted to say how sorry I was to hear about your friend.
WALLACE: Yeah, we got the flowers. Thanks for those, Terry. He'd have hated them.
TERRY: Who gave you those?
VANE: Brunette girl, looked a bit Mediterranean. Nice young lady. I was just saying to these guys, you want to

compliment a girl like that, but these days that's apparently not—

HAWTHORNE: Anyway, thanks, Terry, most thoughtful. How's business?

VOICE 5: Tremendous. We're having themed pub quizzes now, you'd like them. Sorry, just quickly, what did the girl who brought the flowers look like again?

WESTCOTT: Dark brown hair in a ponytail. Pretty. Looked like Conor described. *[Downstairs, Em claws at her scrunchie.]* Why?

TERRY: No reason. Although . . . Oh, look at that. She hasn't put any water in them. I'll go and deal with that now. Back in a minute.

WALLACE: Cheers, Tel.

And then, through the microphone, we hear a lovely range of Foley sound effects: about thirty seconds of pacy footsteps across parquet floor, the swinging of a kitchen door, the squeak of a tap, and finally the brief distressed sound made as Jonny's highly expensive, espionage-quality, omnidirectional stealth microphone bites the dust beneath the stream.

26

Jonny rips off his earphones. 'Shit. Ungood. Triple-plus ungood.' He pulls his bag out and starts scrabbling through it.

'Do you have another one?'

'Of course I have another one.' He's got a small black object in his hand and is tweaking bits of it, trying to hook it up to his computer, typing to unhook the computer from the software of the last microphone with his free hand. 'But I don't have a third one, so if you could all try your hardest not to destroy this one, I would be super-grateful.'

'Who delivers it?'

'Can't be me, Wallace knows my face already,' I say. 'Can't be Em, if the manager's on the lookout for her. Can't be you, Jonny. Elle?'

Elle twists her hands. 'I'm really not a natural.'

'You'll be fine.'

'I don't have the clothes.'

The manager passes the table, shouting about the late-morning spot quiz they're about to have, themed on the Alan Partridge canon. He gives us a suspicious look – either that, or I'm suspicious that he's looking suspicious. He seems to have recognised Em somehow, even though she's shoved a jumper back over her apron and pulled out her ponytail.

He keeps cruising past, and eventually he's gone. We go back to working out what the hell to do.

'Elle, it *has* to be you. You're the only one who hasn't already been spotted or raised suspicion.'

She plants her face in her hands. 'What's the cover? I can't just go in and say I forgot to leave this microphone here.'

'It just needs to be somewhere inconspicuous,' says Jonny. Somewhere nobody will even think of touching for the rest of the meal.'

'There's a big old sideboard,' says Em. 'It's got a load of old plates on it, looks like nobody's moved them for years. You could hide the new mic behind one of those.'

'Is it sensitive enough, Jonny?'

'MI5 use these mics. As long as nobody runs a tap over it, it'll be fine,' says Jonny, not entirely managing to conceal his bitterness.

'Apparently it's not the only highly sensitive part of our team.'

'Leave it, Em. Can I take those clothes off you?'

'No.'

Em's right. The barman is gazing out from behind the

counter with an abstract but faintly troubled air, and shows no signs of going anywhere. If Em stands up, he'll spot her apron and start asking questions.

'Guys, we don't have long to sort this out,' says Jonny. 'Can we just—'

'Yes! God, yes. I'll think of something. For the record, I'm *really* uncomfortable, everyone.' And so, with no proper costume, no cover story, and looking as nervous as a piglet touring a sausage factory, Elle takes the microphone and walks towards the stairs.

We now go live to our correspondent on the first floor:

[*Door opening sound effect.*]
VANE: But that's just the sort of thing you always said he was . . . Sorry, love, can we help you?
ELLE: Oh, hi, I'm just trying to, um . . .

Oh, God. She's screwing it up. She sounds pathetically nervous.

VANE: Have we accidentally reserved the wrong room?
ELLE: Sorry?
VANE: Because we appear to have booked the centre of Piccadilly fucking Circus.
ELLE: I don't—
VANE: First it's that girl with the flowers, then it's the wine, then it's Terry saying hello, then the teenager asking about the food when we've only just got our menu, and

now you. Do you know why people book private rooms? So they can get a bit of fucking privacy. There is a sign on the door, if you can read.

WESTCOTT: Leave her alone, Con.

VANE: No, this is ridiculous. We're here for a meeting. What do you want?

ELLE: Do I look like I work here? If you can keep a civil tongue in your head for five seconds, I'll explain, you patronising shit.

[Downstairs, Jonny's eyes widen. So do Em's. So do mine.]

VANE: Excuse me?

ELLE: And by the way, I don't think it's a great look for a sitting MP, and a relatively senior one at that, to be swearing at a young woman, especially one who's recording this conversation on her phone.

[Stunned silence both upstairs and down at this one.]

ELLE: Now, if you don't mind, I was here last night for a party. We booked this room and I left my watch over . . . *[Footsteps, rifling noises. The doors of the sideboard open and close.]* . . . over here. There. Was that so hard? And now I'll leave you to your dick-measuring contest or whatever it is you're up to, you misogynist worms.

[More footsteps, back towards the door.]

VANE: Excuse me . . . excuse me. Look, I think I should explain. My friends and I are meeting here because we've been bereaved recently. I'm sorry for speaking out of turn.

ELLE: You're lucky I'm in a good mood.
VANE: But you won't play that to anyone, will—
[Door slams.]

Thirty seconds later, Elle rejoins us at the table.
'That was amazing,' says Em. 'Where did you get that from?'
'I just pretended I was you,' says Elle.
'Oh, *babe*.'
'Can we focus?' Jonny gestures at his headphones.
We all re-insert our earbuds and start paying attention to the conversation upstairs.

VANE: . . . thing is, if you apologise to people like that, they just go one step further and start asking you to resign. They're absolutely unbearable. She's probably never voted in her life. Just as well.
HAWTHORNE: At least you handled it with dignity.
VANE: People like that are the reason you can't say anything to anyone any more. Fucking prudes. Like all Becky's friends. Listen to this. She had some of her uni chums round last night, right? And all I say, *all* I say to them is—
WESTCOTT: Can we start our actual business here?
[Assorted grumblings coalescing around 'yeah, all right'.] Right. Thank you. As you know, we have to have the meeting of the Balham Brats today. We'll get to signing the official paperwork later. But we have something much more important to do first, something

the five of us – now four – have been working on for six months now.

VANE: All right, Ben, enough of the drama. We all know we're serious about this.

WESTCOTT: Last autumn, you came to me with your selections. According to the rules of our organisation, we each had a hundred million to invest.

Holy *shit*. A hundred million pounds each? God. No wonder Davy wound up dead. If I was any of these guys, I'd probably have tried to bump off the other three too. It must have been one of them who did it. Or all of them. £25m each? Worth it.

WESTCOTT: So now I can present the results of our investment.

I knew it wasn't a proper charity. I knew five men this powerful and corrupt must be up to something deep and dark. All four of us lean in, ignoring everything around us. Upstairs, Jonny's ludicrously expensive microphone picks up the tiny sound of Ben Westcott clearing his throat, about to give us the evidence we need.

27

'One of us has won the prize pot, standing this year at a hundred and fifty thousand pounds,' Westcott continues. 'And I am pleased to announce that the winner of the Balham Brats Annual Fantasy Football Association Cup is . . . Mr Jay Hawthorne.'

A little chorus of sarcastic cheers erupts around the table: 'Fix!' 'Yeah, who'd you get arrested, Jay?'

'*What?*' screeches someone at our table, and the nice blonde family in the neighbouring booth look across, concerned. I realise, too late, that it's me doing the screeching.

Westcott's voice continues. 'Con is second, I'm third, Rob's fourth. Dave yet again comes a dead last – sorry, poor choice of words there – due to his stupid superstition of fitting players to the same shirt numbers every single year. The most valuable individual player this season was Haaland, in whom three of us invested – Con and Jay, plus myself – and the highest goal-scorer was, of course . . .'

Downstairs, we tune out.

'That can't be right,' Em says. She looks as shocked as I feel. 'Davy's notebook. It had all these sums in, all that money . . . Where is it?'

I dig it out and hand it over to Jonny, who frowns as he flicks to the back page, where the life-altering sums of cash are written out.

'Ah. Right. So. These letters here, just next to the £6.8m, MØ – that's Martin Ødegaard.'

'Who the hell is that?'

'He's a Norwegian midfielder, I believe, last seen at Arsenal. And over here for a cool £13.1 million we have MS, or Mo Salah.'

Even I've heard of Mo Salah. Oh no, oh *no*. They were just playing Fantasy Football.

'Sorry, what were they doing?'

'It's a game, Elle. You pick a team of footballers who you think are going to do well this season, from all the teams. Then at the end of the season you see which players scored most goals, who assisted with goals, all of that, and you work out whose team has done best.'

'What's the point of it?'

'That's where the charity money comes from,' says Em. 'They don't raise it. They just bet an obscene amount against each other, and at the end of each year they give the pot to the children of Balham. I bet they write it off against tax.'

'We can't know that,' says Elle. 'It's still basically a good thing they're doing.'

'I guess so, love. Oh, *God*. This has absolutely nothing to do with Davy's death. It's just a load of rich pricks who like football.'

'Want to keep listening?'

'What? Oh, no, Jonny, stop the recording, it's too depressing. I don't think Wallace is suddenly going to confess Davy's murder to his other three closest friends in the world.'

Jonny hits a few keys and gently shuts the laptop.

I take the notebook from the centre of the table and thumb the empty pages. 'Why would Davy come here today? You're hiding, in fear for your life, and you make two appointments you're intending to keep – one to confess to the police, and one for fantasy football?'

'I think some men just really, really like football,' says Em. 'I didn't know you knew anything about it, Jonny.'

'Oh, I don't.'

'Then how did you spot the initials?'

'I memorised the top two hundred players in the Premier League last year, to test my memory on subjects in which I have no interest.'

'. . . Right. Well, thank goodness you did.'

'Whatever else we say about Davy, he was insane.'

'Why?'

'Picking the same shirt numbers every year. That is the act of a mad sentimentalist. It lowers the odds of you succeeding by . . .' Jonny screws up his face. 'I'll need a minute to do the maths, but he's not done himself any favours.'

Em finishes her drink. 'Shall we go, then? I don't think we're going to achieve much more here.'

As we sit in the Uber home – not home, of course, just back to Balfour Villas – we all stay quiet. At a guess:

Em is thinking about what we can do next. That was just a setback, she'll be saying to herself. We'll work it out soon.

Elle would never admit it because she's identified the dominant mood in the cab, but she's rather proud of how well she acquitted herself after the first microphone took a bath. She's disappointed not to have made more progress with the case, but effectively she's just happy to have helped the team.

Jonny is really gutted about his microphone, which he'd been excited to debut all morning. To avoid any more of his kit suffering the same fate, he's now establishing a mental checklist of tech protocols, which he will circulate to the rest of us later.

And me? I don't have Em's optimism, or Elle's sunny disposition, or Jonny's . . . habit of formulating detailed lists. I don't know what we're doing. It still feels like Wallace is the man with the most questions to answer, but what if the killer was just on the end of one of Davy's laundering scams gone wrong? What if he was simply a client Davy had cheated, who'd sworn vengeance and turned up with a shotgun one night?

Then, of course, we'd have almost no useful information when the police inevitably catch up with us.

Back at the house, we take some time to regroup. I lie down on my bed – just to think for a second – and am disgusted to wake up half an hour later and realise I've had an involuntary nap. I shouldn't be needing daytime naps for another thirty years.

Downstairs, Em and Elle are having an argument, and don't hear me approach, partly because I approach as quietly as possible in an attempt to eavesdrop.

'. . . totally irresponsible.' That's Em.

'Who cares? She's been like that her whole life. But she still owes us.'

'She'll pretend she doesn't. And I'm not giving her the satisfaction.'

'Then we tell her that we'll turn ourselves in, make our surname public, and ruin her career unless she helps us.'

'Unless who helps you?' I can't be bothered piecing it together any more, so I clatter down the stairs. Em and Elle are at opposite ends of the room. Jonny's in the corner, headphones firmly on, still trying to get into Davy's laptop.

'Nobody.' Em is a human scowl. So, to my surprise, is Elle. 'None of your business.'

'Why not?'

'Family stuff. Doubt you'd understand.'

That's rather wounding, but I pretend to ignore it. 'Family?'

'Our sister,' says Elle.

'Half-sister,' adds Em.

'She could help us, but Em doesn't want to even ask.'

'What does she do?'

'Security services,' Em mutters.

'*What?*'

'Not in a way that could help us. She's one of those recognisers. You know? She can look at a crowd of football fans and tell you which one was photographed robbing a bank in Hull three years ago. Except for her it's mostly international stuff.'

'And she's in the UK? I thought you were French.'

'As I said, half-sister,' says Em. 'Our dad was English. Look, there's no point discussing it, because we're not contacting her.'

'What's she called?'

'None of your business.'

'Pretty name.'

'She's called Claudia,' says Elle, 'and I think we're being stupid not sending her a photo of Mr Bowling Ball to see if he rings any bells. Or even Davy.'

'Absolutely not,' says Em. 'She'll shop us. She would *love* it. Can you imagine how pleased she'd be to tell Dad that his favourite daughter was right about the other two all along? It's not going to happen, love.'

Elle subsides, crossly. I wonder who their father is.

'I tell you one thing we have to do,' says Em, in a consoling tone. 'Let's burn that diary of Davy's. We may as well remove one piece of evidence linking us to his place.'

'All right.'

Em retrieves it from her bag. The three of us take a final look at the page containing the footballers' initials, then get a metal bucket from the garden, rip the notebook up, and each light a section using Em's Zippo. ('I didn't know you smoked.' 'I don't. I just like being able to set fire to stuff.') We take some satisfaction watching the pages curl to nothingness.

Jonny, who has taken no part in this pagan ritual, pulls off his headphones.

'Are you guys ready for this meeting?' Three blank faces look back at him. 'With the German guy. Davy's stooge for the companies.'

'Oh, Hans von Gruber.'

'Wolfgang Eisenlohr, yes.' Jonny has his own laptop set up. 'We said eight p.m. Berlin time. He'll be there shortly.'

The Zoom connects. The screen shows one of those computer-gaming chairs, all ergonomic black leather designed so you can sit in it playing *Warcraft* for sixteen hours straight. Behind the chair, it looks like the bedroom of a teenage boy from 2004. Posters of Metallica, women in bikinis, a wolf surmounted by a Native American quote, a cannabis-themed tricolour . . . It's like our new friend was at the closing-down sale for Athena.

After about thirty seconds, a youngish man shambles onto the screen, holding a steaming mug, and sits. He's about my age, I'd say: pale, tall, scruffy fuzz on his jaw, and a thick black hairline that hardly clears his eyebrows. He could be a vampire or a zombie, with an outside chance of human. His T-shirt reads ALL ABOARD THE USB and shows a flash drive with wheels. He and Jonny are going to get on like a Samsung on fire.

'Sorry,' he says. 'I had to sort my Sleepytime tea.' (Imagine all of his lines with a thick German accent, please.) He looks at the screen again. 'Lots of you. There is a problem with Mr David?'

'You could say that,' says Em. 'He's dead.'

'Oh.' He takes a sip of Sleepytime. 'Naturally?'

'No. Someone shot him.'

Wolfgang nods, unsurprised. 'Do I need to be worried about this?'

'We don't know. Has anything unusual happened to you recently?'

'I broke up – you say this phrase, broke up? – with my fiancée, due to a disagreement over my personal habits.'

'I meant in relation to your work.'

'Oh. No, that's all normal.' He really is very relaxed. I'm starting to think maybe Wolfy's mug contains something a bit stronger than herbal tea.

'Sorry,' I say, 'can I just check what your work is exactly? The companies . . .'

'Excuse me for asking, but you are . . . authorities?'

'No.'

'All right then.' He's quite trusting – then again, looking at us, we hardly look like professionals. He takes another sip. 'So, firstly, I haven't done any of this for three years. Mr David – he did not fire me, but he did not send me further work, you understand? He, uh, ghosted me?' It will never cease to amaze me how good the average German is at idiomatic English. 'It caused me a little financial trouble back then, due to some commitments I had made. When I asked for the outstanding money, he sent it, but with no words, no thanks for years of work. So I was disappointed in him, which is why I do not mind telling you all this now.'

'OK.'

'Can you tell us how it worked, Wolfgang?' Em smiles at him, encouraging, although Wolfy doesn't need much uncorking.

'It was simple. Mr David sent me a document, I sign it, he pays me a thousand euros. We did this maybe . . . two hundred times?'

'He paid you two hundred thousand euros just for that?'

'Well. There is work. I have to change the names a bit, maybe the address a bit, maybe the signature a bit. But yes.' He shrugs. 'Other people earn more for doing less. But not many, I suppose.'

'So it's a trick?'

'I believed what Mr David was telling me, which is that he wanted to protect his clients because there were security risks for them. It was not safe for them to keep these companies in their own names and they wanted to stay safe.'

'And,' Em asks, barely suppressing her excitement, 'do you have the list of real names? The people who actually owned all these companies?'

Wolfgang frowns. 'No. Of course not. That would not be the point.'

A Beginner's Guide to Breaking and Entering

All four of us sigh. Em swears under her breath. Wolfgang stares off the screen, rather fuzzily, and seems lost in reflection. One of those awful Zoom pauses stretches out for a while, in which everyone takes a second to reflect that this is how they're spending their one wild and precious life.

Wolfgang pipes up again. 'No, I do not know the names of the owners.' He pauses. 'But I know the name of the man who does.'

28

Five minutes later, we're off the Zoom, and with Jonny's aid we've ordered the biggest pizza available on the dark web. He's even flexed one of his rules and is allowing himself full Coke instead of Diet. We're feeling festive.

'OK, so let me repeat it back so I understand it,' I say. 'Davy was laundering money for various people around the world, we don't know who.'

'Yes,' says Jonny.

'He secured the properties by speaking to motivated sellers, and gave them an extra motivation by slashing his commission if they did it off the books of Harcourt and Wallace. Then his solicitor from the firm did that end of the transaction under the table.'

'Right.'

'But he needed his clients – the buyers, the potentially money-laundering ones – to buy the places via complicated companies owned overseas.'

'Bingo.'

'So in order to avoid naming them on the register, he used Wolfgang as his cardboard cut-out, and Wolfy pretended to be the ultimate beneficial owner of all these firms in exchange for some cash.'

'Yes.'

'And *that* is why nobody talked to us when we went door to door, Em! They were all Davy's buyers, the ones who bought through these shell firms! No wonder they didn't want to say anything! And the two people who know the names of the clients are Davy Harcourt – deceased – and this guy whose name we have here.'

'Yeah,' says Jonny, looking at the name Elle wrote on a Post-it note as soon as Wolfgang said it. 'Marshall Rivers.'

Wolfgang told us before signing off that his principal contact had been a man named Marshall Rivers, and that Rivers was the one who actually set up the companies. He had only ever seen Davy and Rivers on the same screen once, during his first call with both men, but he had been in contact with both about different elements of the transactions. Rivers handled the paperwork, he said, and the payments. I guess Davy wanted to keep at least one bit of the process free of his fingerprints.

As for why Wolfgang was telling us this . . . He seemed quite glad of the opportunity to avenge himself on the employer who'd gone AWOL on their little arrangement and never told him why. There's a chance he was lying to us, I know, but Jonny had done some searching in real time and found a bit of evidence that seemed to corroborate the story. It's also possible Wolfy was so baked his disclosure filters had melted.

'Hey,' Jonny says now. 'Bad news.'

A bit of the room's fizzy mood ebbs away through invisible cracks. Elle pauses the Harry Styles song she's been trying to persuade us to get into.

'What bad news?'

'This Marshall Rivers, the one who organises everything. He's in Nevis.'

'Nevis like Ben Nevis?'

'Nevis like small, underpopulated Caribbean island Nevis.'

'Oh.'

'Yeah. I've been doing a bit of digging' – *doing something useful while Al's been banging on about how he finally gets it*, I sense – 'and Nevis is a great place for an offshore structure.'

'How so?'

'It's basically impenetrable. The data's probably kept in a discreet server in the capital and not online. There's no way of legally getting it, and the only way would be to physically break in.'

'Can't you just . . .' I wiggle my fingers.

'Not if it's not online. You can basically memory-hole your entire fortune there for a few payments to the right people. All perfectly legal.'

'There'll be a government computer you can access, right?'

'Nevis authorities don't have access to bank information. You'd need a court order, which I would guess we're not likely to get.'

'Shit.'

'Yeah. They have a lot of regulations designed to make the world feel comfortable parking anonymous money there.'

I know what Em is going to say next even before she opens her mouth.

'OK,' says Em. 'So we go to Nevis.'

'Don't be stupid,' I say. 'We're wanted for questioning about a murder. I think they have rules about leaving the country.'

'They've only got your name,' says Em. 'And Jonny's prints. Nobody's interested in me yet. They'd be going off a physical description, and I doubt they'd manage that.'

'So who's going?' I ask. 'You and Elle?'

'Oh, not me,' says Elle. 'Not with my allergies.'

'You can come with me, Al. We're more experienced at getting our way. We might need some of your breaking-in skills.'

'No. Not going to happen. I actually, literally can't go.'

'Why not?'

'No passport.'

That stumps her for about ten seconds, before she asserts: 'We'll think of something.'

Once Jonny and Elle have gone to bed, Em and I stay up.

'It still doesn't make sense, though,' I say. 'Not completely. Davy got out of this line of work three years ago – or that's when he stopped putting any work Wolfgang's way. And his ledger dries up at the same time, doesn't it?'

'So Jonny says.'

'So why's it relevant now?' I ask. 'Why would Rob Wallace be so angry to find out that Davy had been doing something wrong when he stopped doing it years ago?'

'I'm sure it would still crush the firm if the truth came out. People don't like being associated with this stuff. Three years isn't so long.'

'Maybe. But would that really be enough for Wallace to murder him? And if Davy had wound up his operation and presumably got away with it, why's he suddenly arranging to go to the police? It doesn't make sense.'

'Yeah,' says Em. 'We're clearly missing something.'

She and I are next to each other on the sofa, and I can feel the same kind of tension I felt before she kissed me last night. Then again, that's the thing about sexual tension. It is entirely possible for only one party to be feeling it, and for the other to be thinking of ways to dodge border control.

I lean a little closer. 'So. I was thinking.' She looks up at me. 'Yes?'

'Why don't we . . .' She glances down as her phone pings. 'As I was saying, I think we should . . .' Her phone pings twice more, in rapid succession, and she breaks off to unlock it.

'Ooh, Al. This is good.'

'What?'

'Elle just texted from upstairs. Charli Harcourt's been in touch. She says she has some information for us.'

This has swiftly dissipated the mood. 'Oh yeah? What kind?'

'She says we should come for breakfast.'

29

I swear, the reason these people are all so thin is that they have so many parties to attend that they just don't physically have time to eat.

We're at the Pentagon Gallery. It's in that bit of London between Piccadilly and St James's Park. The principal businesses here are art dealerships and antiquarian booksellers; on our way here I think we passed an actual yacht showroom. The street above us is Jermyn Street, where a certain kind of posho – or a man passing as one – will happily hand over three hundred quid for a velvet smoking jacket, mostly because it has a label on saying it used to cost six hundred.

The Pentagon is a six-sided building, sitting in the centre of a small eight-sided square. (I don't know either.) Today's exhibition is in the ultramodern style, which is so far over my head I can't even see the contrails. I really try to like art. I enjoy new stuff, and obviously there is nothing less sexy than someone who only enjoys Dutch Old Masters, but there is literally a box here that claims to contain the vapour of a grape, to challenge our preconceptions about nineteenth-century Sicily. I didn't know people *had* preconceptions about nineteenth-century Sicily.

Perhaps I'm feeling irritable about the grape box because Em and I had a tiff on the way here, on the quite important matter of whether we're seriously going to try and fly to Nevis. Nevis! It sounds mad. It *is* mad. Here's how it went:

I told Em I wouldn't go, and she said I had to because she couldn't do it all herself, and I pointed out that I had no passport, and she asked me if there wasn't any way I could get my hands on one, and I paused long enough for her to realise there *was* a way I could get hold of one, and she dragged the truth out of me, which was my own stupid fault, and now we have agreed that once this meeting with Charli is over, I'm going to leave London and head to a small town in the south of England I thought I would never see again, and I feel frankly sick at the thought, and I can't believe it, but I've told her something absolutely true about myself, and it feels like I've lost an entire layer of skin.

So that's where I'm at.

Anyway. The gallery is home to a lot of art-world types – a few veterans of the Red Trouser Brigade, but mostly it's kaftans and eyeshadow. Charli Harcourt is here, chatting with a friend and holding a blini. She's in a deep purple shirt, and leather trousers even tighter on her than they would have been on the original cow. She's also wearing a pair of shoes Em assures me would have cost as much as a new Mini. When she sees us, she waves a languorous hand, excuses herself from her friend, and comes over.

'Tiff.'

'Hello, Charli. You remember Dom.'

'Let's talk somewhere.' Charli gestures, still holding her canapé. We go and stand by one of the unoccupied paintings, which is titled *1200 black squares on a black background, or: mother*.

With her free hand, she hooks a loose strand of hair back where it belongs, and looks at us. She smiles, brief and coy, and for a moment I think she's about to confide in us. Then just as suddenly as it appeared, the smile drops off her face, replaced by iron, and she opens the batting.

'All right. Who are you really?'

Em crinkles her brow. 'I'm Tiff, remember?'

'No you're not. Come on, I don't have time for this bollocks.'

'No, I am. We met at Guggy's, and . . . before that, it was the hotel opening in Mustique, remember? We were on the roof for the fireworks and then the lifts broke.' Well done for remembering that, Em.

'I checked my records once I got home. That hotel's opening party was entirely sub-aquatic. There *were* no fireworks.' She holds Em's gaze. 'So we've never met.'

More crinkles. 'Oh. Really? I must have got confused . . .'

'Knock it off. You two went to see my daughter. Why?'

Shit. 'You told her you're private investigators.'

'We are,' Em concedes. 'But—'

'Who hired you?'

'We can't say.'

'Are you police?'

'No.'

'Then I should have you arrested now.' She looks to one side of the room, as if ascertaining that someone's there. Oh God. In response to Charli's glance, a man is walking towards us. He's not Mr Bowling Ball, but he's in a similar suit and shares the same 'prison gym' build.

'For what, Charli?'

'For approaching my daughter. She's been through a *very* traumatic relationship recently and she's lost her father within the last week. Are you out of your minds? Do you know the laws on harassment? Who even *are* you?'

'We – I – apologise, Mrs Harcourt. I know this must have been an unbelievably difficult time for you. I don't know how you're still standing.'

At that, a bit of Charli's reserve breaks down. For a second her polished exterior cracks, and I think I get a glimpse past the carefully constructed life – the parties, the glamour – to the woman within. Her voice catches faintly.

'You don't know. You have *no idea* what it's been like.' And there's venom there, but there's vulnerability too. She had a husband, a child, everything she had learned to want, then the marriage fell apart, and the child is grown, and she's facing a world where people are murdered, and where all the questions she carefully never asked about her husband's prosperity are drifting to the surface like alligators through a swamp. She didn't want anything especially wrong from this life, I think. Only what most of us are looking for. Just a bit of stability.

Her thug is lingering by her shoulder, and she notices his presence. 'Never mind, Grigor. False alarm.' After a little bonus scowl at us, he recedes.

I pipe up for the first time. 'Mrs Harcourt, we do understand. We know you just want the best for your daughter. But we think there was something going on between your ex-husband and Rob Wallace – they fell out badly and we don't know why – and we're just trying to work out whether it has any bearing on his death.'

'But who *hired* you?' For a moment she looks desperate enough to eat her blini.

'We can't tell you any more than we told your daughter. But we can tell you we're going to find the truth. We will work out who killed David.'

'Do you have any ideas yet?'

'Not really. We know he urgently wanted to see his friends.'

'Ugh. The Balham lot. They were awful.' Charli turns to Em, but nods at me. 'And that stupid pointless game of theirs. Honestly, love, if this one ever gets into Fantasy Football, dump his arse.'

'We're not actually—'

'*And* they were a bunch of wasters. You might want to check out Ben Westcott. I'm sure he's got a conviction for something or other. Bought his way out of it, but it was something to do with a dodgy shotgun licence.'

'Shotgun?' Charli nods, and Em and I file that away.

'We do know Mr Harcourt wanted to tell the police something important.'

Her eyes widen. 'Oh, Dave, you silly sod. What did you get yourself into?'

'And he wanted protection for you, the police think. You and Lulu.' She stays quiet at that. It seems to hurt her more than anything.

'Charli,' says Em, 'did Mr Harcourt ever mention Nevis to you?'

'Mention? We went a lot.'

'Did he ever suggest he might have financial interests there?'

'Apart from the house? I don't think so.'

Em and I look at each other.

'The house?'

30

Three hours later, I'm on the bus.

It's one of the services out of Victoria, heading south and west. Spare seats all around me; there's CCTV on here, but I'm masked to the eyeballs. I wonder if Em and Elle's super-recogniser sister, Claudia, can get people just from the eyes. There's probably an elite tier who can do that.

Charli told us a bit more before we left. Here are the headlines:

- Charli and Davy used to have a house in Nevis. They went every year, and then six years ago Davy sold it. Their marriage had ended the year before and neither of them especially wanted it, so they flogged it and split

the proceeds. In many ways it seems to have been a model divorce. Except:
- Charli definitely didn't know about the Battersea flat. When they split up, Davy got the main residence in the Cotswolds – unusual, but Charli was well set up due to her own financial arrangements (family money?) and she had never wanted to live out in the countryside. That had always been Davy's thing more than hers. She had no desire to join the squirearchy and found the social scene there under-stimulating (her exact words were 'some of these people literally look like they're half pumpkin'.) Anyway, we told her about the flat – maybe he owned that offshore too? – so that was another unwelcome surprise to her. He owed her a lot of support money, which he was reliably paying – money she won't get any longer.
- Charli knew nothing about her husband's business during their marriage. Occasionally he'd tell her about an especially interesting property, but she was content for him to leave his work in the office with 'all those grotty young people'. She had a hunch he was shagging some of his mentees, too, although I have to say we haven't found any evidence for that.
- She says she always liked Rob Wallace, but that she had no idea what he might be capable of. Ben Westcott sounded quite personable when we listened at the Balham Brats meeting – certainly nicer than Conor

Vane, the MP, or Jay Hawthorne, the police officer – but Charli assures us that Westcott is dodgy as.
- And that was it. We left the gallery, came back to the Villas, and discussed our next move with the others. And now, the bus.

We've been going for a few hours and the road is down to one lane, plus passing places. The last half-hour I've seen nothing but fields, plus the faint scent of crops with notes of manure. I don't like the countryside and I've missed lunch. I'd kill to see just one Leon.

Ding-ding. Here's my stop. I'm the only one to get off. The coach pulls away, and I'm left in total silence. I take off my mask. No CCTV here.

I'm on the outskirts of the town. If you don't mind, I won't name which one. It's a small place, and I'd like to reserve the option to go back one day. I can smell the sea, which is a nice change from rural mulch.

This bit of town is a microscopic high street: to a normal high street what a bonsai is to a redwood. There's a fish and chip shop, Almighty Cod, which was always so cheap that it was assumed to be a front organisation for something or other, but it's so run-down that the criminal masterminds behind it are also clearly on their last legs. There's a pub, the Dirty Den, with ripped seats and a sign promising '48 hours of football a day' (they have a second telly). There are three charity shops occupying the storefronts of what used to be a butcher's, a baker's and a Blockbuster. And there's a vape shop, with a banner proclaiming it to be *Britain's #1 Vape Experience*.

It's the middle of the day and there aren't many people around, but there are still enough for me to be sweating. If anyone recognises me and says hi, I think I might run.

I turn off the high street. Here, far enough back to have no sea view at all, we have row after row of 1930s semis that, to everyone's disappointment, the Luftwaffe missed. Then the gaps shrink until the semis become a terrace; eventually, across a few more roads and a scrubby green, there's a block of flats, towering above the other buildings. It's cheap-built and badly clad. It looks deserted, and thank Almighty Cod for that, because if I've timed it right, Flat 204 should be empty today, and the resident will be the same one who was living here when I last visited.

Getting into the building is easy enough. I have a heavy bag, and all I have to do is linger outside, going through it as if for my keys, until someone opens it on their way out: a young mum with a pram, happy for the assistance down the steps from door to street. She buzzes me back in when I explain I've forgotten my keys *again*, but looks at me as if my features are familiar, so I hurry on in.

Second floor, up two flights of cheap stairs; I bet the people living next to the stairwell hear everyone coming and going. Fire exit signs, linoleum tiles on floor and ceiling, neon lights.

Rule 5 again: *Never go back to the scene of a previous interlope*. I'm about to break it for the second time in three days.

But my Hail Mary, Rule 99, will excuse me here: *To save your skin, break any of the above rules.*

I've been leaning on Rule 99 rather heavily of late.

Here we are. Flat 204 is slightly off the main corridor, in the T-shape at the end of the building, so I'm not totally exposed, but it's still going to take me ten minutes to get in. I saw from the street that the blinds were down, which was encouraging. Even so. Plus, I'm at the end of the corridor. If Mr Bowling Ball turns up there's nowhere to go except out of the window, and I don't fancy the drop. Not that it's him I'm worried about today.

I knock hard, then retreat round the corner and listen. A minute later, nobody has opened the door, so I'm safe to approach. I squint into the gap – the deadlock is on. Downside: more work. Upside: greater chance there's nobody home.

For once in this whole sorry story I'm ahead of the curve. Eight minutes later I've dealt with both locks, and I'm in.

One bedroom, one bathroom, one kitchen-dining-living-room . . . it's not a patch on most places I stay, of course. It is a lot more lived in, which makes sense. If you inhabit a one-bed flat about 450 square feet in total, there's bound to be more living per square foot than in most of my residences. This must also be why the air smells of old Thai food.

There's a magnificent TV-game-console display in the living room, and two shelves of fantasy comic books: *Dragonborn, Witchslave, Return of the Swamp Crusader.* That sort of thing. A big one-seat armchair faces the TV; there isn't quite room for a sofa. The dining table is flush with the wall, and there's one chair, also facing the wall.

Yeesh.

Enough idle snooping. Time for some purposeful snooping. The object I'm looking for is going to be . . . where? Where's the space in this tiny box for all the *other* bits of life, the ones you don't use every day?

That's what I don't like about these small flats, there's never any 'mop space'. In about half these places there's not even a cupboard in the hall, so you either have to keep your coat on the back of your bedroom door with your dressing gown, which is weird, or on the one railing you keep all your clothes on because the landlord hasn't provided a wardrobe either.

Small wonder the resident spends all his time escaping into the books and the console. This is why I live the way I do. Because if not, I'd probably be in the flat next door to this one, and all the people living in nicer houses would still be getting away with their careless wealth.

The bedside table is a bust: lots of old rubbish and batteries and loose foreign coins, a broken alarm clock, one pack of condoms with the cellophane still on. There can't be anywhere else in here you'd keep the thing I need. The Hobbit-size wardrobe packed in behind the door? No. Little IKEA bureau for pants and socks and T-shirts? Nothing either in or behind any of the drawers.

Back into the main room. Why's it so much harder searching somewhere small? Video game rack: obviously not. Kitchen cupboards? Unlikely.

Then I turn back to the bookcase, and within thirty seconds I've spotted it, nestled between *Nightmare Realm I* and *Nightmare Realm III*. Of course. Just to be certain, I open it, and flick through until I see a familiar face. Thank goodness. I can work with this.

Someone passes by in the corridor outside, and comes to a halt at the door. They're standing there long enough to give me a micro-coronary – but then I hear keys jangle and the door of the neighbouring flat opens and slams. God, you really can hear everything here.

Time to go – with any luck, discreetly enough that nobody will spot me leaving, or ask the homeowner what they were doing back in the middle of a working day. Although it's not a terribly neighbourly place, I suspect.

I give the flat the once-over, pocket my find, and – masked up again – head down to the street.

31

Em holds the passport at arm's length, squints, then holds it up to me.

'Doesn't look much like you.'

'It got me through security, didn't it?'

'They check again at the gate.'

'Oh.'

We're at Heathrow.

Jonny arranged the flight by various dark online methods. (Or so he claimed. When pressed, it turns out he'd just booked it.) Hand luggage only, and we're booked on a return flight taking off thirty-six hours after we land. We have Marshall Rivers' address; we have a little technical device that will help us immeasurably; we have no phones, nothing that could be used to track us, and about twenty Covid masks. We have everything we could need to make this trip a success. There really is no need for me to be feeling this nervous.

Then it occurs to me that this is just the sort of journey Davy was slated to make, and look how *he* wound up. Even though he missed his flight, and we're about to catch ours, it's not a parallel to spend the next ten hours brooding on.

Em and I are in Departures. I was a little clumsy going through security, and needed a bit of assistance from the distinctly unfriendly staff, and Em told me I was making a scene, so I know now she's as nervous as I am, although neither of us has admitted it, in the vain hope that if we don't comment on the other's anxiety perhaps they won't notice our own.

I think the stress of the last week might be catching up with us, but as long as nobody else is catching up with us, I'm happy.

I'm also trying to keep one particular fact from Em, which I should have known is a fool's errand, but for the moment I've managed it.

'So this is your brother?' She looks again at the picture. 'Frederick. He doesn't look like a Frederick. 1997. So he's younger than you, right?'

I take the passport back and pocket it. 'Do we need suncream?'

'For a trip of twenty-four hours?'

'What, you think you won't burn in a full day of Caribbean sun?'

'Good point.'

I go to Boots and buy the most expensive bottle of factor

30 I've ever seen. Back at our seats, I find Em standing and ready to go.

'They've called us.'

Half an hour later, we're through the gate and on the plane. We have our own row; the third seat is empty for the time being.

'Window or aisle?' Em asks.

'I'll take the window.'

There's a lot of rubbish in my seat – a blanket, a set of headphones someone must have left from the previous flight – so I chuck all that into the third seat and take off my mask. Then I slide in and look out onto the tarmac. A big crawling machine is loading the cases. I'm trying to modulate my breathing, but it's hard to do when you don't want the person you're with to know you're doing it, so I'm conscious of every breath I take, never mind every move I make. Then I look ahead, and see something that makes me gasp.

Two rows in front of us, sitting on top of a torso six inches taller than mine, is a shiny bald head.

Breathe, Al. Lots of people have shiny bald heads. Lots of people are tall and built like weightlifters. It's probably just an innocuous crypto bro, maybe the boss of a chain of gyms. There are plenty of reasons for someone to be that jacked and enormous and on the same plane as us. I didn't see him at the gate, though. Oh, God. I nudge Em. She looks, pales, and slides down in her seat.

'What do we do?' I ask.

'We don't know it's him.'

'Bloody looks like him.'

We mask back up.

'So what do we do?'

'I just asked *you* that.'

'Well, I don't know.'

'I don't know either.'

And then the head swivels, and we realise it's a completely different man. Wrong nose, wrong eyes, wrong everything.

'*Jesus*, Al.'

'You thought it was him too.'

We take our masks back off.

'Why are the seat belts so old-fashioned?'

'They're just plane seat belts.' Em gives me a quizzical look. 'Al, when did you last fly?'

'A few years ago now. It's very bad for the environment.'

'Ah. And they had the newer kind of seat belts on your last flight?'

'Definitely.'

'Where were you flying?'

I was hoping she'd ask me that, because (Rule 9 *Never fewer than two backstories*) I have prepped this one. I answer confidently: 'Algeria.'

'Where'd you fly into?'

'Algiers International.'

She narrows her eyes. 'Al, I'm going to ask you a question now, and I really don't intend any insult. Have you been on a plane before?'

'Don't be ridiculous.'

The plane staff are moving up and down the row, telling people off. One of them, a young man in a waistcoat and tie, arrives beside us and tells me three times to put my tray table away before I understand his drift, and I get so flustered he has to lean over and help me.

'Oh my God,' Em says after he leaves. 'You've *never* been on a plane. In your *life*.'

'Of course I have.'

'Yeah? When do they bring around the ice cream, then?'

'Just after we take off.'

'There is no ice cream, idiot. Oh my God. This is why you've been jiggling your leg since the Uber. *This* is why you didn't want to come.'

'I didn't want to come because this was a stupid way to waste two days. And going through an airport when you're wanted in connection with a murder is the dumbest idea imaginable. And I didn't have a passport.'

'Because you've never been on a plane.'

She's worn me down. 'Fine. All right. I've never been on a plane. Is that a crime?'

'No, it's just . . . it doesn't fit with your Raffles the Gentleman Thief vibe, does it? I bet Raffles had a passport. And the Pink Panther.'

'Yeah, OK.'

'James Bond never had to nick his brother's ID.'

'Shut up, will you?'

I'm relieved by a gravelly announcement, then a security briefing, which I pay close attention to, unlike everyone else around me. I look either ahead or to my left, out of the window, and then examine the back cover of my travel Grisham.

A few minutes pass, crossly.

Eventually a small voice comes from my right. 'I'm sorry, Al. That was mean of me.'

I'm a wall of ice.

'I think you've done great. It took me ages to notice. Most people would have blabbed it was their first flight, looking for some attention. Not you, though.'

The wall of ice is cracking a bit.

'And I think it's amazing you've been doing this interloping for eight years by yourself. Even with three of us and all Jonny's skills, it's still hard sometimes. I haven't told you how impressive I think it is.'

'Oh, all right, you're laying it on a bit thick now.' But I can't help smiling. And five minutes later, when I'm clutching the armrest as the plane rolls down the runway, Em places her hand on mine and squeezes, and it's impossible, physically impossible, not to turn my hand over and squeeze back.

32

Nevis is a pizza oven. I walk smack into the heat at the plane doors, and my pasty London skin is starting to sizzle almost before we reach the terminal.

Indoors is a long queue; slow-moving, which gives me time to slather myself in Nivea. Em and I shuffle and yawn along. You would probably think we were any young couple, clearly doing well for themselves despite my scruffiness – maybe she's a high-powered lawyer with a boyfriend she hasn't shaken off since uni. Or maybe we're just taking a long-term loan from the bank of Mum and Dad. All sorts of nice alternative lives offer themselves up.

But actually we're here chasing a dead man and his money, trying to untangle what the hell he was doing before we get caught ourselves. I suspect a lot of people might find that glamorous. From my current desk in the Information Suite of one of south London's premier prisons, I can tell you: this stuff often feels more glamorous at a distance.

I don't know much about Nevis. It's one of those places that isn't even a dot on most maps. It grew sugar cane for most of the last 300 years, but – as Jonny explained before we went – one of its biggest sources of income today is privacy. Bring your money here, bury it in one of the island's anonymous buildings, and you don't even need to mark the spot with an X – for a modest ongoing annual fee, all your treasure will fit beneath a small brass plate. And from here you can slide it round the world, as smooth and quiet as a curling stone.

For any musical theatre fans reading, Alexander Hamilton was born here too. Another man who knew a bit about dodgy dealing in high society.

As we near the front of the queue, the nerves hit me again. I clasp Em's hand. 'I think we're going to get caught.'

'Don't be daft, Al. Everyone feels like that when they're approaching security.'

'Yes, but most people are travelling under their own names.'

Too late. We're at the front. Em goes to the man who calls her, not looking back. I'm up next. A man in a booth lazily gestures me over.

'Hi there, I'm—'

'Papers.'

I hand over my passport and arrival form, and shut up. Rule 16 again: *Give people no more than they need.*

He looks through the paperwork, glances up at me, looks down again.

'You staying just one night?'

'A conference.'

'What kind of conference?'

'. . . Hats.'

He glances up again, and gives me a searching look, as if I'm taking the piss. I wish I had been. 'Hats' was the only word that came to mind. Eventually, he sighs, thumbs to a free page in the passport and stamps it.

'All right.'

And I've been waved on, and Em's here, and we glide past the baggage carousel and through customs without anyone giving us even a first glance, and out into the sizzling heat of a Carib spring. Almost too easy.

If we get through this without arrest, imprisonment or being killed, and I manage to restore Freddy's passport, there may come a day when he's looking through and reminiscing about all the places he's been, only to find a stamp for the sun-kissed paradise of Nevis. The mystery will – I hope – haunt him for the rest of his life.

My dwindling cash supplies bought us a medium wedge of the local dollars at Heathrow, so we get a cab to the hotel we've picked. Em wanted a resort; I said that would make us more conspicuous if we were only staying one night; she said it would be more conspicuous if we stayed at a hotel with no Westerners in it, and she also pointed out that a resort would be a lot more fun. I said this was ridiculous reasoning, that nobody goes to a luxury hotel for one night, and that this was serious business and we'd have no time for fun. Case closed.

Fifteen minutes later, our cab arrives at the St Agnes Club and Resort, a five-star slab of luxury on the coast. The hotel takes up almost the entirety of a little spit of land running into the ocean, with beaches on both the windy Caribbean side and the sheltered cove opposite it. I'm not sure what the original St Agnes would have thought of the offerings here: couples' massage; Hobie Cat lessons; six restaurants with themes including 'Thai Explosion', 'Classic Diner' and 'Global Melange'. I hope she would have approved.

By the time we're checked in and have been golf-carted over to our room (containing a single king-size bed, which neither of us comments on), I feel like we're already running short of time. The flight got us in soon after noon, thanks to the time difference; it's 5 p.m. in the UK but still lunchtime here. And we only have until our flight takes off tomorrow evening to get what we need out of Davy's in-house offshorer.

I go to the window and open the translucent curtains. If you're reading this in the UK, perhaps on a cold autumn night while rain batters the windows and a chill creeps down the chimney, picture the most ridiculously agreeable beach setting you could imagine. This one's on me.

The sand is an invisible white. The only objects interrupting the sweep down to the gentle sea are a few tastefully spaced loungers, shaded by huge umbrellas. Further along are some simple bamboo cabanas, protected from the sun by billowing cream veils. To our left, a waistcoated waiter is walking along the beach with a tray containing two daft pink drinks, complete with swizzle sticks. Overhead, the sun is a single unwinking eye. On the right, a lone cormorant is wheeling around, as if it's been hired specifically to tick the 'nature' box.

Most guests are sprawled on their sunbeds; a few are bobbing around in the water. Even at a distance, I can guess the clientele: wealthy older couples, their grown-up children they recommended the place to, maybe an Instagrammer or two changing bikinis every twenty minutes and asking their boyfriend to shoot them in a range of semi-decent poses so they can harvest enough content to pay for the trip.

'Why the hell did we just book one night?' I find myself saying.

'Because it isn't fair to leave Jonny and Elle back in London, being threatened with arrest or murder, while we piss about on holiday?'

I concede the point, and we head back to reception, to book a cab into town.

The main town in Nevis is tiny. I shouldn't be surprised; the island's entire population is only about ten thousand. It's pretty quiet at this time of the afternoon, too. As we get out of the cab, we stick out like two sore thumbs.

Marshall Rivers' office is on the upper floor of a two-storey building just off the main street running through the centre of town. Next door to it on the ground floor is a bar, with a fan lazily chopping the hot air, and a barman staring out at the street, motionless. He looks like he's auditioning for a Hopper painting.

Depending how you look at it, our plan is either 'naïve' or 'timeless'. Em is going to winkle Rivers out of his office and into the bar to discuss a private and urgent business matter. She'll keep him talking while I get in, find the files identifying the real owners of all Davy's client companies, and get out. I'll stroll past the bar to indicate to Em that I've got the goods. We'll take separate cabs back to the hotel, dine on the balcony, and fly home tomorrow night. It's *so* easy.

There are contingencies. If Rivers' office is occupied by more than one person, Em will gesture to me to cancel as she passes by. If he's set up unusually heavy security as they leave, she'll do the same. If she's unable to get him out, we'll come back tonight and find the stuff then. If I get in and the kit Jonny provided me with doesn't work . . . I'll think of something else.

Now we're up close, it feels a trifle inadequate, but we're here now, and it's not like we can try this over and over.

'Ready?'

'Of course.' Em shakes her hair out, crosses the street, and presses a button by the building's door. From my position I watch as she listens at the intercom, speaks into it, then pushes at the door and heads in. I retreat to the corner, far enough away to avoid attention, and wait.

Five minutes pass. Have you ever needed to look inconspicuous on a street corner, especially when you left your phone four thousand miles away? It's hard. There's a reason people resorted to leaning on lamp posts and whistling back in the old days.

Finally the door opens and Em reappears, followed by an extremely elderly local guy. He's smarter than I expected: a suit in this heat is no joke. He's dressed like an old blues musician, broad lapels and tall turn-ups, and is shuffling a little as they head across the street towards the bar. Em has hoisted her hair into a messy bun, which is good news. Hair *up* means head on *up*, we agreed. Great. They disappear into the bar.

The door from the street to Rivers' office is unlocked. It opens onto a pastel corridor, paint peeling. To the right there's a door to another office, *Beulah Brothers Law* in gold lettering. Not for the first time this week, I ask myself what I'm doing here. Davy, you're leading us a right dance.

Considering this is a brass-plate operation, I find it disproportionately funny that Old Man Rivers' office is labelled with an actual brass plate: *Marshall Rivers Solutions Associated*. I knock, for safety. No reply. I get out my kit only to find . . . the door isn't even locked. Good grief.

It's about seventeen seconds since I was on the street. This is a new PB.

The office is as you might expect. It's swelteringly hot, poorly lit, with cracks in the paint from floor to ceiling. There's a filing cabinet in the corner, a desk, and a vintage computer monitor. In the other corner there's a tiny kitchenette, not much more than a sink and fridge.

At the back of the room is a small balcony looking out

onto the yard. The shutters are open, and a flimsy curtain is drifting in the breeze.

I pull Jonny's bit of kit from my pocket.

Em and I named it the Frankenstick. It's a rat king of about fifteen different ports, plugs, dongles, you name it, all bundled and funnelled at the other end into a tiny thumb drive. It should work on any computer in the world, he said. As long as I can get into the computer, whichever connection fits should be able to siphon off the information we need.

Oh, my. It's *old*, this machine. It makes the steam-powered computer I'm writing this document on look like next year's MacBook Omega. I move the mouse across a *Seinfeld* mouse mat, and the screen brightens. It's flickering black and green, and showing an ancient programme, one I don't even recognise. Was this something called DOS? I feel like I've just discovered the Rosetta Stone. I'm a bit lost.

From the desk surface, Jerry Seinfeld mocks me with his eyes. All right, forget the screen for the moment. Find the connection. I get under the desk and look at the back of the computer tower. It's roughly the size and shape of the obelisk from *2001*. And as I study the back, I realise with mounting panic that it doesn't have *any* of the connections Jonny predicted. Not one. There's nothing. I go through every port he gave me once, then again. Nothing fits. What the hell?

OK. In this eventuality, Al will . . . work something else out. I get up, brush the dust from my knees, go to the filing cabinet, and open a drawer.

A Beginner's Guide to Breaking and Entering

Cardboard folders. Hundreds of them. Far too many for me to go through. As I start rifling, I find that each one contains a single neatly labelled floppy disk. What sort of nutjob is Marshall Rivers? There's reason in the filing system, I'm sure, but when I pull out the first one, it's just 0001, then a name that begins with F. There's no guide I can see to where the Harcourt disc is. And if it's on the computer, I have no idea how to get to it.

A door slams below. Shit. OK, stay calm. Could just be someone in the downstairs office, of course.

I move to the door, open it a crack, and listen: shuffling shoes, hauling themselves from step to step. They sound like Mr Rivers looked. I ease the door shut.

Rivers is slow on his feet, so I'd guess I have a minute before he's back in the room. Maybe eighty seconds tops.

I look around me. Over on the kitchenette, there's a roll of bin bags.

As he opens his door, Mr Rivers smiles to himself. The young woman had an interesting cover story, and it's rare for anyone to be sent directly these days, budgets being what they are, but she was so clearly from a law-enforcement agency that it was practically insulting. He told her what he told all the others when they came with their flimsy stories: sorry, but I can't help you hide your money. Nobody's allowed to just approach Mr Rivers, not without a rock-solid introduction from one of his three matchmakers. It's simply too much fuss to break the rules for one person, because then you'd have to break them for everyone, and Mr Rivers has done quite enough rule-breaking for one life.

As he opens the door, he looks round at his comfortable old office, and smiles. Nice to be taken out for a drink by a pretty young woman, though. And he got wise to the trick and came back before anyone could get in and do any damage. A couple more hours of work and he'll head back to the bar for a sundowner.

He ejects the floppy disk that was in his machine, goes to the filing cabinet, opens the second drawer, and stares down in dismay.

Behind him, a gentle breeze blows from the open balcony door. And I am out on the street, hailing a cab to take me back to the St Agnes Club and Resort.

33

Em and I don't speak much on the flight home.

Firstly, we're exhausted from the jet lag, and secondly, we slept together last night, which seems to have brought us to a bit of a verbal truce.

Now, I've led with the least important bit of news there, but the most scurrilous. I'm sure you are only interested in how the case is going. So here's the worthy stuff:

I jumped from the first-floor window of the office, managing to bust my ankle all over again as I did. But I had the presence of mind not to use the bin bag as a cushion. Em and I rendezvoused at the hotel an hour later, and went through every single floppy disk in the bag until we found the one labelled *Harcourt*. We neatly stacked the rest, re-bagged them, taped the bag up, and left them in the room, with an apologetic note addressed to Old Man Rivers. He'll doubtless work out which of his clients' disks is missing eventually – he'll have an even cleverer backup somewhere – so I hope we haven't inconvenienced him too much. Rule 37: *Don't make enemies if you can help it.*

As for the rest of the evening . . . We celebrated a bit at the bar with a round of St Agnes Slings, of course, then got some food, then another round of drinks. Night fell around us, and we found a couple of empty loungers on the breezy side of the island, looking out at the Atlantic, and talked. We weren't drunk. We talked about anything and everything except our professional lives, we laughed, and we relaxed for the first time since this all began. And slowly we stopped trading little barbs, until we both ran out of things to say, because we were avoiding saying anything bigger. Finally, she drained her glass, stood, and announced she was going to bed. I was flummoxed, trying to work out what I'd just said wrong, until she turned at the end of the sand, and asked:

'Are you coming, then? Or are you going to sit out here moping all night?'

And that was that, and now we're next to each other on the plane, and I'm struggling not to grin.

I'm feeling completely daft about how happy I am. She's not my *girlfriend* or anything. Once this is over, whenever that is, I'll never see her, Elle or Jonny again. But it did seem to – this isn't a romantic way of putting it – resolve things between us, or rather to make sense of them. There was a moment of clarity when she was asleep and I was staring up at the ceiling fan, feeling that pleasant emptiness and thinking: I'm glad I knocked on the door at Balfour Villas.

I mean, I'd prefer not to be wanted by the police, and for Mr Bowling Ball to have no idea who I am. But things could be worse.

No alarms go off at Heathrow, either, which is the second nice thing about today. That's something. I bless Freddy for his passport, and for not upgrading to the biometric variety so I get through without being spotted with the wrong face. I'm going to try really hard to return it to him.

We walk through the airport masked, board the Piccadilly Line, and change at King's Cross for Highgate. Em's got a missed call from her sister and a voicemail, but we want to surprise them by turning up with the answer to all our prayers, so we hurry onto the next Tube.

At the other end, we stroll towards 17 Balfour Villas, chatting happily as we go. Like an idiot, I still don't see anything wrong as we pass through the gate.

It's not until we're at the front steps that we realise the door is hanging wide open, the hall slicked with the rain that fell earlier and an air of abandonment about the entire place.

I breathe in to shout Jonny and Elle's names, but Em's a step ahead, because she grips my arm and whispers, '*No.*'

The wind rustles the foliage at either side of the house. We stand there, panicking, trying to work out if we're about to be arrested. Or worse.

We mask up on the porch, for what little good it will do us, and hurry back to the street.

'Where now?' I whisper.

'I don't know. Let's just go.'

Oh God. Bowling Ball must have turned up when we were away. He's got Jonny and Elle somehow. He got them and he's been waiting for us to turn up, and now he's going to get us too. We pace along the street, back towards the station, not really thinking about anything at all.

Em gets her phone out and dials her voicemail, to hear the message Elle left.

'I'll never forgive myself if . . . I can't believe . . .' She stops and listens. 'They're . . . Oh, God.' She stops walking, reaches out and flaps at me to stop.

'What?' She hangs up and walks out into the middle of the road. 'Em. Where are you going?'

'Thirty-four . . . thirty-six . . .' She squeezes through another set of iron gates, left just a crack open.

Elle and Jonny are standing in the doorway of 38 Balfour Villas, looking like proud homeowners.

'Hi!'

'We set up a camera,' says Jonny. Em runs up the steps and hugs her sister for about twenty seconds, while Jonny and I say hello, then wait for them to finish. Number 38 is even grander than 17, from the exterior.

Eventually Em pulls away from her sister. 'You *have* to text telling me you're safe the next time you pull something like that.'

'Sorry. Jonny said I couldn't. He used the term OPSEC a lot and I didn't like to ask.'

'Operational security,' Jonny murmurs. Em hugs Jonny too, then stands back.

'How was your trip?'

She looks around, and even though we can't be seen from the street, she shoos the others into the house. 'No. Not after what you've just put us through. First we get a drink.'

Two hours later, it's mid-morning. So the clock says, anyway. My body's been jet-lagged then briskly de-lagged twice in the last forty-eight hours. My circadian rhythm is thumping pretty far off the beat.

Number 38 is much blingier than the semi-abandoned 17. Right now we're in a tiled room decorated to look like the Alhambra. Jonny says the house belongs to a famously thick mobile phone entrepreneur who just happened to be in the right place (Britain) at the right time (the late 1980s), and who is definitely in the Caribbean now, based on his social media feeds, perhaps on Nevis. According to Jonny, it's genuinely possible he's forgotten about this place.

'Amazing,' says Jonny, fiddling with the metal strip on the floppy disk. 'Genuine nineties shit.'

'That's great, Jonny. Any progress?'

Ten minutes ago, a young man from the internet turned up on an electric Chopper bike, dropped off a disk drive and took £50 away with him.

'Give me a minute.'

'What *happened* to you two, though?' says Em.

'Jonny says it was the man from when you went to Davy's

flat,' Elle replies. 'You're right. He does look like a bowling ball, from the cameras. Pretty good-looking guy, although I'm sure he's a hard man to love.'

'He was actually there? At number seventeen?'

'Oh, yes. He looked unhappy too.'

'How did you get away?'

'We were out. I was getting a haircut and Jonny was picking up Davy's laptop from Nikola T.'

'Who?'

'Some computer specialist. Claimed he could get it open in half an hour.'

'And did he? Jonny?'

Jonny is fiddling with the disk drive. 'Nikola's a bullshitter. Took him much longer than that. Do you want to hear about the laptop or this disk?'

'The disk. Sorry. Keep going.'

'But what about Bowling Ball, Elle? What did he do then?'

'He went through everything he found. But thankfully Jonny had taken his phones and his computer when he went out, so there wasn't much for him to go through. So he just smashed the place up a bit. Real temper on him.'

'And left?'

'Not straight away. Jonny's cameras tripped on his phone, so he rang me at the hairdresser's and said we had to find somewhere new to stay.'

'Oh, God. So Bowling Ball might still be in number seventeen now.'

A Beginner's Guide to Breaking and Entering

'He isn't,' said Jonny. 'He missed one of my gatepost cameras. He left an hour ago.' We didn't avoid him by much. I feel sick at the thought. Jonny keeps talking: 'And now . . . we have the information on this disk. Open Sesame.'

The four of us gather round to see exactly what has been worth all this fuss.

It's a table. The columns are simply labelled: property, date of purchase, purchase price, name of cover company, name listed on register, name of actual beneficial owner. Some names in that final column stick out. About half are British-sounding, half from everywhere else.

'I know that name. He's famous, I think.'

'And her. She's minor royalty.'

'He had a Christmas Number One, I seem to remember.'

It's a treasure map. All the people who laundered their money through Davy, and Wolfgang, and Marshall Rivers, over the years. I feel so relieved that it's real. There are dozens, hundreds of lines here, each one another thread of proof about what was really going on before Davy died and how he made his money.

The names are extraordinary. Captains of industry, philanthropists, celebrities . . . every single variety of eminence is on there. There's even a bishop. All of them pouring dirty money into a magical funnel, and at the other end of it, cranking the handle to transform it into lovely clean houses in smart bits of town, is Davy. Was Davy.

'Can you make copies, Jonny?' Em asks.

'On it already. But, I'm sorry, does this help us at all?'

There's an awkward pause. I speak up. 'Why wouldn't it? Isn't it everything we've been looking for?'

'Well, it just proves beyond doubt that Davy was involved in money-laundering. But it certainly doesn't show we didn't kill him. It's not like it tells us which client he angered, or betrayed, or anything like that. In fact, us having this is quite good circumstantial evidence that we did kill him so we could get hold of his money.'

'But we didn't,' says Elle.

'I know, but the police might be a bit cynical about that.'

'Ugh,' says Em, speaking for all of us.

'Maybe it was one of these people who killed him,' says Jonny. 'But we don't know who. We also don't know whether Rob Wallace found out about the laundering and had Davy killed to shut it down. We haven't nailed it. And if we go to the police with this list, they'll take it off us, thank us, and then nick us.'

There's a long silence as the other three of us absorb the implications of this.

'Actually, while we're on bad news, what about Davy's fees for all this work?' says Em. 'There's no sign of those anywhere.'

'Ah,' says Jonny. 'There, we have a bit of good news.'

34

On the morning we'd left for Nevis, Jonny had taken Davy's computer to his associate Nikola – the computer guy's computer guy. It had taken two days, but Nikola had managed it, and the computer was now fully Open Sesame-d.

This is what Jonny found:

'There's a spreadsheet in here, containing—'

'Oh, God, another spreadsheet?' says Em.

Jonny says, rather stiffly, 'I don't have to show you if you don't want to see it.'

'Ignore her, Jonny,' says Elle. 'Go on.'

'All right. Well, it's more properties. But these are different, in a few interesting ways. Firstly, the list starts three years ago.'

'So just as Davy's last scam ends, or as he wraps it up, he starts this new one?'

'Looks like. The second interesting thing is that the properties are very different. They're nothing like this' – Jonny gestures around at the mad tiled faux-harem we're sitting in – 'and there are loads more low-quality, low-budget lettings.'

'Wouldn't they be much less lucrative?'

Jonny looks like a proud teacher who is only slightly irritated that his top pupil has stuck their hand up before he's finished writing on the whiteboard. 'Well. Yes. But despite the properties being cheaper, the fees here are far bigger than in the first file. So Davy was doing something different.'

'What?'

'Not sure.'

'I know,' I say. 'He was a mentor. The colleague I met in his office – what was he called? Sami, I think – he said Davy ran a mentoring scheme. He had a network of young agents who he would help, then place at other agencies. Always low-rent ones. Not the kind of properties Harcourt and Wallace dealt with.'

'That's worth following up.'

'I'll get Sami's number.'

Jonny continues. 'OK, so there's that. Have you got it pinned?'

We all mumble yes.

'Right. Well, the last two things I found on here are super-interesting. Firstly, in the drafts folder, there's a message that just says *hello*.' No recipient in the address line.

I pipe up. 'Is that interesting? Sorry, but I've done that with emails before. Start it, don't know what to say, give up, find email in drafts folder six years later, delete.'

'It might be that,' says Jonny, 'except that it's the only draft. If this computer is the centre of the new scam, it might be for a reason. Like: he shares the inbox with someone.'

'Oh!' Elle perks up. 'I've seen a Netflix documentary about that. It was how a woman caught her husband having an affair. He kept all the messages to his mistress in his drafts folder, because he thought there's no email trail that way, because the email has never actually been sent.' She sits back. 'He lost everything, but then he got famous because he was *such* a love rat. He has a podcast now.'

'Exactly,' says Jonny. 'Drafts that aren't sent are much harder to trace than actual sent messages. So that might be what was going on here.'

'OK,' I say. 'What do we do with that?'

'I think whoever Davy shared his inbox with might know who killed him. And I don't think the message was outbound, either. I don't think he wrote that *hello*. I think the person he shared the inbox with wrote it, as a test. So we should write back.' Jonny swivels the screen. Beneath the first message, there is a second *Hello*. As you would expect of Jonny, he's capitalised it and added a full stop. Never change, Jonny.

'So we just wait and see if anyone responds?'

'Pretty much.'

'OK. Great. What was the other interesting thing?'

Jonny smiles. 'This one I've saved specially.' He taps, and swivels the screen again. A grey-on-grey panel, with four boxes.

'What is it?'

'It's a portal, run by a private bank in the UAE.'

'You think this is where all the fees went?'

'I reckon so.'

'What do we need to get in?'

'These sets of numbers.' He points. 'Sort code, account number – the local equivalents of them – but also two passcodes, in this last box here. Two sets of fourteen digits.'

'Before Davy died, he said the money was in the outbuilding,' I say.

'The non-existent outbuilding.'

'Yes. Is this the . . . outbuilding?'

'Why would "the outbuilding" be an account in a private Middle Eastern bank?' This is Em.

'Could be a nickname?' Even as I say it, it doesn't sound likely.

'Why are there two passcodes, Jonny?'

'This bank is pretty niche. It lets you pick the account number, even gives you a boutique sort code. And it lets you set a number of passholders, each with their own access code. Davy will have had his own code. But you need two to get in.'

'So he shared the account with someone.'

'Yeah. The way these normally work, he wouldn't have been able to access it without their code, and they wouldn't have been able to access it without his.'

'Lulu said her dad was skint,' said Em. 'Remember?'

'Yeah,' I said. 'What are you thinking, Jonny?'

'I'm thinking that maybe all Davy's commissions from the laundry work are in this account. Which he couldn't get at without the second access code.'

'So,' Em says, counting on her fingers. 'We know that until three years ago Davy was doing classic money-laundering. We know the names of all the people he was doing it for. We also know that three years ago he developed a new trick, and abruptly cut off his previous clientele for a new system, which we haven't cracked. We think it has something to do with these cheap properties, and maybe the junior agents he was mentoring, and we think the money from it went into this private bank account in the UAE.' She taps Jonny's screen before he can pull it back, and he gets out a small polishing cloth. 'Fair summary?'

'Yeah.'

'But we can't get into the account, and from the looks of it we couldn't get in even if we found his code, because we don't know who his accomplice was. And none of this helps us with who was holding the gun that night.'

'No.'

'Hmm.'

Elle chips in. 'Our working assumption is that it was Rob Wallace, right? They were heard arguing by the woman running the office.'

'It's not enough,' I say.

'And Al, you got a killer vibe from him?'

'Sure. But again, the Crown Prosecution Service have quite a sceptical attitude towards vibes.'

'He didn't seem terribly comfortable at the Fantasy Football lunch,' says Elle. 'He kept pretty quiet. And he didn't seem happy talking about Davy's death.'

'Still zilch in prosecutional terms.'

Em says, thoughtfully: 'One of the guys at that lunch was an MP, right? What was his name?'

'Conor Vane. The one who was horrible to Elle.'

'He might know something,' says Jonny.

'Hey. Listen to this,' says Em. 'I just googled him.'

'And?'

'"A senior MP and member of a powerful select committee has been criticised as 'totally in the pocket of the offshore financial industry' in a new report published by a transparency organisation." Says here Vane spent a lot of time a few years ago lobbying to keep a loophole open so businesses could maintain offshore operations.'

'He might have been involved with Davy.'

'Or Wallace.'

'Or both.'

'He seems to be doing OK, though,' says Em. 'He's the one pushing this deal with the Qumaris.'

'What deal with the Qumaris?'

'It was on the news the other day. We're about to sign a megadeal with them.'

Now, for those of you who aren't familiar with Qumar, it's a gigantic trading power located a few thousand miles southeast of Knightsbridge. It's absolutely loaded with all sorts of goodies and crunchy mineral and hydrocarbon assets, which the British Empire had a good go at extracting back when they were the only game in town. However, times have changed, the colonial shackles have been melted down and re-forged as friendship bracelets, and Britain is now the junior partner, reduced to turning up with a rather hungry look and asking for the price of a cup of tea.

I'm no geo-strategist, but even I know that the trade deal Britain's about to sign is slightly controversial. Qumar's unique security situation has necessitated a rather old-fashioned approach to law and order, in that their secret police hang anyone who proposes minor constitutional changes, and they have thousands more people locked up for a bit of good old-fashioned re-education. Nevertheless, Britain is bravely wearing the blinkers of trade and the nose peg of necessity, and holding out its hand to seal the deal.

You may have noticed that I've also changed Qumar's name, from a country you will be familiar with to a fake country they used in *The West Wing* when they needed somewhere for President Bartlet to bomb. If Aaron Sorkin objects to me lifting the name, he can sue me. I'm literally writing this from prison and have no fear of copyright infringement.

'OK, so Vane's going to be busy,' says Jonny.

'I'm sure he could spare five minutes, though,' says Elle. 'These MPs are always having little meetings. If Vane knows anything more about Rob Wallace, he might talk to us.'

'Where will he be tomorrow?'

Jonny's at his computer. 'His constituency is miles away. But this is a big vote week, it looks like. So most likely he'll be in Parliament.'

'Oh, *no*.'

Em looks like she's just won the lottery. 'Yes, Al. Yes.'

35

It was depressingly easy to get an appointment with Conor Vane MP.

We sent an initial email telling him someone from a parliamentary committee on standards wanted to meet him on an urgent matter. Jonny tricked up a spoof address specially for it. We got nothing back. After two hours, Jonny was getting impatient, so he set up another account pretending to be the representative of the Emir of Somewhere, saying he was putting together a Middle East trade trip. A vital trade and outreach mission, five nights all-inclusive, seven-star hotels, perhaps twenty minutes of work a day. In return, Vane might be asked some minor, perfectly legal questions about petrochemical refineries in the UK, and the regulatory framework surrounding them.

Vane's secretary replied to the Emir's secretary (Jonny) within three minutes, practically biting our fingers off and saying we could come and meet Mr Vane any time tomorrow.

So now I'm here, with Em, in a little waiting room on the other side of the Whitehall entrance to Parliament, not far from the Red Lion. Thank God I've still got Freddy's passport, the gold standard.

Vane actually saw Em briefly when she was doing her waitress act at the Bombardier, but we're going to have to take the chance, so she's changed her hair and put on some glasses. He doesn't seem like he's an especial student of women's looks – not from the neck up, at least – so we might get away with it.

I'm in so far over my head I can't see the surface from here. My natural furlong is empty houses, not Parliament. We have a vague question list and we'll probably have about three minutes to get through it before security reaches Vane's office. This is *mad*. The number of cops with guns is rather unsettling, too.

Em and I didn't say much about our trip to Nevis in front of the others yesterday. What do you say? 'By the way, we're sleeping together now'? And nothing happened last night. Our new house has so many bedrooms we'd have been up half the night finding each other anyway. But this morning Elle definitely gave me a rather appraising look, as if she had to consider me more seriously now. Jonny treated me exactly as he always has done.

Vane is one of the lucky ones who's bagged himself an office in the Palace proper; most MPs are on the other side of the main road, in Portcullis House. After a short wait in reception, an early-twenty-something assistant in a pencil skirt and grey blouse picks us up and walks us through the warren of ancient corridors, texting constantly as she goes. Poor thing, I think. Vane's office can't be much fun.

Up, round, through, occasionally crossing paths with various other scurrying creatures who look just as young and nervous as our guide. Once or twice someone grand comes the other way, and our party practically flattens itself against the wall as the charismatic megafauna go by. Even the grandest grandees look pretty unimpressive. It's easy to see the attraction of being an MP if you're a certain kind of man. You might be far from home, overworked, underpaid (in your opinion) and physically under-blessed (in everyone else's), but there's subsidised booze, an agreeable clubby feel, and plenty of young people around who will worship you like an actual god.

Speaking of which, as we are ushered into Conor Vane's office, I watch his eyes, which linger determinedly on his assistant's bottom as she leaves the room.

The office is spectacular. It's bigger than a studio flat, with a huge oak desk the size of a billiards table and gorgeous wood panelling. There's also a vast Union Jack hanging limply on a stand in the corner, which he uses as the background for his self-aggrandising TikToks (his channel is called VaneyVidiVici). The walls are coated with framed news stories about the man himself, plus some cartoons of him which he clearly bought no matter how unflattering they are.

Our task is simple: ask Vane what links him and Davy. Tell him we know about Davy's scam. See if Wallace was involved or if he might have had something to do with Davy's death.

He will almost certainly prevaricate, obfuscate, stonewall and chuck us out, but there's a chance – just a slim one – he'll give us something useful.

'Please. Sit, sit. Did someone get you coffee? No? Can I . . . You're sure? All right. But no hospitality is too great for the representatives of our friends from the East, ha ha . . .' He's actually rubbing his hands.

Em opens the batting. 'Mr Vane, I'm sorry, but we're not actually the representatives of the Emir.'

Vane's hands stop. 'Then . . . Sorry? What about the trip?'

'There is no trip,' says Em, patiently. 'We're investigating the death of David Harcourt' – Vane groans – 'and we have a few questions we'd like to ask.'

'God,' he says, looking disapprovingly at me. 'I should have known. The Emir wouldn't send anyone with a collar that scruffy. Vanessa!'

I love that a man as self-absorbed as Vane has managed to find an assistant with a first name almost identical to his own surname. This isn't the time to consider that, though. And as footsteps approach Vane's office door, Em speaks fast. 'If you give us five minutes, we won't go to the *Guardian* with the emails of you accepting a lucrative offer from a foreign state and offering them access to British industry.'

Vane's assistant pokes her head round the door. Vane gives us a look of deep, deep loathing, and says, 'Never mind, Vanessa. I thought our guests wanted coffee – you would think they would – but they've just told me they actually want nothing of the sort. They're very inconsistent.'

The baffled Vanessa retreats. Vane's sneer deepens. 'On whose behalf are you investigating the death of my old friend?'

'We're freelancers.'

The lip-curl deepens. 'You've got four minutes.'

'Mr Harcourt donated to your private office, correct? Did he want to keep the loophole open for firms based offshore buying properties in the UK? Did you campaign on it to keep his donations coming in?' (This was a Jonny find. He did a deep dive into an online database called the Register of Members' Interests, which is basically all the people bunging cash at MPs in the hope of getting a bit of influence, and found Davy had given Vane several thousand pounds a few years ago. Nobody picked up on it at the time.)

'I declared David's donation, perfectly within the rules. All in the register. There's no rule against receiving donations from concerned citizens. And every time I spoke on this subject in the House, I declared my interest. I'm scrupulous on that.'

'We'll check.'

'Free country. It's all in Hansard.'

'We know Mr Harcourt was involved in offshore sales, most likely for money-laundering.'

Vane speaks carefully now. 'I have no knowledge of that. I assumed David's interest was because he appreciated and valued the harmless, legal use of offshore structures. I would never accept money from anyone engaged in criminal activity.'

'Was Rob Wallace involved in Mr Harcourt's death?'

Vane frowns. 'David's business partner? I've never met the man.'

'You had lunch with him at the Bombardier in Putney a few days ago.'

That pushes him back. He spends a few seconds thinking about it. 'There are laws in this country against harassing innocent members of Parliament. And there are a lot of heavily armed police in this building who would love to practise ejecting disruptive individuals.'

'We just want to know what happened between Rob Wallace and David Harcourt.'

'As far as I know, both men are perfectly legitimate estate agents.'

'We know they argued. We know Wallace got wind of whatever racket David was involved in.'

Vane sighs, apparently depressed at the amount we know already, and appears to fold his cards on this particular hand. 'All right. Rob was in the middle of firing David and taking full ownership of the business, at ruinous expense. David was going along with the buy-out, as far as I know. There was a big payday coming for him, and he could have kept practising as an independent agent. There's no reason for Rob to have taken any . . . drastic action. And I can assure you this sort of thing is totally irrelevant to our little charity. Anything else?'

'Did you know Mr Harcourt was going to the police?'

'No. I would have thought the police would be the last people he'd want to contact, if what you say is true.'

'When did you last speak to him?'

'To David? A year ago. We weren't close. Apart from those

annual lunches, we never saw each other. He stopped donating a few years back, and my work here allows for very little socialising.' I don't believe a word of this, or that Vane is incapable of socialising and getting something for himself at the same time.

'Who killed him?'

'I have no idea. If I knew, I'd go to the police. And speaking of the police, I'm calling security now.'

'No need,' says Em. 'We're leaving.'

Vane bestows on us a grin with all the humanity and warmth of a dental close-up. 'Vanessa will escort you out.'

We walk back through the warren, saying nothing. Vanessa seems to have picked up on the froideur in the room and has taken her employer's side against us. Even her back seems frosty as she leads us through the building. Once again, she's texting as she walks.

And then, just as we're about to leave the place and never come back:

We're in the rather grubby side-door reception. I'm about to pass through the turnstile, and breathe freely for the first time in forty minutes. Em already has gone through.

'Oh. One last thing.' Vanessa holds up her phone. 'Mr Vane wanted you to see this.'

Her phone is open on the Signal app. On the screen are the words: **WALLACE DID IT. WATCH YOUR BACKS.**

She presses a button, and the message disappears for ever.

36

Back at 38 Balfour Villas, Em is giving me a look.

'Come on, Al. How would he know?'

'Maybe Wallace confessed at the pub when they were having lunch.'

'Would that be before or after the results of the Fantasy Football? "By the way, I killed one of our best friends, lovely catching up with you all, see you next year"? Come off it.'

'I'm serious. These people all go way back. They tell each other everything.'

'White Illuminati,' mutters Jonny.

'Thank you, Jonny. I mean, I'm pretty sure the original Illuminati were also white. But yes.'

'No,' says Em. 'Clearly Vane was just trying to protect

himself from any involvement with this mess. Maybe he suspects Wallace but doesn't have proof. If he had proof, he'd probably go to the police himself.'

'Slippery bastard like Vane? No way.'

'Shall we go over who we're looking for again?' asks Elle. She's drawn everything up on the kitchen blackboard.

WE NEED SOMEONE WHO:
- *Knew re Davy's appointment with police (how?)*
- *Was involved in laundry scheme?*
- *Got Davy his clients?*
- *Has access to shared inbox with him*
- *Shares Dubai bank account access*

She's written a second list beneath this one:

MORE QUESTIONS WE HAVEN'T WORKED OUT YET:
Where is 'outbuilding' full of £? Is that Dubai account?
What is deal with crap new properties?
Who killed Davy???
When can we stop doing this?

'Yeah, good shout, Elle. OK, so Davy had clearly got out of his original money-laundering game,' Em says.

'What if Marshall Rivers and that German guy, Wolfgang, killed him? They teamed up to do it,' I say.

'Motive?'

'They'd been cut out of his original scam. They wanted revenge.'

Em frowns. 'Three years later, from several thousand miles away, with no prospect of getting at the money? I doubt it. It's something to do with these new properties of his.'

We look at the map of the UK Jonny has drawn up on his screen. It shows all the properties on Davy's second, more recent list. As you hover over each pin on the map, it brings up the Google Street View for that place. They include graffitied pillboxes; bedraggled terraces; flea-bitten apartments above rat-infested shops in no-horse towns. Places you wouldn't want to live in; frankly, places you wouldn't want to walk past.

'They're all mega-scuzzy,' says Jonny. 'Not one of them sold for more than £250,000. And those are the ones in London. The ones outside it, some of them were under a hundred grand. They're some of the cheapest, nastiest places on the entire market.'

'Why would you launder money through cheap properties?' asks Elle. 'If you wanted to do that, you'd just buy a block of flats, wouldn't you? So all the rents ended up as clean money too?'

'Elle, you have a brilliant criminal mind,' I say, and she blushes. 'And yes, you would. So maybe he wasn't laundering at all. Jonny, is there anything else on his computer?'

'Nothing. I've crawled all over it. There are no clues. No signs of who the beneficial owners are. No company names, even, for these places. Just the addresses. It's like not even Davy knew what was going on.'

'Wouldn't he have had an offshorer for this part of the operation too, another Mr Rivers?'

Jonny shrugs. 'Maybe. But there are no contacts, nothing in the inbox, no incriminating messages, no documents. It's like it's all been scrubbed from the other side.' That gives me a little shiver. If even Davy hadn't written it down, how the hell are we going to find out?

'It feels like when we know what the trick was here, we'll find out everything else.'

'Maybe.' He looks at the screen, and his eyes widen. 'Guys.'

'What?'

'Did one of you open this up?'

We all confirm we haven't touched Davy's computer.

'Then . . . OK. We've made contact.'

'With who?'

'With whoever Davy shared his inbox with.'

We look over his shoulder, at the draft that originally just said *hello*, and to which Jonny added a second *Hello*. The page now looks like this:

hello

Hello.

who is this

'When did you last check that, Jonny?'

'Three minutes ago.'

We all stand around the computer, looking at the new

words. Someone's at the other end of the line. My skin tingles with the weird modern horror of being surveyed remotely.

Jonny keys in some tentative words: *Friends of Davy. Who is this?*

A second later, jerky type starts appearing on the screen: *colleague of Davy. Good bloke. Shame what happened to him*

'Jonny, can you track this? Work out where it's coming from?'

'No. Sorry.'

'Can I type?' Em takes Jonny's seat.

Did you kill him?

The response comes: *He killed himself*

Em: *??*

Making an appt with police like that. Silly bastard. Should have guessed I'd find out. Which one of you is typing now? Probably one of the foreign girls right? We watch, not saying anything, as the words crawl across the screen. *Or the tall black guy? Or the skinny white boy?*

'Double-ungood,' murmurs Jonny.

Id tell you to back off. But bit late for that. My associate will find you. Big guy. No hair.

Em types: *Where do we meet him?*

Dont worry. Hell find you

She has one last attempt: *We didn't kill Davy. We don't know what he was doing. We just want out. What can we do to make that happen?*

No reply.

37

We shut the laptop, put some tea on, and sit in silence for a bit, all creeped out by the encounter with Davy's inbox friend. Eventually Elle pipes up.

'This is like a nightmare.'

'Yes,' says Em. 'But we have to keep going.'

'Why? Can't we just go overseas?'

I surprise myself, and the others, by saying: 'No. We've come this far. We've managed it without being arrested or caught. We can work it out. And when we *are* arrested, we'll hopefully have a decent set of answers which we can swap for . . .'

'Our freedom?'

'Certainly a reduced sentence.'

'Terrific,' says Em. 'So we need to find out about Davy's

last con, the one that appears to have killed him. There's no paper trail, there's no evidence, there's nothing except these addresses. What do you suggest?'

I wiggle my fingers. 'My turn to do the thing I'm good at.'

I've never interloped anywhere quite this bad.

The next time you hear someone talk about the 'north London elite', they're probably not talking about this bit. We're in one of the grubbier outskirts. On the way here, I've passed wrecking yards, mothballed factories, and all sorts of dodgy mews. These are not like the traditional inner-city mews, where a two-bed goes for £5m and your next-door neighbour is the Duke of Rutland. They're more the old-fashioned kind where stolen cars get surreptitious spray-jobs by day and johns get unenthusiastic hand-jobs by night. Nobody here reads *Mews of the World*.

Just to give you a bit more context, I'm holding a clipboard and wearing a hi-vis vest. These are probably the only reason I'm alive to type these words now.

The others are all in a cheap café near the station that has no CCTV, facing away from the door and wearing masks. Lucky bastards. I'm in a cramped, horrible street, making my way towards 139 Endersby Road. The whole area is somehow pulling off the trick of being simultaneously low-rise and crowded; the houses are small and cheap, but rammed together. That won't change any time soon. No developer in their right mind would think this place, even inside the M25, could ever appreciate in value. It has a distinct 'built on an ancient Anglo-Saxon burial ground' feeling of cursedness about it. It was the closest property on Davy's list, hence us starting here. Now, I really wish we'd picked the second closest.

Number 139 is an end-of-terrace. The only property adjoining it, 141, is a burned-out husk, with scorch marks at the windows, and you can see right through from the front to the back, which has been creatively remodelled by a bad house fire.

In the distance, a weapon dog barks.

Number 139 itself used to be a two-storey place, now extended at the top by a dodgy dormer. I slow down as I approach. The brickwork is old and grimy, the front garden stinks of fox scat, and the tiles between the squeaking gate and the peeling front door are losing a battle against triffid-esque weeds. The rooms look dark – even if they weren't, grubby net curtains are shielding all activity within.

What the hell would Davy want to sell this place for? And who would want to launder money through it?

The only life around is a man shuffling along across the street who has clearly clocked me as new to the area. He's got stringy hair, and he's wearing an old leather jacket covered in sewn-on patches of bands older than I am. After his second suspicious glance, I keep walking, past 139, until I round the corner it sits on, and he heads in the other direction. Once he's gone, I return.

I'm a long way from my preferred interloping beat. My comfort zone is either in Kensington, with luxurious properties where you can hardly see the front door from the street, or in the suburbs, at the end of a driveway, like Mr Lethbridge's place. In my whole career, I've never lock-picked a door so visible from street level. Rule 18: *Avoid passing traffic* isn't an option.

Good news, though – no smart doorbell. Nor is there a box advertising a burglar alarm. There's no security of any kind, as far as I can tell. And from the look of it, the deadlock is open, meaning there might well be someone home.

Rat-a-tat-tat.

Thirty seconds go by. Sixty.

Rat-a-tat-tat. Just to make sure. People have naps, or shuffle slowly down the stairs. Some ignore a knock at the door completely, because it's only ever bad news.

Another minute, glancing back to see if I'm being observed from a window opposite.

Zip. Zilch. Bupkis.

I fish out my tools, and within half a minute, the door is open before me.

'Hello?' I say to the empty hall. 'Gas company here.' It just about passes muster. This place looks like the sort that might be behind with its bills. Some rogue utility firms still use enforcers to squeeze a bit more money out of their valued customers, even though they claim not to.

I've put the snib up on the door in case I need to leave fast, and it gums shut behind me.

There's a door on my left – classic three-bed terrace design; this will be what the Victorians called the downstairs parlour – so I open it.

My first impression is darkness. The net curtains are backed by some heavy blackout lining, and no natural light gets in. The second impression is noise, a huge humming sound, and the darkness is interrupted by some winking lights. I get my phone out, noticing my hand is shaking a bit, and turn on the torch.

The whole room is full of computer servers.

Six rows of black cabinets, full of whatever makes these computers run. They're connected by that thick ribbony fibre-optic cable, and they're chittering away to each other in the dark.

What the *hell*?

Above me, I notice three extremely professional-looking security cameras. They're the kind that are actually monitored, rather than the dummies on most high streets, and – even worse – the kind that produce crisp 4K images rather than the old-fashioned 'blur in a hoodie' variety. At least I've kept my mask on throughout this whole process. I back into the hall, assuming I don't have long left to look around before someone turns up.

Upstairs, or back to the kitchen? This feels like one of those old choose-your-own-adventure books, the ones where almost every option leads to a grisly death.

No matter what this place is for, you'd usually keep the kitchen operational, so it's probably just a kitchen. Upstairs it is.

I climb, pausing and panicking at each creak, and at the first-floor landing go straight to the bedroom at the back of the house. This one has daylight, at least. As I open the door, I see two pairs of bunk beds on either side of the room:

unoccupied. There's also a small desk that has on its surface a pile of paperwork, a tablet computer, and a shredder half full of word spaghetti.

I lean over the documents, and they're all in a language I don't recognise. I don't understand any of it, of course, but I grab my phone and photograph the top few sheets, before I hear a little noise from downstairs.

That, it turns out, was the sound of the relaxing part of today ending.

I'm no longer alone in the house.

38

I've still got my hi-vis on, and my clipboard, and my mask. For a moment I consider trying to style it out in character as an idiot bailiff, but then I think again. This place feels *official*.

The window at the back of the room I'm in is . . . of course it is. Bolted and barred, with no key in sight. I'm going to have to get back to the street.

One rule I've never written down, a rule I didn't think I'd ever have to observe or number, is simple: no physical violence. I have a horrible worry I'm about to break that rule now.

There are footsteps approaching up the stairs. These ones aren't like old Mr Rivers' in his Nevis office. Nor are they like those of Mr Lethbridge, crunching crossly across his gravel drive. I feel like I've become a real connoisseur of slowly approaching footsteps in the last fortnight. These, I would say, are the footsteps of a fit and healthy young person.

The door opens.

By the time it does, I've slid myself under the bottom of the bunk bed, facing the door. I look to my left, and see something that's either a baton or a very aggressive sex toy. Just terrific.

The feet I can see are clad in rough old trainers, the laces already undone.

The owner of the feet isn't moving suspiciously, at least. They potter back and forth to a small wardrobe in the corner of the room. I think they're undressing – the shoes are eased off, socks shoved into them. Small feet. A few more rustles of cloth. Then I feel a terrible *squeeze* from above, along the length of my torso. My new friend has got into the bottom bunk, and from the feel of it, they've landed right on top of me.

It doesn't matter how petite someone is, if they put their full weight on your torso, you'll know about it. Right now, I can hardly breathe. My vision is going haywire. Is this how I die?

After thirty seconds of this, the body above me shuffles, and the pressure relents. They've shifted, thank God. I guess lying on me isn't comfortable either. I reach up to my face, and silently claw my mask down so I can breathe better.

A few more minutes pass, and the body above me shifts once or twice more, then is completely still.

The breathing from up there sounds regular. They're not moving. I should have waited behind the door, and charged out of the room as soon as it opened. Easier still not to have come here in the first place. The easiest thing, really, would have been to stay in Nevis, settle down with Em, and start a new life as a conch farmer.

I'm just going to have to go for it.

You may not remember, but earlier on, I said that there are two ways of moving surreptitiously – the first is to proceed more or less as normal, the second is to go at semi-snail pace, take an age, don't disturb a single floorboard. And I recall confidently asserting that the first method is by far the most simple and natural. I wish I'd practised the second a bit more now.

Here goes nothing. With agonising slowness, I reach out and transfer the trainers out of the way. Then, for about three minutes, I eeeeeease myself sideways. It's bloody working. The breathing stays regular. No further shifting. I'm almost out . . . little bit more . . . I've made it. I'm beside the bed on all fours, my arms trembling from the exertion. All I have to do is get up and leave.

And then, from the crumpled trousers that have been tossed on the floor, a phone *dings*.

I look sideways. Staring into my face, maybe eighteen inches away, is a rather bleary-eyed young Chinese woman.

We both react at the same time. My move was going to be to slowly raise my finger to my lips, to reassert some control over the situation, then walk out of the house and sprint back to the station.

Her move, on the other hand, is a bit more direct, which is to open her mouth and scream blue murder. I run.

As I go, another door opens further up the house, and I

hear footsteps descending towards me. I take the stairs four at a time, nearly breaking my neck, heave the door open, vault the low garden wall, ignore the rising swell of shouts behind me, and I'm gone.

'This is not good.'

'Stop saying that, Jonny. None of this is good.'

We're back at our new home in Balfour Villas. We keep discovering more rooms: this one is a home gym with a huge screen and plush red seats at one end, which we have dubbed the 'gymema'. We're in the front row. It got late somehow, and it must be close to midnight. Outside, the weather's kicking up a fuss, and occasionally a loose branch taps the window, reliably terrifying me.

I ran the ten-minute walk back to the station in – I would estimate – about fifteen seconds. By that time I couldn't see anyone chasing me. There had been nobody outside guarding the house, which would have created further complication. I didn't look back for the first half of the route, but I'm pretty sure I had given them the slip. At the station, I phoned Em, told her I was getting on the train without explaining further, and was on the first southbound Tube before they could catch up with me.

On the train, I did the usual things – changed carriage three times, switched lines, took my jacket off when I was confident I was out of the cameras' field of view, masked up, changed masks so they'd have a harder time identifying me, all of that.

Thanks to my mucking about underground, the others

reached Balfour Villas about half an hour before me. I explained what I could about the weird server house, then fell asleep for a few hours until Em came in and woke me up because she was sick of waiting to talk more.

The only thing I salvaged from the house was the photos I took of the top few sheets of paper on the desk. Jonny took the photos from my phone, then put them up online to be translated, using some dodgy Chinese expat intermediary on one of his illegal websites. And he's now telling us things are 'not good'. No shit.

'No, I mean, this is really a disastrous development.' Things must be bad if Jonny isn't even using *Nineteen Eighty-Four* references.

'What is it?' Elle asks.

'It's official government shit. Chinese government.'

Em asks, 'Which bit of the government, Jonny?'

'Unclear. Lots of terms my correspondent didn't recognise. But he thinks it's an espionage thing.'

'Oh, *great*.'

I still haven't quite adjusted. 'Sorry, but it sounds like we're saying I broke into Chinese government property today. Are we saying that?'

'In mitigation, you didn't know it at the time.'

'I'm sure they'll take that into account when they catch up with me.'

'I read something about this,' says Em. She taps on her phone. 'Yes. That's it. Look.' She holds it out. Elle and I read it together.

'What the hell is a dark police station?'

'It's basically an unofficial embassy overseas,' says Jonny. 'You base a few of your people there, but you don't register them the same way you do an embassy or a consulate or whatever. And once those people are installed, they can do various things on your behalf without being acknowledged by the host government.'

'What are they for?'

'It's all in the piece, Al.'

I read on. 'Pressuring dissidents to return . . . secretive bases overseas . . . Oh, wow. We're talking proper George Smiley stuff here.'

'I don't think they would get the reference, but yes.'

'Says here we asked them to shut them all down.'

'Guess they must have forgotten this one.'

Em gets up and walks the length of the room and back, kicking the treadmill as she passes it.

'This is what Davy started doing three years ago,' I say. 'He was setting up these secret police stations for the Chinese government. Bad places, places you wouldn't think to look for them. Near Chinese communities too, I suppose.'

'It won't just be China,' says Em. 'There will be lots of countries running similar things.'

'This is what he wanted to confess,' I say. 'He got too uncomfortable with it, wanted to get out, contacted the police . . . then someone he was working with found out he'd made the appointment and whacked him.'

'Who?'

'Whoever's in his shared inbox. Whoever he has this UAE account with.'

'It doesn't feel very *espionage*, turning up at someone's door and blowing them away,' says Em. 'It feels more gangland. I still think it was one of his colleagues from his end of the operation.'

'But either way,' says Elle slowly, 'this is what Davy was up to.'

'Yeah.'

'So now we have potentially caught the interest of agents from dozens of hostile foreign powers.'

'I *told* you it wasn't good,' says Jonny. He's back on his laptop.

'And we still don't know who Davy told about his appointment with the police. It was in his diary in code, and he didn't make the booking through Mrs P from his office. Even that Kate woman didn't know what he was going to confess. He was being *careful*.'

'Not careful enough,' says Em. 'What are you typing, Jonny?'

'Checking our online security. This bloody weather has smashed up two of my cameras outside. Although I doubt I can do anything if the world's top intelligence agencies want to know our whereabouts.'

'There was another story about this kind of thing recently,' says Elle. 'I feel like it was . . . on TV. When did we last watch TV?'

Em and I think. Jonny keeps typing.

'I haven't seen any TV since the moment we discovered who Davy was,' I say. 'It was on the news, remember? At the other Balfour Villas place.'

'Yes. That's it. And there was something else . . .' Elle gets her phone out. 'Some other news story that day. It was after the report about Davy.' She types, frowns, narrows the dates down, then, as Em and I look at each other, she quietly says, 'Bingo.'

'What?'

She holds out her phone. 'The other story was about an Iranian spy ring being busted on the south coast. Remember?'

'So what?'

'Do you have Lulu Harcourt's number?'

'I've got it,' says Em. 'Are you saying there's a link between Davy and that story?'

'Maybe. Wasn't Lulu's first story, the one before she told you about her dad, about an Iranian guy?'

'Oh, shit. Her ex-boyfriend. The one who took photos of her asleep. What was his name?'

'Faisal,' I say.

'Exactly. Jonny, where are you going?'

'Installing two new cameras outside,' he says, waving some kit. 'Won't be a moment.'

'Be careful, please.' As Jonny lumbers into the hall, Em continues. 'Where was I?'

'Hang on,' I say. 'You're saying Faisal went out with Lulu and took those threatening pictures not because he was a creep but to send a message to Davy?'

'Maybe. Davy's doing these deals, setting up dark police stations all over the country. He does a deal for the Iranians. It goes wrong somehow and they're at risk of exposure. The Iranians hold him responsible – maybe he screwed up. They go to him and say they want new premises pronto. He refuses. But they've got his daughter as leverage and they start gathering photos to send as a threat. Only it doesn't work, because Lulu gets in the way and their operation gets busted. But Davy makes the connection, and he's so freaked out by the threat to Lulu that he makes an appointment with the police. He wants to confess everything, get some witness protection for his immediate family, get out.'

'That could be what he argued with Rob Wallace about.'

'Or Rob Wallace found out about the appointment with the police, was worried he was going to confess everything and tank the business, and offed him. Either way, that's how it goes.'

'It's a nice theory, if the timings stack up,' I say. I'm struggling a bit. Considering one government's overseas espionage operations was a bit much for one day. Two is overload.

'I really think we should give Claudia a call,' says Elle. 'This is exactly her line.'

'*No,*' says Em. 'How many times do I have to say it? We are not begging for her help.'

'It's not begging, it's—'

'Just stop it, Elle. She can find out about all this afterwards, when we're vindicated and the whole thing has been dealt with without her stupid help.'

'You're being petty.'

'You're being sentimental. You don't remember what it was like growing up with her,' says Em.

They scowl at each other, and a cold wind blows through the gymema.

'Jonny must have left the front door open,' I say. 'I'll just pop and shut it.'

I head out, leaving them to their argument: through the main living room, the subsidiary study, and into the large Romanesque hall, with its embarrassing squillionaire's chandelier thirty feet above and its unforgiving marble tiles beneath. The door has indeed been left open, although that's not the main thing I focus on as I pull up. Here's what draws my focus instead:

There's a man in the hall. He's not Jonny. I can tell because of a few key differences.

1) Jonny is a foot taller than this guy.
2) Jonny isn't Chinese.
3) Jonny doesn't habitually carry a fucking big knife.

39

He may not be tall, but he's muscular. Dressed in black. He doesn't look military, but I wouldn't say he's a civilian either. He's . . . somewhere in between.

I'm the first one to shout; he's the first one to move.

'Em!' My voice sounds a bit strangled. I can hear the panic in it and I hope she does too. But there's no time to say anything else, because at that moment the man jerks towards me, hefting the knife as he approaches. It's practically a claymore, but he's not struggling with it a bit. I find myself thinking, *He must spend a lot of time in the gym*, and then, *No shit*. Then I run.

For some reason – a faint desire to draw the guy away from Em and Elle? – I sprint out of the hall in the other direction than the one I approached from, towards the kitchen and dining room. The ground floor of the house is arranged in two big loops, and I know it better than him, so I gain a bit of ground as we go. But I risk a look over my shoulder as I round the kitchen island and he's uncomfortably fast. And I only have the advantage of greater familiarity with the place once. If we do a second lap, he'll catch me.

By the time I'm back in the hall, the girls have arrived, and they scatter away from me in opposite directions before they even see the guy chasing me – Elle back into the living room doorway, Em towards the front door. The guy pauses as he hits the hall. I'm in the middle, right under the chandelier, with nothing but empty space for ten feet around me. Any manoeuvre that could get me and the girls out of the house would be best, I think, and then realise, no. Why would that be? Look at this guy. We're not equipped to deal with him in *any* environment.

I wish he would say something. He hasn't said a word yet, and if he'd only tell me what he wanted, maybe we could . . . No point in that either. The knife makes it pretty clear what he wants. He's still focused on me, although he's clocked the girls too. He looks grim, as if this job has already gone slightly wrong, and he's having to adapt to keep the show on the road. Join the club, mate.

He moves towards me, and I stumble backwards to the foot of the stairs. Yes. That's an idea. If I can draw him upstairs, the girls can get out and away. OK, there's the ten-second plan of retreat. We'll work on the following ten seconds in the fullness of time. He comes towards me, and I turn and flee up the staircase. He follows. Good.

The staircase is a grand one, which splits into two halfway up. I take the left fork, and he follows. I move backwards along the gallery, and see the girls are coming up behind him. What the hell are they playing at? I try to gesture at them to go, but there's no time, because the man's about to bulldoze me to the very soft carpet.

Some people say that in life-threatening situations they find an extra reserve of strength that allows them to lift the crashed car off their loved one, punch the bear, whatever. I just want to put on the record that this doesn't happen to everyone, and as he shoulders me to the ground, I have never felt weaker or flimsier. The one thing I do remember is to kick. I'm wearing my nasty heavy boots, and from my position on the ground, as he's starting to bring the knife down, I jerk back like a grasshopper and go for a kneecap.

Whatever I hit, it crunches satisfyingly, and puts him off his stroke. I scrabble away while the guy yelps – the first noise he's made so far – and get back on my feet, saying a little prayer of thanks to the man who just saved my life, Dr Marten.

I stumble backwards and turn another corner. We're on the cross-beam bit of the landing now, running from the left side of the house to the right. There are bedrooms all round this landing, none containing any blunt instruments.

I edge past a wooden podium with a gorgeous old vase on it. It's the only ornament on the whole landing. I reach out to try knocking it across his path, as if it would slow him down at all, but he lashes out with the knife and I pull my hand back. The blade leaves a thick wound in the solid oak of the podium. Over his shoulder, I can see the girls trailing, the idiots. Why won't they leave?

He's past the podium now, and he makes a couple of experimental little slashes in the air to make me jump backwards. He glances over his shoulder at the girls, but doesn't seem worried. I can see him winding up his legs for a proper spring at me, this time with the knife first. He's not even going to bother knocking me down, he's just going to lunge.

I know that reading this, you're thinking I should just parry the blow, but the first eighteen inches of this guy's attack are going to be all knife. If there is an effective parry for that kind of move, I don't know it. He growls, and crouches, and I just pray it happens fast enough, or that Em and Elle use the tiny bit of time I've bought them to get out of the house. I knew this was coming, at some level, ever since we saw Davy's body. I've had a good run, stayed in some nice places. I even made some friends recently.

'Hey.'

The guy swivels, just as Em hits him on the ear with the vase.

It makes a very satisfying noise, the sound of a couple of million pounds' worth of porcelain disintegrating. It even produces a little cloud of blue-white powder, which dissipates around him like a halo. I would have hoped – you might think – it would be enough to knock him out cold, but he just shakes his bullet head and coughs.

A Beginner's Guide to Breaking and Entering

He's muzzy, though, and I realise: this is the moment. This tiny reprieve is the only possible opportunity I have to seize the advantage before he recovers and resumes his attempt to get my guts out of my torso and onto the parquet floor.

What the hell.

I run headlong at the guy, clamp my arms around his torso, drive him into the landing rail in what any rugby referee would consider an illegally high tackle, and over we go together.

40

As we pivot over the rail, I can feel his knife at my side, but I have the guy in a bear hug, and he's still so shocked to be going over the edge of the landing that he's not able to do much with it. If I land on the blade, I'll have yet another problem, but my thinking is now short-term enough that anything which keeps me alive for the next second and a half feels like a good bet.

As we go, we bounce off the chandelier – hard enough to smash it half to bits, not nearly enough to slow our descent. And then we're tumbling together, upside down, and a few confused impressions push themselves through my brain without me having time to focus on any single one. I shouldn't have bothered giving up smoking for my health. I should have met these guys years ago and travelled around with them, having fun, rather than leading a solitary existence with only my rules for company. I should definitely have slept with Em a second time.

That's enough of that. The hall floor is rapidly becoming the biggest thing in my field of view, and there's nothing to do but see who lands on top.

Drum roll . . .

No, don't be daft. I land on top. Obviously. Which is why this book is not called *My Time As an Elite International Assassin*.

There's a *crack* as we hit the ground. It's organic. I roll off, and can tell as soon as I peel away from the guy that he's dead. Not a bad way to go. Quick, certainly. What about me? I think I've fractured my wrist, which was partly beneath him, and took not only my weight but plenty of his. Even if it isn't broken, it hurts like hell. And – oh, *fuck* – there's blood coming from my mouth. I put my hand to it and examine it for a bit. I can't quite make the connection between the two. There's a word for when you've hit your head this hard. What is it again?

Em gets to me first, and makes the kind of comforting, sensitive comment she's been trotting out since the day we met. 'Al, you tit.' She kneels and gingerly takes my functioning hand.

'Yeah,' I manage to say. I'm a bit winded.

'Where's this blood coming from?'

'Don't know.' It feels as if the plates of my skull are sliding over each other. Thinking is a bit tricky. Where am I again?

Elle catches up, and takes over from her sister. She squeezes my mouth open and looks inside with a phone torch. 'It's all right. You've just bitten your tongue. It'll bleed for a bit but it'll heal fast. And this . . . this isn't even fractured as far as I can feel. Maybe a hairline.' I wipe my mouth on my spare sleeve as she gently lowers my wrist, and glance sideways at the man who was trying to kill the three of us about a minute ago. I'm still a bit confused, and as I look at his body, I think, *God, pal, what happened to you?* before remembering that I did.

'Can you move your other arm? OK, good. And your legs? All right. I think you're OK to move. Uuuup we get.'

Em is looking at me with bafflement. 'Al, we'd have thought of something else. Why did you do that?'

'I'm sure . . .' I pause to breathe. My thoughts are clearing a little. 'Sherlock Holmes . . . did it once.'

'You silly bastard.' She's still holding my hand, though, even though I'm on my feet. 'You all right?'

'I think so.'

'Good. Don't do that again.'

Elle has taken the dead man's pulse at his neck – although his neck is at such a surprising angle that you wouldn't think she'd need to – and gets her phone out of her pocket. 'I'm ringing Claudia.'

'Now? When someone has died and we were the ones who . . . when we were present? Are you insane?'

'It's Claudia, Em. We can trust her. I won't tell her you're here. If we do have any hostile powers after us, I'd like us to know for sure.' Elle gets out her phone, takes a picture of the guy's face, and starts texting.

Em thinks of something else. 'Shit.'

'What?'

'Jonny.'

She helps me up, and together we run and hobble to the door, which is still wide open, and look out into the dark front garden. 'Jonny?'

A shape looms up before us – a tall, unruly shape, with none of the feline grace or poise of an international man of mystery. Its T-shirt reads DON'T BLAME ME, I TOOK THE BLUE PILL in neon green. The figure opens its mouth.

'What's up? Sorry. Gatepost cameras took a bit longer than I thought.'

'*Jesus*, Jonny.' Thank God. He's absolutely fine.

He looks at me and frowns. 'What's going on in here?'

We pull him into the front hall and fill him in, although the corpse does most of the work for us. He nods. 'Quick exit?'

'Very quick.'

Jonny lumbers off to pack up his kit. We're all ignoring the dead man, surrounded by fragments of chandelier, but Elle is on her phone, and looking worried. 'Em.'

'What?'

'Claudia's texted back already. She's working late.'

'And?'

'We were half right. This guy is government.'

'Which government? Chinese?'

Elle shakes her head.

'Somewhere like it? North Korea?'

She grimaces. 'British.'

The others help me gather my things together, and in about six minutes we're ready to head. By then I'm feeling much better – physically, anyway.

As we finish piling our things in the hall, we look back at the man on the floor. It's not like Davy. He genuinely looks all right. If it wasn't for the angle of his neck, he might be having a nap. If it wasn't for the huge serrated knife, he might just have been a homeowner who met with a terrible accident. And if it wasn't for the mountains of DNA evidence tying us to the place, we wouldn't need to worry at all.

We did discuss burying him in the garden, but it wouldn't do us much good. With the way things have been heading lately, we'll be lucky to get through the next week. Elle asked if anyone wanted to say anything, but I don't know what you can say about someone you've known for two minutes who you then killed in self-defence, so we just put a big tablecloth over him for a touch of propriety, and I mutter, 'Sorry.'

All our things are at the front of the hall. Em and I have been discussing where we go next. Between Bowling Ball and this, Balfour Villas is now officially subprime. I know a place over in Richmond, a nice house belonging to a TV presenter who I happen to know is filming a home renovation show in Puglia for the next three months.

None of us has thought about the fact that the man lying

behind us is – according to Em and Elle's sister – a British spook. And Claudia isn't going to get the chance to track our whereabouts either, because Em turned her sister's phone off, and confiscated it for good measure. I saw the screen over her shoulder. Claudia was texting every three seconds when Em got to it. The last two messages I saw were *Wait* and *You should know*. With adamantine self-control, she switched it off even with the three little dots on the screen, and dropped it into her bag.

The Uber is en route to us, two streets away, so we're going to scurry through the dark garden just as it arrives, hop in, get to the centre of town, split up and reconvene at the new place.

We bundle out, shut the front door behind us, and cart the bags across the garden. As we go back and forth, Jonny dives into the undergrowth to retrieve all the cameras he just installed.

Em, Elle and I are in the street, huddled around our little pile of bags. What a forlorn bunch we make. My teeth still feel loose in my head.

'Who was he?' That's Elle. 'Who would send a British spy?'

'I don't know, love. We'll work it out at the next place.' Em is trying, but she doesn't sound convinced.

Just as the Uber turns the corner, before we can even give it a wave, there's a shout from behind us, followed by a bang. It's a noise – I am beginning to recognise, although I wish I wasn't – that could only be made by a gun going off at close range.

41

I'm sorry to be vague at this point, but about four events happen and I can't work out the order. Everything just sort of congregates on a single point in time. Here they are. You're welcome to put them whichever way up you like.

1) *Another* black-clad figure appears on the road, bursting out of the front garden of 38 Balfour Villas about twenty feet down from us. It's holding a stubby stick. It sprints in the opposite direction and is almost immediately lost to the night, dodging the pools of street light as it goes.
2) Elle screams and runs back into the front garden, leaving me and Em staring after her.

3) A motorbike engine starts up halfway down the road and screeches away.
4) Our Uber pulls up.

1) and 2) might be the other way round, or 2) and 3), but I'm certain 1) comes before 3). Then again, 4) might come before any of the above. At the end of the sequence, we have a silent UberXL waiting before us with its hazards on, Em has followed her sister back into the garden, and I'm facing the driver, who has popped the boot. I gesture to him to wait, just one minute, and follow Em.

She's up ahead, crumpled on the ground beside a domed figure in a stupid T-shirt. Oh, shit.

'OK. Up we come.' The girls are on either side of Jonny, and I lend a hand to get him to his feet. I can't see exactly what's wrong, but his shirt is wet.

'Hospital?'

'We're five minutes from St Catherine's,' says Elle. 'They have an A&E.'

'Ambulance?'

'We shouldn't wait. We have a car here.'

'OK.'

'You talk to the driver, Em.'

Em goes, and Elle and I help Jonny walk slowly to the car. He's mumbling: 'Bag.'

'We've got your bag, Jonny, that's all right.' I grab it as we lurch past the rest of our stuff. It's the only one containing anything incriminating, I think; there are no particular grounds for arrest in my old pants. We leave the little cairn of our belongings on the pavement as the Uber accelerates away.

Em clearly did a good job explaining the situation to the driver, because we're at the entrance of A&E in two minutes forty-five seconds. Em is up front. Jonny's back left. Elle's back right. I'm in the middle, wedging Jonny upright. I can hardly read his T-shirt any more. Maybe it's just the bad light in the cab. That must be it. That must be it.

Elle phoned ahead as we went, and there's a little welcome party waiting for us on the ramp up to the doors. At least we did this on a quiet Tuesday night, because even in this light, I can see that Jonny's face has turned grey, and he topples out of the cab. He would have cracked his head on the ground if there hadn't been two paramedics waiting to scoop him up.

I try to pay the driver from my dwindling roll of banknotes, but he refuses point-blank. God bless you, Ibrahim, wherever you are now. May your back seat never be so insulted again.

And then we're inside, as a team of doctors gather around Jonny, agree he's suffered an abdominal gunshot wound, and consider what they're going to do about it.

As someone who's only ever arrived at A&E after micro-accidents and quasi-emergencies, I've never witnessed a full crash entrance before, and how they handle it. God, it's impressive. You'd think there would be a lot of shouting, but there's none. It's more . . . controlled urgency.

The doctors come and go like bees. They're talking,

assessing, throwing comments to colleagues, catching them without even making eye contact, fitting drips, removing personal effects, scanning, pressing, assessing. They're like one consciousness divided between eight bodies.

A theatre is being prepared for Jonny, someone says. *He won't like that*, I think, *he hates the theatre*. I remember him saying that on one of our car journeys. He says it's an 'imperfect rendition of human behaviour' and, like most other art forms, 'struggles to faithfully replicate to the audience the complexities of navigating the decision matrices the world presents to us'. Plus, he finds the seats uncomfortable.

Christ, I hope he lives.

And then they're wheeling him away. The three of us trail behind the trolley like lost children, until we reach a doorway where it's made clear to us: this far, and no further. Jonny shrinks away from us as they pull him along the corridor. His eyes are closed, there's an oxygen mask over his mouth, and his stupid geeky T-shirt has been cut off him and binned. Then they swing him round a corner, and that's it.

Because this isn't a US daytime TV drama, there is no observation room from which we can watch the surgery while looking nervous. And now we're alone, we are no longer the devoted friends of a seriously injured young man. We are just three more obstacles to a clear corridor. We find an empty bench, facing one of the hospital's main stairwells, and sit watching as all human life walks, paces, shuffles, or wheels past us.

After ten minutes of silence, I go and get a few cones of

water from the machine. As I arrive back, a young doctor is in my spot, speaking to Elle and Em. He's about my age, dressed in scrubs, and irritatingly handsome.

He's saying: '... do of course need to ask you some questions.'

'Of course,' says Elle, and Em gives me a nervous look.

I've stopped next to them now, and the doctor takes me in too.

'What sort of questions?' I ask.

'Well, we'll have to contact the police.'

'Don't do that,' I say, a bit too fast.

'Why not?'

What do I say? If I say Jonny was shot by someone we know, they'll say it's vital we talk. If I say he was shot by a stranger, they might be quite interested in tracking the gunman who's been shooting random passers-by. I can't think of anything. I've completely run out of lies. I open my mouth, close it again, look at the girls for help. Em saves me.

'Because we *are* the police.'

The doctor's face is a mask. (Given that we're both in a hospital and post-Covid, that is a confusing sentence in two separate ways. To be clear, he's not wearing a mask, he just keeps his expression blank.) 'Are you? With the Met, or a different department?'

'The Met. This was a plain-clothes operation. He shouldn't have been anywhere near it, but it went wrong. We've notified our colleagues.'

'Do you have your ID?'

Em pulls rank. 'Mate, do we look like we gathered our stuff properly? Our colleague's been shot.'

He nods. 'Oh. Well. You'll be following your procedures. I won't disturb you any further.' He stands, and stretches his arms. 'Can I help with anything else?'

'Is our friend going to be all right?'

The doctor looks at me. 'I hope so. But I'm afraid it's not really my department.' He saunters off, looking just a bit too cool. I am a diehard supporter of the NHS, but I would cheerfully see that guy struck off.

Once he's out of sight, Elle says, 'Nice one, Em.'

'All right,' I say. 'So the guy who shot Jonny was clearly the associate of whoever was in the house. That must mean—'

Elle interrupts me, and I think it's the first time I've ever heard her interrupt anyone. 'Al. Seriously. Stop. Just stop for a second. We talked when you were getting the water, and we've decided something.'

'Decided what?'

'If we get out of the hospital without being arrested, we're just going to go to ground.'

I'm genuinely confused. 'You're suggesting we give up?'

'Al, we have just – between the three of us – killed someone who turns out to be a British spy. And Jonny's being cut open right now. You really think we're getting out of this with one more deduction?'

'Yes, I—'

She does it again. 'Just *stop*. You're being ridiculous.'

'Ridiculous would be quitting after everything we've been

through. We are so close to working it out. I mean, this is huge, it's . . .' I gesture expansively, then tail off, because both Em and Elle have their arms folded and are giving me the same look. Em will back me up, surely. 'Em, you must see what I'm saying here. We are so close to finding out who killed Davy. And where he left the money. And then—'

'Al, have things got better for us since we started all this?' Em gestures at the corridor. 'We've got nothing. We have a vague hunch about who might have killed Davy, a few conflicting theories, and not much evidence. The whole thing has been a catastrophe. You were right, we should have got the ferry to France in the first place.'

'Yes, but—'

'Oh, just shut up. I wish I hadn't suggested we even start along this stupid path. I wish I'd let you go when you were trying to run that first night. All you've done is lie, and make things worse.'

'Em, that's not fair. I haven't lied. We have to trust each other.'

'Trust? You haven't told us who you are, nor where you come from. Nothing. We don't even know your name.'

'I did tell you who I am.'

'You gave Elle a version of your life that was clearly bollocks. You told me you had a brother, and I only know that's true because you stole his passport from him. That's the one fact you've given away. You don't believe in us. You don't seem to believe in people. You don't know why you're doing this either. You just want to stay outsmarting your marks, for ever. Some of us want more than that.'

'*I* want more than that.' As I say it, I realise I really do, and the thing I want more than anything is to stay with these guys. But I stumble over the words, and they clearly don't believe me. They're wrong, *wrong*. I must make them see it. 'If we give up now, it was all for nothing.'

'I'd rather be arrested and maybe get some police protection than be hunted down by whoever killed Davy.'

'Hang on, it was an *actual spy* who shot Jonny. You think we're safe from anybody from now on?'

'Obviously not. But if we do get out of here, we can go to ground, find somewhere quiet, and then just live. We'll take Jonny back to France, do a bit of piscining there until he's properly better, settle down. And if we're arrested, we'll take that. Don't try to change our minds, Al. Or whatever your name is.'

Em has the look on her face of someone who's run out of patience. I remember that look from about a decade ago. I've worked quite hard to avoid anyone knowing me well enough to look at me like that again, and yet here we are.

'Why can't you *see* . . .' Oh, shit. I stop, because I've just seen something much more important.

There's a uniformed police officer standing at the other end of the corridor. And the clean-cut young doctor who was talking to us before is at his side, pointing our way. That viper.

'We have to go. Police.'

Em looks round, sees the officer – who is now walking our way – and shrugs. 'No, Al. We're staying here, with Jonny.'

The copper is about fifty feet away. 'Please. We can get away. I know it.'

Neither of them moves. The copper's moving faster.

'*Please.*' He'll be here in fifteen seconds. They do not move.

I swear, pitch out of my seat, and hurl myself at the stairwell.

42

Nine million people in this city, and not one I can trust.

I'm on a coach, hauling out of town along the same route I took a few days ago. I got out of the hospital all right. The police officer didn't seem especially interested in giving chase, not that I knew it as I threw myself down two stairwells and crashed out of a side gate and onto a main road, where I managed to snag a passing bus going to Victoria, and then a coach heading south-west.

I blagged the coach fare, which is something. I know I never steal personal possessions, but on this occasion I think MegaCoachCorp can give me a break. I'm masked up, still sweating even though I sat for twenty minutes waiting for us to set off, and nobody's paid me the slightest bit of attention.

Unless there's a discreet spy on board, I'm safe for the next couple of hours.

I go through my pockets again. I'm not exactly overburdened with useful tools. Two last lock-picks. Throwaway phone, passport in someone else's name, light wallet. No keys – never any keys, of course. The wallet contains a few bank cards, all of which will get me traced and netted within ten seconds of using them. The bundle of notes I always carry around as insurance is a shadow of its former self. I have ... sixty-five quid. Not much in this economy. *Jack Reacher gets by with less*, an accusing voice says. It sounds a bit like Em.

Jesus. I just killed someone. All right, I might as easily have been killed myself, but I'd forgotten about the guy until now, believe it or not. Subsequent events got in the way. I saw a glimpse of his face as we went over the railing together – nothing but surprise on it. But I'm not feeling guilty, not yet, at least. He's the one who came into our home with a big knife. I wish he'd told us what he wanted. Why would a British spy want us dead?

The feeling keeps occurring to me that I'm stuck in a room, and every time I stop focusing on the walls, a giant hand pushes them in a bit. The room is getting smaller and smaller. I know there's a door somewhere, but I can't quite see it yet.

Keep looking for that door, Al. Keep on looking. I wonder if the girls have been arrested, and fall asleep.

I wake on the outskirts of the town I'm heading to, press the button almost too late, apologise to the driver, who had to slam on the brakes, stumble down and out. Over a decade avoiding this dump, and now I'm back for the second time in a few days.

The ten minutes I spend getting to the apartment block should be twenty, but I'm pacing fast, neither looking nor feeling my best. Even so, once I'm there, it's a small matter to bluff through the main door – tailgating this time, some twenty-somethings back from the pub who hardly notice me as I slip in behind them.

I've decided to swallow my pride and seek help from the one person in the world who can't refuse it.

Footsteps approach the door and stop just on the other side of it. I can see the light of the peephole eclipsed as he puts his eye to it.

A voice says: 'Who is it?'

'It's me.'

The door opens, and my brother looks at me. He's surprised, to put it mildly.

'Hi, Fred. Long time no see.'

'What are you doing here? Are you here because of the . . .' And then he remembers he's not speaking to me, hasn't spoken to me for years, and clams up.

'Can I come in?'

'Why?'

'I'm in trouble.'

'That means nothing in this family. As you know.'

I try to take that in the spirit of constructive criticism I'm sure was intended. 'Yes, I know. But I mean, real trouble. Like, "someone wants me dead" trouble.'

'Who wants you dead?'

'I'm not sure. I may not have met them yet.'

'If they want you dead they probably know you pretty well.'

'Very funny.'

The next door along the corridor opens, and some busybody neighbour sticks their head out to see what the noise is. Fred gives them an appraising look – more trouble to have me outside the flat or in it? – and eventually stands back from the door. He's still looking a little shocked.

I make the usual noises of appreciation as I enter, but Fred's not buying it. He gestures to the armchair, puts a glass of water down in front of me, and takes the dining chair for himself. 'You look like shit.'

'Yeah, well, it's been a long decade.' He gives nothing away. 'OK. Here's what happened.'

You would definitely recognise the version of events I tell Fred over the next ten minutes. It's as if I strained everything you've just read and boiled it for a bit, to kill off any suggestion of impropriety. I don't give him the full account. But I do tell him about Davy's house, and about Mr Bowling Ball, and about Nevis. I don't mention whose passport I left the country on.

As I talk, he seems not to be listening. I use everything at my disposal: I give him pity, humour, inspiration . . . None of it works. It's like I'm speaking to a jury of one, a jury who's already received clear instructions from the bench. The confidence drains from me, and I feel myself shrinking even further in his sight. Eventually, I finish, and sit back.

'So you're not here for any other reason.'

'Fred, do I need another reason? People are trying to kill me. Will you help?'

He tells me straight out, at least. 'No.'

'What? Why not?'

'Because the police got here before you.' For a horrible moment I think he's about to say, '... and they're here tonight!' like Michael Aspel in *This Is Your Life*, and the detective and his colleague Kate are about to climb out of the kitchen cupboard, arm in arm. But Fred keeps talking: 'They came here a few days ago. They know who you are. They know you killed this man Harcourt. And I'm not going to help you get away with it.'

'Fred. Please. I haven't killed anyone.' (Yes, I know this is a lie, as of about four hours ago. What I mean is, I haven't killed the specific guy the police think we have.) 'You know me, I hardly even shoo pigeons. You think I shot someone in cold blood? What the hell is my motivation?'

He just picks up his phone and addresses it: 'Timer: ten minutes.' It squawks confirmation back at him. 'When that alarm goes off, I'm ringing the police and telling them you're here.'

'Fred. This is crazy. I'm your brother.'

He looks at me. 'Do you know what Mum and Dad did, after you left?'

'This isn't about—'

'They *hoped*. For years, they tried getting in touch, until you changed your number, and after that they just hoped you'd come back.'

'There were things going on, things that—'

'Oh, yeah, things in your life. You were nineteen, you silly twat. Everyone's messed up at nineteen. You haven't asked after either of them, I note.'

'Someone tried to kill me tonight, and you—'

'Dad's in a home, just so you know.'

That gives me a knock.

'What?'

'He went in three years ago. In case you'd ever wondered.'

'He's not old.'

'Ten years older than when you last saw him. Mum couldn't cope.'

I look my parents up occasionally, just to see if they're in the same place – I don't contact them, you understand, just observe from a distance. The last time I checked, they were both fine. Has it really been more than three years since then? In the pit of my stomach, I know it's been more like five. You know how it is. It's like going to the dentist. You keep thinking you'll make the appointment. You never do.

I've been sitting in silence for about thirty seconds before I think of the obvious question. 'What about Mum?'

'Don't contact her. She thinks you're dead. Easier if you are.'

I don't have much to say to any of this. After a while, he glances at his phone. 'Six minutes to go.'

'Why are you doing this, Freddy?'

'I'm not doing anything. I'm just having a normal life.'

'Enjoying it?'

'Not really. I work in a shop. My dad's in a home. My only brother left a decade ago and my mum thinks he's dead. But I'm in a choir. I read a lot. There are worse ways of living.'

He's practically shouting the subtext: *like breaking into other people's houses*. After a long pause, he speaks again. 'Did you even get my messages?'

'What messages?'

'You should have had some texts.'

I get my phone out and open the messages, the *Time is running short* and the *I know who you really are*, all that menacing crap. 'This was you? Jesus, you nearly gave me an aneurysm.' He shrugs. 'Why?'

'I hired an investigator to track you down. He got both your phone numbers, but couldn't trace you. He even set up a honey trap of a job with your firm, although you didn't go for it.'

Bloody hell. Jasmine wasn't trying to set me up, she was actually passing on a message. I owe her an apology once this is over. And Fred still hasn't answered my question.

'But why track me in the first place? If your life was so much better without me in it?'

He looks around, not meeting my eye. 'Curiosity, I guess. When I saw you at the door, I thought you'd worked it out and you were coming back to . . .' He tails off, and shrugs. After a silence, he checks his phone. 'Four minutes.'

I waste another two minutes sitting in silence, thinking about Dad, and wondering what Mum is doing right now. Eventually I remember I've got quite a lot else on.

'Fred. People are trying to kill me. And a lot of other people want me arrested for something I didn't do. I'm asking you one more time to just . . . help.'

'Absolutely not. But if you like, I'll give you a snack for wherever you're going. You look done in. I don't think that counts as aiding and abetting.'

'What have you got?'

'Should have a Kit Kat somewhere.' I laugh, then realise he's serious. He goes to the kitchen, opens a tin, and hands one over as he returns. Orange flavour. I pocket it.

I get up and move to the door. 'I'm really sorry, Fred. But I didn't do it. Not this particular thing, I mean. I know I screwed the rest up.' He shrugs, and I don't blame him. He leans past me and holds the door open. I stand in the corridor, looking back, trying to work out what to say to him for the last time. At that moment, his phone alarm sounds. He props the door open with his foot, takes a business card from his wallet, enters a number, and dials. With the phone to his ear, he says, 'See you.'

'See you, Fred. Oh, one more thing. Almost forgot.' I dig in a pocket and hand over his passport. 'I could have used this to flee the country, just so you know.'

At the other end of the line, someone has clearly just answered, because he's caught for a moment between staring at me and listening to his phone. Then he says, 'Hello?' and looks to the side, and I turn and head down to the dark street.

43

The next coach back to town isn't until tomorrow, so short of breaking into someone's car, I'm down here for the night.

I know where to go. At least there's no CCTV to follow me through the streets.

The beach is dark, and bloody cold. April's still rough on the coast. The walk down is steep, too, and before risking my neck I pause at the top of the cliff path. There's a lonely tanker on the horizon, and a few tiny fishing boats bobbing off to the left, near the old harbour. The air is clean, and empty, and there are more stars above than I've seen for months.

Down at beach level, I turn right, past the little tin café, and count. One . . . two . . . three . . . here we go. Fourth hut along. Round the back, dodging the little creek, across the cracked slabs, kick the nettles away from the back wall . . . There's the lock box. Code: 1994. Back round the front, I unlock the door, fetch a torch from the kitchen cupboard, use it to find the little Calor heater, and set up a folding chair.

It's pretty in here. Little framed drawings on the wall, all of seasidey things – gulls, the huts themselves, striped towels on a washing line. There are threaded shells, bunting on the benches, cushions shaped like biscuits. It's chintzy, and fun, and just the sort of place I'd usually sneer at without good reason. It's just . . . nice.

This is the first place I ever interloped.

What am I doing here?

At that moment, it's like all the lies I've ever told team up into one enormous lie and stand before the beach hut, blocking my exit.

Fred didn't use my name tonight. My real one, I mean. Not the one I've given you, or Em and the others, or my firm. If he had done, I'm not sure I'd have recognised it.

Right now, it occurs to me that I really am the person I seem to be, for the first time in years. I'm a vagrant, a youngish man whose only skill is breaking and entering, a parasite who's about to be collared for something he didn't do, but who absolutely deserves to be caught for all the things he did.

All this sounds a bit mawkish, doesn't it? And I'm not too manly to admit it: I indulge in a bit of a cry. If I could think of one person who might help me, I'd call them. But there's nobody left. It's been a long day, a long eight years. And then, with the little stove warming my feet and lower ankles and nothing else, I fall asleep.

I wake to find a tall, hairless figure stooping over me, its arm reaching out.

'Christ!' I kick out, which knocks the stove over, and between us the figure and I spend a scrambled thirty seconds stamping to ensure it doesn't set the hut alight. The figure says 'sorry' throughout, which reassures me I'm not about to be murdered. Eventually the stove is upright, and although I've burned my thumb, I'm otherwise intact.

He's about twenty, I'd say – a weathered twenty. I thought he was bald at first, but he's actually more in the first-fluff stage of someone who shaved their head a few weeks ago. He's in a tracksuit, and his shoes are open-toed sandals with socks beneath them. 'Sorry, mate. I was just passing and saw the light. Just snooping really.'

'That's all right. I shouldn't be here either. Help yourself to a chair. Warm yourself up a fraction.' He nods, grateful, and quickly opens up a chair beside mine, as if I'm about to change my mind. He pulls off his sandals and socks, and exposes his bare soles to the tiny warmth of the stove. His feet look like they've seen far more of the outside world than any feet should.

'How'd you end up here?'

I think about answering, but in the end I just shrug. 'Long story. You?'

He's called Len. He's got the kind of story I used to give people – except he's more convincing. It's the usual stuff:

family break-up, debt, addictions, and then the slow spiral until all the options have run out, all the sofas have been surfed and all the spare places crashed. He's been on the street for four months.

On balance, I'd say Len is a bit worse off than a spoiled teenager who just had a row with his family and walked out one day, then never bothered to get back to them, carelessly throwing away an entire accumulated life on the strength of a few adolescent arguments and a large dose of self-pity. That seems like a fair appraisal.

I want to help him somehow, but offering interloping advice feels presumptuous, and I can't think of anything else, until inspiration strikes.

'Want a Kit Kat?'

'You sure?'

'Yeah. I'm trying to cut down on sugar.'

'Thanks.' He pockets it.

I'm so tired. God, it was only this morning we visited Conor Vane in the Commons. Then Balfour Villas, the spy, the landing, the landing *from* the landing, the Uber, the hospital, the coach, Fred . . . There are years where little happens, and nights where your life is turned upside down and squeezed.

I can't stop wondering where Em and Elle are. Were they arrested? Were they allowed to stay with Jonny? What's happening to Jonny? I'd take any punishment going if I could trade it for him being all right.

Len is looking at me expectantly, and I realise he's just said something. 'Sorry?'

'I said, where are you going from here?'

'I'm not sure.' This is the truth for once.

'You can't stay in this hut for ever,' he says. 'I've tried it.'

To be honest, I was thinking how you could interlope this place on a semi-permanent basis. Only use it after dark, when there's nobody else around. You'd have shelter, warmth, light . . . God, what am I, a caveman? Al, you once spent three weeks in the Duke of Westminster's house, telling the neighbours you were on a ducal exchange scheme. Aim a little higher.

'I'll probably . . .' I could run, of course, I've got enough of my wits remaining to blag a ferry. French can't be that hard. Make my way south, wind up in Nice or Marseille, get a tan, work on a boat, just live. Don't be daft, Al. But it's tempting. 'I'll probably just drift for a bit.'

Len shoots me a look of pity, as if I've given the wrong answer. I'm tempted to explain to him that I woke up last night in an actual mansion in London. He would nod, and smile, and chalk me up as the sort who needs a fantasy to cope. You meet them a lot, in this trudge of life. Everybody deceives themselves about something or other, and normally I'm the one helping people deceive themselves, but right now it's me who seems delusional.

'I hope you don't mind, Len, but I think I need to sleep now.'

He nods. 'All right, mate. I won't disturb you.'

With the aid of a stuffed Bourbon cushion and two custard creams, I nod off. When I wake, he's gone, and – for Christ's sake, Len – he's left me half the Kit Kat.

There's a grey light out there beyond the sea. Dawn's coming.

I get a few sheets of paper from the shelf – something for the children to draw on when it rains – and, for want of anything else, a brown Crayola. Then I write down everything I can think of, in the wrong order:

Davy; luxury places; mentoring scheme; Battersea flat; Wolfgang the German stooge; UAE bank (two have access); laundering; Nevis; Rivers; Charli and Lulu; Mrs P; Rob Wallace; Kate McAdams; Balham Brats (Fantasy Football); Conor Vane; flights to Dubai; dark police stations; spies why British spies; outbuilding outbuilding OUTBUILDING; what was he confessing to?; who was he working with?; who did he trust?

There has to be something in this mess, something I can tease out. Someone's lying; and when someone lies, they leave a little fissure between what they've said and reality. Find those gaps. Find where the light shines through.

I look through my phone at the wide electronic trail I've left behind. I don't have access to Davy's inbox, but pretty much everything else in the last fortnight links me to the crime. I've got Davy's number saved, Charli and Lulu's numbers, the number of Kate McAdams from the National Crime Agency (I swiped it before we chucked the phone we spoke to her on), and numbers for most of Davy's friends, everyone except Jay Hawthorne.

Wait. There it is. A gleam of light.

And . . . it's gone again. Something snagged at my brain for half a second there. Somewhere a tiny revelation flashed a fin, a phrase spoken in the course of all those meetings that offered a theory I could test. What was it? Stay calm, Al. Don't thrash. It'll come around. Just gently meander back, let your eyes wander across the page again, stand motionless in the middle of the stream . . .

There. I have the thought, cradled between my hands. I slowly gather it up, ring two of the words in Crayola, link them together, and step back. It'll take a few more hours before I can make the call, but I have time. I should have a few hours yet.

44

One thought follows another, and by half past eight – that's a decent hour to start ringing round, isn't it? – I have three calls to make.

Call One is to Mrs P. She's at her desk already, the good woman, and she's not totally surprised to hear from me again. In an amused tone of voice she promises to send over a photo I've asked for.

Call Two is to the local council in Bridling, to their planning department. I need to wait until nine for this lot, but they answer eventually, and although they're a bit cautious at first, they're willing to help a nephew of poor dead David Harcourt who is doing his best for his uncle's surviving relatives. They, too, agree to send an image over to me.

A Beginner's Guide to Breaking and Entering

Call Three is to Ben Westcott, the president of the Balham Brats, chief Fantasy Football wrangler and Davy's sometime best man. This call requires more tact than the first two, and I get through several cups of tea in the hut just thinking about how I'll approach. Eventually, I decide on the most dangerous option: the truth.

At the end of my calls, I look at what I've assembled, and it stands up from every angle. I have a decision to make.

If I call the person I think was Davy's co-conspirator, the one with whom he shared access to the bank account in the UAE, I think I could persuade them to split the money with me. Even if it was 80–20 in their favour, it would be enough to set me up for life.

I genuinely could go back to the Caribbean then. Or just to Europe. I could buy a chalet somewhere, get a bit of security ... it could work. I can't see all the way across the Channel from the beach hut, but I know the continent is somewhere over there, and it's bloody tempting. I'd never have to interlope again. I could become a completely different person, this time for good.

The only problem is that it would involve leaving the killer at large, with Elle and Em either at their mercy or facing arrest, and Jonny too, assuming he survived the night.

Ugh. This is why I don't like working with people. They lead you to make stupid, silly, weak decisions.

I do look up the price of ferry tickets, then a few property portals to see how much the average mountain chalet sets you back these days (a *lot*, it turns out; these ski people must be made of money and still they choose to go somewhere cold? Insane), but my heart isn't in it.

Oh, God, it's no choice at all. The laws of self-preservation and sanity are telling me to flee, and yet I'm not listening. I'm not even listening to *myself* any more. That's how screwed up those three have got me.

My fourth call is to Em.

She lets the phone ring for a while, which I don't begrudge her. There's also a good chance she's been arrested. But eventually she picks up, with a typically Em opening offer.

'What?'

'Hi. How's Jonny?'

'He's going to be fine.' I release a breath I hadn't realised I was holding. 'No arteries hit. No vital organs either. The gunman was either very unlucky or very good. A few days of bed and he can start being up and about. But he's on his back for the moment.'

'Is he awake?'

'Awake and typing. He's already had a stand delivered to balance his computer on. Built a 3D model of the hospital to direct the delivery guy to his bed. He keeps saying he's "fully operational".'

'What happened with the police?'

'We said we didn't know Jonny, that we were at a bus stop and someone drove by and shot him, and we were the ones who got him to hospital. It was late, there won't be other witnesses from Balfour Villas, and we claimed we got a black cab instead of an Uber so they won't be able to track the driver. The police have false names and numbers for each of us.'

'Where are you?'

'Still at the hospital. Feeling pretty horrible.'

'You're amazing.'

'Sure. What do you want?' She sounds unhappy, as you might imagine. She listens as I tell her I know who killed Davy, how they can be lured in. But that I can't do it alone, for a couple of reasons. If I'm being honest, I *could* do it alone, but I don't want her to know that. She's exactly the sort of person to back out if she thought I was doing anything to save her neck. At the end of my pitch, there's a long pause as she relays the idea to Elle, then she comes back on the line.

'I'm sorry, Al. We don't want any more trouble.'

'Em – Elle, if you're there – we left all our shit on the street outside a house with an open front door and a dead spy inside. We have twenty-four hours maximum before we're done for. We may as well get someone else arrested at the same time.' I can still hear the reluctance down the line. 'What could I say to change your mind?'

'You could tell us who you really are.'

'Would that help? Really?'

'It would.'

I take a deep breath, and Em speaks again.

'Hang on a second. I'm putting you on speaker.' The sound changes.

I get rid of the first deep breath, take a second one, then I start telling the truth. I am about to break the first rule I ever came up with.

Rule 1: *Nobody gets your real name.*

. . . And no, I'm not going to repeat what I said to her. Are you mad? That's private. You already got quite enough of an idea who I am from when I went back to Freddy's place. But what I tell her now actually is true. What happened, how I started, why I kept going . . . She gets all of it, even the bits that don't reflect well on me. There are a lot more of those bits than I thought. At the end of it, I run out of things to say, and I feel wrung out. I gaze at the grey sea while she and Elle muffle the phone and confer. Then the mouthpiece clears.

'What would we have to do?'

'You just need to put a message in the shared drafts folder. We know they're checking it regularly. Do you still have Davy's computer?'

'Yes. By Jonny's bed.'

'All right. Write a message saying you've fallen out with me, that I screwed you over and tried to go it alone, but that you know where I've gone. Tell them I'm the only one who knows how to get into Davy's half of the strongbox account. And name the cut of the proceeds you want for bringing them to see me. Say where we'll all meet.'

'Do we have to be there in person?'

'If you don't mind, I'd like you to come along.'

'What do we tell them they'll get?'

'A few things. They'll get my head on a spike, they'll get the perfect corpse to pin Davy's death on, and they'll get whatever's in this shared bank account. They're probably quite keen by now.'

'Tempting.'

'Mm.'

'I'm tempted myself, to be honest.'

'Then, of course, they'll want to kill you, but ideally they won't even manage to kill me, which will be higher on their agenda.'

'You'll send us the where and when?'

'Yeah. Take care of yourself. Love to everybody.'

Em snorts, and hangs up, muttering *love to everybody* as she does.

I start packing up the beach hut. I don't have long.

45

I've just realised, I've no idea where the name 'Bridling' comes from. I do like a bit of amateur etymology – eventually when you've stayed in enough villages with weird names in off-season you start to get a bit nerdy about local history – but I never got around to researching Bridling. There's Bridlington up in Yorkshire, which apparently means something like 'the estate of Berhtel' in Old English, but nobody has any idea who Berhtel was and it seems unlikely he had a second home in Oxfordshire. You get to reflect on these things when you spend twenty hours a day in your cell. Anyway.

This chapter opens with me back in – surprise surprise – Bridling, the village that started this whole farrago, the village containing Davy's very big house in the country. The one we last saw in the rear-view mirror as we got out of there at triple the speed limit.

And now here I am again. Tariq provided a car on credit. I told him I needed not to be conspicuous, and in the sorrowful tone of a slandered man he said, 'Al, my friend. When are my cars conspicuous?' He even sent a lad from Mr Toad's Motors down from London, all the way to the coast, after I explained the outer edges of my current difficulties. Thoughtful man. I picked the little Hyundai up without trouble, and drove, carefully and methodically, to the Cotswolds.

If I ever get out of this mess, I'm going to give Tariq first refusal on my first-born son.

I'm sitting on the bench outside Davy's front door. The gate opened when I pressed '0' on the keypad, so I just drove in, with no difficulty. The house is locked, although if you squint through the outer door you can see the shattered glass of the inner hall door. I haven't been in yet. It's important that they can tell I definitely haven't been in.

One of the porch's upright beams has a yellow ribbon tied round it, which seems romantic and mournful until I look closer and realise it's police tape.

There's a crunch from the other end of the gravel, and the gates swing open. Em and Elle hop out of a cab. They don't say anything until it's left again, and the noise of the engine has faded to nothing.

Em gives me a wary look. 'Hiya.'

'Hi.'

'How's it going?' asks Elle. I knew she'd crack first.

'So-so. How about you? How's Jonny?'

'*Really* good.'

'He's fine,' says Em. 'He keeps saying he's double-plus stable, so at least the bullet didn't knock the Orwell out of him. He's trying to persuade the hospital to let him plug into the NHS IT mainframe.'

'They should absolutely not do that.'

'No.'

The silence between me and Em at that moment is so thick and forbidding that not even Elle is willing to skate out across the surface. She turns and wanders along the front of the house, examining the wisteria. Em and I are left together.

'I'm really sorry for how I . . .' I was hoping we'd both start speaking at the same time, which would give me a good reason to tail off, but Em lets me twist, and so I have to continue. 'How I behaved. Throughout.'

She shrugs. 'We don't have to talk about it now, Al. Still want me to refer to you as Al?'

'I think so. Maybe I should change my name to that. You know, by deed poll. So I'm actually telling the truth from now on.'

She doesn't quite smile, but it's close. 'Well, *Al*. You think this will work?'

'Maybe.'

She wobbles her head in agreement, then looks out at the drive.

'So, did they buy it? They didn't mind coming out here?'

'Seems like it,' she says. 'I told them that you'd only meet us here at the house, and I think they liked that. Gave them a little sense of drama. Hard to tell over a draft email, but they seemed to *love* the sound of betraying you and splitting the proceeds. They think we're going to get into the account, drop you as soon as we're in, and then they say they'll split the money with us.'

'Well, if they do shoot me as soon as they're in, try to take them up on that before they shoot you too.'

'But who is it? Who are we waiting for?'

I pat my pocket. 'I'll show you afterwards, assuming I was right. Anyway. Only the person who has access Davy's inbox knows we're here now. And they've as good as told us they killed him.'

She's not listening to me. Her attention is on the gates. 'Look lively. Here we go.'

A third car is approaching up the gravel drive, a grey Audi which looks almost respectable but for the tinted windows in the front. We're not the only ones who know how to get round security codes. Elle comes back over to where we're standing and takes her sister's hand.

The Audi pulls up next to my car. The driver's door opens, and Mr Bowling Ball unfolds out of it. He's formally dressed, which makes him look more than ever like a manosphere vlogger arriving for a court appearance. His shoulders are giving the suit's seams a hard time, along with the gun he's clearly got holstered under his arm. He gives my borrowed Hyundai a look of pure disdain as he walks round the back of the Audi and bends to open the rear door.

Out of the car steps . . . Conor Vane. No. Wait, what? The person who gets out is, inexplicably, not Conor Vane. Conor Vane is who I was hoping for, who I'd have bet my last £65 on. Conor Vane is the man whose name I wrote on a piece of paper with brown Crayola to impress Em with once he arrived.

And yet, indisputably, out of the car steps Davy's ex-wife, Charli.

She's looking fab, as per. No coat, just a purple satin blouse, spray-on jeans and a clutch bag big enough for a single five-pack of Vogue Slims. Her heels are as thin and metallic as kitchen skewers, and she trots neatly to the front door despite the inches of gravel underfoot.

The impression she gave in the past was so shallow, so – will you forgive me for using a gendered term here? – so *ditzy*, that it's quite hard to recognise her now. Her face seems to have rearranged itself. But then I remember how she looked when I first met her at her friend Guggy's launch party, and the thought that fleetingly occurred to me. Even in those fluffy, self-helpful surroundings, something suggested she had known difficulty, and was determined she would never know any more of it.

Shit.

As Charli approaches, Em leans over to me. 'Was that who was on your piece of paper?'

'. . . No.'

'Thought not.'

'Good morning, all of you,' says Charli. She addresses Elle.

'I don't think we've met. Related to this one?' Elle nods, and Charli looks her up and down. 'Mm. Two years younger, I'd guess, always in the shadow of big sis, never quite worked out how to be yourself, compensated by being terribly nice and hoping someone would notice? Thought so. This is Alfie. He's met you a couple of times, I believe, and you've made his working life very stressful. Alfie, can you check the exterior?'

Alfie nods. He gives me a look of particular venom, and the girls one of subsidiary grumpiness, then stalks off to examine the house.

'I must say, you all look a bit surprised to see me. Were you looking forward to making a speech about why it was whoever you thought?' Charli plucks a vape from her tiny bag and puffs on it.

Nobody else is saying anything, so I suppose it's my turn. 'You killed Davy?'

'Hope so. And you were here, on the other side of the door. Nice to have these little reunions, isn't it? How's your friend?'

'He's doing much better.'

'Oh, that's marvellous. Should never have happened, of course. Botch job. You want something done in this country, do *not* ask a professional. They're all unionised time-servers.' My head is swimming.

Alfie is back from the exterior. 'They haven't been in.'

'Oh, good.' She plucks a key from her micro-bag, unlocks the front door, steps around the shattered glass still lying in the hall – treading on the outline of her husband's neck– and leads us through to the back. Alfie follows us.

Once we're in the study, Charli takes a seat behind the desk, and the three of us are plonked once again onto the sofa. Last time we were here, Davy was pointing a gun at us: this time, Alfie's gun is still in its holster. So actually we're doing much better, thank you.

Charli thinks of something. 'Alfie, can you do a sweep of these three and the room? Don't want to be recorded, do we? I mean, we'll be in a non-extradition country this time tomorrow, but there's no harm in maintaining operational security.' OPSEC again. She and Jonny would get along.

Alfie gives us a pat-down and I get a glimpse of his gun under the suit. Perhaps I could grab it? Upside down? And then, what, blow these two away? Don't be daft, Al. Remember the rules and you'll be all right.

I can't remember a single one of the rules.

Calm down, Al. God. You've been in worse trouble than this before.

Don't check the truth of that statement, it'll only upset you.

After some heavy petting, Alfie seems satisfied that we're unarmed, and gives the room itself a good search for any cameras or microphones. This takes about ten minutes, which we spend sitting in awkward silence, but eventually he pronounces himself happy and stands behind Charli, looking like a shaved Dobermann.

'I thought it was Conor Vane who killed your husband,' I say.

She exhales a cloud of strawberry. 'I mean, he's involved, but he's not *committed*. Why him?'

'The phone records. Davy was so hopeless that Mrs P at his firm did his phone contract for him. So she got all his bills, itemised. I rang her, and she sent them over. Conor claimed he hadn't spoken to your husband in the weeks leading up to his death, but in the fortnight before Davy died, they spoke eight times. I assume Davy was asking about dark police stations, and Qumar, and what he should do.'

'They did speak, yes. And Con had a good reason to lie about it, even to a friend and donor. Doesn't mean he killed Dave. You think a sitting MP would murder someone? Con isn't clever enough to do it without being caught, but he's also not stupid enough to try.' She sighs. 'Yes, Con has been helpful. And Dave *was* asking his advice about Qumar, because he knows all about Con's interests in the area and wanted to know what was best, who could be trusted, whether he should blow the whistle, whether he'd be safe. Con sensibly advised him to book an appointment with the police, then phoned me and told me. All I had to do was track Dave down before the meeting.'

'So . . . you were his accomplice, all these years?'

'I think "accomplice" is a rather hierarchical word, don't you? If anything, he was mine. I was the one who came up with the thing in the first place.'

'Your Instagram,' says Elle. 'Nice cover.'

Charli shrugs. 'You've got to travel all over the world to meet these people. Lots of them can't legally come to London. You may as well stay somewhere nice. Nobody pays attention to some clueless rich-bitch divorcee enjoying herself at luxury resorts in various, ah . . .'

'Dictatorships?'

'States with cultures of muscular governance. Potayto, potahto.'

'Which let you meet everyone there who wanted to launder money.'

'Yeah. I reassured them, discovered how much they needed to clean, and Davy found the places they needed.'

'But all his money goes to Lulu,' says Em. 'You had an interest in him staying alive.'

'If I'd wanted his main estate, yes,' says Charli, waving her hand through the vape mist. 'Which consists of one ratty Cotswolds vicarage, a few hundred grand in ISAs, and the London flat you sniffed out. She's welcome to it. But with him dead, all I need is access to our account, and I stand to make a much larger sum.'

'You told us you and he were reconciling. Was that true?'

'No. But another good cover, right?' She drags on the vape again. 'You'll have seen from his phone records that I spoke to Dave a lot. More than mutual-parenting one sulky student would require. But if we were getting back together, it works.'

'Why was he so worried about Qumar, though?' Em asks. 'What made him book the appointment with the police?'

'Oh, well, it was this new line of work. He'd never been totally comfortable with it. Kept wibbling that it was *treason*. Silly bastard. I kept telling him, it's all people stashing money here via other places. Half of our original clientele were from the UK. But he worried away about this dark police station stuff. Said he couldn't trust the mentees, said he was getting cold feet . . . Then an operation we'd set up for some Iranians fell apart a month ago – did you see that? – and they blamed him for it. Sent some twit boy to threaten Lulu in Brighton. Once Dave found out, he hit the roof.'

'So the Iranian thing started it?'

Charli tuts like I've made a point that might be accurate but isn't relevant. 'The Iranians were the trigger, but they're not the main clientele. That's the Qumar lot. They're about to launch a big expansion of their operation over here. Hundreds of thousands of Qumaris in this country; they need keeping an eye on. So Dave rang the police. He thought he could get himself and Lu into witness protection and me into prison if he confessed. Didn't trust his friend Jay Hawthorne, which was sensible. Anyway, that had to stop.'

'And then he booked a flight to Dubai, and holed up here.' Charli shrugs yes. 'But you weren't in the country. We checked the records of that jet. It came back the day you said it did. So you must have sent someone else.'

'You think he'd have opened the door to Alfie?' Charli looks round at her bodyguard. 'Some days *I* don't want to open the door to him, and I'm his boss. No, it had to be me.'

'But how . . .'

'Did you check the previous flights for that jet?' I look at Em, who looks at Elle, who looks at me, and Charli sighs. 'It had just done another run from Dubai to London, then back. I was on the earlier return flight. It's not that hard to tweak a name from one passenger list to another, not when it's a private plane.'

'And Dave opened the door to you. Because he trusted you.'

'Afraid so. He was basically a nice man.'

'What about Lulu? Is she involved?'

'God, no. I'll see if she wants to visit me in a few years, but she's a big girl now, she can look after herself. Especially once she inherits two homes and enough money to hang around in Brighton her whole life. Such a shame. She takes after her father.'

'You'll miss it, won't you? Life here, all the parties, the glamour?'

'Like a hole in the fucking temple.' Charli shakes her head. 'Do you know how many parties for shoes – genuinely, shoe launch parties – I've been to in the last month? Three. I'm going to get to a beach somewhere and start reading the complete works of Trollope.'

Elle pipes up. 'Aren't you worried they're going to catch you?'

Charli's brow crinkles as far as is possible. 'Who?'

'The police.'

She shakes her head. 'They're all following *you*. Nobody is looking for me. They bought the private plane alibi, and they've seen the finances. They agree that I would have wanted nothing more than for Dave to keep earning to support our darling girl.' Her tone changes. 'Plus, I'm a particular friend of Jay Hawthorne, which is useful too.'

'So Hawthorne won't bother trying to find Davy's actual killer. And Conor Vane wants to protect the relationship with

Qumar, and he doesn't mind you benefiting from the dark police stations as long as nobody blows that open.'

'You're bright for squatters, I'll give you that.'

'What about Rob Wallace?'

'What about him? He found out about the laundry operation a month ago. Broke his heart. He had to fire Davy, as he saw it. They were working on his exit from the firm when the Iranian thing happened and it all got messy. Rob has a very old-fashioned interpretation of criminal law.'

'Oh.' All this time, Rob Wallace was one of the few demi-angels in this story. Good grief.

'Right,' says Charli, briskly. 'Are there any more piss-about questions before we do what we came here for?'

'Oh. One, yeah. Why did you send spies to kill us?'

Charli looks surprised for the first time. 'I didn't. I sent Alfie and he bollocksed it right up, as you know.' Alfie looks like he's been tapped on the nose with a rolled-up newspaper.

'Two people came to our place a couple of nights ago,' says Em. 'One of them died, and the other ran off after shooting our friend.'

'Nothing to do with me,' says Charli. 'I assumed you'd pissed someone else off along the way. All right, can we crack on? You have access to Davy's half of the account, I believe.'

'I want to know you won't kill us once you're in.'

'You have my word I won't.'

'I mean . . .' says Em, 'you killed someone last time we were here.'

'I did have a reason for that. It's not a *habit*.'

'Just as well. Because we filmed you as you arrived and got out of your car. We've already uploaded the clip, tagged with the date and time of filming, to a secure server, and if we're found dead, the footage will automatically be released to a pre-set list of police and media.'

'For Christ's sake, nobody's going to kill you.' Over her shoulder, Alfie looks briefly disappointed. 'We've had quite enough of all that. Once we're in the account, you'll be as complicit as we are. And once you've got your twenty per cent . . .'

'Forty.'

'Twenty.'

'Thirty-five.'

'Twenty.'

'Twenty-five.'

'. . . And once you've got your *twenty per cent*,' Charli snarls, 'we'll all be able to hire security and we never need to see each other again. OK?'

'No,' says Em. 'Sorry. Not a good enough guarantee.'

'Look,' says Charli, and I can sense her fashionista bonhomie wearing rather thin now. 'If we get into the account, Alfie and I are leaving the country. I, of course, will be going on a tour of all the places my darling husband and I visited during his tragically shortened life. Nobody will believe you if you claim I was involved, so it makes no difference to me whether you're arrested or not. And frankly, it's far *more* suspicious if the three of you are found murdered. I'm better off with you alive and imprisoned. So once we're in, and you have your cut, you can do what you like. Now can you *please* just get us all into the account?'

The girls and I look at each other. Em nods at me, although her face is grim.

'All right,' I say. 'Here's what you do.'

46

Interloping, as I may have said before, is largely an exercise in misdirection. You're managing the flow of people's beliefs about you, in a direction very slightly different from the truth but which nevertheless ends up depositing them just where you need them to be. And the other thing I've said before is that most people don't need active deceiving; more often than not, they deceive themselves. Here's why:

1) Most people like to believe other humans are basically good. If you buy someone's story, you are buying into a world where strangers don't lie to you for no reason. That's a nice world to live in. I'd like to live there myself.

2) Most people are basically good themselves. I haven't always relied on the kindness of strangers – usually I'm relying on their empty second homes – but there is a basic benevolence about people that would move me to tears if I was sentimental. For example: Len in the beach hut and that half Kit Kat.
3) It takes a bit of mental energy to poke holes in someone's story, and most people can't be bothered to do it. Asserting something with confidence carries the day nine times in ten.

Occasionally, of course, these principles don't apply, which is where my work gets harder. And right now, I'm faced with Charli Harcourt and her human Rottweiler. They don't believe other humans are benevolent, they aren't basically good themselves, and despite their busy schedules, they would gladly trot out of their way to tear my story apart. Deceiving them would be impossible. Which is why I'm not going to even try.

'It's simple,' I say. 'You need three sets of numbers, yes? The sort code, the account number, and the string of digits to get you in.'

'We don't need the sort code and account number, idiot,' says Charli. 'I have those already. We just don't have Davy's personal access number.'

'Can I tell my friends anyway? It took me ages to work it out, and I'm proud of it.'

'Ugh.' But Charli subsides momentarily and I keep talking.

'Remember what Davy told us before he died?'

'He said the money was in the outbuilding,' says Elle.

'Which doesn't exist,' says Em.

'Exactly. But he stored the information somewhere on the premises. Because he wanted Lulu to get access to his serious money. Charli, I'm sure you'd guessed that already. If Lulu had Davy's code, plus the sort code and account number, she'd have half control of the whole account. That's why Davy was so keen to put her and Ben Westcott together. And if you remember, Jonny found out that these accounts are so specialised, they'll let you pick your own numbers for all three elements.'

'OK. So where's the outbuilding?'

'At the local planning office,' I say, and draw out the wad of paper in my pocket (shuffling the sheet with IT WAS CONOR VANE written on it to the back). 'Davy had lodged plans with the council to build a long, low shed in the field next door, a miniature barn. Look at the way the dimensions are written.'

'08-12-68,' Em reads. 'Eight feet high, twelve across, and . . . sixty-eight deep? It's written like that again here.' She and Elle scan the document. 'And here.'

'Bingo. Davy had permission to build three years ago, but never bothered. He just kept renewing the permission. Building it wasn't the point. The plans simply ensured it existed somewhere, in the hope that Lulu would work out that the dimensions were the sort code.'

'What about the account number?'

'Look at the front wall of the plan.'

The outbuilding is prettily designed. It has the name PENELOPE written above it.

'Who's Penelope?'

'Lulu. It's her middle name. Remember?'

'He only ever called her Penny,' says Charli. 'Just to annoy me. And he's still trying to annoy me in death. Stupid name. Old-fashioned. You ever see a model called Penelope?'

'What about Penelope Cruz?'

'She's the exception.'

'Penny Lancaster?'

'Oh, shut up.'

'Try typing the name "Penelope" on an old mobile phone,' I say, 'which was Davy's preferred variety, and you get 73635673. Which is—'

'The number he picked for the account, yes,' Charli says. 'You've taken about half an hour explaining two things I already know. Do you have his personal access code or not?'

'I do. Em and Elle, do you remember going to the Bombardier in Putney a few days ago, and what they were actually up to?'

'Yeah. The Fantasy Football thing.'

'And do you recall why Davy had come last?'

Em doesn't. But Elle does. 'That man Westcott, Davy's best man. He said that Davy picked players with the same shirt numbers every year.'

'Which Jonny pointed out was insane for anyone actually trying to win a Fantasy Football tournament. But then I remembered just how much you, Charli, said you hated his

Fantasy Football habit. And Ben Westcott is Lulu's godfather, isn't he?'

'Not my choice,' Charli murmurs. 'Are you saying his stupid fake football numbers are the code?'

I turn over a sheet of paper. For the last twelve years, Ben Westcott has recorded the details of all the Fantasy Football teams of all five men. The shirt numbers picked by the other four are completely indiscriminate. Davy's are a grid of the same numbers, in the same order, year after year.

'Davy knew Lulu was allergic to football too. But he had one hope – that she would work out the truth about the outbuilding, that Ben Westcott would realise the football thing, and the two of them would piece it together without you knowing, Charli. That's why he wanted Lulu to contact her godfather, and why he phoned her saying as much a few days before he died.' I lean into my bag and get out Davy's laptop. 'It didn't work, of course. But that's how we get into his account, and how we all get our money.'

I say the last words with a flourish, and the audience react in four different ways. Elle claps and gives me a thumbs-up. Em shakes her head, a bit grudging but basically impressed. Charli looks furious, presumably that she didn't work it out herself. Alfie: no change. He's still looking at me like he's a Dobermann and I'm two pounds of wet offal.

'Can I see that?' Charli takes the sheet of paper with the football strip numbers on, and studies it, shaking her head. 'Dave, Dave, Dave. You silly bastard. We needn't have gone through any of this.'

A Beginner's Guide to Breaking and Entering

I open Davy's laptop, but Charli interrupts: 'Ah-ah. No thank you. The last thing I want is you draining the account God knows where and then us having to kill you and find the money all over again. You just give the laptop to Alfie here, there's a good boy.'

Reluctantly, I agree. Alfie takes it off me as Charli opens her own tablet. Then he looks over his employer's shoulder and pecks the address of the Dubai banking portal into Davy's laptop.

'All right. Pop that down just next to me. Thank you, dear.'

First, Charli enters her own three strings of numbers on her tablet: the sort code, account number and her private PIN. I can see on the screen that the account details appear in grey.

I pipe up. 'How much is in there, if you don't mind me asking?'

She swivels the screen round. I read out the number, slowly and carefully: '£34,287,961.'

'Bloody hell,' says Em.

Next, Charli grabs Davy's laptop and puts in the same sort code and account number, then consults the sheet Ben Westcott sent me and enters Davy's code.

We hear a little *blip* noise, a friendly one. She's in on both devices and they've lit up – one knows she's Charli, one thinks she's Davy. Now she can transfer the money anywhere she likes. Open Sesame. She gives a sigh of revolting satisfaction.

'Ten years of work, of course, ten years of sucking up to proper scumbags, but it's a decent amount.'

'And twenty per cent of that is ... nearly seven million quid,' Em says.

Charli looks blank. 'So what?'

'We're splitting the money eighty–twenty.'

'Ah. Yes. Probably a slight tweak in that plan, now that I'm in.' Charli smiles.

'Oh, what a surprise,' says Em. Charli merely shrugs.

I have one more question I need to hear Charli answer. 'Was it worth it?'

'Was what worth it?'

'Killing your husband.'

'Ex-husband. And for this amount of money? I'd have been mad not to. Frankly, I'd have done it pro bono, but earning a lifetime of comfort makes it the single best decision of my life so far. Yes, it's worth it.'

'Glad to hear it.'

'It's about to be worth killing the three of you, too. Gun, Alfie.'

Alfie looks a bit baffled. 'I thought you said we weren't—'

'Gun.'

He digs in his holster and hands over the pistol. This one isn't the kind of antiquated revolver Davy was waggling around from the corner armchair a week or two ago. This one is snub-nosed but massive, and looks like it'll be a lot better at finding our vital organs.

'Cute move filming us as we arrived,' says Charli, 'but it won't do you any good.'

'Why not?'

A Beginner's Guide to Breaking and Entering

'Because I'll be out of the country before anyone sees the footage. When the police get here, within about half an hour, they're going to find a house full of wonders. They'll find me shrieking on the gravel because I walked in on a scene of total carnage. They'll find your bodies, the dreadful squatters who killed my darling husband and stayed squatting here after the police left. Last of all, they'll find Alfie, my faithful bodyguard, who went in first to secure the place and was overpowered by you thugs.'

'What?' This is the first full sentence Alfie has said for a while. It's also the last thing he says, because Charli levels the pistol at him and pulls the trigger.

Alfie falls backwards, into a reproduction bust of a different Caesar, which shatters beneath him, and slumps to the ground, propped up by the wall. He looks down at his chest, then up at her, with a little outrage.

'Sorry, Alf. You'd have done the same to me within about twenty minutes of the money transferring.' Charli covers the three of us with the gun.

'And now the three of you, who attacked my poor innocent security man as he swept the premises. He fired, but even after he wounded you, you wrestled the gun off him and killed him before succumbing to your injuries. Or maybe you turned on each other. It's going to be a dreadfully unpleasant room to walk into. But privacy has its costs. And when my funds are all safely in my own . . .' Here Charli glances at the laptop. 'Wait, what?'

From where I'm sitting, I can just about see Davy's screen,

where the value on the account has changed. The top line now reads: ACC BALANCE: £0.11 GBP.

Charli's head swivels round. 'What have you done?'

Then it changes again: ACC BALANCE: £265,754,932 GBP.

Her face is now as grey as Alfie's.

The balance disappears, and then new text appears over the top in jerky type: ACC BALANCE: TOMATOES. HELLO CHARLI.

'What the *fuck* have you done?'

'Nothing,' I say. 'But our friend Jonny might have created a spoof version of the portal that only works on Davy's laptop.'

'So when you logged in with the correct details, it looked like it was letting you in, but actually you got bounced to a site he created,' says Em.

'One that activates the computer's webcam and microphone,' adds Elle.

'And because you showed us how much was on the screen in the real account, I was able to read it out loud, meaning he could listen in and replicate it exactly in the few seconds it took you to log in,' I explain.

'He's very clever, our friend Jonny,' says Em.

'And,' I say, as I hear footsteps crunching on gravel, and the shouts of enthusiastic armed response teams running towards the room from either side, and the crackles of Tasers itching to bite someone, 'he has a great sense of timing, too.'

47

Alfie's fine, FYI. I knew you'd be concerned, so just to reassure you, he's definitely going to live. Turns out Charli was about as good a shot as her ex-husband.

He suffered a little light lung-puncturing, of course, and lost about a gallon of blood, but I think that's only fair after what he put us through. Even so, Charli managed not to hit anything essential, and luckily for Alf, the police who charged the building within a minute of hearing the gunshot had brought some paramedics as backup. I feel like he's going to grow as a person when all this is done.

Sorry, that's not the relevant bit.

They arrested Charli first. That was good. She had thrown the gun away from her as the police ran into the room, but it didn't do her much good, because a) her prints were all over it, b) the three of us were sitting on the sofa and clearly hadn't just shot anyone, and c) Davy's webcam had captured the entire scene in glorious 4K.

They arrested us too, of course. Kate McAdams, our police friend from the restaurant, was in the second wave through the door, and was very happy to see us again. When I asked what the charges were, she said they'd think of something, and in due course, they did.

There was a great moment when they were wrestling Charli off to the van and she screamed, 'You're going to believe a bunch of fucking *squatters* over me?'

Em heard it and shouted back, 'We're not squatters. We're interlopers.' I could have kissed her. If it wasn't for the officer grinding my head into the Axminster, I would have done.

Elle had masterminded the police side of things. The first person she'd phoned was their sister Claudia, the super-recogniser, who had been trying to trace the girls without success ever since their last contact. Then Claudia pulled a few levers and got the police involved, including Kate McAdams. It was quite a multidisciplinary operation and a proud example of modern global Britain punching above its weight.

Not that I was aware of any of that at the time. For me it was all a bit of a blur – separation from the others, wrenched shoulder, hot van, interview room, badly made tea. Annoyingly, I didn't get to tell anyone that I wasn't going to say shit without a lawyer present, because they provided a lawyer immediately. He's called Richard, he's even younger than me, and he's spent most of his time since he qualified defending really grim cases and keeps telling me this one is going to be 'super-fun' by comparison. I'm just glad to be spreading a bit of happiness around.

There are heaps of charges, but none of them are for murder or money-laundering or espionage, so all in all I don't feel too hard done by. And one of the ones they are apparently determined to make stick is unlawful entry of the home belonging to . . . Mr Paul Lethbridge. Remember him? Captain Coaster. I freely admit, that is funny.

Nobody bailed me, of course. I didn't want to ring Freddy and bother him again; he'd made it clear he wasn't interested.

And now here I am, in the Visitors' Room, waiting to see who turns up. Whoever was visiting didn't fill in the form properly, so I'm just waiting without knowing who I'll meet.

After fifteen minutes of sitting listening to the low buzz of inmates all around me chatting to their families, I see Richard, the legal beagle, through the porthole window, being escorted in by the guard. He puffs over, ditches a few files on the floor by his chair, and flaps his jacket around a bit, trying to get some fresh air.

'I have some news.' He's trying to put a brave face on it, but I can tell he's seriously perturbed.

'OK. What?' This doesn't sound great. He's sighing and rolling his eyes like he'd rather be anywhere else than here.

He mutters something.

'What was that, Rich?'

'I said,' and he's almost got tears in his eyes, 'they're dropping the charges.'

'All of them?'

'All of them. Apparently this is such a sensitive case they're just going to sweep you under the rug. They think they have more than enough evidence on Charli Harcourt without dragging you into it. And they'd rather not admit all that awkward stuff about the, er . . .'

'The British agents who were sent to kill us? Very wise.'

'Yes,' Richard says. I suddenly realise why he looks so absolutely crushed.

'So that means . . . no trial?'

'No trial.'

'I'm sorry, pal. I think you'd have done a brilliant job.'

'Thank you.'

'There'll be another case like this. You just have to believe in British criminals.'

'I hope so.'

And after muttering some congratulations he clearly doesn't mean, Richard steps out of my life, so far for good. You didn't get to spend any quality time with him, I'm afraid, but he's awfully busy and I'm not sure he enjoys life so much. Mothers: warn your children off a career in the law. As he leaves, he turns and says:

'You have another visitor, by the way.'

Thirty seconds after Richard white-rabbits off to his next perp, Kate McAdams of the National Crime Agency enters the room, scans it, then makes a beeline for me. She looks much more comfortable in uniform than she did in the restaurant where we first met her. She sits and gets out a greige folder, labelled in head-girl copperplate.

'Hello . . .' She consults her notes. 'Which of these names am I using?'

'Al is fine.'

'I'm here to talk through the details of the agreement you're going to sign. It shouldn't be me really, but they thought you'd react well to a friendly face.' This is pushing it. She looks like a child's drawing of a frown.

'Well, thank you, Kate.'

'So. These are the terms.' She pushes a sheet of paper over to me.

'Is it common for the police to ask people to sign NDAs?'

'Nothing about this story is common. But if you keep your mouth shut on this one – for ever – we're willing to drop the charges, as your lawyer should have told you.'

'Even the Lethbridge one?'

'You will have a totally clean slate. Plus, if you do keep your mouth shut, it means you probably won't be targeted by the Qumaris. Or the Iranians. Or any of these crime families Mr Harcourt had worked with over the last decade and whose houses you turned up at asking personal questions.' She slides over another sheet of paper with a lot of names on it.

I give it a read. A few names jump out at me. I point at one. 'Didn't they get a podcast made about them?'

'You've annoyed a lot of people.'

'These ones are the actual Mob, aren't they?'

Kate remains impassive. I sign the NDA.

'Any questions?'

'Thirty or forty. What happened to Conor Vane?'

'He's in custody. He was arrested actually leaving the House of Commons. Great bit of theatre.'

'He told us Rob Wallace was involved in Davy's murder.'

'Yeah. We think he was just trying to throw you off. Probably panicking. We've found out quite a lot about Mr Vane since you saw him last.'

'Was it him who sent the spies after us? The British ones, I mean?'

'Yes.' Despite being Scottish and therefore having almost translucent skin, I'd swear Kate is blushing a little. 'Obviously Charli Harcourt was the one who had the financial interest in you staying alive, at least until she'd tracked you down and got access to Mr Harcourt's half of the account. But after you visited Vane, he just wanted you shut up, and he was worried enough to pull the biggest lever available to him. He phoned some . . . contacts in the security services and persuaded them that it was in everyone's interests that you be removed from the board.'

'Right. Is that going to happen again?'

'No. They've been, er, called off. One of them is dead, and the other one won't be bothering you any further. He's been reassigned, by about eight thousand miles.'

I wave the bit of paper. 'And signing this means I can't even go on *Loose Women* to talk about it.'

'No.' She takes the NDA and files it back in her folder.

'Ugh. Fine. Oh, I've thought of another one. Where did the money go from Charli's account?'

'It's been impounded. I think not even you could get your hands on it.'

'And Charli herself?'

'One murder confessed and another attempted, all on film, plus the evidence of her accessing the account, and the transactions over the years? She'll be keeping us busy for a while. I think that at last count there were nine separate agencies gathering evidence on her.'

'Rob Wallace?'

'On a long sabbatical from the agency. He'll be back. He's done nothing wrong, outside the usual for estate agents.' I like that. I didn't think Kate had a sense of humour.

'What about your bent copper? Jay Hawthorne?'

'He's retiring at the end of the month. Very distinguished career.' Kate's face suddenly has all the plasticity of a Japanese theatre mask.

'Is Lulu Harcourt all right?'

'I believe so. She's putting her father's properties on the market.'

'Sensible girl. And . . .' This is the one question I really care about, so paradoxically I've saved it until last. 'What about Jonny, and Elle, and Em?'

Kate McAdams consults her notes. 'Jonny is still recuperating, in a secure military hospital. Elle is in a safe house in Surrey, which I believe she is attempting to refurbish without permission. And Em . . .' She glances down at the piece of paper in front of her. 'Your friend Em is on the other side of that door.'

Clearly McAdams has a taste for the theatrical too. She's also gathered from my expression that I'm no longer interested in anything she has to say, so the next things she gathers are her paperwork and her jacket. 'For what it's worth, I'm rather impressed, although this could all have been done much more cleanly if you'd just told me everything in the restaurant.'

'Next time, eh?'

She twists her mouth and leaves.

Once she's gone, I promise myself I'm not going to stare at the room's outer door like a lovesick puppy. I will be bold, nonchalant, Cool Hand Al. This act lasts for about eight seconds, after which I stare at the door like a lovesick puppy until Em walks through.

She's dressed down for the occasion – jeans, jumper, trainers – but she looks wonderful. Her hair is bigger than I remember. Sorry, I'm not good at describing this romantic stuff.

'Nice place you have here.'

'It's a house share, but it's decent. All food laid on and the gym is refreshingly simple. Broad range of life experience in here too. It's no Balfour Villas, of course, but . . .' I shrug.

'You holding up all right?'

'Not bad.'

'They're dropping the charges, I hear.'

'Just as I was getting the hang of this place.'

'What are you going to do?'

'I have a few apologies to make.' I think of Fred, and – although I have no idea how I'm going to deal with the situation – of Mum and Dad. I'll manage it somehow. Maybe Fred can help reintroduce us. Eventually.

'You'll need somewhere to stay,' says Em. 'And something to do.'

'Yeah, I don't imagine I've still got my old photography job. I think the police will have asked after me enough that my old bosses won't be interested in employing me any further.'

She smiles. 'In that case, you might like to know we've had an approach.'

'Oh. I can't talk to anyone, I'm afraid. That McAdams woman made me sign a vow of silence about the whole thing. Plus, I'm not sure I'm really a morning television kind of guy.'

'Not that kind of approach. A job offer.'

'From . . .'

She holds her phone out so I can see the screen. 'They call themselves social engineers. They test weak points in corporate security – getting into places they shouldn't be, reporting back. Kate McAdams says she put them on to you. To us.'

'You're saying . . . interloping for a living?'

She shrugs. 'Might beat working. For a little while.'

'Sounds a bit legal for my taste. And yours. I've always thought of myself as a poacher-staying-poacher.'

'I'm sure we can find ways of making it interesting.' She smiles at me.

There's one other thing I want to say to Em, and I don't know how to say it, so I'm just going to start and follow where my mouth leads. This breaks Rule 25 (*Only start a line if you know how it finishes*); right now, I don't care. 'Thanks for coming back.'

'Thanks for asking.'

'Were you not worried that I didn't know what I was doing? I mean, *I* was.'

'I don't think any of us knew what we were doing there. We'll be better prepared next time it happens.'

'Very funny. I'm serious, Em. I don't know what I would have done without any of you.'

'Well, that's good. Because I've been looking, and I think between the four of us, if this new job pays anything decent, we might be able to secure a three-bed somewhere.'

'Only three bedrooms?'

'Well, you've got to economise somewhere.'

It's my turn to smile.

'Am I allowed to kiss you goodbye?'

'Even if you're not, I don't think they could get to you in time to stop you.'

It turns out I'm right about that. And as Em is politely escorted from the room, I get the feeling – just an indication, you understand – that from now on, everything might just be completely fine.

There should probably be a rule for this sort of moment, but right now I'm afraid I can't think of a single one.

Acknowledgements

Plenty of people did a great deal to help make this story absolutely true to life and the way modern Britain works, and it is frankly impressive that with the wealth of expertise available to me, I will still have managed to get lots wrong. Nonetheless:

My *Private Eye* colleague Richard Brooks writes about real-life money laundering and offshore properties, and provided lots of patient advice about registers of beneficial ownership and other complicated subjects. His books (like *The Great Tax Robbery*) are fascinating. Oliver Bullough also provided very helpful guidance about the offshore world and shell companies, and his *Butler to the World* is another rollicking guide showing how our country got this way.

Dr Steph Grohmann, one of the few academics to have

Acknowledgements

walked the walk and lived as a squatter herself, was very helpful both in her printed work and over email about the life of real squatters, who spend most of their time being demonised in the media and treated as punchbags by the government. Rachel Ozers advised on how to track people down. Estate agent James Fenwick offered plenty of advice about the current state of the regulations, as did Henry Pryor. Kate Shouesmith offered useful thoughts about what reputation managers actually do. My friends Anna Lea and Maisie Glazebrook have both spent lots of time in Other People's Houses (a rejected title for this book), albeit perfectly legally, and I'm sure I nicked lots of inspiration from them en route. Ruaraidh Maclean provided a sharp-eyed early read.

On the publication side of things: Peter Straus and his colleagues at the RCW agency remained tremendously helpful from the first moment Al sidled into my imagination. At Penguin Random House, my editor Selina Walker provided fantastic editorial support all the way through. Any of the bad bits that didn't end up in the book were cut thanks to her, and any bad bits that remain are because I was stubborn. Joanna Taylor, Jane Selley and Charlotte Osment all worked wonders in the editing process, and Ceara Elliot designed another fantastic cover. Najma Finlay and Dusty Miller on publicity and Sam Rees-Williams' marketing chops will be the main reasons anyone hears of the book or buys it.

Penultimately, a little wave should go to Leo in King's Cross station, who expertly relieved me of £20 one night, and provided a little germ of inspiration for Al's character. I hope

Acknowledgements

you're doing all right, and I'm quite sure that wasn't your real name.

My final and biggest debt of gratitude is to Molly, who was the main reason I didn't go bananas writing this book, as per, and who remained a font of good humour, good vibes and bad tea all the way through. Thank you.

Bringing a book from manuscript to what you are reading is a team effort, and Penguin Random House would like to thank everyone at Hutchinson Heinemann who helped to publish *The Beginner's Guide to Breaking and Entering*.

PUBLISHER
Selina Walker

EDITORIAL
Joanna Taylor
Jane Selley
Charlotte Osment

DESIGN
Ceara Elliot

PRODUCTION
Nicky Nevin

UK SALES
Alice Gomer
Olivia Allen
Kirsten Greenwood
Jade Unwin
Evie Kettlewell

INTERNATIONAL SALES
Richard Rowlands
Linda Viberg

PUBLICITY
Najma Finlay

MARKETING
Sam Rees-Williams

AUDIO
James Keyte
Meredith Benson

Discover more from *Sunday Times* bestselling author Andrew Hunter Murray

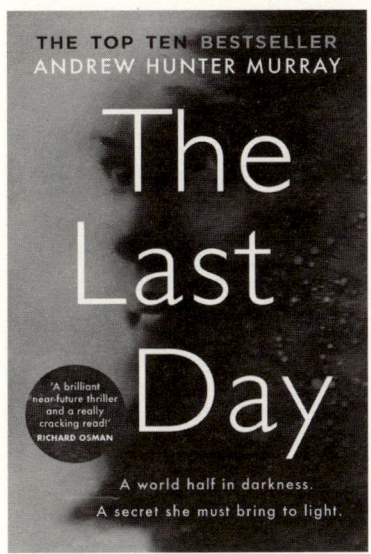

'A fabulous achievement'
Stephen Fry

2059. The world has stopped turning.

One half suffers an endless frozen night; the other, nothing but burning sun. Only in a slim twilit region between them can life survive.

In an isolationist Britain clinging on in the twilight zone, scientist Ellen Hopper receives a letter from a dying man. It contains a powerful and dangerous secret.

One that those in power will kill to conceal . . .

'A brilliantly clever thriller'
Richard Osman

Sanctuary Rock is a perfect place. A remote island, owned by a wealthy philanthropist who is building a brand-new world on the ruins of the old one. Ben only came to the island to bring his fiancée Cara home. But when he arrives, he is rapidly seduced by the vision of a better way of life.

Before long, he decides to stay. But the island holds darker secrets than he could ever have suspected. And his own life may be in terrible danger . . .

Follow Andrew on social media @andrewhunterm